# COMPLIANCE
## THE DUST CHRONICLES
### BOOK TWO

# COMPLIANCE

## THE DUST CHRONICLES
### BOOK TWO

## BY MAUREEN MCGOWAN

SKYSCAPE

## SKYSCAPE

The characters and events portrayed in this book are fictitious.
Any similarity to real persons, living or dead, is coincidental and
not intended by the author.

Text copyright © 2013 by Maureen McGowan

Amazon Publishing
Attn: Amazon Children's Publishing
P.O. Box 400818
Las Vegas, NV 89140
www.amazon.com/amazonchildrenspublishing

Library of Congress Cataloging-in-Publication Data is available upon request.

ISBN-13: 9781477816530 (hardcover)
ISBN-10: 1477816534 (hardcover)
ISBN-13: 9781477866535 (eBook)
ISBN-10: 1477866531 (eBook)

Book design by Alex Ferrari
Editor: Margery Cuyler

Printed in the United States of America (R)
First edition
10  9  8  7  6  5  4  3  2  1

# CHAPTER ONE

THE GLOW FROM ARABELLA'S EYES SEEMS A HUNDRED TIMES brighter than the glow from the moon light projected onto the sky. It's hard for me to call the dome's inner surface the sky now, or the synthetic light the moon, but I must. No one can know I've been Outside.

As I lead Arabella down the narrow alley, tall dark buildings press in from both sides and as much as I appreciate the extra light her eyes create, it's dangerous. If someone spots us, she'll be tossed outside the dome to be torn apart by Shredders. So will I.

I stop. "Take some deep breaths," I tell her. "Calm yourself down."

"I'm sorry, Glory." Her voice is small and shaking. "My eyes glow more when I'm scared." She seems much younger than her thirteen years, and her breaths quicken so much that her chest heaves. Phosphorescent green tears spill and then fade as they trail over her cheekbones. "I'm such a freak."

I give her frail body a reassuring hug. In spite of her small stature, her clothes are too small, and the shoulder seam of her coarsely woven shirt needs mending. "You're not a freak," I tell her. "And where you're going, lots of people are Chosen."

"Chosen?" she asks.

"Chosen is another word for Deviant. Nicer, don't you think?" And appropriate in Arabella's case.

My Deviance, on the other hand, is a curse and I won't ever use it again. Not to kill.

Arabella's shoulders slump. "If I'm Chosen, how come my parents hid me away? How come Management wants to kill me?"

"People are afraid of what they don't understand." I wipe a tear from her cheek. "How many of your friends don't need to carry a torch to see in the dark?"

She looks down. "I don't have any friends."

My throat tightens. "Don't worry. Where you're going, you'll find lots of new friends." And, I hope, someone to take care of her now that I've ripped her away from her parents.

For an instant, I wish I could go with Arabella, return to the safety of the Settlement and see my dad and brother again, but it's not possible. Besides, here I'm saving lives, working undercover for the Freedom Army to rescue Deviants from inside Haven and get them to safety.

Looking up through the narrow space between two

factories, I tilt my head to find an unobstructed view. Exhaust belches from the factories and wafts high above us, snaking and searching for a way to escape. The vents here must need repair; but through the smoke I make out the faded blue panels of the sky. They slope sharply in this part of Haven, and based on the angle of the moon light's glow, we're going to be late to meet Clayton.

Arabella's the thirty-seventh Deviant I've rescued in the three months since I returned to Haven. It's a perfect record and I'm not about to fail now.

"I know this is scary," I tell her. "But you're going to be safe. I promise."

Arabella shakes her head, and her nearly white hair floats up around her frail shoulders. I hug her again, keeping my breaths long and even, hoping to transfer a sense of calm to her. When I found the young teen, she was living behind a false wall at the corner of her parents' tiny apartment, barely able to move. Once her mom and dad discovered her Deviance, not long after she turned twelve, they hid her and almost never fed her, from the look of things.

Arabella's parents' relief when I claimed I could help her was obvious. They barely questioned me before handing over their daughter to a stranger, releasing them from the need to dispose of her body.

I'm being unfair. I probably gave them the first hope they'd known since Arabella's Deviance surfaced and she began her year in captivity. When we left, they told her they loved her, and their relief was more likely because I spared them the pain of watching her die.

"I was thirteen, too, when I lost my parents." I pull back from our hug. "Three-and-a-half years ago."

She looks up and the green glow in her eyes fades. "Did they die?"

"My mom died." My heart clenches, but I push the memory away and look up at the crumbling bricks beside us. "My dad's still alive, but for three years I thought he was dead. My brother and I thought he died when our mom did." That's enough truth. She doesn't need details.

"So you and your brother were all alone for *three years*? No parents?"

I nod.

"Why did your dad leave? Where did he go?"

"Same place you're going." I rub her back. "His name is Hector Solis. Say hi to him for me, okay?"

"How did you survive without parents?" Her voice catches.

"I just did. You will too." I check the moon light's angle again. We need to move.

"What's your brother's name?" she asks.

"Drake." I scan the alley for movement. "He's Chosen, too."

"Your brother's a Deviant?" Her eyes widen. "Did he get exed?"

"No. He's safe and happy." At least he was three months ago. "I helped him, just like I'm helping you."

"Are *you* a Deviant?" Her voice has grown stronger, her eyes less bright.

"Time to get moving." I pretend I didn't hear her. "If you

hold onto my shirt"—I hand her the back hem—"can you keep your eyes nearly shut?"

She nods. "I can't control my Deviance. I'm sorry."

"Don't be sorry. Your Deviance is cool. I wish I could see what's in front of *me* in the dark."

"Really?" A half smile drifts onto her sad and terrified face.

"Yes. But right now your eyes draw too much attention." I make sure she's holding onto my shirt; then we move down the alley, starting more slowly and gathering speed as Arabella gets used to walking blindly. I can't risk leading anyone to the hand-off location Clay and I use. If it's discovered, he'll have to find another, and I won't be able to save more Deviants until he does.

I'm due to get a new list of targets at tomorrow night's briefing with Clay, and I'm itching to see it. There's only one name left on the list I have now, and I haven't been able to find her.

Arabella's eyes flash, lighting the street. I wince, fearful we'll be discovered, but she quickly casts her eyes back down, and I slow my pace, imagining her terror.

Finally, we reach the exchange point, and as we approach, the top of Clay's bald head pokes out of the manhole cover that once was in the center of an ancient street from Before The Dust. The round, metal disk now spans a third of the remaining street's width.

My tension unfurls. We arrived just in time.

Seeing us, he drops down, and I turn to Arabella. "You need to climb down this ladder." I point to the hole.

She shakes her head wildly and her eyes glow, bright green illuminating the entire alleyway.

"I'll go with you." I'm not supposed to go down—Clay will have to leave the cover open longer—but of all the people I've helped, Arabella's the most fragile, the most frightened.

Taking her shoulders, I steer her over the opening and bend with her, guiding her foot onto the lowest rung she can reach. She's shaking and I'm not even certain she's strong enough to climb down a ladder alone. I grasp her under her arms and then put my foot at the edge of the same rung she's on. "I'll help you. Step onto my foot."

She does, and she weighs almost nothing. I move my other foot down. "Now the other one."

She obeys, and with my arms still tucked under hers, I let my hands slide over the street's surface. Wishing I were holding a rung, I step down with her foot above mine, and my bent back scrapes on the edge of the hole.

We slip. Her body tenses, but I grab the top of the ladder just in time. "Don't worry," I tell her. "I'm right behind you. You won't fall."

She grasps the ladder without me having to tell her and we descend together. "Right, left, right," I whisper to prepare her for each step and keep us in sync.

When we reach the bottom, Clay flashes his torch in our direction, grunts, then strides over and looks up the ladder. "This is getting too dangerous," he says. In the glow of Arabella's eyes I can see he's equal parts impressed and annoyed that I came down. The cool, damp air sparks goose bumps on my arms.

"Arabella," I say, "this is Clayton. He'll take you from here."

Her eyes brighten.

"Don't worry," I tell her. "He's saved lots and lots and lots of kids like you." Clay must sense her fear too because he forces his tanned face to smile, revealing teeth that glow in the light of Arabella's eyes.

"My parents t-told me never to talk to strangers, even before they knew I was a Deviant."

I place my hands on her shoulders. "My parents taught me the same lesson, and it made it hard for me to trust the boy who helped me and my brother, but do you know what I figured out?"

She shakes her head, her eyes wide and glowing.

"I figured out that it's one thing to be cautious and another to never trust *anyone*."

She nods, but her eyes are still full of phosphorescent worry.

"Do you trust me?" I ask her.

"I . . . I think so." Her nose wrinkles. "My parents said I could go with you, but they didn't mention anyone else."

"I trust Clayton—completely. So that means you can trust him too."

"O-okay."

Clayton steps slowly toward us. "Can you walk on your own?" he asks, and Arabella nods.

"Terrific. Why don't you sit for a moment and rest up while I have a word with Glory."

She backs over to the wall and slides down to sit, pulling

her knees into her chest and wrapping her thin arms over her shins.

Clayton steps in the other direction, turns to me and whispers, "You shouldn't have come down."

"Now that I *am* down, do you have my new list?" I need more names, more Deviants to rescue. I've been half-dreading and half-hoping to see my friend Gage's kids on one of Clay's lists. Gage was expunged the same day I escaped Haven, and if either of his kids are Deviants, I hope to save them.

Clay shakes his head. "Rolph has ordered us to slow down."

My shoulders snap back like I've been slapped. "Why? Doesn't he think I've been dong a good job?" When Rolph, our FA commander, asked me to go back inside Haven to save other Deviants, it didn't take long to convince me.

"You're taking too many chances," Clay says.

"I'm careful." I lift my chin. "And I'd take any risk if it meant saving more Deviants."

Clay's hand lands on my shoulder. "We're slowing down on extractions for now."

"But why?"

"Rolph found out you're training to be a Comp." He shakes his head. "It's too dangerous."

My cheeks burn. "It was Rolph who asked me to work undercover. What part of *that* did he not think was dangerous?"

"He figured you'd get a low-profile work placement, not something as exposed as Compliance Officer Training. I should have told him where you were placed sooner." Clay rubs his nose.

"But COT is the very best work placement for me to have." I tighten the string holding my ponytail. "I've got way more access, way more freedom. I might not be able to hack into the System like you can, but in my COT classes I get access to the HR database. Plus, I'm learning combat skills and getting stronger."

Clay frowns. "All *that* is what makes it too dangerous."

"All *that* is what makes me better at my job." My throat tightens. I need to convince him. If I can't save fellow Deviants, why am I in here? Why am I separated from my family?

And how will I make up for everything I've done?

Clay frowns. "It's not just you who's exposed; it's all of us." He widens his stance. "It's decided. Rolph issued his orders. You're off duty until further notice."

I grab his arm. "Fight for me. Tell him he's wrong."

Clay shakes his head. "The Comps are upping the security for the President's Birthday celebrations. They've installed new cameras and it'll take time to figure out which ones actually work. I think Rolph's right. Your involvement in extractions is too much of a risk."

"What?" Sweat tingles my skin, despite the cool air. "How many Deviants have I found and brought to you?"

He cracks his knuckles. "Must be close to thirty."

"Thirty-seven counting Arabella."

"It's too many, Glory. Too fast."

"Is this because I didn't find Adele Parry?" She's the only name Clay gave me that I couldn't find. And one of the only adults. Deviant abilities typically appear around puberty so most Deviants I've rescued have been young teens. Like my brother. "Do you have anything else on Parry? She wasn't at the work placement you gave me, or the address, but I'll find her. I will."

He shakes his head. "Rolph assigned her to someone else."

"Who?" My stomach twists. "I'm the only FA soldier with a valid Haven ID. I have the most freedom to move around. I should be the one to find her, to find everyone."

"Stay out of it, Glory. She's no longer your responsibility."

"But I can find her." Saving Deviants is why I'm here. It's all I have, all I am.

"Glory," he puts a hand on my shoulder. "It's not just me and Rolph who are worried about you. Your dad is too."

My breath catches. "Is Dad okay? Did he send a message? How is Drake?" My younger brother turned fourteen since I last saw him.

"They're fine. Drake's grown. And he's one of the fastest runners in the Settlement now. Other than Gage—of course." Gage's Deviance is speed—he moves like lightning.

"That's amazing." My brother, a paraplegic for three years, regained use of his legs once he was outside Haven and exposed to the dust that's lethal to most humans.

Clay rubs his eyebrow. "Drake begged me to bring you home."

A lump forms in my throat. I want nothing more than to see my family, but if I leave Haven again, there will be no coming back and there are too many others to save. "I can't. But tell him I wish that I could."

A light flashes above us in the alley. Voices drift down. Comps.

# CHAPTER TWO

"**W**E'VE GOT TO MOVE," CLAY SAYS.

I gesture for Arabella to get up. "Good luck."

She flies forward and dives at me, hugging me tighter than I thought possible with those spindly arms. "Thank you."

I help her jump up so Clay can carry her piggyback. Then he shakes his head and looks up the ladder. "Rat dung," he curses.

He needs to close the manhole cover. I'm too small. Clay lets Arabella's legs go and she slides down his back. "Come with us, Glory. Leave Haven. You've done your part. Time to retire."

"No." I push Arabella back onto him. "You guys run. I'll go up and draw the Comps away from this alley. I'll figure out a way to get the cover back on. I'll create a diversion. Don't worry."

I hug Arabella. "Good-bye."

"Will I see you again?" Her eyes glow.

"Some day." I do hope that some day I'll leave Haven and reunite with my family, but it's hard to imagine that I'll live long enough.

"Come with us." Clay's voice is hard, stern. Another light flashes above. It won't be long until the Comps spot the open manhole.

I leap onto the ladder and climb. When I near its top, the ladder vibrates in my hands and I look down to see Clay. "Come," he mouths.

I shake my head and peek out. A spotlight traces down the alley, missing the manhole by inches. I push out onto my belly and look back down, planning to tell Clay to run, but he's already gone. The glow of Arabella's eyes has vanished.

I push the heavy metal cover. It doesn't budge. The spotlight traces along the wall opposite me, several feet up.

It passes. Stops. Traces back.

A Comp's communicator buzzes, but I can't make out the words. I flip onto my back, brace on the wall, and push with my feet, straining, grunting. Sweat rises on my face, but the metal slides and clangs into place.

A light shines from the end of the alley. "Stop! Compliance Officer!" a Comp yells.

I run.

The farther I can get from the manhole the less chance they'll realize that one opens. I reach the corner and turn left, checking over my shoulder.

A single Comp's chasing me and his armor crunches

and thumps with each step. He's already passed the manhole and shoots his Shocker gun. I leap around the corner and its electric-charged tag arcs in the air, striking nothing.

Ahead, a rope dangles down from the edge of a roof. I leap, grab it, and climb, arm-over-arm, even as it swings from the momentum of my jump. Reaching a window ledge, I brace myself, then haul the rope up behind me, hoping to pull it above the Comp's notice before he passes.

I'm too late. A tag from his Shocker flies, but I dodge out of its way. I loop the coiled rope around an exposed beam that juts out near the window. Not having a rope might slow the Comp down.

He uses his communicator. Soon I'll be surrounded, and my being enrolled in COT won't help me get out of this one. Even as a Comp trainee, I'm not supposed to be outside the barracks at this time of night.

Clay's right about one thing: I have been taking risks, but I've snuck out dozens of times, and this is the first time I've been chased.

I fly up the rope, shoulders and back flexing and straining, working in efficient tandem. An almost-grin forms on my tense face. I wouldn't have willingly chosen to be assigned to COT, but as a side benefit, I've become stronger.

Able to climb ropes since I can remember, I'm now so much faster. And I no longer rely solely on observation or guesswork to know the Comps' protocols and procedures, making it easier than ever to roam Haven at night unde-tected.

I know exactly how many Comps are assigned to this

sector tonight. Three. There are fewer posted in the factory district than in residential areas—even the Pents where I grew up. More Comps will come if the one chasing me issues a Code Yellow, but I should have time to get away before they have me surrounded—if I find a good route.

When I reach the top of the rope, I scan the roof. No Comps yet. I roll onto the hard surface and race to a ladder leading up a building to the side, then climb. Twenty feet above, a window's open about six feet to the right of the ladder. Too far to reach.

At the window's height, I study the crumbling brick surface of the building. Not ideal, but my only chance. Moving to the edge of the ladder, I stretch but miss the first visible handhold and swing back to the ladder. On my second attempt my fingers catch hold.

Pushing off the ladder, my weight transfers to my fingertips. My foot catches on the edge of a worn brick and I bring the second one to join the first. Digging the tips of my fingers into the small groove, I free my other hand to find another crevice.

I slip. The toe of my sneaker scrambles over bricks, sending tiny pieces of mortar and dried clay to the roof below. But my foot finds purchase and I slide over to find another handhold, fingers scraped and sore.

Finally, I stretch out my leg and it lands on the sill of the open window. I hook it to brace myself as I find another place for my fingers. When I'm close enough, I slip inside the building.

The room is dark. And big. I blink, urging my eyes to

adjust to the dim light. I don't dare crank up the small torch I have stashed in my jacket pocket. A strong chemical smell burns my nostrils, and the shapes of what must be machines form in the dim light. Luckily, this factory doesn't have a shift of workers tonight. All is quiet and the Comps haven't found me. Yet.

I creep across the room and discover a gaping hole with a steel cable hanging at its center. After cranking my torch, I shine the light into the shaft, and the cable reaches up as far as I can see. Below, there's a dead end about forty feet down at what must be street level.

It's an elevator—we learned about them during our building structure class—and it must be used to move materials between the floors of this factory. Before The Dust they were also used in residential and office buildings for people too lazy to climb stairs or use ropes and ladders, but most of the elevator shafts from BTD were converted to living space. I haven't encountered an elevator during practical training sessions yet, but I'm sure to before graduation.

There's no use climbing down—roofs are safer for travel than surface streets for me—and I need to get my bearings and plan my route back to the barracks. Climbing up, I'm sure to find another opening from the shaft, if not at the roof, maybe at a level with a bridge to another building.

After turning off my torch, I stash it inside my jacket, then jump and grab onto the cable. My brick-scraped fingers aren't happy, but I wrap my feet around the cable to help, then climb up, hand over hand. Darkness engulfs me, and

I ascend what feels like ten stories without finding another opening. They're all sealed off.

About twenty feet from what looks like the top of the shaft I strike pay dirt. An opening. Through the faint light I see a staircase going up at the other side of the room. Roof access.

Comp boots stomp above me. They're on this roof.

I lower myself until I'm not visible through the elevator shaft opening and wait.

According to protocols, the Comps will search for me for no more than twenty minutes. There are too many other places to patrol for them to waste time on a girl out after curfew.

My hands and feet are tired and sore, my legs shake, but I focus, drawing deep breaths until the pain becomes part of me. I imagine I'm somewhere safe, somewhere Outside. I imagine I'm floating in a lake, cool water around me, hot sun above, my hair fanned around my smiling face.

Haven employees have no idea such places still exist, but I've been there. With Burn. Thinking of him makes me feel braver, stronger. Makes me remember what I'm capable of and why I need to survive. I need to save other Deviants like he saved Drake.

If Clay refuses to give me more names, I'll find more Deviants myself.

But no matter how many I save, it will never wash away my biggest regret—my shame, my guilt for what I did to my mother.

• • •

I'm still not asleep fifteen minutes before the alarm's due to ring to signal that we have six minutes to report for our morning run. I don't need a run. Sweat's pouring off me, and my heart rate refuses to slow. In the bunk below, my roommate Stacy, the only other girl in COT, is snoring. Although it keeps me awake many nights, at least my heavy-sleeping roommate doesn't rouse when I frequently sneak out.

My body's sore and tight, and I stretch, hoping to clear lactic acid and coax my muscles to relax. We've got a live chase simulation today and I need a moment of sleep. Behind closed eyelids, I imagine Arabella's expression the first time she sees the real sun, a lake, a tree. I imagine a smile bursting onto her face the first time she sees the Settlement, where Deviants live alongside Normals, safe from the Shredders.

Then that happy scene is erased by the faces of other Deviants—their faces distorted in pain as they're tortured by Shredders. What would have happened if they'd been exed before I found them.

Somehow I'll convince Rolph to put me back on active duty. Tonight, I'll report to my briefing with Clay as if last night didn't happen. I need to find Adele Parry. That will convince them I'm indispensable.

I drift, skirting sleep, until finally, my muscles relax. I sink into the mattress, feeling weightless, boneless. I'm falling . . .

The alarm rings.

The lights snap on illuminating the dark brown water

stain above my bed. Stacy grunts from the lower bunk and rolls over, shaking our bed's frame.

I stretch one last time before twisting to get down from the bed.

At least last night I did something good. I saved a young girl and gave her a fighting chance at a safe life Outside. How many more will it take to make up for my past?

I'll be paying for the rest of my life.

# CHAPTER THREE

DENSE AIR SPEWS FROM ROOFTOP VENTILATION UNITS, AND the plumes of steam spread and slither across the sky. With my back pressed against the metal side of a vent, heat penetrates my skin and scorches my lungs. The air's too thick up here for deep breaths, and if I move from this corner, I'll risk capture.

In today's training exercise, I'm playing the part of a Deviant. Irony abounds.

The door from the building's stairwell slams open and Comp trainees pour out. Their armored uniforms reflect the low light as heavy boots crunch over gravel and shake the roof's surface. Spotlights probe the night, bouncing off the sky about twenty feet above me.

I tense, ready to spring, weighing my options, but the Comps have the advantage of night vision goggles.

I don't stand a chance of staying hidden. I need to run.

"Over there," one shouts and races toward me. "The Deviant. I see her."

Squeezing into the small space between two vents, I wince at the hot rush of pain and the smell of baked skin. A red dot from a Comp's laser sight strikes my arm, but I pull further into the gap. The Shocker gun's tag strikes metal, leaving a dent before it binds. One of the Comps slams into the vent I'm behind, and the vibrations push through me as I press out the other side of the gap to the open rooftop.

I've got nowhere to hide now, but they need to get around the far side of the large metal unit before they can shoot. I have a few seconds.

Adrenaline flowing, I race to the roof's edge and leap.

My leg stretches through the air, reaching for a place to land, but the next building's too far. I misjudged the distance.

Sixteen's too young to die. I'm not ready.

The sole of one shoe scrapes down the roof's edge but I drop, throwing my arms out, grabbing for something, anything. My fingers catch on the lip of the roof, and by some miracle, my left foot lands on something hard, solid—maybe the top trim of a window.

I don't care what it is; it's enough to support me as I gain a better grip.

Pushing off with my foot and down with my arms, I fight to get my weight onto the roof, shifting, twisting. Almost.

A boot lands between my arms—a Comp's boot—and I lose my hold. Sliding back, I claw the rough surface, hoping my foot will rediscover that ledge, but heavy-gloved hands grab me under the arms.

I'm caught.

I won't give up. As soon as the Comp pulls me far enough that I won't slip back, I twist from his grip and roll to my back.

Grabbing his boots for leverage, I jackknife at the waist, bringing my feet back to slam into his gut.

He staggers, more startled than hurt, and pain from the impact of thin shoes against armor shoots from my soles to my spine. Still on my back, I spin to face him. He reaches toward me, but I brace one foot on his chest and kick with the other, wishing there was a vulnerable spot in the armor. At least my braced leg keeps him from reaching me, although he could use his gun.

"Stop it, Glory," the Comp says.

"Cal?"

My legs drop and I scramble to my feet. With their dark, visored helmets, it's impossible to tell one Comp from another. Even one who's my official, HR-department-sanctioned dating partner.

"Why aren't you with the rest?" I gesture to the opposite roof where our fellow COT recruits are disappearing back into the building, having clearly decided not to follow my lead and jump. They'll likely cross at a lower floor on one of the many bridges between the two buildings. "What made you come over here?" I ask Cal.

He lifts his visor and when I see his handsome face, my heart skips. "I know how you think." He grins and his blue eyes brighten the dingy world of Haven's rooftops. "I figured you wouldn't head up to that roof unless you had an escape route. It was just a matter of checking the relative heights of the surrounding buildings to guess your plan. Although"—he steps to the roof's edge and looks down—"cutting it a bit close, don't you think?"

"I've never been up here before. I thought it was closer."

He spins back. "You jumped that blind?" His voice cracks. "You could've been killed." One of our classmates died the last time we did a live chase simulation. Two others flamed out—quit the program.

"Why take such a huge risk? It's just an exercise."

That danger was nothing. I face worse every day. I bite the side of my lip to hide a proud smile. "Aren't you going to tag me?"

"Shooting you is a technicality at this point." He grins. "I've got you."

He hasn't got me. Not until he fires that training-tag-loaded Shocker that hangs at his side in a loose grip. I could still take him down.

One kick to his gun's base, a fast, lunging grab, and I'd have it pointing at his chest, the trigger pulled, his armor tagged with shame. He'd have a dozen negative points against him, and I'd replace him as the top ranked member of our COT class. But given all my secrets, it doesn't seem smart to draw too much attention. It's enough to know I *could* be first.

"You'd better shoot." I laugh. "Haven't you heard? I'm a Deviant. Dangerous. A suspected terrorist." I'm grateful Cal doesn't know what I'm saying is true. Some of it anyway.

"Are you telling me you're really a Deviant?" Cal raises his free hand and shakes it. "I'm so scared."

He smiles softly as his fingers reach for my face.

I pull back.

Hurt flashes in his eyes and his expression drops. Regret creeps up my spine. I still like Cal—a lot. I've always liked him, but I'm no longer certain I love him. Not like that. Not after what happened with Burn. Besides, I don't have time to think about boys.

I raise my hands over my head. "Hurry up. Shoot."

"Glory, I . . ." He puts a gloved hand on my shoulder and lowers his head toward mine. "You've been through a lot. I get that. But how long will it take for things to get back to the way they were before you were kidnapped? People will question our license."

"I'm sorry."

The intense concern in his eyes washes over me, making me feel happy and guilty at once. But he doesn't know a tenth of what I went through. I wish I could tell him that I wasn't really kidnapped, and that Burn helped me get my brother to safety, but if anyone inside Haven learns the truth . . . I can't think about that. My emotions build and my eyes tingle, signaling the build-up of my Deviance.

I drop my gaze before I risk any harm.

A noise startles Cal and he looks over his shoulder. The rest of the recruits have arrived.

"Shoot me," I mouth and raise my arms to the side. "Larsson will be furious if you don't." Since I'm involved, he'll be furious no matter what we do.

Cal scrambles backward five or six feet to lessen the ferocity of the impact, then aims at my thigh and pulls the trigger. The tag strikes. Gritting my teeth against the sharp pain, I drop to my knees, hands laced behind my head in surrender. Hundreds of tiny sharp barbs at the tag's back poke through my thin pants and grab hold. That's going to leave a mark.

The rest of our training group falls into a semi-circular formation around me, guns raised. Laser sights dot my chest like pox.

"Cut it out, guys." I drop my hands to my sides. "You got me. I lost."

"Oh, the little girl is scared," Thor taunts. "If you can't cut it, flame out."

Most of the group lowers their guns, but a Shocker fires and a training tag slams into my chest, knocking me back, taking my breath. Panic rises. I can't breathe from the pain of the impact. Who shot me?

A large shape plants itself next to my body, kicking a few stones at my face.

Larsson, our Recruiting Captain, crouches. I close my eyes. It figures he was the one to shoot.

*Breathe. Breathe.*

He grabs my chin roughly. "Look at me."

I open my eyes but keep them cast at his chin.

"I said, 'Look at me!'"

I stare into his narrowed, ice-green eyes. My ears roar

and the backs of my eyes tingle. My Deviance is coming on and I can't control it. My chest constricts. This is bad. Really bad.

If I hurt the Captain—cause even a pinch of pain to one of his internal organs—this exercise will become real. Quickly. He'll know I'm a Deviant and I'll be exed. Fear shudders through me along with memories of the Shredders who rule outside the dome.

"What's the matter, Princess?" Larsson mocks me and presses the heel of his hand onto my chest over the bruise where his tag struck. My cheeks burn with rage.

To quash my emotions, I rub the place on my finger where I wore my mother's ring, before I threw it away out of guilt and self-pity.

"Is this too much for you?" Larsson asks. "If you want to be a Comp, you've got to be tough."

"I am tough."

"Not tough enough." He yanks my back off the roof. "You're so scared you can't even look at me."

My Deviance continues to build, but I turn my gaze his way. Rubbing my finger isn't working, so I count in my head, run through the times tables, recite items from the P&P manual. I fill my head with mindless details to shield my emotions and control their fatal powers.

"I told Belando we shouldn't accept you," Larsson says. "Are you ready to flame out yet?"

"No, sir." I can't quit COT. My insides tremble and I fight to keep my emotions at bay. I'm more effective at saving Deviants from inside COT, no matter what Rolph and Clay think. If I were working fourteen-hour shifts in a factory, like my friend Jayma, I wouldn't have found a quarter of the kids I've saved. Plus, if I'm out of the program, I'll no longer be useful to Mr. Belando.

I will not quit.

Once I graduate, I'm supposed to work undercover for Mr. Belando, the Junior VP of Compliance. He thinks the time I spent with my kidnapper gave me insight about Deviants who are conspiring against Management, and he wants me to infiltrate their organization and betray them. I don't trust the reasons Mr. Belando gave for choosing me as his spy, and there is no chance I'll do what he wants, but he didn't give me a choice.

If I do anything to displease him, he claims he can produce evidence that my kidnapper turned me, and that I support Deviant Rights. I don't know if he knows the truth— that I wasn't kidnapped, that I've been Outside, that I *am* a Deviant—but I'm certain he can deliver on his threat. If I quit COT, he'll have me exed.

"You're not cut out for this." Larsson shoves me down. "Even if you survive training, you won't last a week as a Comp."

My breath is knocked out of me and I can't breathe. Good thing because I want to scream at him to stop taking his frustration out on me. Captain Larsson resents my being in COT and that his ultimate boss, Mr. Belando, forced him to accept me.

Cal steps toward us. "Just because she's small doesn't mean she won't make a good Comp."

"What was that?" Larsson jumps up, grabs Cal's utility belt, and pushes him to the edge of the roof. "Did you fasten your buckle correctly, Recruit?" Larsson spits as he yells. "If you fall, the little princess won't have anyone to help her cheat her way through training."

"Yeah," Thor says, nudging one of our classmates. "She cheats. How else could a girl be so high in the class standings?"

Cal's jaw hardens and his eyes narrow. "Glory doesn't cheat."

I fight for breath as Larsson tugs on Cal's belt. My dating partner waves an arm to catch his balance.

"Does this recruit think he knows better than his captain?" Larsson says.

"No, sir." Cal's voice is deep and strong, but a thin trail of sweat traces from his forehead past his left eye.

"I'll bet this recruit is a Deviant." Larsson turns back toward the group. "Maybe he's not afraid to fall because he can fly. I'll bet he's got a tail that can grab onto the edge of the roof. Or a spear that will come out of his guts to impale me. He'll make sure he's not the only one to die if I drop him."

Cal's jaw shifts. His foot slips and I reach toward him, trying to cry out, but I still can't make a sound.

"Is that it, Recruit?" Larsson's voice is loud and ugly. "Are you a Deviant? One of the freaks trying to destroy Haven, take our home?"

"No, sir."

"What's that?"

"No, sir. Not a Deviant, sir."

"And what do we do to Deviants, Recruit?"

"Hunt them, expunge them, kill them, sir."

Larsson's free hand gestures toward me. "And who was this recruit in today's exercise?"

"A Deviant, sir."

"You think I should go easy on Deviants?"

"No sir."

"You a Deviant sympathizer?"

"No, sir."

Larsson yanks Cal forward. He stumbles at first, then straightens.

"What did we learn here today?" Larsson asks the group.

"Glory cheats," Thor says, and a few others laugh.

Larsson frowns. "It's important to remember"—Larsson voice is all instructor now—"that not all Deviants are easily identified. Some only show their Deviance when threatened. If either of these recruits actually were Deviants, they'd have shown their true colors under pressure."

Apparently Cal just passed a test. So did I.

Cal picks up his gun and straightens. Breathing better now, I stand, and Larsson points to the tag still stuck into my leg.

"That strike wasn't fatal," he says to Cal. "If this weren't an exercise, this Deviant might have killed you. With the President's Birthday less than two weeks away, we have to be extra vigilant. No points today."

Cal tagged me and should be awarded the points. Nowhere in the rules does it say the tag strike needs to be lethal.

Inside Haven, the Comps only carry Shockers, their electric charges effective as long as their barbs penetrate clothing—and they penetrate every clothing material except leather, which is rare in Haven.

Larsson's ignoring the logic of his own exercise. He's punishing Cal for talking back, for being my boyfriend.

"Got a problem with that?" Larsson asks Cal.

"No, sir."

A loud boom pulses through the air, pounding into our ears and our bodies. My arms fly up to cover my head. We all duck.

Shouts and screams rise in the distance, and Larsson puts his hand to his ear, presumably to turn up his communicator.

"Terrorist attack," he tells us. "One of the factories in Sector ES4 was hit."

My heart races. ES4 is where Jayma works.

"Report back to the barracks," Larsson shouts. "On the double."

Most of the group head for the door to the building's stairwell, but I crane my neck, trying to pinpoint the blast's location. Terrorist attacks were rare in the past, but this is the eleventh one in the last three months. Please let Jayma be safe.

Cal grabs my arm and leads me after the others. "Bloody Deviants," he says. "Every one of them deserves to die."

# CHAPTER FOUR

CAL CHECKS OVER HIS SHOULDER, CONSTANTLY SCANNING. Both of us grew up in the penthouse slums, and being back in the cramped upper floor of this residential building makes me feel both safe and sad. The smell of cooking rat meat mixes with the tang of too many people and the chemical smells that cling to the sky all over the Pents.

"Relax." My fingers graze the upper arm of Cal's t-shirt. "No one saw us leave the barracks."

"You're right." He puts a hand on my shoulder. "Every Comp who's awake is dealing with the terrorist bombing. We're clear for at least another hour or two."

At least that long. Cal has no idea how often I sneak out of the barracks.

"I couldn't have slept tonight," I say, "without knowing that Jayma and Scout are safe."

"Me neither." He swallows. "Let's check the roof."

At the end of the corridor, I reach through the hole in the wall to make sure the rope that leads to the roof hasn't been found or moved since we were last here. Labor-level employees, especially those who live in the Pents, don't have access to e-notes, so there's no way to check on Jayma and Scout without coming over. I heard that there used to be a System screen in this building, but it was deemed unnecessary and re-commissioned before I was born.

Cal runs his fingers over his closely shorn hair. I miss the way his blond hair used to drape over his forehead, falling close to his eyes. But even with it cut short, Cal's undeniably handsome. He turns and light from outside the window glints off his face. My fingers itch to trace over the light stubble on his sharp jawline.

Shaking off those thoughts, I lean out, grab the rope, and climb. It grows taut below me as Cal follows. At the top, I peek over the roof's edge to see Scout and Jayma there—making out.

Passion wafts from their entwined bodies, and Scout shifts, pulling Jayma tighter. My cheeks heat and a hint of longing erupts inside me. Keeping my gaze down as if I haven't seen them yet, I clear my throat and climb onto the roof.

"Glory!" Jayma leaps up.

Bent to avoid hitting her head on the sky, she races toward me, pulling me into a huge hug. She's working too hard in her new job, burning way more calories than she's taking in, and her ribs form hard ridges under my fingers. "I didn't think I'd see you until the Quarter End Free Day."

Cal and his brother give each other backslapping hugs.

"Are you on leave?" Scout asks. "You guys in COT get a lot of time off. Tonight, the QEF Day, and then the President's Birthday—all within a couple of weeks. Wow."

"We're not exactly on leave," Cal says, and I shoot him a look. Better if Jayma and Scout don't know how much trouble we'd be in if we were caught outside the barracks.

"Just time for a quick hello." Cal straightens as far as he can and puts his hand on a beam as he passes between the roof and the sky. "And we're probably going to be on duty for the President's Birthday. We don't get that much time off."

"We came because we heard about the bombing," I tell Jayma. "We wanted to make sure you were okay."

"It was horrible." Her eyes fill with tears. "The blast went off two buildings over from mine. Everything shook, and the smell . . ." Scout runs to her side and wraps his arm over her shoulders. Her HR-issued dating bracelet glints in a beam of light as her hand rises to his chest.

Cal steps next to me. His arm rises to follow his brother's example, but I shift forward, removing his opportunity. I'm so grateful for his patience, and I twist my dating-license bracelet.

The FA Commander ordered me to maintain my dating license when he sent me back inside Haven. Rolph figured that making any changes in my personal life would draw Management suspicions and cast doubt on the kidnapping cover story that I used to explain my nineteen-day disappearance from Haven. It's impossible to know whether Rolph is right, but the stakes are too high to test, so I can't end things with Cal.

"Did you know anyone who got hurt in the blast?" Cal asks Scout.

"No, but what a mess," he answers. "Five workers died and seventeen were taken to the Hospital." Scout shakes his head. "Worse than dead."

"We don't know that," Cal says. "No one knows for sure what happens in the Hospital."

Jayma frowns. "Comp training has changed you."

"No it hasn't." Cal shakes his head.

"I still can't believe you've both joined the enemy," Scout says. "The Comps are practically Management."

"Someone's got to keep Haven safe." Cal squares his stance. "If it weren't for the Comps, who would catch the terrorists and Deviants?"

"But Comps do more than catch terrorists and Deviants." Jayma's face flushes. "I don't understand why you want to be one. Hasn't Management caused us enough grief?" She looks down at her feet. "You've forgotten what it's like up here in the Pents."

"All I'm saying"—Cal leans on a beam above his head and his pectoral muscles press against his t-shirt—"is that I don't think you should assume every bad rumor we've heard is true. 'Haven Equals Safety.'"

Her head snaps up and her cheeks flare. "I can't believe you're quoting slogans."

Cal draws a long breath. "Once Glory and I are Comps,

we'll be able to help you guys too. We'll all eat better. We'll all have an easier life."

"And that makes it okay to put innocent people into the Hospital?" Jayma turns to me. "Glory, why are you so quiet? Are you going to defend the Hospital and Management too?" Her eyes probe mine and my stomach squirms.

I turn to Cal. "Have you ever heard of someone being released from the Hospital?"

"No, but—" Cal shifts.

"But nothing," Jayma says. "I don't know what they do to patients in that horrible place." She shivers. "I'm not sure I want to know. It's enough that no one ever comes out."

Cal slams his fist against his open palm. "None of those workers hurt today would even have been sent to the Hospital if it weren't for those Deviant terrorists."

My stomach tightens. "You don't know for sure that the terrorists are Deviants," I say. "They're just as likely to be Parasites, or even Normals fed up with Management policies."

"Of course they're Deviants." He spins toward me. "Who else would commit terrorist attacks?"

*Why would Deviants commit them?* I want to ask, but I don't. I've got so many secrets from Cal it's a wonder I don't burst. I don't know who the terrorists are, but I don't believe that they're Deviants even if Management claims they are. If they understood Deviants, they'd know that we don't draw attention to ourselves. We stay hidden.

Jayma and Scout sit on the roof as a unit, wrapped in each other's arms.

"Tell me about Comp training." Scout's voice is full of

excitement. "Have you guys captured any Deviants yet?"

Cal sits, and his chest broadens as he leans back on his arms. Always strong, his body has filled out since we started Comp training, both from the exercise and the better-quality food. His biceps flex and his shirt hugs his hard torso. Being up here with Scout and Jayma, it's like time has rolled back, and the feelings I had for Cal flick through me like flames.

"The training's tough, but great," Cal says. "Glory's a star." He pats the gravel beside him.

I sit as close as I dare, feeling his heat in the air between us. "He's exaggerating," I tell them. "Cal's the top of our class, and just today he bested me in an exercise."

Cal doesn't correct me or elaborate. Maybe that's the way he saw it too.

"Aren't you scared?" Jayma asks, looking at me. "What if you come face-to-face with a Deviant? I've heard that some can tear out your heart with their bare hands—worse than the Shredders." She shivers and Scout pulls her closer.

Cal shifts toward me, and his bent leg touches my thigh. "We're well trained," he tells her. "Plus, we carry weapons and wear armor."

"And a lot of those stories you've heard are just that," I add. "Stories. Fairy tales to scare little kids." I shake my head.

*Pulling hearts out?* When he's enraged, Burn could do that. But even if any of the other Deviants I've met *could* do that, they wouldn't. Except maybe in self-defense.

"Not all Deviants are dangerous."

Cal spins to face me. "Don't let Larsson hear you say that. He'll think you support Deviant Rights." I don't respond and he turns back to Jayma. "Don't worry. We Comps keep Haven safe. I'm hoping our class will be assigned active duty on the President's birthday." His hand grazes down my back to rest low on my hip.

Heat, then guilt race through me. I can't bare the thought of losing Cal's friendship, but I don't want to lead him on or make him think things might go back to where they stood before. And yet I don't have the will or energy to fight the physical feelings burning inside me. My body wants comfort, wants to turn back time, wants to lean into Cal's touch.

I reach out a leg and tap Jayma's with my foot. "Today, *your* job was dangerous, not mine. I'm so glad you're safe."

"I wish we had the same work placement," Scout says. "The second my shift ended, I raced to find her." He kisses Jayma's forehead. "If I'd lost you . . ."

Scout pulls Jayma into a tight embrace, and Cal's thumb strokes my hip sending delicious, warm ripples through my body. In this moment I want to risk everything. I want to let Cal back into my heart; I want to let him get close; I want to tell him my secrets—what I am.

Regaining self-control, I rise. "We should get home." My fingers slide over Cal's shoulder, and his hand grazes the back of my thigh. I lean away and hug Jayma. "I'm so glad you're safe."

# CHAPTER FIVE

"**W**HAT'S THE BEST WAY TO KILL A SHREDDER?" ANSEL asks from one of the front desks in the class.

"Slice its effing head off," Thor answers, and some of my classmates struggle to contain their laughter.

"That's enough." Mr. Shaw, our Enemy-Phys instructor, holds up his hand. Deep wrinkles carve valleys between his eyebrows. "I will not tolerate off-policy language in my classroom."

Thor leans back in his chair, hands behind his head, and stretches one leg out from under the small desk. Bright red spots flare on Shaw's cheeks at the blatant lack of respect.

"Does anyone have a *serious* answer for Recruit Ansel's question?" Shaw asks.

Cal raises his hand. "Gun blast to the brain."

Shaw nods. "Yes, that is often effective."

I killed a Shredder by exploding its head, using my gathered emotions. Shuddering, I sink lower in my chair, hoping to stay invisible.

Shaw points to the projected image on the wall behind him. "Shredders have been known to survive severe wounds to the chest and abdomen." He swipes his hand in the air and another image appears.

Half the class visibly shifts back in their seats as we're shown a gruesome image: a Shredder lying on a metal table, its torso cut open down the middle. The creature's insides are dark brown—nearly black—and shriveled.

Shaw clears his throat and points at the cadaver. "This shows the dissection of a Shredder less than fifteen minutes after its death." Several recruits gasp and I lean forward for a closer look. The body looks dehydrated, like it's been dead a long time.

"Shredders live off of the dust," Shaw says, "with little or no liquid in their diet. Therefore, their blood becomes thick. They dehydrate."

"How do they stay alive?" one recruit asks.

"Our scientists are trying to determine the answer to that question, and to others." Shaw displays another screen showing a Shredder spread-eagled in chains, and a Comp in full body armor slicing across its chest with a huge knife.

"Cool," someone says from the back.

"When do *we* get to do that?"

"We should do a live dissection."

More suggestions erupt from my classmates, and Shaw

changes the screen to show the same Shredder, but with what has to be a ten-inch gaping wound across its chest.

"Notice the time stamp on this image." He points to the lower left-hand side of the screen, then gestures for the image to change. "Now *this* time stamp."

Several recruits gasp. The second image was taken less than ten minutes later, and the wound's healed with barely a black mark where the Comp sliced the Shredder's chest open. "Is that the same day?"

I'm not certain who asked, and I don't really care. I already know way more about Shredders than I care to.

"If they heal so quickly," Cal asks. "How can you be certain one's dead?"

"Try kissing it," Thor says. "You're into freaks." He looks back at me.

"Enough!" Shaw strides to Thor's desk. "One more interruption and I'll report your behavior to Captain Larsson."

Thor shrugs. Thor is clearly one of Larsson's favorites, and even our instructors know better than to raise Larsson's ire.

Cal offers me a supportive smile, but I can tell from the tension in his jaw and his shoulders that it's all he can do to keep from challenging Thor. I get that they bother Cal, but I don't care about Thor's taunts. I *am* a freak.

Shaw returns to the front of the room. "Let's move on to Shredder behavior."

The door to the classroom opens and a woman walks in. Shaw turns toward her, clearly startled. The red spots on his cheeks spread and deepen. I'm beginning to understand why

Shaw's an instructor and not on active duty. He can't even handle the stress of teaching.

Our visitor's crisp, white coat drops to the knees of grey slacks that brush the floor over black shoes with heels that click as she crosses to the center of the room.

She nods to Shaw. "Continue. Please, don't let me interrupt."

My stomach tightens. This woman is clearly Management and her presence makes me nervous, on edge, even if outwardly everything about her should do the opposite. Her voice is soft, her tone cheery, and when she turns to face the class her expression sparkles.

Dark brown hair, a shade darker than mine, falls in shiny curls around her face. I've never seen anyone quite so pretty. She looks my way and I divert my eyes from her gaze.

"Class," Shaw says, his voice full of nerves, "Please say hello to Mrs. Kalin, VP of Health and Safety."

A collective gasp fills the room and everyone, even Thor, straightens in their desks. "Hello, Mrs. Kalin," the group says in unison. At least now I know why she makes me uncomfortable. This is the VP responsible for the Hospital.

Mrs. Kalin looks around the room like she's making an effort to greet every student individually. Her eyes fall on mine. Cheeks burning, I look down. I'm too nervous to trust myself with eye contact.

"Mind if I take a seat?" she asks Shaw.

"Of course. I mean, yes, please do." He gestures toward a chair in the back, then slaps the side of his head. "But today's topic is Shredder physiology. You should teach the class, not me."

"Nonsense," she says. "I'm certain you're doing a terrific job." She smiles at him and his shoulders drop as if the tension's melting off his body.

Mrs. Kalin trails her fingers over the desks of the recruits she passes, smiling and nodding at each student. Realizing the only empty seat in the room is behind mine, I stare at the scratched wooden surface of my desk hoping to go unnoticed, but she touches my forearm as she passes.

I look up to meet her eyes and, for a moment, warmth calms my nerves. She reminds me of my mom.

I look back down. She's Management.

Shaw continues to tell us about Shredders, and I keep my lips shut, even though I know that some of the information he's teaching us isn't true. Shredders can talk. They are sentient. They do make plans and live in groups. I've heard it. Observed it.

When the class ends, I wait until nearly everyone is gone before standing. Cal is just outside the door, waiting for me and talking to Quentin.

Shaw walks back toward me, red spots flaring again. *Great*, I think. *What have I done to draw his attention?* Then I remember that Mrs. Kalin is sitting behind me.

Her chair slides back. "Thank you for letting me sit in on your class today, Mr. Shaw."

"If you have any pointers . . ." Shaw looks like he might bow down and kiss her shoes.

"None. You did well." She pauses, and Shaw continues to gape at her as if he's mesmerized by her beauty.

"Don't let me keep you," she finally says and Shaw shakes his head as if waking up, then turns and rushes out of the classroom. I rise, wanting to sneak out and wishing I'd left with the group for once.

"What did you think of today's class?" Mrs. Kalin asks.

The only one in the room, I stop and slowly turn. "It was . . . interesting." I'm not sure what she wants me to say.

She steps toward me and my gaze rises from the points of her shiny black shoes to her face. "Do you think there's more to Shredders than Mr. Shaw told you today?"

I look into her shining brown eyes, and despite her danger-loaded question, the tension drifts out of my shoulders. I feel them unfurl. "Yes," I say. "Shredders must be able to talk and think."

"Why do you say that?" she asks.

"Because when someone gets exed, the Shredder attacks. They look planned."

"That's an astute observation, Glory."

I cock my head to the side and study her face, searching for motives in her eyes. How does she know my name? I try to recall if Shaw used it during class. Either way, she took notice. Took notice of me. My lungs expand. I feel taller.

"Are you interested in science?" she asks.

I nod.

"I thought so. When I was your age I was full of questions about the dust, about Shredders, about Deviants. I knew there had to be more than what we learned in GT."

"I know. Right?" I bite my tongue, but she doesn't seem upset by my outburst, and I feel I can trust her. It's been so many years since I've trusted freely—not since that horrible day I'd rather forget. How strange that I want to trust Mrs. Kalin, a member of Management no less.

"We're always looking for bright people in H&S." Her hand touches my upper arm. "If you'd like to talk to me about your career, you let me know."

I nod, then look down. I squeeze my eyes shut, still reeling from the glow of her attention. I force out the good feelings and remember what really matters.

I can't trust her, and there's no way I'd ever work for H&S. Not a chance. Even if she looks like my mom, even if she made me feel good, I can't forget who this woman is: my sworn enemy.

# CHAPTER SIX

ROM BEHIND HIS DESK, MR. BELANDO, THE JUNIOR VP OF Compliance, beckons without lifting his head. The silver stripe at his temple glints against his otherwise black hair. Not a single strand moves, and if I weren't so creeped out, I'd want to touch it to test if it's real. Meeting Mrs. Kalin today almost gave me hope, but Mr. Belando is a quick reminder of what most people in Management are like.

As I slip into the chair opposite him without being asked, I can't resist running my hand over the chair's smooth leather and the brass studs at the edge of the seat. Such opulence is unheard of in the Pents. Few people I knew growing up even had chairs.

Mr. Belando types on his projected keyboard with such fervor that I worry his wooden desk will form dents, and I wish I'd been here when he typed in his passcode. If Clay has cut me off, I need a new way to find targets. Belando's pass-code will give me access to all the information I need. Clay will still have to escort the kids out of Haven, but I doubt he'll refuse to help once I've found them.

Mr. Belando grunts and snaps back in his chair. I straighten, but he returns to typing. He acts like he's forgotten that I'm in the room or that he summoned me to this meeting.

Anxiety builds inside me, a taut rope from the back of my throat to my belly, and I focus on the painting behind his head—a farm scene from BTD. Except for the faded red barn, it could be a painting of the Settlement.

"Young lady," Mr. Belando says, "your attention, please."

I jump. "Yes, sir."

"Well?" He leans onto his desk.

I squirm, unsure what he's asking me. "Sir?"

"Do you plan to apologize?"

"I'm sorry?" Heat burns low on my cheeks.

His expression's so smug. "Why do you keep provoking him?"

"Who, sir?"

"Captain Larsson." He squeezes his waxy lips together and shakes his head. "I pulled strings to have you exempted from the Entrance Trials. I went to a lot of trouble to get you into Compliance Officer Training and how do you thank me? By causing trouble?"

"Trouble, sir?" I honestly don't know what he's talking about.

He leans back in his chair. "Larsson wants you kicked out.

He went above my head to the Senior VP, Mr. Singh. Insubordinate piece of rat dung." His eyes narrow and he leans forward. "I don't think you appreciate all I've done for you."

"I do, sir."

"Because if you're finding Compliance Officer Training too difficult, I *will* have you removed." One side of his mouth lifts.

"No, sir. It's not too difficult, sir." I know what he means by "removed." I'll be exed. Mr. Belando has the power to do it, no questions asked.

His chair creaks as he rocks back and puts his feet up on the desk, crossing his legs at the ankle. Even the bottoms of his shoes are pristine and shiny.

"You say you understand what I expect from you," he says, "yet you draw attention to yourself. Make trouble. If you want to survive COT, you'll learn not to provoke your Captain's ire."

"Yes, sir."

Dropping his feet to the ground, he stands and leans onto the desk. A tiny vein above his left eyebrow appears and my stomach churns.

I leap to my feet. "Captain Larsson is trying to force me to quit. I won't."

"No, you won't." He strides around his shiny wooden desk and puts a hand on my shoulder, close to my neck. "I've taken a big chance on you, Glory. I expect to see some return on that investment. The Deviant problem is growing worse by the day." He pauses and I can barely breathe.

His hand is heavy on my shoulder. "Experts from the

Health & Safety department assure me that you'll remember more details of your kidnapping soon. Details that can lead you back to him and begin your undercover work to catch them all." He bends close to my ear. "Did your kidnapper tell you his bomb targets? Where is he hitting next?"

"He's not setting the bombs." The words burst out of me before I think, and my guts twist.

"How can you know that?" His fingers dig deeper, pinching. "What have you remembered? What aren't you telling me?" His voice is edged in steel.

"Nothing, sir. I told you everything I know." My heart pounds so fast and hard he must hear it, must feel it under his hand. He's quiet for an impossibly long time, his breathing loud beside me, and my anxiety builds as I fight the urge to elaborate on the story I gave the Comps when I returned to Haven.

I want to defend Burn. He'd never hurt innocent people—on purpose. None of the Deviants or FA Soldiers I met would, but I know that adding more details to my story will only make him want more and will only cast doubt. So I wait.

Mr. Belando's fingers dig into the back of my neck. "Are you secretly working for the terrorists? Helping to set those bombs?"

My chest constricts. "No. Never." His fingers dig deeper, pinching, and my voice is tight with pain and tension. "My friend was almost killed by that last bomb. I'd do anything to stop the Deviant terrorists." My neck cramps under his hold, and I'm not sure I'll be able to turn my head once his hand moves, but I don't dare show signs of pain.

A beep comes from his System. He releases my neck, moves back behind his desk, and swipes his hand under a laser beam to activate his screen and keyboard.

I suck in a sharp breath and resist the urge to raise my hand to my neck. He's going to re-enter his passcode. I have to get it. His laser keyboard projects onto his desk, but from this angle all I can see are red lines. I shift until the letters and numbers start to appear in streaks and dots. If I just move forward and a little farther to the right . . .

"Sit down." He looks at me sternly.

Heart pounding, blood rushing in my ears, I focus my eyes past him to the back wall and watch his hands out of my peripheral vision. I can't see the keyboard, but can watch the pattern. His fingers strike the desk twelve times—three letters, three numbers, five letters, one number. I burn the pattern into my head. If I can figure out the first letter, the rest will follow.

He frowns and lines appear on his shiny forehead. Up to this point I wasn't sure his skin was pliable.

He looks up and I move back. "We live in troubling times, Glory."

I nod.

"Yesterday's terrorist bombing was a surface symptom of the pestilence lurking inside our fair city. Deviants will steal Haven from us Normals, given a chance."

"Yes, sir." My heart beats so loudly, I'm sure he can hear it, and I dare not look him directly in the eyes. Instead, I remain focused on his way-too-perfect lips.

"Do you know what the real threat is?" he asks.

I shake my head, praying he doesn't mention the FA—or me.

"Our own people." He leans forward so his face is mere inches from mine. "Moles, spies, traitors within."

I press the soles of my feet into the floor to make sure my legs don't shake.

"There's a traitor in the COT program. Possibly a Deviant."

Blood rushes in my ears. My stomach implodes. "How is that possible? Everyone in COT is screened, tested, even before they're recruited." Does he mean me?

He narrows his eyes. "I just received a report. We uncovered evidence that someone from COT is involved." I want to press my heart back into my chest. His jaw shifts as he raises his chin. "A training tag from a Shocker was discovered in the same location where the terrorists assembled their bomb."

I jump up and lean on his desk. "You know where the terrorists meet? Why don't you send the Comps to catch them? If you can stop the explosions—" The terrorists are undermining what the FA is trying to do, making things worse for all Deviants.

He bangs his fist on the desk as he stands. "Do you think I'm a fool, young lady?"

I shake my head.

"The terrorists change meeting locations." He shakes his head. "They won't use the same place again."

"What do you need me to do?" When Mr. Belando asked me to work undercover, I never imagined I'd find a reason

I'd want to. Hunting down the terrorists is much better than betraying fellow Deviants. And even if he and others are right, and some of the terrorists *are* Deviants, if I find them, I can tell them about the FA and assure them there's hope, that they're not alone, that their violent methods are not the answer. I can make Haven safer for everyone.

"Time is of the essence," Mr. Belando says. "We need to neutralize the terrorist threat before the President's Birthday. It's less than two weeks away."

"Why before then?"

"Enough questions." He flicks his hand.

"But, what do you need me to do?" It's another question but he looks straight at me.

"Keep your eyes and ears open." He slides his manicured hands across his desk. "Listen for subversive discussions, support for Deviant Rights, expressions of sympathy for our enemies. From your instructors too."

"Yes, sir." I can't imagine there are Deviant sympathizers inside COT—besides me—yet my chest bubbles with excitement and a regained sense of purpose.

His eyes narrow. "Now that I've given you an assignment, it won't do to have you observed with me." He strokes his chin. "I can't have anyone know of our arrangement—especially anyone in COT."

I nod, not wanting to mention that if Larsson knows that Mr. Belando forced me into COT, our arrangement is already suspect.

"From now on," he says, "we must take greater precautions. I can't have you seen coming onto this floor."

Fine with me. I hate coming here. "Where will we meet?"

"Here." He looks at me like my question's ridiculous. "But after office hours."

"But how will I get into the building?" Procedures dictate that I register at the entrance with a guard who logs my employee number against an appointment record. I don't see how we can keep that part a secret. It goes into the System.

Mr. Belando holds his hands as if cupping a large sphere, then turns them. His screen shifts to an angle where I can see it too. He presses a key and a nine-digit code appears on the screen. "I've disabled the cameras on the roof of this building," he says. "This is a passcode for the roof access door." He looks up at me. "Got it?"

I quickly memorize the nine-digit number and nod. "How do I get on and off the rooftop without getting caught?"

He turns to me, a slight smirk on his face. "Surely a promising Comp recruit and future spy can solve such a small problem." He twists his screen back so that I can no longer see it. "Prove yourself worthy."

My stomach clenches, but he's right about one thing: I am adept at sneaking around Haven. And once again, I wonder how much Mr. Belando knows that he's not telling. But if he knows what I am or who I'm working for, why wouldn't he just kill me?

"In fact," Mr. Belando says, "I think you should leave via the roof tonight."

"But, sir, I'm logged in with the guards. If I don't leave through the front entrance, I'll be flagged."

He types on his projected keyboard as I say this, and I'm

not certain whether he's heard me. He presses one final key with a flourish and leans back. "You are no longer in this building."

My breath catches, but I nod. Of course he can access the guard's log. He's the Junior VP of Compliance; he can probably access any part of the System he wants to. The power at his fingertips makes me vibrate with excitement.

I need his passcode.

He continues to type and, after a moment, flicks his hand. "That will be all."

Outside Mr. Belando's office, the corridor's empty. I race to the end and slip through the stairwell door. The latch clicks behind me, and I grimace at the unnecessary noise. Taking the stairs two at a time, I race up thirty-one floors, past the upper floors housing the offices of the lower-level managers and support staff, to the top.

As I climb, the air becomes hotter, more polluted, even in this fancy Exec Building, and I'm panting when I reach the roof level. In the faint light, I type the nine-digit code on the keypad. One wrong keystroke and an alarm will ring.

There's a slight pause when I finish. My muscles tense in fear, but a green light flashes and the door clicks open. Relief floods through me as I exit.

The roof of the Exec Building isn't as close to the sky as the ones in the Pents and it's possible to stand, but I keep low as I cross, out of habit and to decrease the chances I'll be spotted.

Hearing a sound in the corner, I drop to my stomach,

pressing myself against the rough roof surface, fighting to slow my breathing, still fast and heavy from the climb. Squinting to focus in the low light, I see the unmistakable shape and movement of rats. Smiling, I spring up to a squat. Who'd have thought there'd be a stash of free meat on the top of the Exec Building? I want to laugh.

I creep toward the rodents. If I hurry, I can bag a few, get them over to Jayma, and sneak back into the barracks before lights out.

My speed and agility have improved during Comp training, and I bet I can catch some rats with my bare hands. That won't break my vow about using my Deviance.

Crouching near the rats, I sense someone watching. The hair on the back of my neck rises, and I twist to search the adjacent rooftops, then scan the beams of the sky. There's nothing. I check behind a large metal structure, but find nothing there either.

Still feeling the electricity of unseen eyes, I look for surveillance cameras. Mr. Belando assured me that he disabled them, and I can't think of a reason why he'd lie.

I wait until I'm certain there's no one up here besides me and the rats; then I return my attention to hunting. Selecting a rodent near the edge, I creep forward, placing each step down silently, keeping my breaths slow and even.

The rat turns and sees me. Its whiskers twitch but it doesn't move as I take another cautious step forward. The rat bares its sharp teeth and I spring forward, grabbing the creature around its stomach before rolling to the side to absorb the impact of my dive. Twisting its head, the rat tries to bite, but I break its neck before its teeth have a chance to dig in. The other rats scatter, and I wait for them to calm down before landing a second, then a third, and soon I have a small pile of rats ready to skin and bring to Jayma.

Loneliness eats into me for a moment—it's hard not to see her every day, especially now that I'm separated from Dad and Drake. I rest for a moment, closing my eyes to regain my center and push down emotions I can't afford.

Feeling better, I open my eyes. A rat's staring at me. My shoulders jump. Fear rouses my Deviance and before I can think, my eyes are locked onto the rodent's, my Deviance focused on its brain.

I vowed not to use my power to kill—ever again—but now that I'm locked onto the rat, I'm tempted. More meat for Jayma.

The rat falls to its side. I gasp and rush forward as the other rats scatter away. My heart thumps and tears rise up in my eyes. It's not about the rat; they're expendable—meat. Killing rats is something I won't apologize for, ever, but I've broken my vow. I've used my ability to kill.

I want to believe that I'm not a bad person, that there's more to me than my deadly power, but what do you call someone who kills with her eyes, if not bad, horrible, evil?

Reaching out, I tentatively touch the rat's side and snap my hand back. It's not dead; it's still breathing, still alive.

Did I fry its brain?

The rat's eyes are open, and I lie down to get closer, looking for a sign that the rat still has a functioning mind.

*Wake up*, I think as I look into its eyes. I sense his brain waves, moving slowly. *I'm sorry, so sorry. I didn't mean to hurt you. It was an accident. Wake up.*

The rat blinks, I break our link, and it leaps up and races away.

Trembling builds inside me and I lie flat on my back to slow my breathing, to will my heart rate to decelerate. I have no idea how I rendered that rat unconscious or how it woke up. I'm not even positive I had anything to do with either. I wish there were a guidebook to help me understand the bounds and limitations of my Deviance, to help me learn to control it.

I shake my head and look up at the sky. What good would that do? Even if I figured out and learned to control every facet, my mother would still be dead.

The LED stars dotting the sky blur as tears fill my eyes. I can't reverse what I did at thirteen before I even knew I was a Deviant.

I've known the truth for over three months, and the pain weighs on me like a building collapsed on my chest. I can't bring my mother back. I can't even keep my promise to her memory that I'll never use my power again.

Guilt clutches my body, snaking along the inside of my skin, zapping my energy, my hope.

But I refuse to indulge it. I can't wallow. Saving others is the only way I can make up for even a fraction of the terrible thing I did.

# CHAPTER SEVEN

NOISE BOUNCES OFF THE TUNNEL WALLS, ECHOES OF ECHOES of echoes so loud and constant that I can barely think. We're under a building near the outer edge of Haven, and everyone in our Comp training class is talking at once, excited about the mysterious "adventure" Larsson promised—more like threatened.

Although the tunnel's well lit, it brings back memories: some great, some I'd much rather forget—all about Burn.

Cal leans down toward me. "You okay?"

"Fine." My cheeks flush. I have to stop thinking about Burn, especially when I'm around Cal. It's not fair. It's not right.

Cal's fingers brush mine, but I pretend not to notice, and I raise my hand to scratch my nose.

"Hey," Stacy says from behind us, "*I'll* hold your hand."

I spin to face her. So does Cal.

"You want to hold Glory's hand?" he asks, a mischievous smile on his face.

"Very funny." Stacy pushes in between Cal and me. "That's not exactly what I had in mind."

"Glory and I are dating, Stacy." He holds up his bracelet for her to see.

My roommate's shoulders are nearly as wide as Cal's, and she's only a few inches shorter. In fact, only three of the boys in the group are taller than Stacy, and her complete invasion of the space between Cal and me is like an itchy powder on my skin. I see enough of her as my roommate; I don't need to deal with her now.

"I was only joking." She grins at Cal. "No offense to Glory, but everyone thinks you're a great guy for staying licensed after everything that happened. Who knows what that Deviant kidnapper did to her?" She puts a hand up to mask her lips from me, but whispers loudly, "Damaged goods."

I roll my eyes.

"Show some compassion, Stacy," Cal says.

"You're too kind," she says to Cal, then looks at me with fake sympathy. "But maybe it's time to admit the truth and move on."

"What truth?" I ask.

She sneers. "That your dating license is bogus and should be revoked."

"It's not bogus," Cal says. "We're perfectly legitimate dating partners."

"If you say so." Stacy gives him a conspiratorial grin. "Is this new?" She runs a hand over the sleeve of Cal's plain gray shirt. The same shirt he's worn since we started training. "Or have your arms grown?"

"I am getting stronger," Cal flexes his arm.

"Oh, look at that." Stacy touches him again and my itching powder gets worse.

She continues to natter and I block it out, let it blend with the cacophony of voices, hoping it will temper my urge to scratch her eyes out. The tunnel narrows and Cal doesn't seem to notice as Stacy uses her broad shoulders to force me to walk behind them. Fine. It's not as if I feel like talking.

Stacy brushes her shoulder against Cal's arm. "Glory doesn't even let you touch her. No one would blame you for revoking the license." Her hand brushes down his bare forearm to catch on his bracelet. "You have options."

Her voice pierces through the din of lower male voices, but I can't hear Cal's response. She laughs at whatever he says and slaps his arm playfully. I scratch my shoulder.

Stacy is beyond rude but she's right about one thing: I can't have it both ways.

I try to imagine Cal with Stacy, try to imagine being happy for him like a friend would, but I can't. The thought of them together leaves me nauseated. Since I got back, I've been keeping him at arms' length, but seeing this display makes it clear: I don't like the idea of Cal dating someone else. And that's not fair.

Cal notices I'm no longer beside Stacy. He stops and gestures for her to go on ahead. While his back's turned, she scowls at me then stomps off.

"Do you like Stacy?" I ask Cal once she's out of earshot.

Maybe I can learn to accept them together. He deserves to be happy and we have no chance at a real future. He doesn't even know what I am.

"Stacy's okay, why?" He turns toward me. "Are you two getting along?"

"Not really."

"Oh, I'm sorry. It must be tough with her being the only other girl who got into COT.

"I'm fine." Saying it helps to convince me. "Stacy sure seems to like you." I bump my hip against his and bob my eyebrows.

Grabbing my wrist, he stops and lets the few people behind us pass. "Don't let her get under your skin. You have nothing to worry about." Unable to endure the intensity in his eyes, I look down. "I'm yours," he says. "I don't want anyone else—ever."

"Cal, I'm sorry. I know I've been distant . . ."

He crooks a finger under my chin to tip my face up. "I get it. You've been through a lot. I can be patient. We have our whole lives."

"But . . ." My mouth dries, my mind blanks, my ears fill with cotton, and I can no longer hear the noise of my classmates. Looking into his blue eyes, standing this close, I feel so safe, so comfortable, and it's easy to forget the reasons we can't be together—the reasons he doesn't know and can never know.

"Recruits!" Larson's voice booms down the tunnel. He's standing at the entrance to a room about forty yards ahead. "Inside. On the double. We're closing the doors."

Realizing we've dropped way behind, Cal and I race after the group, and when we enter the room there are only two seats left. One in the very back row and one in the front near a dark curtain covering the wall. I take the seat in the back, but Larsson steps over and grabs my arm.

"Short ones up front." He drags me forward, dumps me into a chair, and whispers, "You'll flame out after this."

I straighten and cross my arms over my chest.

"Excited?" Ansel, the recruit beside me, asks. The smallest boy in our class, Ansel's been trying to make friends with me, but being my friend is dangerous. I don't want to make him a Larsson target too.

"Do you know what's going on?" I ask.

An eager grin spreads on his face and he straightens his glasses. "Someone's getting exed. We get to see it live."

TV screens hang on each side of the big curtain. "Live? Don't we always see expungings live on the screens in the Hub?"

"Live and up close," Ansel says. "My dad took me to one of these viewing rooms last year to try to talk me out of applying for COT." He taps his heel so quickly it vibrates against the floor.

I want to press down on his knee to make him stop. "What work placement did your Dad hope you'd get?"

He shrugs and looks up to the side as if realizing he's already said more than he meant to.

"Management Training?" I whisper.

He nods, then leans in close. "Don't tell the others, okay?"

Some of the other recruits pick on Ansel, and if certain

boys—especially Thor—found out that Ansel's father is in Management, his life would get even worse.

I mime zipping my lips.

"Your parents are Management too, right?" Ansel asks. "That's how you got accepted into COT?"

I shake my head. "My parents had factory work placements."

His brow furrows. "But Larsson was forced to take you, like me."

I hold up a hand to cut him off. "We'd better be quiet."

I get why Ansel wants to bond over something he assumes we have in common, but although I was forced into COT, it's not the same—not at all.

His heel continues to tap a rapid rhythm on the floor, and the curtain pulls back to reveal a floor-to-ceiling glass window. The recruits gasp as they view Outside just twenty feet ahead.

Larsson knocks on the window. "This reinforced glass is one of five layers between us and Outside, so don't think you're risking your life by sitting here, like the Officers you'll see Outside. You are nowhere near prepared for that."

Glass is a rare commodity inside Haven, and I've never seen a single sheet so large, never mind five. The closest window has a mesh of metal running over or through it, dulling our view, and the glow from the sun isn't nearly as bright or as golden as I remember.

The pale blue sky barely permeates the blowing dust that's carried on a strong wind and swirls over chunks of debris and ruins. Our field of vision is much larger than we normally see on the TV screens, but between the gusting dust that drifts up the glass and the ruined buildings in the distance, it's impossible to make out the wall I know surrounds Haven about a mile out from the dome.

"It's like we're out there," Ansel says, wonder in his voice.

"Is that the real sky?" someone asks from the back.

"Silence." Larsson plants himself at one side, legs spread wide. "Observe. Pay attention to the details. There will be a quiz."

I don't want to watch the gruesome scene on the other side of the window. It's too horrible, too familiar, and it brings back too many memories, too many fears of what might yet happen.

I flick my eyes away, but Larsson stares at me and shakes his head with a knowing smile. I look back through the window. He clearly thinks I can't take the gore, and I refuse to give him the satisfaction of being right.

The boy exed today looks about fifteen, and sharp spikes stick out from his forearms and the backs of his hands. I assume his spikes only appear when he's in danger, but it's not like I've seen the kid any other way.

A Shredder circles. Its eyes are bloodshot, nearly red, and bulging from a head that's more like a skull covered by brown and red scabs than a face. I realize in disgust that the Shredder has small bones and teeth woven into its matted hair.

The Shredder lunges. The boy swings, slashing his spiked arm across the monster's chest. The dry flesh on the Shredder's torso tears and it roars, revealing stubs of brown teeth between nearly black lips. We can't hear the sound of the roar live, only what comes through the TV screen speakers, but I swear the glass vibrates. Shredders' voices are both loud and grating, like metal scraping on metal.

I swallow my urge to shout a warning the boy couldn't hear anyway; then another Shredder kicks the Deviant from behind, knocking him down. Dust rises up around the boy's body in a cloud.

The recruits cheer. If anyone in this room is a Deviant sympathizer, he's hiding it well.

Beside me, Ansel slides to the edge of his chair and his leg vibrations accelerate. The teen Outside tries to rise, but the Shredder who kicked him leaps and lands on his back, forcing his chest down to the dust. Another Shredder, with sharp horns protruding from his head like an extinct forest animal, takes a huge spike and drives it through the boy's hand, pinning him down. The boy swings his other arm, trying to dig his spikes into anything he can strike.

For a moment, I wonder why the Shredders haven't used ropes or chains to neutralize this Deviant's weaponized arms, but that wouldn't make an exciting show.

And this show has a purpose.

Fear of Shredders and dust keeps everyone trapped inside Haven and working for Management's benefit. But at the same time, Management wants to fuel our hatred of Deviants. They don't want these fights to end quickly or generate sympathy for those Expunged. The Comps probably took the Shredders' chains.

The smallest Shredder, limping on a leg that's bent at an unnatural angle, takes a long knife from a sheath on his back. My stomach contracts as the knife slices long gashes down the prone Deviant's back. The boy writhes in pain as blood soaks his shirt.

I want to yell, to tell him to breathe in more dust, that it will help him to heal, but believing what we've all been taught, he's actively keeping his nose and mouth from the ground. The Shredders take turns slicing into him with knives, slamming clubs into his back and tearing off slices of his skin to keep as trophies.

A loud noise booms through the TV's speakers. The ground rumbles.

I jump up off my chair. "What was that?"

Even Larsson looks surprised. We stare out the window and what looks like a huge wall of dust rolls toward Haven from far away. A regiment of Comps, all in full armor, march in the distance toward the dust cloud.

The TV screens turn to static. Clearly, the broadcast inside the Hub has been cut off, but it's not clear whether this was intentional to censor the action or whether the explosion cut off the feed. The noise can't have been an earthquake. We would have felt it more strongly inside.

In the distance, a group of six Comps peels off from the larger formation and heads toward us. Not toward *us*, exactly, but toward the battle between the Shredders and the boy, who's still fighting with everything he has. Most of our group is on their feet. A hand lands on my shoulder and, startled, I look up. It's Cal.

"Did you come forward for a better view?" I ask, distaste in my voice.

"Down in front," someone shouts.

I sit and he crouches beside me. "I came up to make sure you were okay."

Cal gasps, and I turn back to the window. The six Comps who peeled off have opened fire with huge guns—Auts that shoot three bullets a second. Even though Larsson assured us that there are layers of bulletproof glass in front of us, the gunfire's loud, like slabs of concrete dropping off a building.

A few of the Shredders charge the Comps, but it's no use. Bullets tear into their dry flesh, smashing bones until the Shredders drop to the dust. Our recruit class falls silent. I'm not sure if anyone's breathing.

The exed boy's still lying face-down, one hand pinned by the spike. Is he dead? The Comps turn to leave, and I pray that he's faking his death, that he'll get that spike out of his hand and escape once the Comps leave. Maybe he'll even be found by an FA Soldier. They monitor the broadcasts, and if they don't already know that this kid was expunged, they will soon.

A few yards away, two of the Comps stop, turn back, and stride toward the prone boy. My throat closes. The Deviant remains still even as the Comps stand directly above him.

They ready their guns, and the boy grabs one of their legs by the calf, pulling the Comp off his feet. But this last-ditch effort is futile. The other Comp opens fire and the dust around the boy darkens with blood.

# CHAPTER EIGHT

EXHAUSTED, I STARE AT A SYSTEM SCREEN IN THE STUDY room. My muscles are so tired that I feel like I was the one expunged this afternoon instead of that poor kid, but my mind's still running at full sprint. As much as I know I need sleep, I'm not sure I could drift off even if I had time to lie down.

I don't have time.

Later tonight, I'll go to meet Clay. He's supposed to be in our designated meeting place every night at 1:00 AM, and I'm supposed to go at least weekly or whenever I have something to report. I've been going nearly every night these past three months, but with the bombing and my meeting with Mr. Belando, I haven't seen Clay since we saved Arabella three nights ago.

Even though I haven't found Adele Parry yet, I'm going

tonight to convince Clay to give me more names. COT recruits only get access to the most basic HR records, but I'm determined to find new clues. Finding Adele would convince Clay that Rolph was wrong to slow me down.

I've clicked through search menus for what feels like hours, but I can't get to the parts of the System I need. I'm also keeping my eyes open for Mr. Belando's mole, but I'm more focused on my main purpose—saving Deviants, finding Adele.

"What are you doing in here all alone?" Cal's voice comes from the hall.

He's standing in the doorway, his body silhouetted by the light behind him.

"Studying." I shut down my screen.

He crosses the room and rubs my shoulders. "Everyone's in the rec room playing on the SIM. There's a tournament. You should come."

I shake my head. "Too tired. I think I'll turn in."

"You won't make friends if you don't make an effort to get involved."

"You and Scout and Jayma are enough friends for me."

Disappointment mixes with the concern in his eyes. He's right. I should try harder to get along with our classmates. This very small thing for Cal is the least I can do. Plus, I'm supposed to be spying on my classmates for Belando. If there's even a chance I can play a part in stopping a bombing on the President's Birthday, that's a valid cause too.

I push back my chair to stand. Cal stays close and his hands glide over my torso as I turn to face him. It feels as if the air between our bodies is pulling me forward, but I resist the urge to bridge the short distance. Something holds me back. My work for the FA? My betrayal of Cal? Burn?

"Cal!" A voice comes from down the hall. "Your turn."

He doesn't react, so I slide from the space between him and the table. "You're being paged."

"Are you coming with me?"

I nod. "You're right. I should spend more time with the others."

He grins. "I'll bet once you make some friends, Larsson will stop picking on you. The others won't let him get away with it."

As we walk down the hall to the rec room, our hands brush close to each other but never quite touch, and I can't tell whether I'm disappointed or relieved. The noise gets louder as we approach, and when we enter the room, it's deafening.

"Cal. Finally," someone I can't see shouts. Cal offers me a reassuring smile before moving to the center of the room to face a section of bare wall. Within moments, the display for the SIM fills the blank space, projecting from a small laser projector latched onto the ceiling.

The rest of the boys and Stacy are crowded around Cal and his opponent, whom I now recognize as Quentin. Those at the back are standing on chairs and benches, and Ansel gestures for me to join him on top of a crate.

Watching the others, I find it hard to believe that one of them might be a mole for the terrorists. I wish I could turn back time and watch everyone's reactions on the roof when that bomb went off. At the time everyone seemed horrified. Then again, if the mole's in our group, he'd be good at deception.

Regardless, I'm happy on the sidelines, with no pressure to interact, yet not alone. Cal was right. I'm glad I came.

"Will you have a go?" Ansel asks.

"Not a chance."

"You should. It's fun." Ansel shifts to improve his view.

Cal takes a SIM controller, nods to Quentin, and the boys take their ready positions. As they press the thumb buttons on their controllers, two images appear on the wall.

I gasp. Cal's avatar is human, huge, and wearing a long, flared coat. *It looks like Burn.*

The Burn-like avatar sports chin-length dark hair, heavy eyebrows, and strong features. The game designer obviously based this game character on Burn's image that was posted all over Haven after my alleged kidnapping. Only his eyes are different—a mixture of bright red and orange like they're about to shoot fire. Maybe they will.

Quentin sees his avatar—a Shredder—and laughs, then slams his fist against his chest. Mirroring Quentin's actions, the avatar's fist hits its chest on the screen, and bits of skin and flesh fly off its torso. My nose curls up in response. Through the game speakers, Quentin's laugh transforms into a roar that's not nearly as gruesome as Shredders sound for real, but it reverberates through the room and hurts my ears.

Facing them, Stacy steps between the two boys. "Good luck." She winks at Cal.

He smiles back and my skin crawls.

"And begin!" Stacy steps out of the way and the two boys turn to the screen to start their bout.

The spectators cheer, but instead of watching the projected fake gore and the action on-screen, I keep my eyes on Cal. My life is strange and complicated enough. I can't watch Cal control an image that looks like Burn.

Cal ducks, legs flexing, then leaps and kicks. Based on the cheers and the way Quentin steps back, I assume that Cal's avatar landed a hard blow somewhere on Quentin's torso.

As they continue to fight, I watch Cal and imagine what it would be like if he knew the truth about me. Would he suddenly want to report me, to fight me, to kill me? Or would he understand and still love me? Maybe if he knew the truth, I could fully love him back, like he deserves.

He's already proven his loyalty by not turning my brother in, and by standing by me after my kidnapping. Cal's hatred of Deviants is grounded in misinformation—the same misinformation everyone in Haven's being fed—and maybe if he knew the truth, things would be different.

The cheers grow louder. Cal raises his hands above his head and shouts. The match is over. He won. I turn to the screen, and the Burn-like avatar is shooting flames from its eyes. I almost laugh.

I jump off the crate and push through the crowd, planning to congratulate Cal, but Stacy gets there first. Acid burns in my stomach. I'm about to charge forward and push her aside, but someone else challenges Cal, pulling his attention from Stacy. I turn back toward my spot on the crate. Ansel's gone.

Shouts rise above the chatter and something, or someone, bangs against the wall so hard it vibrates. I get up on the crate to see. Thor pulls Ansel forward by the shirt, then slams him into the wall—hard.

"If you're not a Deviant, then prove it." Thor punches Ansel in the gut.

"Fight!" several voices shout in tandem, and the crowd forms a semicircle around the pair.

Thor slams his open hand into the wall next to Ansel's head. "Come on, Deviant. Let's see whatever you do that makes you a freak."

My hatred for our class bully expands, and I wonder if I could convince Mr. Belando that Thor is the terrorist mole. The idea's laughable—no one hates Deviants more than Thor, and from what I've seen, he's not bright enough for deception.

I doubt that reporting him would help stop the real terrorists but at least it might get Thor kicked out of COT.

Fists raised, the bully curls his upper lip and beckons Ansel, taunting him, daring him to attack. Ansel steps away from the wall. "I'm not a Deviant."

"Then you don't have anything to worry about," Thor says. "You'll pass my little test."

Thor charges, but Ansel ducks and comes up from below, landing a punch on Thor's nose. Blood trails down the bully's upper lip and then flies off when he roars. He rages forward, arms flailing, fists landing on Ansel's tucked body. Thor's not using any of the combat techniques we've been taught, but his wildness is proving surprisingly effective against his smaller opponent. Ansel might not survive.

I jump down and my heart thumps loudly in my ears. I try to get closer. Someone needs to stop Thor.

Before I get there, Cal pushes his way to the front of the semicircle.

Fear tightens my stomach. Someone does need to stop this, but not Cal. I don't want him hurt. Fighting with the SIM controllers is one thing; this is another. "Stay out of it," I shout, but the sounds of my classmates are too loud.

"Stop," Cal shouts. His booming voice cuts through the din, but both boys ignore him.

Cal lunges for Thor, grabs him, and pins his arms back. Thor struggles, but Cal, using skills learned from our prisoner restraint class, kicks the back of the bully's thick legs, forcing them to bend until Thor's on his knees.

Ansel looks as if he's about to kick his downed opponent in the face, but Cal shakes his head. "Don't even think about it." Ansel stops mid-kick and backs up.

Cal releases Thor and the thick boy lands prone on the floor.

"Who do you think you are to tell me what to do?" Thor scrambles to his feet and backs up to the wall, glaring at Cal. "No one put you in charge."

Cal lifts his hands. "We're all on the same team here. Whatever beef you two have, this isn't the way to sort it out."

Cursing, Thor charges Ansel. "The little shrimp is a Deviant." Blood and spit fly from Thor's lips.

Cal steps to the side to block Thor's path. "Why do you think he's a Deviant?"

The bully's face reddens, veins bulge at his temple, and blood drips from his nose. "He doesn't belong. He's too weak, too small. If we have to serve with him, he'll get us all killed. Just like your girlfriend. Neither of them belongs. Larsson knows it. We all know it."

Cal's jaw flexes at the mention of my name. "Ansel got into the program, same as the rest of us."

"Yeah, but . . ." Thor runs the back of his hand under his nose to clear some blood. "But someone must have pulled strings. He sucks. No way did he get through the Entrance Trials." Thor looks around the group. "He wasn't there on my day. Did anyone see him on theirs?"

A few boys shake their heads.

Cal shifts again, staying between the two boys. "Even if you're right, and I'm not saying you are, Ansel's got to pass COT just like the rest of us."

Thor narrows his eyes. "He's using Deviant tricks to get by. It's not fair."

"What tricks?" Cal asks him. "Tell me what tricks he uses."

"That's what I was trying to figure out, you idiot." Thor shoves Cal.

Cal straightens and widens his stance. "That doesn't make sense." His hands flex at his sides. "We were all carefully screened before getting into the program. No way is anyone in COT a Deviant. If one of those monsters even tried to get near the program, they'd be expunged."

"One might get through." Thor's voice is calmer. "They have special powers."

Cal claps him on the arm. "Listen. You prove that one of us is a Deviant"—he gestures around the room—"and I'll *help* you kill him."

I press my palm against my stomach to quell its churning.

Cal reaches for the game controllers. "Work out your differences on the SIM." He passes the controllers to Thor and Ansel. "Let's see a fair fight. After that, we'll sit down and talk this out."

"I'll cream him," Thor says. "No matter which avatar I get stuck with."

"Bring it on." Ansel takes a set of controllers and strides in front of the screen.

Thor wipes the blood from beneath his nose onto the back of his forearm. "Let's go."

Cal stands to the side, arms folded over his chest, as the match begins. He's a born leader. I've always known this but it's never been clearer, and I've never felt more grateful to have him as a friend—as a dating partner too. Pride swells inside me, pushing out some of the dread. If it weren't for Burn, I could fall for Cal again—hard.

But this fight proved my love would be doomed. If he finds out the truth, Cal won't just hate me. He'll want me dead.

# CHAPTER NINE

RELEASING THE LADDER'S LAST RUNG, I DROP TWENTY feet to land in a crouch. Keeping still, I listen and observe to make sure I'm alone in the dark alley. The moon light has been bouncing off the sky for six hours already and its pale gray-blue tint casts a pallor on my skin. Deciding it's safe, I run down the alley to the nearly hidden metal door of the room where I have my briefings with Clay.

Instead of taking rescued Deviants all the way to the Settlement, like Burn did with Drake and me, Clay hands off the kids to a transport team waiting outside the wall.

After checking again for observers or newly repaired surveillance cameras, I tap on the metal door twice, pause, then three times. The door swings open but wherever Clayton's standing, he's shrouded in darkness.

I slip in, shut the door, and a dim light comes on.

My breath catches. It's not Clayton.

It's Burn.

My stomach flips at the sight of his heavy, dark eyebrows, his chin-length brown hair, and his broad body under that long, swinging coat. My pounding heart pushes all my blood to my face and ears. Poised on my toes, my body wants to spring forward, to race into his arms, but my brain holds me back. I feel turned inside out, every nerve ending exposed and firing at once.

Should I hug him? Shake his hand? Nothing feels right.

"What are you gaping at?" he asks, his voice flat and cold.

My throat clenches. "I—this is a surprise." My tongue feels coated in dust. I glance around the ten-by-ten room with its piles of plastic containers sorted by size. "Where's Clay?"

"Like you don't know." His voice is strange.

"Why would I know?"

He frowns. "You actually thought Clay would be here?"

"Of course I did. Clay's my Extractor."

"Not anymore."

"That's not fair." I fight to calm my rising anger, to slow my thudding heart. "I've done a great job and I'm careful. Rolph can't cut me off like this." My voice holds a desperate tinge. "I need to save more Deviants."

"You *need* to?" He smirks. "This isn't about you."

"I know." I look down at the dusty floor and another possibility rises. Is Burn my new Extractor? When I first agreed to work for the FA, I hoped I'd work with Burn, and I try to imagine what it will be like to work with him now, to see him a few times every week.

Merely being in the same room, I remember how it felt to be engulfed in his strong arms, captured by his lips. But I know it's not possible. When we act on our attraction, our Deviant abilities are too dangerous. If it happens again, one of us will end up dead.

"Why are you here?" I step forward. "It's dangerous for you inside Haven. You're wanted for my kidnapping."

He grunts.

I look down. "It's good to see you."

He crosses his arms over his very broad chest. "What?"

His tone is like a punch. Maybe he's seen me with Cal. But where and when? At least my desire to kiss him is waning. "Why are you acting so cold?"

"Cold?" he asks.

"Like you barely know me."

"I *do* barely know you." He shakes his head, the disgust in his voice unmistakable. "And it's already more than I want to." Each word's like another stab. Looking at him now, I feel as if every connection between us has been severed, like there's a wall, or a force, keeping us apart, and I'm not sure whether it stems from him or from me.

I lift my chin, trying to keep my body from shaking. "Burn, stop pretending that I mean nothing to you, or never did. Stop pretending that we didn't spend hours together out in the dust, that we weren't attacked by Shredders, captured by sadistic military freaks. Stop pretending we never . . ." I can't voice the last part. My cheeks flare.

"Oh. That." An ugly smile snakes onto his face. "I get it. You *like* me."

I remain still, shifting my jaw, but my head feels like it might explode. I need to ignore his taunts. Who cares why he's acting this way as long as he gives me a new list of targets, as long as he works with me to save fellow Deviants.

"Admit it. You're into me." He flares his coat and strikes a strong pose. "I can smell the teenage lust from here."

Hurt roils into anger. "Shut up." I stomp my foot. "You're being such a jerk."

"Sorry, little girl," he says. "I'm done with you. I've moved on. Found a real woman."

"Don't call me a little girl." My words come out through gritted teeth, especially since that's exactly how he's made me feel.

"But that's what you are." One side of his mouth crooks up and he struts around me, his face in a half-sneer. "A little girl, not qualified for this assignment. Not qualified or properly trained for the FA. I told the Commander he shouldn't risk the lives of qualified soldiers—of anyone—on you."

My hands form fists and it's all I can do not to use them. "Rolph *chose* me for this undercover mission. He *asked* me to do this." Burn recommended me to him, but if I remind him, he'll likely twist it some way to salt the emotional wounds he's already slashed open. "This is my job. I'm good at it."

"Rolph was clearly desperate when he asked you," he says. "Speaking of desperate—so was I."

"What?" My insides collapse. I can't breathe. My mind flashes to the last moment I saw Burn, to his huge arms wrapped around my body, holding me as if I were the most precious thing in the world.

And now he says this?

Clearly *I* was the one who was desperate. My throat's nearly closed with regret and anger. When I first met Burn I thought Cal had betrayed me. That warped my judgment. If I'd known the truth about Cal, I never would have let myself feel anything for Burn.

Burn knew the truth all along and made me turn against Cal, the boy I always loved, the boy I was—and am—officially dating. Burn made me betray Cal.

And now Burn's making it clear that I never meant anything to him.

Fine. He means nothing to me. I swallow the hurt. Refuse to let it control me.

"Cat got your tongue, little girl?" He crosses his arms over his chest.

I lunge forward, anger exploding out of me like I'm a broken air vent. "I am an FA soldier, not a little girl, you—you—rapist!"

"Rapist?" He laughs. "This *is* getting interesting."

I lift my chin. "Given your Deviance, I don't doubt you've raped *someone* by now. I feel sorry for your new girlfriend." Cruel words. He deserves them.

"Oh, she has no complaints." He leans against the wall and his biceps bulge against the fabric of his coat.

My chest is so tight, my ribs are crushing my lungs. "Great. Good for you. I get it. You're happy. You were only using me. Fine. But that's no reason for you to act like you *hate* me."

He shifts forward. "I've got plenty of reasons to hate you. It's a mistake to use a Haven employee for extractions. Especially you."

My shoulders shift back. "Why especially me?"

He sneers. "Because you're related to Hector Solis."

At my dad's name, my heart rate takes off and I step toward Burn. "Do you have a message from my dad? Is he okay? Is Drake? Is something wrong?"

He shakes his head.

"How about Gage? I'm trying to find his kids." Burn saved Gage, Outside, and showed him how to safely breathe dust. Maybe mentioning him will bring Burn back to his senses. "Do you know their names, where I can find them? Do you know if either of his kids are Deviants?"

Burn looks at me like I'm insane. "I'm not giving you any information. No way. You're one of *them*."

"One of *them*?" Fists form at my sides. If I didn't think he'd kill me, I'd slug him. "You're a Deviant too." Plus, we're the same age so his "too young" and "little girl" insults rankle.

"Not a Deviant, stupid. An *employee*. One of the brainwashed masses."

His words fuel the burn in my cheeks, my anger, my hurt. "I am not brainwashed. And I am not stupid." I can barely sort through all the malicious things he's saying, can barely contain my emotions. My Deviance might kill him. Why has he turned against me like this?

I breathe slowly, trying to figure out what's going on, trying to get my ability under control. Burn knew I was coming back into Haven, and he never gave me the slightest indication that he was against the plan. In fact, I thought my coming back here, risking my life to save others, made him proud. What's changed?

He's like a different person.

But whatever's changed, all I can do is be professional. I need to remember what's important: it's not me, it's not Burn, it's not Cal—it's saving Deviants. That's why I came back.

I clear my throat. "I need more names. There's only one left from the last list Clay gave me: Adele Parry."

His shoulders shift back. "Stay away from her. She's none of your business."

"Adele's name is on the list that Clay gave me, so it's my responsibility to find her, and yours to get her to safety." I fight to keep my voice even. "I'll continue to report to this location every night I can at 1:00 AM—just like I did with Clay." I straighten my shoulders. "I'll do my job. You do yours."

"You think I'm your new Extractor?" His nostrils flare. "No thank you. I'd rather not get killed."

"You're right." I shake my head. Clay will do it. "It's not safe for you in Haven."

"No one's safe working with you."

I lift my chin. "I've been part of thirty-seven successful extractions."

"And got your Extractor killed."

My head snaps back. "What?"

"Clayton's dead." Burn steps toward me, crossing his arms over his broad chest. "Dead, because of your incompetence."

"What happened?" My voice comes out in a breath that empties my lungs. They won't refill.

"Killed," he says, "along with your last target."

I double over. "No." Arabella? I gasp for breath, desperate for air. I straighten. "I saw the last expunging. It wasn't them."

"Management doesn't put on a show every time someone's exed. Especially not when it's a skinny little girl with glowing eyes who looks like a freaking angel."

Huge stones clog my throat. Arabella's dead. And Clay. "What happened?"

"They were picked up before they even got out of Haven. We didn't have a chance to mount a rescue mission before the Shredders dragged them off to one of their camps. By the time we found them, there wasn't much left."

My breaths quicken. I feel sick. "What went wrong? What can I do differently next time?"

"There won't be a next time. You're done," he says. "Out of the Freedom Army. You'll have no further contact with any of us."

"No." I feel as if I'm being crushed under a thousand tons of rubble. "The FA can't cut me off. I'll save more Deviants with or without you."

"Clay was a good man." Burn's voice shakes and he charges toward me, raising a fist.

It's all I can do not to duck, but he stops short of striking me. My heart thunders. "Were you and Clay close friends?" I ask softly.

His wince makes his answer clear. No wonder Burn's

been so strange. He just lost a good friend. So did I, but clearly Clay meant a lot to Burn. They probably knew each other for years, working side by side for the FA. Burn never knew his real parents.

Did Clay raise him? I realize how little I know about Burn.

My determination to regain his trust—and Rolph's—grows. I'm devastated that Arabella and Clay were caught, but whatever happened, I'm certain that the Comp didn't see me coming out of the manhole. I refuse to believe that I was the reason they were caught. If I could talk to Rolph I'd tell him that, but I suspect making my case to Burn won't help. Not right now when he's so angry.

If I find Adele Parry, they'll both see how much they need me.

I reach for the doorknob. "I'll report back here every night. I'll let you know when you can extract Adele. I'll find her."

"Good luck with that."

He sneers at me, and I study the strong, hard line of his jaw, the look in his dark eyes, trying to find a hint of the boy I knew. I try to find a glint of his bravery, a shadow of the wounds inside him, a trace of the way he used to look at me.

All I see is disdain.

I avert my gaze to avoid murder.

Three months suddenly feels like ten lifetimes. I thought that seeing Burn would make me feel closer to my family and ease some of my loneliness, but it's made me feel so much worse.

Until three months ago, I'd seen Drake every single day of his life, and without my brother around, a chunk of me is missing. Burn's attitude makes my loneliness worse. A deep, dark ache opens in my chest like a wound, a hole only my family can fill.

"Turn off your torch so I can open the door," I tell him, my voice cold.

The room goes dark and I slip out into the alley.

# CHAPTER TEN

STINGING AND STUNNED, I SLIP THROUGH THE AIR VENTS, following them down from the roof, and then drop from the opening into the barracks hallway. If I can't rescue Deviants anymore, then why am I in Haven? Why am I putting up with the loneliness, the danger, the stale air? And almost worse than all that, I'm shattered by Burn's complete and utter rejection.

He's the only person who fully knows me and accepts me. The real me. He's the only person who gets how it feels to lose control, how it feels to discover you've used your power to kill and not even remember. Both Burn and I have killed; we share the weight of that guilt. I thought we shared more.

Loneliness lands like dust clogging my throat, like a deep ache in my bones. Burn's indifference made the time

I've been separated from him and my family feel like hundreds of years, and the distance like thousands of miles.

Muscles shaking with fatigue, I slide into the hallway, then replace the grate. I have less than three hours before the morning bell rings.

Three nights in a row with barely any sleep. Once I find Adele I'll regain my place in the FA, but tonight I'm too tired to sneak into the System room to attempt another search. Eyes cast down, barely open, I head for my room.

"Where in Haven have you been?" Stacy says way too loudly and I jump.

Whispering is outside Stacy's skill set. Why didn't I check the hall? Did she see me come through the vent?

"I was using the toilet," I tell her, and then realize the women's toilet is past us both in the other direction.

"Liar." Her short brown curls bounce like springs as she shakes her head. "I'm reporting you to Larsson." She bumps my shoulder with hers as she passes, no doubt headed to follow through on her threat. My overly tired mind refuses to devise a solution.

"Wait."

Stacy turns and looks down at me with scorn. Her shoulders must be twice as wide as mine. She'll be way more plausible in the Comp uniform than I'll ever be.

"I was taking a walk," I tell her, "stretching my legs." I flex my foot and I don't need to fake a wince. "I had a cramp."

One side of her mouth twists up. "You could have walked your cramp out in our room."

"I didn't want to wake you."

Her lips squeeze together. "It's against regulation to be in the men's end of the barracks past 2100 hours."

"Then Stacy"—we both jump at the sound of Cal's voice from behind me—"why were *you* heading that way?"

Stacy runs a hand over her short curls and tips one shoulder forward as if wanting to make herself seem smaller, more feminine. "You're up late, Cal." Her tone is cloying. "Can't sleep?" She twists one of her curls. "Anything I can do to help?"

"I'm just making sure Glory gets back to her room."

"Haven't got around to revoking your license yet?" She gestures toward the dating bracelet on Cal's wrist.

"Stacy," Cal says evenly. "I've told you. Glory and I have no intention of revoking our license."

"You two sure don't act like a couple." Her eyes narrow. "She cringes when you touch her."

Cal's nostrils flare. "Our relationship is private."

I feel ill. Stacy's focus on Cal has revealed things I hoped no one would see.

Stacy reaches for his arm and leans in. "Is she holding something over you? Forcing you to stay with her? If your license is bogus, HR should know."

"Stacy, you need to drop it." Cal moves away from her and drapes his arm over my shoulder. I try not to stiffen, but thinking about it makes it harder.

"We're a real couple," I say.

"Could have fooled me." Stacy's jaw twitches. "You look like you're ready to run."

I lean into Cal.

"You'd really accuse us?" Cal appeals to Stacy. "I thought you were my friend."

"Yeah, well . . ." She's clearly torn between her crush on Cal and her hate for me. "I still don't know what Glory was doing out here in the hall. There's no way I'm buying her leg cramp excuse. I was awake an hour ago and she wasn't in our room then, either."

Cal's arm tenses behind me, but then he leans toward Stacy and whispers, "She wasn't there because she was with me."

Stacy's face twitches as if she's holding back her reaction. "You're lying. You guys weren't together. I don't believe you're even a couple. I'm not sure what kind of game you're playing, but if you're committing fraud, HR should know."

"You want proof we're a couple? Fine." Cal tilts my head back and kisses me full on the mouth.

I tense, but I need Stacy to believe Cal so I relax, soften my body, my mouth. Cal deepens his kiss and the pressure of his lips, the warmth of his hands, the tension and heat of his body reawaken something inside me and ignite what I used to feel, what I've felt for Cal since I was eleven and he was thirteen.

Cal is one of the best people I know—strong, generous and loyal—and at this moment I could fall back in love. Maybe I already have. Fatigue can't fully explain my wobbly legs, the stirring inside me, the heat. Without his hands for support, I feel certain I'd melt on the floor.

"Okay, okay." Stacy's voice cracks. "I get it. You can stop."

Cal pulls back from our kiss. Questions are mixed with

the passion in his eyes, but all I can offer him with mine is gratitude.

His lie was risky. He put his record on the line by tying himself to my absence. Stacy can't report me without reporting him too. Let's hope her desire to stay on Cal's good side outweighs her urge to hurt me.

Cal presses his warm lips to my forehead and then I walk on jelly legs, following Stacy to our room. When I reach the door, I turn back. Cal's watching, making sure that I'm safe, but the heat's vanished from his expression, leaving only questions.

Cal pulls me aside on our way out of the gym at the end of hand-to-hand combat training. "We need to talk."

"Larsson wants us in our full gear for the next class." I wipe a towel across my sweaty face. "Can we talk later?" I've been avoiding being alone with Cal all day, not wanting to face questions about last night.

"No." His hand's hot and firm on my bare forearm. "Now."

I could break out of his hold—I practiced the technique in class today—but don't want to hurt him. Plus, a few of our class members are still milling around and I can't cast further suspicion on our relationship status. If Stacy's questioned our dating license, perhaps others have too. Drawing attention is the last thing I want. I can't do anything that gets in the way of my saving more Deviants. Especially now that I'm on the outs with the FA.

I bend one leg and rest my foot on the wall behind me

so that my knee forms a barrier between us, a safety margin; because if he tries to kiss me again, I don't think I'll have the willpower to stop him. Based on my reaction last night, my body wants to be back together—for real—but I'm still confused and not ready to face his questions. Besides, I have more important priorities.

"Where were you?" he asks.

"Combat training. Same as you."

"Not now." He brushes sweat off his forehead with the sleeve of his t-shirt. "Last night." His eyes are filled with concern.

Guilt drapes over me and I drop my foot to the ground. "I was getting Jayma some contraband rats."

"In the middle of the night?"

"When else am I going to do it? Did you see her? She's so skinny. She needs extra meat."

He leans with his forearm flat against the wall next to my head. "I love that you're so generous and thoughtful, but"—his lips brush my hot forehead—"you need to be more careful. Take me with you next time."

I try to keep eye contact but can't. Gigantic secrets gnaw at my insides. How can he not see them? "I'm worried about Jayma."

"Scout will look out for her," he says. "Don't go out at night alone. Please. It's not safe." He leans, his breath hot on my face, his lips drawing closer.

It would be so easy to kiss him right now, to let his strong hands soothe the aches in my body, to let his lips transfer those aches other places.

But I slip to the side, escaping the closeness. "We'd better get changed." I stretch one arm across my chest, holding it across my body with the other hand.

He takes my arm and moves it down, removing the barrier between us. "What is it?" His voice is serious. "What aren't you telling me?"

"Nothing." I try to look into his eyes, but they disobey and flit away.

"Don't lie, Glory." His voice sounds more hurt than angry, but his jaw is hard, and I want to reach out and trace my finger along the sharp, hard line, to relax his features and mold them into the expression I love—the way he used to look at me with love in his eyes.

I want to share everything with Cal. I want to tell him every truth, but instead I smile in the way other girls smile at their boyfriends when they want something. I smile in the way Stacy smiles at Cal. "Can't a girl have a few secrets?"

His head jerks back. "Why are you acting like this?"

"Like what?" I tip my head to the side and touch his arm lightly.

He backs away.

"What?"

"You can't manipulate me, Glory, so don't even try."

I straighten against the wall, guilt and regret hardening every muscle inside me. "I . . . I . . . I'm sorry."

He crosses his arms over his chest. "Glory, I love you. But something's going on."

"There is a lot going on, but nothing you don't know. I

lost my brother, remember?" Cal thinks Drake is dead. "And I was kidnapped. I'm trying to get over it, but it's hard." My voice sounds tight. I can't fake sincerity. Not with Cal.

"There's something else." He shakes his head slowly. "I've known you your whole life, and if you can't be honest with me, well . . ." He runs his hand over his shortly cropped hair. "Maybe Stacy's right. Maybe you and I are over."

I gasp. His expression is hard and his words shoot into me like thousands of tiny spikes. Even if letting him go might be the right thing, the honorable thing, I can't lose Cal. It may be selfish, but I've lost too much.

"Is that what you want?" I ask, my voice small. "To revoke our license?"

His eyes fill with sadness. "No. Not at all. But I can't—I won't—go on like this."

He runs his hand lightly down my arm, stopping to hold my wrist. His thumb traces the edge of my bracelet and his touch ignites little fires inside me, opens a deep ache in my gut. I didn't realize until he threatened to take them away that Cal's support, his friendship, his love, are the only things keeping me stable, keeping me from dropping into the gaping dark hole of loneliness. Cal's the closest thing I have to family right now.

He takes my hands, intertwining our fingers. "You've always been secretive." He leans in closer. "You had to keep secrets from me because of your brother. But you don't need to keep secrets anymore. Not from me. You can trust me. I tell you everything."

I nod but can't speak. I feel transparent under his gaze, and for a second I wonder if I *am* transparent. Maybe Cal is a Deviant with some kind of a truth-sensing ability.

But that's ridiculous. Cal's transparent to me too, and I hate that I'm hurting him right now, that I've deceived him. Cal doesn't keep secrets—not from me—and I'm terrible to keep them from him. Especially after he gave me an alibi last night.

It's not fair. This has to end.

I look up into his eyes. "If you want to be with Stacy, I'll go with you to HR to revoke our license. I'll tick whichever box you want so our stories concur."

He wrinkles his nose. "I don't want to be with Stacy."

"Good." The word is out before I can think.

"I want you to be honest."

I squirm, wanting so badly to have someone else know my secrets, especially Cal. "If I tell you," I whisper, "you can't tell anyone."

He leans closer. "I promise."

I close my eyes for a moment. "When I sneak out at night,"—Am I really going to do it? My stomach twists, my mouth dries. I open my eyes—"it's to meet with Mr. Belando." I can't tell him more.

His eyes widen. "Why?"

I look around to make sure no one else is near. "Belando thinks there's a mole inside COT. Someone working with the terrorists."

"Really?" Cal's grip on my arm tightens. "Why did Belando come to you?"

"He thinks I can help him find Deviants because of my kidnapping. That's why he got me into the COT program."

Cal nods as if everything that's happened in the last three months suddenly makes sense. "Let me help." He's unable to hide the excitement in his voice.

"No. You can't." I look into his eyes. "And no one else can know about this." I press my palm against his chest. "No one."

He nods. "I promise. Who do you think it is?"

"No idea." I look around to make sure we're still alone. "Mr. Belando thinks the terrorists are planning to attack the President's Birthday celebration."

His body tenses. "Half of Haven will be there."

"I know."

"Don't worry." Cal pulls me into an embrace so tight I can feel his heart beating through my skin. "If Mr. Belando knows about the plan, the Comps will stop it. But be careful. I can't lose you. Not again. When you were kidnapped, I thought I'd die."

I relax, encased in Cal's protection, his love. Maybe it *is* time to unburden all my secrets, my guilt. If I tell Cal everything I know about Deviants, about Shredders, about the dust, about life Outside, maybe he'll accept me for who I am, especially if I tell him about my vow never to use my ability to kill.

The rest of the truth bubbles inside me, but I swallow hard to keep it down.

The risk is too high. The timing's not right and I need to keep focused on my most important goal. Once I find Adele and prove to Burn and Rolph that I deserve to stay in the FA, maybe then I can tell Cal everything.

I pull back and look into his eyes, now filled with heat.

"I shouldn't have told you," I say softly. "If Belando finds out, he'll kill me. I promised not to tell *anyone*." And by telling Cal, I've put him in danger.

"You can trust me, Glory. With anything. You know that, right?"

Pressing me against the wall, Cal bends to capture my lips and I yield, letting the swirling thrill of his kiss erase my fears, assuage my guilt, annihilate the weight of everything I can't tell him.

# CHAPTER ELEVEN

THE TENSION IN THE GYMNASIUM IS THICK AND ELECTRIC. IN front of us, a Shredder thrashes against chains, holding his outstretched arms between two metal poles.

Several of the recruits yelp and jump back, but I stand stock-still, fighting to control my hatred and fear. And fighting to understand why Larsson brought this monster not only into Haven but into our gym. This explains why he had us dress in full combat uniforms for class today, but we're unarmed and I know firsthand what these demented monsters can do.

The Shredder appears to be shirtless, but his clothes might be plastered to his skin with dried blood. Gashes gape on his neck and their symmetrical placement, three on each side, make the openings look like part of his anatomy rather than injuries. Perhaps his gashes are gills?

I shiver with the knowledge that if I ever became addicted to the dust, it might turn me into one of these monsters. I'd rather die. I've managed to commit enough atrocities without dust madness.

"Recruits." Larsson rubs his hands together. "Time for your real training to begin." The entire group moves back like a ripple on the surface of a lake. *Cowards.* I'm left out front.

"I see we have a volunteer." Without seeing Larsson's face under his visor, I can picture his cruel, derisive expression.

Another recruit steps up to join me. It's Cal, and I resist the urge to shift closer to him.

"Bring in the cage," Larsson yells, and a group of at least twenty Comps carry in sections of linked metal walls bounded by steel bars. They clamp them together until they form a box around the Shredder who continues to fight against his bindings, foam forming at the edges of his cracked, nearly black lips.

My fellow recruits hoot and holler. Now that the monster's caged, their bravado awakens, and shouts of, "I could take him," and "He doesn't look so bad," circulate around the group, building in volume and bluster.

I grit my teeth. These idiots have no idea. They haven't been up-close witnesses to a Shredder tearing into a human body or ripping off strips of skin. They haven't seen Shredders' mindless cruelty even toward each other.

And none of my classmates have actually killed a Shredder.

The crowd cheers as the Comps bring in a dead body on

a stretcher. Bile rises in my throat. It's a boy of about fourteen or fifteen, his curly blond hair wet against his head as he lies lifeless, dressed in only a pair of shorts. I try not to shake my head as I imagine the Comps' plan. My best guess is they'll toss his dead body into the cage so we recruits can see a less-gruesome version of a Shredder in action.

A man wearing a white coat over his suit takes out a needle and injects it into the dead boy's neck.

With a scream, the boy bolts upright on the stretcher—not dead—and looks around with open-eyed terror. "Where? What?" His words are barely audible through his hoarse voice and over the roars of my fellow recruits, most of who seem to find this spectacle exciting, not appalling.

Larsson blows his whistle and we all quiet down. "This Deviant has been condemned to death," he says. "Mr. Singh, the SVP of Compliance, has agreed to let us use his execution for this demonstration rather than schedule an expunging."

The group cheers. I don't. Instead, I hope this kid's Deviance is something that will help with his self-defense. Not that he'll live, even if he survives the Shredder.

Then I see the boy's hands and feet. They're webbed like the pictures of ducks and geese from the extinct animals textbooks from history class. His webbing won't help him fight this Shredder. I imagine that's one of the main reasons he was selected.

The boy jumps off the stretcher and runs, but he's quickly surrounded by Comps and restrained, arms pinned behind his back. He thrashes and kicks his feet, clearly realizing his fate.

"Solis. Up front." Larsson calls my name and my insides clench. "Asani, you too." He calls out Ansel's last name.

Cal moves forward with Ansel and me, and I'm grateful that Larsson doesn't seem to notice or care.

"Closer." Larsson lifts the visor on his helmet. "All of you. Up here. Now." He moves within a few feet of the front corner of the cage. "If you graduate, which you two won't, the lives of other Comps will be in your hands. I can't abide cowards. Especially not weak ones."

Refusing to be pushed from behind or to show fear, I march forward until I'm standing less than a foot from the closest wall of the cage. Through my visor, I look toward the Shredder and see what looks like terror in its eyes. But that's impossible. Just a reflection of mine. I know Shredders can think and plan attacks, but they don't experience fear.

"Lift your visors, cowards," Larsson barks, and with a rumble of snaps, everyone complies. Viewed without the dark plastic between us, the Shredder's skin is even harder to look at: brown and red and black, with pale-yellow patches on his chest, a color that might once have been white.

I recognize the off-white patches and nearly wretch. It's three of his ribs, exposed through dry and ravaged flesh. I cast my gaze down, less to protect myself from the vision than to protect the Shredder from my eyes.

"What's the matter, Recruit," Larsson yells, and before I'm certain who he's speaking to, he grabs my arm and throws me forward so I slam into the bars of the cage. The Shredder howls and struggles.

"Leave her alone," Cal says, and my muscles clench.

*No*, I think. *Stay out of this, Cal.*

Larsson stands stock-still, anger simmering under a strange and terrifying calm. "I told Belando it was a mistake to take dating partners into the same COT class. He's an idiot." He shakes his head as if he's discussing a misbehaving child, not his boss. "The girl will put you in danger," he says to Cal. "She'll get you killed."

"No she won't, sir."

In a flash, Larsson's fist, covered in heavy Comp armor, flies forward and smashes into Cal's exposed face. Cal's head snaps back and blood rushes from his nose.

"No," I cry out. Cal's bent at the waist, his hands covering his face. With all the blood, it's hard to tell how much damage was done.

Larsson glares at me but instead of acknowledging my outburst, he shoves the slumped Cal and yells, "Clean up your mess." He points to the puddle of blood.

The Shredder howls, probably at the scent, and I start to question my vow. If I caught Larsson's gaze right now, my look would most certainly kill.

Someone tosses Cal a cloth and he wipes his face, then holds the fabric down to slow the bleeding. I want to comfort him, to help, but I don't have a death wish and would likely make things worse for Cal.

The clang of metal on metal draws my eyes. The Comps open a door on the back wall of the cage, and throw the Deviant inside. He presses his back against the iron bars, but the Comps slam their guns into his body, forcing him forward.

The still-restrained Shredder bucks so ferociously I fear it'll tear off its own hands to free its arms.

With a loud snap, the clamps around the Shredder's wrists release. Its arms drop to its sides. For a moment, the creature's startled and confused, then it spins to face the Deviant who's trying to climb up the side of the cage, but his webbed hands and feet won't grip the bars.

The Shredder lunges and scrapes his fingers down the boy's back, leaving what look like claw marks. The Shredder's three middle fingertips resemble knives and I gasp in realization. He gashed his own neck with those hands, explaining the symmetry. I look away. I will not watch this. I've witnessed enough horrors.

Larsson grabs my chin and pulls me forward. "Watch."

My neck strains against the force, refusing to turn back.

"Watch, or flame out." He leans in close to my ear. "I'll break your neck if I have to."

I don't doubt him for a second. His hand forces my face back to the cage, but he can't force my eyes open. My Deviance tingles and sparks behind my eyes. I can't control it. A scream fills the room and I'm not certain whether it's the Deviant or the Shredder.

"Open your eyes. You need to see this for your own good." Larsson's voice is hard, but calmer than I expect. I comply, and the Deviant boy's directly in front of my now-opened eyes, his face pressed against the bars.

Our eyes lock and I fight against my power. It's no use. I've lost control. My Deviance has triggered and I'm locked onto the boy's brain.

Killing him would be the merciful thing to do—and I could. To end this more quickly, to spare this fellow Deviant from the torture, all I'd have to do is squeeze his brain, or twist his heart, or snap his carotid artery, or any of a number of things. I can hear and feel his heart beating loudly, as if it's inside me.

But I won't kill him. Never again. I lower my lids to break our connection.

Still gripping my chin, Larsson pushes me to the side and I stumble to the floor of the gymnasium, my hand sliding into the puddle of Cal's blood.

"Who wants to do the honors?" Larsson holds a large Aut-gun over his head. It's the kind of gun they use Outside, and it shoots in rapid succession—real bullets, not like the Shocker tags the Comps use inside. After three seconds of stunned silence, all the recruits yell out, begging to be the one to shoot into the cage. We've only used Auts twice and only during controlled lessons on a range.

Larsson tosses the gun toward Cal who has to drop the bloody towel from his face to catch it. "Let's see what you've learned."

Cal's eyes narrow. He assumes a wide-legged stance for the shot, not showing any pain in spite of the damage to his face and the blood gushing from his nose. The whole left side of his face is askew, swelling and bruising, and his normally prominent cheekbone is no longer visible.

I'm quite sure Cal didn't ask for the gun, but now that he has it, duty and responsibility pour off him faster than the blood from his surely-broken nose. Cal doesn't have a cruel or vicious bone in his body, but he honestly believes that killing both the Deviant and the Shredder is justified. Maybe he's right.

Cal raises the Aut. The rest of the group gives him a few feet of room. Strong hands pull me back so I won't get showered by red-hot spent shells. It's Larsson. Cal hesitates for a moment and I wonder if he's trying to decide which one to kill first, but then I realize his tactic. He's waiting until he can line them up and take both down with a single burst of gunfire.

The Shredder grabs the Deviant, and Cal fires. Rapid bangs puncture the air—I will never get used to that sound—and the faint smoke of spent gunpowder hits my nostrils before it's replaced by worse smells from inside the cage.

"Good job, Recruit." Larsson slaps Cal on the back. "If you can keep your mind off the little girl, you might just make it. Get that face looked at. Have someone take you to the Hospital."

"No," I scream and grab at Larsson's arm.

He shakes me off as if he barely felt me. "Recruits. To the barracks."

Our class marches out of the room in formation, leaving Cal and me alone with Larsson. I can't let this happen. I can't let Cal go to the Hospital.

"Going to the Hospital" is another euphemism for execution, another way for Management to get rid of the weak and the sick, to dispose of employees no longer useful to Haven.

Larsson's found a way to get one of us out of COT. I'll

bet he expects me to flame out once Cal's gone. Cal's visibly shaking although it's not clear whether it's caused by the prospect of the Hospital, his pain, or the loss of blood.

I put myself between Larsson and Cal. "You are not taking him to the Hospital."

Cal staggers forward to stand beside me. "She's right. I don't need the Hospital. It's not that bad." He touches his face, and his body lurches as if he's trying not to vomit.

"Recruit, you need medical attention." Larsson grabs past me for Cal's arm, but I stay in between and draw his attention.

I'm not the one hurt, but I can barely breathe. "No." I focus on Larsson's eyes. Saving Cal is worth breaking my vow. Cal cannot go to the Hospital.

Larsson's cold green eyes lock on mine. His heart's pumping more slowly than I expect. He doesn't care about the damage he's done and doesn't realize the danger I pose.

I squeeze, just a bit. Not nearly enough to kill, but enough to let him see I mean business. Larsson grimaces, but looks confused. So am I. What am I doing? I'm showing him who I am. He'll have me expunged.

Unless I kill him.

With only Cal as a witness we could claim Larsson collapsed. Cal might even believe that story. But who am I kidding? I can't do it. I can't kill. Not even someone as horrid as Larsson. It's wrong. I break away.

"Did someone call for medical help?" a female voice says.

Mrs. Kalin strides into the room and I suck in a sharp breath. She really does remind me of my late mother, down to the same confident stride as her heels tap the gymnasium floor.

"Mrs. Kalin." Larsson straightens and salutes, then drops his hand to his side as if suddenly realizing his instinctive gesture was wrong.

"What happened here?" She steps up to Cal and surveys his face. "Looks like a broken nose, but I can't be sure about your cheekbone with all that swelling. Not sure if it's broken or badly bruised. Come with me, young man, and we'll get you fixed up."

"No." I grab Mrs. Kalin's arm. "Don't take him to the Hospital. Please." I press the heel of my hand into my squeezing chest.

"Recruit." Larsson pulls me off her. "This is Mrs. Kalin, the VP of Health and Safety. Show some respect."

"Nice to see you again, Glory," she says.

Larsson looks startled, then glares at me.

Drawing deep breaths and trying to think clearly, I keep my gaze on the toes of her shoes, which shine against the dull gymnasium floor. I've just argued with one of the most powerful VPs in Haven. I'm dead.

Her hand softly takes my chin and tips my face up, but I refuse to look into her eyes. If I do, I'll hurt her. I can't. Not even to save Cal.

"I admire your concern for your dating partner." She brushes her thumb over my cheek. "Don't worry. I'll help your young man."

I remain between her and Cal. "Don't take him to the Hospital. Please. He's fine. He'll heal."

"He needs medical attention." Her voice is calm. "His nose is broken."

"I'm fine," Cal says but his voice is distorted and he's clearly having trouble breathing through the blood.

"Glory," Mrs. Kalin says. "Would you like to come with us to see for yourself?"

Blood rushes in my ears. "To the *Hospital*?" If I don't do something quickly, we're both dead.

"I don't think the Hospital will be necessary," she says. "The Executive Building is closer and I have a room there that's suitable for treating this kind of accident."

I nod slowly, and the tension in my shoulders eases. I don't fully trust her, but at least we're not going to the Hospital.

"Why don't you take off your helmets," she says. Both Cal and I remove our headgear, and she brushes stray hairs from my sweaty cheek to behind my ear. "My, you really are pretty."

My cheeks heat and I keep my gaze down.

"Now, let's get your young man's nose fixed." I flick my gaze up to her face as she sends me a reassuring smile. "You can be my assistant."

# CHAPTER TWELVE

ERVES FIRING, I STEP UP TO CAL WHO'S LYING ON A METAL table. His left eye's swollen shut, his nose no longer follows a straight line, and his cheek's turned an alarming shade of crimson.

"How do I look?" he asks.

"Fabulous." I grin. "Handsome as ever."

Mrs. Kalin steps to a counter at the side of the room and gestures for me to follow. "You knew someone who died in the Hospital, didn't you?" She squeezes my wrist. "Was it your mother?"

I pull my arm from her grip. "No."

She leans on the counter. "But you did lose your mother."

"How did you know?" My throat's tight, my voice strange. Did she look up my HR file? If she did, she knows the answer.

"It's not hard to see." She rests her hands on my shoulders. "The way you carry yourself, your strength, your sadness. I can tell you're alone."

I break down and lift my gaze. The instant I look into her smiling brown eyes, I relax—at least enough to control my ability. The kindness she projects is palpable.

"I can see the weight of the responsibility you've carried. It's right here." She squeezes my shoulders. "You had to grow up way too fast, didn't you?"

My throat tightens. Her even tone and her kindness remind me so much of my mother that I want to crumple and fall into her arms. I want to be comforted. I want to be loved. I want my mother back.

I look down, feeling overwhelmed by emotions.

"Every young girl needs a mother. If you ever need to talk—about anything—you let me know." Her hands drop from my shoulders.

"Okay."

She opens a metal cupboard and removes some supplies. "So why are you so nervous about the Hospital?" she asks.

"No one ever comes out." My insides freeze. Why did I open my big mouth?

She seems unfazed. "How many people do you know who've been admitted to the Hospital?"

"One." Just Jayma's brother. H&S had the Comps take him to the Hospital when Jayma and I were only ten. We never saw him again.

"And you jump to such conclusions?" She turns back to me and smiles softly, her eyes full of such kindness.

I feel safe. "I've heard of others."

"What others? How do you know it's not all a bunch of terrible rumors?"

I scan my memories and realize she's right. Everything I've heard about the Hospital is based on rumors. Jayma's brother was sick with the flu when he went in. It's possible H&S told Jayma's parents the truth when they claimed they couldn't save his life.

She raises her eyebrows. "A bright young girl like you who's interested in science—you shouldn't jump to conclusions without facts."

I don't sense any malice or deception in her eyes. "You're right." It's unbelievable how safe I feel with Mrs. Kalin. How at ease. How at home.

She selects a small vial of liquid. "If you're interested, I'll take you on a tour of the Hospital."

I look into her eyes to make sure she's serious. Her suggestion's oddly appealing considering my fears, but if I see the Hospital for myself, I'll know the truth. Assuming I come out alive.

Taking Cal's hand, I bend to kiss his undamaged cheek. Mrs. Kalin steps up to the table, a syringe in her hand. Cal's eyes widen with alarm.

"It's okay," I tell him. "She'll make you feel better." As I say this, I realize I believe what I'm saying. It feels odd to trust Mrs. Kalin—trusting is not in my nature—but it feels right. Maybe I've learned that lesson. I didn't trust Burn when he was trying to save Drake. I didn't trust my father when I first saw him again, either. Not until I learned the truth. It's time to trust my own judgment, and Mrs. Kalin hasn't given me a reason not to trust her.

Cal's fingers nearly crush mine as she injects the clear liquid, first high into his cheek, then another dose closer to his nose. His grip relaxes and I bend forward, pulling our clasped hands close to my chest. "It feels better, right?" My voice trembles.

He nods and I let out a long breath.

"Is it starting to feel numb?" Mrs. Kalin lightly prods his nose and he turns to face her.

"Yes." His voice is calm. "The pain has dulled. It's tingling."

"Then we're ready to begin." She smiles at him as she gently presses on his face from several angles. "Your nose is broken, but the good news is the cheekbone's only bruised. Glory, I need your help. Hold down Cal's shoulders."

She looks at me with reassurance in her eyes and I do as she asks. Mrs. Kalin takes his nose between her palms and the cracking noise sends chills down my spine. Cal barely resists my hold.

"There," Mrs. Kalin looks down at her handiwork. "Now, young man, I think you could use some rest." She injects another syringe, this time into the crook of his elbow, and within seconds Cal's eyes shut and his breathing slows.

"Is he okay?" I ask.

"He's just sleeping. Don't worry." She puts a manicured hand over mine, and her skin feels soft and warm.

"Why are you being so nice to me?" As soon as the words are out, I want them back in. Distrust is a hard habit to break.

"Why wouldn't I be nice to you?"

Feeling ashamed of my suspicions, I look down, unable to face her.

"You're a bright girl," she says. "Mr. Belando was smart to take you under his wing."

I snap my face up toward hers. "How did you know about that?"

Her eyes flash as she tips her head to the side. "Nothing to be alarmed about. Mr. Belando and I don't have any secrets. I'm glad you have a mentor in Senior Management, but a girl needs a woman's guidance." She squeezes my hand. "I'm so sorry about your mother."

I feel the ache in my heart that never goes away. Tears well in my eyes.

"All alone at such a young age. You deserve better."

"No"—I choke down a lump—"I don't." I turn my head to the side and catch a glimpse of my reflection in the shiny cupboard door, then quickly look away.

"Of course you do." She turns off the bright overhead lights, and the one left bathes the room in a comforting glow.

I shake my head. "I was horrible to my mother." If she had any idea what I did . . .

"Everyone has done *something* they regret." She smiles softly.

I fight my emotions, my rising tears.

"I'm sure your mother loved you," she says, "no matter what you did. It's important to move past it and forgive yourself. Making mistakes is an important part of growing up."

A sharp pain stabs my throat. I will not cry. But her

words, her presence, have made me feel the safest I've felt since my mother's death. I remember few details from that horrible day, but I do know my last words to my mother were harsh. She died thinking I hated her, and I can't believe I caused her so much pain.

"You're not alone, Glory." Mrs. Kalin's voice is calm and soothing. "I've done things I regret, things I'm ashamed of. That's how we learn, how we grow. We make mistakes, learn from them, and move on."

My chest heaves as I choke back tears.

"Oh, sweetie."

My shoulders collapse forward. That's what my mother used to call me.

She wraps her arms around me. "What we've done in the past is less important than what we do now and what we hope to do in the future. The key is not who you were or what you did; it's about who you are right now and who you want to be. Look at me."

I raise my eyes to hers. She's so pretty in the soft light, her expression so kind and sincere.

"If you let me, I can help you reach your potential."

Tears stream down my cheeks. She pulls me into a tight embrace and I let my guard down. My body heaves as I sob, as if every slice of pain, every stone of guilt, every bound-up emotion I've felt since I learned the truth are pouring from me at once. As if every wall I've built to constrain my emotions crumbles.

Mrs. Kalin strokes my back, my hair, and with each slow caress another layer of pain flows away. She's right. I can't take back what I did. I can't change it. All I can do is move forward. All I can do is be a good person, now and in the future. And my work with the FA, saving other Deviants, is helping with that. I need to regain Rolph's trust.

I lean back and wipe my face on the sleeve of my t-shirt. Smiling, she hands me a square of white cloth.

"What's this?" I ask.

"A handkerchief. Use it to dry your tears, to blow your nose."

"But—?" It's hers and the thought of soiling its gleaming fabric is horrifying.

"Keep it. It's yours now." Looking directly at me, Mrs. Kalin smiles, and I feel like I've fallen backwards into a pile of soft blankets, like I'm floating in a lake with the hot sun on my face, like I'm being hugged by my mother.

It's been ages since I've felt so calm and safe. There's no one inside Haven who knows the full truth about me and I wish I could tell Mrs. Kalin who I am, what I did, what I'm doing to make up for it. The truth tingles on the tip of my tongue, gurgling up so insistently, I fear I'll choke in my efforts to contain it. I want to tell her how many Deviants I've helped and still hope to help. How I'm sacrificing myself to save others. I want her to be proud.

"Thank you so much." I look down, unable to trust my emotional control enough to maintain eye contact. My breaths come faster.

Nearly hyperventilating, I grow dizzy and close my eyes. It's been so long since I cried, and my mind's thick and clouded. I struggle to sort through my confusion, my divided emotions. Have I let myself be sucked in by Mrs. Kalin's kindness out of guilt and loneliness? Am I that desperate to feel loved again? To be forgiven?

Keeping my eyes closed, I shake my head. I can't forget who this woman is. I mustn't. She might be kind. She might be insightful. She might even be sincere in her wish to mentor me, but she's still Management. I shouldn't trust her—not fully. And I can't let myself be distracted by my selfish need to feel loved.

# CHAPTER THIRTEEN

IN THE MANAGEMENT MALL, SITTING IN THE CHAIR IN A ROOM that Mrs. Kalin called a Salon, I run my hand down my hair, unsure how to react. It's softer and silkier than I imagined possible and feels so different without the permanent ridge from my ponytail string.

Spending ration points on something like cutting my hair seems frivolous. Most people I know learned how to cut their own hair by age six. I glance into the mirror and instantly feel uncomfortable, like rats are crawling over my skin. When I was little, we had a small mirror in our apartment and I'm not sure where it went.

Once the mirror was gone, I had no ration points to replace it, and looking at my reflection for the first time in years, I shudder. My hair flies up, then falls back into place—perfectly. It must be a result of the smooth, sharp cuts—a feat not possible with the knife I use. I look down.

"You look beautiful," Mrs. Kalin says from beside me.

My gaze snaps back to the mirror. It's kind of true. I barely recognize myself. My skin shines from the lotions the lady put on after scrubbing it, and my bruises barely show through the make up she dabbed on my cheeks.

"I can't get over it." She bends and puts her cheek next to mine, nearly touching. "We might be mistaken for mother and daughter."

Our eyes meet in the mirror and warmth floods up from my chest. Tears heat my eyes.

She spins my chair around to face her. "What's wrong?"

"I—nothing. This is so lovely. Everything you're doing for me. Thank you."

"You miss your mother." She bends and takes my hands in hers. "Of course you do." She runs her hand over my hair. "I was never blessed with a daughter, but if I had one, I'd want her to be exactly like you."

I keep my eyes down.

"What's wrong?" Mrs. Kalin rests her hand on my shoulder. "Are you worried about Cal?"

I shake my head.

"Don't you like your hair?"

"It's wonderful. Thank you." Not wanting to face her, I twist my chair back and keep my gaze away from the mirror.

"But *something's* troubling you." Her finger tips my chin up, but I focus on a foggy patch on the mirror instead of our reflections.

"Nothing's wrong."

Even I can tell my words aren't sincere, and my skin prickles under her attention. I don't deserve the happiness she makes me feel. As much as she reminds me of my mom, she's not, and I can't yield to the comfort my traitorous subconscious seems determined to accept.

She slides an arm over my shoulders and bends so that our cheeks are nearly touching. I assume she's looking at our side-by-side reflections, but I stare above at the reflected image of a laser-projected sign that advertises the President's Birthday celebration. Apparently there's a banquet that only executives can attend.

"It's so fortuitous that we found each other, don't you think?" Her voice is so bright I let our eyes meet in the mirror for an instant, and smile. "If I can do anything for you, let me know. Please. Anything. Just ask."

I look down. Her tone is almost pleading, as if my asking her for something would be the key to her happiness. I glance into the mirror again, and her expression's so warm that I let my gaze linger on the reflection of her eyes—brown and deep and caring. Instantly I feel safer, calmer. I know that it's only because of how much she looks and sounds like my mom; I know it's only because I'm missing my mother; but it's been years since I've been so relaxed. Surely it can't hurt to absorb this feeling a few moments longer. Logic dictates that I should be terrified of this woman, hate her, but it's just the opposite. I'm realizing that I've never felt less afraid.

"Maybe I can help with whatever's troubling you," she says. "Is it your young man?"

I shrug, fighting the urge to tell her everything I've been dying to tell someone—anyone.

"He'll be fine. Or is it something besides his injury?" She squeezes my shoulders. "You know, only 63.4 percent of dating licenses result in marriage contracts. Don't worry. You'll find the right boy."

"He is the right boy," I blurt. "I'm the wrong girl." It's uncanny how she reads me.

"Look at me." Her voice is stern and I lift my eyes to focus on hers in the mirror. "Don't say that," she says. "Ever. You are absolutely the right girl, the most special girl I've met, and I won't have you think otherwise."

She doesn't know all the reasons she's wrong, but her words ease my discomfort and I suddenly want to confide in her, to ask her advice. Maybe she can help me feel like less of a freak. Or figure out how I can feel so much for Cal after everything that happened with Burn. Or why it hurts so much that Burn's being cruel. Or why I could let anything happen with Burn in the first place, when I knew how much Cal loved me. Or whether it's possible to love two boys at the same time. Or whether someone like me can ever experience love.

With so many questions, I don't know which to ask first and I look down at my hands.

She straightens and smoothes her dress. "We're all done here. How about we find you some nice clothes."

An hour later, I tug at the fabric covering my ribs. The dress shows too much of my figure—a figure I didn't know was there. I'm not sure I've ever seen a reflection of my whole body at once. Who knew mirrors came in such big sizes?

Mrs. Kalin rises from her chair in the curtained-off section of the clothing store. "I think this is the one." She brushes the fabric covering my shoulder. "The red makes your hair gleam and deepens your eyes."

I glance back at the mirror and study the dress as objectively as I can. She's right: dressed like this, I'm prettier than I thought. "Thank you, but I don't need this dress. Where would I ever wear it?"

The woman who works at the store steps closer. "You can wear it on the President's Birthday," she says brightly and I don't point out that I'll be in a Comp uniform, on duty that day.

"Your daughter is very beautiful," she says to Mrs.Kalin. "You must be very proud."

"Thank you," Mrs. Kalin says before I can open my mouth. Contradicting her in front of this stranger seems rude. The saleswoman's lips are bright pink, in a shade that couldn't be natural, especially paired with her brown skin, and I assume she's got some kind of colored wax or paint on them. I make a note to ask Mrs. Kalin about it later.

"That will be all," Mrs. Kalin says, and the woman returns to the front of the shop where she was busy arranging an entire rack of similar dresses when we arrived.

Mrs. Kalin stands next to me and smoothes my hair. "I'll keep the dress at my apartment if you like. That way your friends won't be jealous."

"Thank you." I smooth the skirt, trying to keep focused.

I'm still feeling overwhelmed and lightheaded. Everything here is so brightly colored—the store even smells nice—and I draw a long breath, trying to pinpoint the scent. I realize it reminds me of Outside, of a fresh breeze coming over the fields. I wonder how they get the air so clean down here. "I didn't even know stores like this existed."

"Lower paygrade employees aren't meant to know of such things," she says.

"Why not?"

"If employees are exposed to goods and services they can't afford, it's bad for employee morale."

"That doesn't seem right."

She takes my shoulders and turns me toward her. "You have a generous heart—it's one of the reasons I admire you—but you know that not every employee can earn ration points at the same level. The economy would collapse if they did. Pay rates vary according to responsibility and ability. Otherwise, no one would accept the more challenging jobs."

"But—" I remember how hard my mom worked in the sewing factories, how she came home with her fingers cracked and bleeding. I think of how many Sky Maintenance workers are killed every year in accidents. I look into her eyes, studying her expression and trying to judge whether or not I should state my opinions, but before I start, I realize she's right. If I'd known that such lovely things were available for purchase—new—I would have resented it.

I look away from Mrs. Kalin's eyes and down to the shiny, soft fabric of the dress and wonder where such fine weaving was done. I can't quite get my head around the fact that, according to the storekeeper, no one has ever worn this dress before—ever!—and staring at the tiny woven threads, dizziness overtakes me. My vision blurs.

Something shifts in my mind, like when one of the TVs in the Hub has interference, and I remember that nothing's as black and white as Mrs. Kalin makes it seem. Cut off from my family and worried about Cal, cut off from the FA and sliced to bits by Burn's cruelty, I'm too vulnerable right now. I'm letting memories of my mother and Mrs. Kalin's kindness cloud my judgment.

"Employees who grow up in the Pents"—I don't look up—"never have a chance to train for the jobs that earn enough ration points for things like this. Everyone in Haven works hard—not just Management."

Stomach churning, I brace myself. Will she rip the dress from my body and have me expunged for speaking out against the P&P? I lift my eyes to gauge her reaction. For a split second I think she's frowning, but then realize I'm wrong.

Empathy and understanding emanate from her in warm waves. She crosses to sit in a plush, two-person chair next to the mirror. "I agree that we need policy reforms," Mrs. Kalin says. "As safe as the P&P makes life for every employee, there's always room for improvement. As a senior member of Management, I'm always open to hearing suggestions—especially from a bright, young employee like you. How can we in Management change things if we don't know what needs changing?"

"You think things should change?" I make a conscious

decision to close my gaping mouth. Surely she's not criticizing the P&P, criticizing Management.

"Yes." She leans close. "Not every senior executive feels the way I do, but I hope to make Haven a better place for everyone."

"Really?"

She nods. "The P&P was never meant to be a static document. Policies can and should change."

"What about Deviants?" I say.

Mrs. Kalin tips her head to the side as she rises. "What about them?"

My stomach tightens. I've said too much. But this might be my chance to affect real change inside Haven, real change without bloodshed, without terrorist bombs, without more FA soldiers like Clay dying needlessly. It's time to be brave. I lift my gaze from the shiny silver floor to face her.

"How come Management tosses Deviants out into the dust, no questions asked? How can you be sure that all Deviants are dangerous? I mean, maybe they're just different. Different isn't always bad." I chew on my lower lip.

"I agree." Mrs. Kalin's voice is a conspiratorial whisper. I snap my eyes up to look at hers and find no deception. She leans in close. "But don't tell anyone I said so." She takes my arm, draws me over to the big chair, and we sit together. My red dress nearly glows against the plush, dark blue fabric.

"Understanding what makes Deviants different," she continues, "is one of my top priorities for Health & Safety. One of the primary research projects at the Hospital."

"Really?" Excitement scrambles inside me. "You're doing

experiments to discover why some people became Deviants after the dust?" Is it possible that Mrs. Kalin might save us all?

"Yes." Her expression intensifies and fills with what looks like pride. "I knew you had a head for science."

"What have you found out?" I ask, breathless.

She glances up to the front of the store, as if she's checking to make sure the woman's not listening. "My current hypothesis is that Deviants hold the key to the ongoing survival of mankind. Deviants adapted to the dust. It behooves us to understand that, not fear it."

My excitement nearly bursts through my chest. She gets it. She understands. Better than that, she thinks Deviants are the key. I am the key.

"It is true," she continues, "that some Deviants have committed horrible crimes, but if we treat Deviants like criminals, what should we expect?" She shrugs one shoulder.

It's the first time I've felt so accepted, so understood by an adult, and I have to remind myself that she doesn't actually know that I'm a Deviant.

Or maybe she does. Maybe she's saying these reassuring things to let me know it's okay to tell her. Maybe this is her way of letting me know she's on my side—no matter what.

Warmth surrounds me, fills me, and I feel more loved and confident than I have since my mother died—even before that. I'm as close to Mrs. Kalin as I ever was to my mother and I long to tell her.

In fact, I should tell Mrs. Kalin everything I know about

Deviants, about the dust, and about life Outside. It might help her research, might help save humanity. Thousands of thoughts and words scramble inside me, and looking into her eyes, I feel as if I could tell her anything. I truly feel that once I tell her the truth she'll accept me for who I really am.

My head feels like it might burst, and I feel my Deviance rise. Breaking eye contact, I stare at my hands, and they move in and out of focus. Dizziness invades and I blink to clear my head. So many emotions at once have made me feel strange. I nearly told her too much.

I cast my gaze down. "I'm glad to hear you have an open mind about Deviants. I was scared to say anything." I pause. "Sometimes I have subversive anti-policy thoughts."

"Every bright young person does," she says. "It's normal to question authority, especially at your age." She sounds so sincere, but could she be lying? I wish I had some way to be certain I can trust her. I wish my Deviance let me hear thoughts.

I draw a deep breath.

Outside, when my father was pulling me up a cliff, I thought I heard his thoughts—but I'm not certain.

I hurt him that day. I know *that* with certainty. So, even if I can hear thoughts, can I do it without hurting the person? And more importantly, can I do it without Mrs. Kalin figuring out I'm a Deviant?

It's worth the risk. I need to try. I need to be brave. This isn't just about me. It's about all the other Deviants inside Haven. I need to know if I can trust Mrs. Kalin.

Fear and anxiety fuel my Deviance and I look her straight in the eyes. I lock on immediately and focus on her brain—but instead of twisting, I listen.

*So special. So alone. So hurt. I wish she'd fully trust me. If only she'd call me Mother.*

My anxiety washes away. I blink, breaking our connection, and give in to the smile that spreads on my lips. "Thank you," I say on an exhale. "I can't tell you how much that means to me."

"Thank you for what, dear?"

I shake my head. I almost revealed too much again. "Thank you for treating me today. And for saying that my subversive thoughts are normal. Sometimes I feel like such a freak."

Did I really hear her thoughts, or just imagine what I wanted to hear? I wish I had a way to be certain. I look through the store and out to the mall where crowds walk by, all in clean, well-repaired clothing. How can there be so many new things?

She pushes my hair behind my ears. "Honey, there's a big difference between being special and being a freak—and *you* are special." She clears her throat. "But that's enough serious talk. This outing is supposed to be a treat. How are things going with Cal? How long have you two had your license?"

"Just over three months." My cheeks heat. "It's going fine."

"Just fine?" She winks. "Has he kissed you? Do you have any questions about what you're feeling when you're around him?"

I look up at her and smile through my embarrassment.

Cal is a safer topic than Deviants or Haven policies. "I like him. A lot. I have for years, even before we applied for our license."

She smiles. "But?"

"But sometimes I wonder if he's the right boy for me. The one meant for me—the only one—you know?" An image of Burn—the bulk of his body, the intensity in his dark eyes—reignites how he made me feel. My body tingles and heats, but I shake my head. I need to forget Burn. Even if acting so coldly was his way to cope with seeing me again, he made his point. We're done.

I clear my throat. "I don't know why I've got doubts about Cal. I'm so lucky to be licensed to him. He's wonderful. It's a miracle he wants to be with someone like me, and I'm nuts to think there might be someone better. I'm not so special."

"Glory,"—she cups my face—"you're so wrong, and in time I hope you'll understand just how special you are."

# CHAPTER FOURTEEN

THE CORRIDOR IN THE EXECUTIVE BUILDING IS DARK EXCEPT for a battery-powered safety light high in the far corner at the end. I slip from the stairwell onto the fifth floor and head toward Mr. Belando's office. After getting back from my outing with Mrs. Kalin, I contacted him claiming to have intel about the mole. I don't. Not really. But I plan to get him to type his code with me watching.

Today's outing gave me hope for the future, but in the meantime I need that code. Once I have it, I'll be able to find Adele Parry, and once I've found her I can get back to finding more Deviants. First on my list will be my friend Gage's kids.

Even if I can't convince Rolph that he needs me, I can use Belando's code to find Deviants on my own. Burn might be acting like a jerk, but I know if I find any Deviants, he'll save them. And perhaps I can use the passcode to help find the mole and stop the terrorists. The President's Birthday is a week from today. The stakes have never been higher. I can't fail.

Listening for activity, I strain to hear anything above my heartbeat. I'll never get used to the stress of being on the posh lower floors of the Exec Building, the domain of Senior Management. Especially not now that I have to sneak in.

Light spills from under Mr. Belando's door and I creep forward, pausing at the edge of each office to make sure it's unoccupied. The soft carpet cushions my footsteps, and my back hovers over pristinely painted walls decorated with art works he told me were in a public museum BTD.

His door's closed and I'm not sure whether I should go in, knock, or wait. Knocking will make noise I can't afford so I reach for the handle.

I snap back. Voices. He's not alone. Pressing against the wall beside his door, I slide along it into a shadow about six feet away.

Belando's office door opens and light floods the hall. A large man in a dark grey business suit steps out of the office, then turns back to shake Mr. Belando's hand. My chest freezes. It's the President. I've only ever seen him on the screens in the Hub, but he's unmistakable. Tall, broad shouldered, and although he looks no older than Mr. Belando, his hair is silver like highly polished metal.

"Congratulations, again," he says to Mr. Belando. "I'm sorry the circumstances are so unpleasant, but the honor is deserved nonetheless."

"Thank you, sir," Mr. Belando says.

"I personally selected you for this position." He claps Belando on the shoulder. "I put myself on the line for you."

"I won't let you down."

"I'm certain you won't." The President faces me, and my throat tightens with each rapid beat of my heart.

Although I'm shadowed, he sees me. I'm certain he sees me.

But the President turns away and strides down the hall, his gait strong and silent, as if he weighs nothing, even though he's one of the largest men I've ever seen—besides Burn. At the end of the hall, the light from the corner glints off his hair and he traces a long-fingered hand over the unnatural silver, as if he knows someone's watching. I can't breathe.

When I'm certain he's rounded the corner, I creep forward. Reaching Mr. Belando's door, I push it open with one hesitant finger, like it's booby-trapped.

"Come in," Mr. Belando says with more lightness in his voice than I expect. "You're late."

"I—" Better not to tell him I saw the President. No telling how he might react. "I'm sorry."

"Sit." He motions toward the chair across from him and then runs a finger over the top edge of a brass plaque on his desk. The plaque reads Mr. Belando: Senior Vice President, Compliance.

"You were promoted."

He leans back in his chair, lifts a glass filled with an amber liquid, and takes a long sip. His cheeks are flushed—something I've never seen on the normally polished man—

and I wonder whether it has something to do with the drink or the President's visit. For all I know, both Presidential visits and amber liquids are regular items on Mr. Belando's daily schedule. "Yes, I was promoted."

"Congratulations."

He sets the glass down and the liquid sloshes. "Tragic, really. Mr. Singh, my predecessor, hasn't been heard from in days. No one's certain where he is, but the position couldn't be left unfilled, could it?" A satisfied grin drifts onto his face.

I don't respond and can't help but wonder if Mr. Belando played a part in his former boss's disappearance, or how a man in his position could simply disappear. If Mr. Singh is gone, he was either tossed out of the dome in a secret expunging, or simply chopped up in the compost factory. Clearly, he is dead. I shiver. I have no doubt that Mr. Belando could make *me* disappear, and get rid of any trace of me in the System too. It would be like I never existed.

Mr. Belando tips his hand back and forth a few times, and the amber liquid sloshes up the sides of his glass. "What do you have for me?" His expression resurfaces with a serious veneer. "It had better be good. We're running out of time." He sets his glass on his desk.

Time to launch my plan. "You asked me to report anything unusual at COT."

"And?"

"There was a fight in our rec room. One of the recruits accused another of being a Deviant."

Mr. Belando leans forward. "Which one?"

"I didn't see the accused, but I did see his accuser." There's not a chance that I'll give him Ansel's name, but I need to give him something to put my plan into action.

"Who was it?"

"Thor Kwaraski." The second his name is out of my mouth, my throat thickens. With my accusation, he'll be guilty until proven innocent. "Sir, to be clear, I don't think that Thor's the mole. No one in our recruiting group is more loyal."

"Excessive loyalty could be the boy's cover." His hands slide toward the light that will activate his System terminal and I learn forward to get a better angle. His fingers stop short.

"I don't think it's Thor, sir, but the fight got me thinking about connections between the recruits in our class, connections that they have to other Comps, connections to Management."

Mr. Belando nods, interested.

"It would be helpful to know whether any of the COT recruits had relationships to each other before training started, or whether they're related to any of the instructors or to other Comps or to anyone in Management or to any known Deviants or other offenders." I fall into a couple of those categories myself, but Mr. Belando knows that.

He frowns. "How would that help?"

I draw a long breath. "Do you think the mole is someone with a prior relationship to anyone else in the COT program or Management?"

"Not likely." He frowns and drums his fingers on the desk. I'm losing him.

"That's what I thought too," I say brightly and slide forward in my chair. "If I cross-reference the COT recruits' HR files I can rule some people out and narrow my search." I can feel my pulse throb in my throat.

Mr. Belando stills in his chair, and I can tell that I've captured his interest. So far so good. I move even further ahead in my chair until I'm almost at the edge of his desk. "My security level doesn't give the access I need for that kind of database query." I just need to see him type in his code. I'm sure if I had access to the right information I could narrow down the mole suspects, find Adele, and find more Deviants—all three. Everything's riding on my seeing this passcode.

Mr. Belando stares at me for what feels like an hour. His chest rises and falls in a slow rhythm, and my heart beats so hard I fear he hears it. He drains the rest of the amber liquid, sets the glass down, and the ice cubes clink.

Nerves scramble over my body like a thousand rat feet. At any moment I'm going to break out in a sweat. He yanks his chair forward.

I jump. My heart slams against my ribs like it wants out.

"Do you expect me to change your security level? Is that it? Do you expect me to circumvent the P&P?"

I shake my head. "No, sir. I only wondered if you might do some database searches for me." I swallow. "If it's convenient."

He grunts, but then swipes his hand to wake his keyboard and screen. I lean to better my angle. I have three theories about the key that starts his code. If I can become sure about that, I can figure the rest from its pattern.

"Your theory's worth a shot." He starts to type his passcode and I lean over the desk, straining to get a better view.

He started on the J—I'm certain—and in my head, I recite the numbers and letters as he types them, burning the pattern into my mind as his thick fingers pound the desk. I've seen him type his code seven times now between all my visits to his office and the pattern's remained the same.

I think I've got it, but I'm not sure.

He looks up and I bounce back from the desk.

"I've submitted a rush request to the Audit department," he says. "They'll complete your searches. Normally these requests take months, but you should have the results in two to three days. Let's see how many names your loner theory kicks out." He stands.

"Thank you, sir. I'm sure these searches will be helpful."

His code will be helpful. My only problem is deciding which to do first: find the mole, find Adele, find Gage's kids or find more Deviants to save?

He narrows his eyes. "You'd better find the mole soon. The President's Birthday is one week from tomorrow."

When I get back to the barracks, I check on Cal. He's in his room, nose taped, and still sleeping off Mrs. Kalin's medicine. Happy to see him safe, I get back to business and take the seat in the study room farthest from the entrance. The room's about half full of recruits. We have twenty minutes before lights out and everyone's using the System to study for our policy exam tomorrow.

Crowded room or not, I can't wait. What if Belando changes his code?

I swipe my hand under the beam of light to activate the screen and keyboard. With an empty feeling in the pit of my stomach, my fingers fumble as I type in the code. Hovering for a moment on the ninth of twelve characters, unable to choose between the Z and the X. I select X.

*Beep.*

I look up at the sound. My heart rate soars but no one even turns, and I realize I could claim to have mistyped my own passcode. I'll get three tries before a real alarm sounds.

A drop of sweat traces over my temple, and I close my eyes and imagine Mr. Belando typing in his code. Yes, a Z, not an X, but I'm no longer confident whether it's a T or a U following it. The numbers are easier because he moved his right hand over to the number pad and that's more compact and easier to watch.

I open my eyes, draw a deep breath, and try again, choosing the Z and the U.

*Beep.*

My chest constricts and I suck in a ragged breath. One more chance. My hands tremble. I look around the room. No one's watching, but it feels as if I have an audience of thousands.

Thinking of all the Deviants who need saving, I try one last time, opting for the Z and T. Closing my eyes, I strike the last key, a 6.

No beep.

I open my eyes as the screen appears before me, reading, "Good Evening, Mr. Belando."

My eyes dart around. No one's watching, but it's not

hard to imagine that somewhere there's another set of eyes looking out from this screen and seeing that I'm not Mr. Belando. My shoulders tense. Even if no one looks at my screen, it's all too possible that someone, somewhere, will review the log of Mr. Belando's System access. I'm hoping that, since he's in charge of Compliance, I only have him to fear. I'm not sure how I'll explain what I'm doing to him, but I need to be brave, and I'll cross that bridge if I come to it. Chances are he doesn't review his own accesses.

The next screen reads COMPLIANCE across the top. Below that, the menu options list virtually every other department inside Haven. I've always known the Compliance department was powerful—its employees oversee the performance of every other department and audit their adherence to the Haven Policies & Procedures Manual—but until this moment, with every detail in Haven literally at my fingertips, I hadn't fully understood that power.

Blocking those thoughts, I select HR RECORDS, and I'm about to search for Adele Parry, but I reverse my priority list and enter Gage's name instead. If one or both of his kids are Deviants, this might be my one and only chance to access the full HR database and find them. I can't pass up this chance to help his kids.

TERMINATED appears on the screen under Gage's name. Dead.

If they know he's still alive, it's not recorded here. His profile is still linked to his marriage contract partner, Theresa. From her HR record I discover they have two children:

Kara's fourteen and Tobin's eleven. I wish there were some way I could safely get news to them that he's alive. They deserve to know.

As much as I hated my father when I thought he was the one who hurt Drake and killed Mom, I wish I'd known he was alive.

I memorize their address, the department Theresa works in, and the location of the GT center that both Tobin and Kara attend.

There's a flag next to Tobin's name in his GT class list. I touch it and a message box appears. "Absent twenty-three consecutive training sessions. Parasitic behavior reported to Compliance." I gasp. It's a note from his instructor from at least a month ago.

I search through menus until I find a list of open audits and then search through the open investigation list for Tobin's employee number. It's not there.

Either I'm too late or no one in Compliance has acted on the note from Tobin's GT instructor—yet. There's one small benefit to all the Comps being so focused on finding the terrorists: it's created an audit backlog.

Backlog or not, assuming Tobin's GT absences were to hide a Deviance, I need to find him quickly.

The study room door opens, and I swipe my hand to close down my screen; but it's just one of my classmates whose name I've forgotten or never noticed. He nods before taking a seat at the other side of the room.

I use my own passcode to open the study files on my screen and pretend to review the material, but I can't concentrate. Besides, I'm already feeling prepared for the exam.

After five minutes, I gather the courage to use Mr. Belando's code again. This time, before I look for Adele, I perform some searches on my COT classmates' HR files, hoping to find a key to the mole's identity, but I don't find anything of interest. At least now, if the unthinkable happens and Mr. Belando realizes I used his code, I can demonstrate how I was looking for the mole. I doubt that will make him forgive me, but I can't let that fear stop me.

Giving up on my mole queries, I search for Adele. Her name brings up the work placement and residence that Clay gave me, but I already know she's not there. I've checked. I then discover a feature to show the full employee list for her former work placement.

There she is. Her ID photo shows a square face, short dark hair, thick eyebrows, and an angry expression.

What happened to you, Adele? Why is there no transfer or termination record? I split the screen and compare the lists of employees at her work placement now and a year ago. The only other change is a female who was transferred to some place called a laundry. On a whim, I look at her photo in the list of laundry employees. It's Adele.

Somehow Adele has assumed another woman's employee number and records. I quickly take note of her details. Heart pounding, I take a huge risk and send an anonymous e-note to Adele, asking her to meet me tomorrow night.

Tomorrow is the Quarter End Free Day, but it's too risky to approach her during daylight hours. Better if I can get her to meet me at night. I sign it, "A friend."

I know from class that these notes aren't ever *really* anonymous, that even low-level auditors can trace them; plus, her supervisors at the laundry will be able to see it if they choose to. But I'll worry about that if I'm caught.

Hoping to cover my tracks, I go back to the list of transfers from Adele's old job and follow a few more links, thrilled when I actually find the parent of one of my fellow COT recruits. That will help my cover story with Belando should I need one.

I search for other records at Gage's wife's work placement too, then I do more searches on our Comp class and our training instructors, leaving a complicated trail I hope Mr. Belando will find plausible. I'll claim I didn't want to wait for the audit reports.

Adrenaline surges. I was made for spy work. If I continue to be smart and careful, I might live beyond seventeen.

"What are you doing?" Captain Larsson asks.

I jump and press the kill key to completely shut down my screen. "Studying," I blurt. How did he creep up on me?

He narrows his eyes and leans over the table toward me. "Didn't look like studying to me." He points to his eyes and then to me. "I'm watching you, Solis. Be careful."

I lift my chin and look at him calmly and evenly. "Yes, sir."

*Too bad Larsson*, I think. I am Glory, super spy. You can't scare me.

# CHAPTER FIFTEEN

THERE ARE FEWER PEOPLE IN THE HUB TODAY THAN ON most QEF Days, but it's still crowded. With the President's Birthday only six days away, some people must have decided to stay home, but more will come that day. Many more people will be here that day and if the terrorists strike then, so many lives will be lost. Scanning the crowd, I wonder whether anyone here is one of the terrorists. It's not clear what they want other than to disrupt our lives and make us lose confidence in Management. They're nuts. Setting bombs is not the way to do that.

But I don't want to think about terrorists right now. The bright lights from the Hub screens shine and bounce off the glass and steel buildings—such a contrast from the dark alleys and rooftops at night—and my skin almost sings at being outdoors while the sun light's turned on. The feeling doesn't compare to real sunlight; still, it's great, and I'm determined to enjoy this short respite from my stressful and busy life.

There's little I can do right now anyway, and everything's falling into place. Adele responded to my e-note and agreed to meet me tonight in the laundry. As long as Burn—or someone from the FA—shows up at the meeting spot tonight, I can let him know I found Adele. It's my best chance to get back on the team.

"Isn't the Hub beautiful today?" Jayma tips her head back and spins.

"I did that." Scout touches her shoulder and points up to a new billboard with a photo of the President standing in front of the Haven logo and grinning ear to ear. The colors are bright and the President's teeth gleam with blinding white.

"You painted it?" Jayma stares at Scout in awe.

"I put it up." He puffs out his chest. "Well, my crew did. It was difficult to get it straight."

"Why aren't there more people here?" Jayma asks.

"Not sure," Cal says. "It's kind of odd for a Quarter End."

"It's the terrorists," Scout says, then wraps his arms around Jayma's waist from behind. "People are afraid to come to the Hub since that last bombing."

"Don't worry." Cal slides his hand up my back to my shoulder. "There's too much security for anything to happen here." He gestures with his head to the Comps lining the Hub's perimeter.

In addition to the Comps we all see, Cal and I know from class that there are a minimum of eleven Comps posted in buildings around the Hub. But Shocker tags—even bullets—won't do anything against bombs.

"The terrorists are cowards." Cal claps his younger brother on the back. "They'd never come near the Hub. Plus, assuming they're Deviant freaks, we'd spot them."

"You're probably right," Scout says, "but people are scared." He looks up at a large screen that's flashing the Haven motto: Haven Equals Safety. "Haven used to be such a safe place."

I suppress a grin. We graduated from GT just last term but Scout's talking as if he's an old man looking back on his youth. And the Haven slogan is laughable. Terrorists aside, no one in Haven understands what safety means, or real danger for that matter.

"Hey there, stranger." Stacy bounds up to Cal and grins, totally ignoring me. Ansel, Quentin, and the handful of other recruits who are with her nod their hellos.

"You found us." Cal says, and Stacy leans in for a hug, clinging to him even after he drops his hands. He smiles an apology at me.

"How's your nose healing?" Stacy asks. "You were so brave that day."

"It's not that bad," Cal says, and she rubs his arm.

I turn away. Cal said he doesn't like Stacy in that way, and I believe him, but that doesn't mean I want to watch her flirt with my boyfriend.

I gesture for Ansel and the others to come over to meet Jayma and Scout, and after I've made introductions, everyone chats and admires the new lights and sights in the Hub as if we're all good friends.

Ansel pulls me aside. "You okay with that?" He crooks his head over toward Cal and Stacy. She's still standing way too close and laughing.

"It's no big deal," I tell Ansel, but I wish I could convince the bands of elastic tightening around my stomach.

"No, *you're* the best," Stacy says to Cal. As much as I try to ignore her, I can't.

"Really?" He runs his hand over his cropped hair.

"And you deserve the best too," she says. "You should upgrade."

"Upgrade?" he asks.

She grabs hold of his wrist and circles her fingers around the edge of his dating bracelet.

*Enough.* I stride over and slip under Cal's arm.

He squeezes my shoulder and smiles. "Stacy's trying to convince me that I'm the best in our martial arts class." He shakes his head.

"You're the best in my eyes." I reach up to his neck and pull his lips down to mine, kissing him harder than I should in public.

"Wow," he says quietly when we come up for air. "Where did that come from?"

I shrug and give him a small smile.

Cal bends his lips toward my ear. "Let's get out of here. I want some time with you. In private."

My whole body buzzes, and I pull back a tiny bit. The

level of license we have does not permit activities that might result in procreation.

Stacy stares at the ground, arms crossed over her chest, and I know her discomfort shouldn't make me happy, but it does.

The music from the Hub loudspeakers swells, and the screens pulse with changing colors to get our attention. An image of the President appears on the screens, beaming down.

"Welcome," he says, "and thank you so much to each and every Haven employee who's working hard to make the Hub beautiful for my birthday celebrations." He gestures as if he's actually up there on the screen and surveying the surroundings. "I hope that you'll all attend."

The crowd murmurs.

"In fact," the President continues, "I've declared my birthday a Haven-wide holiday!"

The crowd cheers, and without thinking, I'm cheering too. It's hard not to get caught up in the excitement, especially when it's about something nice, like a party rather than someone getting exed. And I'm still on a high from the kiss.

"And now," the President continues, "I have a special treat."

The crowd's spellbound.

"Today's exercises will be led by none other than the VP of Health and Safety herself, Mrs. Kalin."

The crowd cheers, the President steps to the side, and Mrs. Kalin, looking very fit in a brown jumpsuit, steps into the frame. "Thank you, Mr. President." She turns to the camera and smiles. Normally we do the exercises at our work placements, led by our supervisors or instructors when we were in GT.

I look into Mrs. Kalin's eyes on the screen—so much easier without the risk of revealing my Deviance—and they're warm and inviting. My shoulders drop and I realize how tense I've been these past days—past months.

I remember my pledge to take advantage of this free day and forget about Adele and the FA, forget about the mole, forget about Burn. Right now, I'll enjoy this special treat of having Mrs. Kalin lead our exercise routine.

"Why is everyone cheering for the witch who's in charge of the Hospital?" Jayma asks, and I peel my gaze from Mrs. Kalin's eyes on the screen. Jayma's facing the ground. Scout and Cal are jumping and cheering with everyone else and getting set up to do the exercises, and neither of them has noticed Jayma's discomfort.

I touch her arm. "I've met Mrs. Kalin. She didn't seem that bad."

Jayma pulls her arm back. "H&S killed my brother."

"The *flu* killed your brother."

Jayma glares at me. "I can't believe you're saying that."

"I know. I know." I shake my head. "It's just that . . ." It's just what? It's not like I fully trust Mrs. Kalin. "I wanted to hate her when I met her. I really did. But she's been really nice to me, and she helped Cal when he broke his nose. And she cut my hair." Not exactly true, but how could I explain the Salon?

I look back up to the screen. Mrs. Kalin asks whether

everyone has been taking his or her vitamin powder. She smiles and it feels like it's meant just for me.

Happiness pushes out my negativity and I remember all the things Mrs. Kalin told me, and I turn back to Jayma. "After meeting her, it's hard to believe that they're doing anything that bad in the Hospital—on purpose anyway. It could all be rumors."

Jayma's jaw twitches.

"Listen," I smile, "let's not think about anything sad today. I almost never get to see you anymore. Let's not waste it."

"You're right." She hugs me. "But I'm going to do the routine from memory. No way am I looking up at that witch on the screen."

I open my mouth to protest, but there's no point in arguing with Jayma. She hasn't met Mrs. Kalin, and to be honest, I can't believe I let myself lap up even an ounce of the woman's kindness. Maybe it's a symptom of my loneliness, of my frustration at being cut off from the FA. Once I get back on track . . .

"Now that the President's gone"—Mrs. Kalin winks at us from the screen—"I want to ask for your help. Let's make his birthday extra special. He's declared a Haven-wide holiday, so spread the word. Tell all your friends and family to attend. Let's see how many employees we can pack into the Hub!" She clasps her hands together. "There will be plenty of surprises. You won't want to miss it."

Every time I look up at her image I'm reminded of her kindness, and the way she talks about the Birthday Celebration makes me excited, even though I know about the bomb threat. It seems Mr. Belando hasn't told Mrs. Kalin or the President about the danger—if there is danger. I trust Mrs. Kalin a lot more than I trust Mr. Belando.

"Come on, you two," Cal says from beside us.

Jayma and I set up to exercise with the rest of the crowd, and the routine Mrs. Kalin chooses is my favorite. With the louder speakers here in the Hub and the lights moving in time to the music, exhilaration floods through me. Cal's grinning too, and I can't help but stare at his flexing muscles as he drops down to do push-ups beside me.

"You're beautiful," he says when we jump back up. "I love your new haircut."

I feel beautiful. I feel strong and happy—happier than I've felt my entire life.

Yes, my life is dangerous. Yes, I've hit a setback, but no one's better equipped to handle these challenges than me. Soon I'll be back to rescuing Deviants again.

And I won't stop until every Deviant in Haven is safe.

That night, I slip off my bunk and land without a sound. Only one of my shoes is at the end of the bed and I feel around in the dark for the other. Stacy's not snoring yet, but if I don't leave soon I'll be late for my meeting with Adele.

"You're so lucky," Stacy whispers.

"You're awake." I turn on my torch to help me find my other shoe.

My light flashes past her. Her eyes are red and she slips the back of her hand over a wet cheek.

"What's wrong?" I find my shoe and slip it on.

"Like you care." Her voice is shaky and tight.

I take a deep breath, then crouch beside her bunk. "If you don't want to talk about it, fine. But after the way you've treated me, don't accuse me of not caring."

Tears well in her eyes and she turns toward the wall. "Say hi to Cal." Her voice cracks.

I sigh. "You flirt with my dating partner incessantly, then expect me to feel sorry for you?"

She turns back. "You don't know what it's like."

"What?"

"Being a freak.

I suck in a sharp breath. Is Stacy a Deviant? What if she's the mole? "You're not a freak, Stacy." I keep my voice calm and even.

"You don't get it."

"I get it more than you think." I certainly know how it feels to be different, to think you're alone. "Sometimes I feel like a freak too."

"Yeah, right." She sniffs. "You're all tiny and cute."

"I am not."

She snorts. "You have no idea what it's like to be the big girl, the tall girl, the girl whose shoulders are wider than most of the boys'." She blinks and tears slide down her cheek and into her ear. "I look like a monster." She pounds the bed with her fist. "I hate myself."

I reach out and tentatively touch her shoulder. It's damp with sweat. "I'm sure you'll find the right guy."

"No, I won't. Most boys never even notice I'm a girl."

"I'm sure that's not true."

"Cal's the only boy who's nice to me, but of course he doesn't want me. Of course he'd choose someone like you."

I draw a long breath. "Cal's a good guy—and he likes you—but he and I have known each other since we were kids." Guilt turns my stomach to stone.

My time with Cal has an expiry date. Some day he'll find out what I am and we'll be over. I hate thinking that I'm keeping him from finding a girl who could move forward to a marriage contract with him. I've been selfish in taking him back. If I were a better person, I'd set Cal free. And maybe Stacy's not as bad as I thought. "Are you okay?"

"Leave me alone." Stacy turns to her side to face the wall.

"Stacy . . ." I'm not sure what else to say. Plus, I'm late. "Maybe if you'd stop being so mean, you and I could be friends."

She swings an arm behind her and slugs me in the shoulder.

"Ouch."

She doesn't apologize, but rolls onto her back.

"Are you going to report me for sneaking out?" I ask. One way or another, I have to leave.

She throws one of her shirts at me. "Get out."

I'd feel better if Stacy really were the mole. Then I'd feel more certain she wouldn't report me to Larsson for leaving the room.

# CHAPTER SIXTEEN

STEAM RISES FROM THE HUGE LAUNDRY VATS BEHIND ADELE, and long wooden paddles rest against the concrete brick wall. Strong chemicals burn my throat and nose. I pity Adele for having to work in here every day. She's going to love the fresh air once she's on the Outside and away from the dust that's especially concentrated near the perimeter of Haven.

"Trust me," I tell Adele. "You're not safe anymore, but I can help."

"You?" She narrows her eyes and crosses her arms over her wide chest. "You couldn't help a speck of dust."

"Yes, I can." I can't tell her how I found her or how many other Deviants I've saved—not without blowing my cover—but the fact that I tracked her down proves that I've got what it takes to remain a key part of the FA. Burn will see that, Rolph will see that, and I'll be reinstated. I can't let my pride get in the way of this mission. "It's not just me. I'll put you in touch with others who'll help you."

"I don't *need* help." Skepticism seeps from her every pore. She draws her hands together and her biceps flex. I have no doubt she could crush me with those laundry-strengthened arms, or snap my neck.

"The Comps are on to you," I tell her. They must be if she was on Clayton's list. "They're going to arrest you. You'll be exed."

"How do I know you're not one of those Jecs kids," she says, "here to get me to admit to something and then turn me in?" She told me that we're alone in here, but her voice is too loud and it sends nerves snaking through me.

I glance around. "I'm not a Jecs." My stomach churns. I'm not part of the Junior Ethics Committee who spy on fellow employees, but she's closer to the truth than I'd like. What if she finds out I'm in COT?

"What can you do?" she asks.

My shoulders relax. "I'll take you to meet my contact, two nights from now. He'll get you to safety."

"You misunderstood." She crooks up one side of her mouth. "What. Can. You. Do."

I shake my head.

"Your *Deviance*."

"I—" This doesn't feel right. Not at all. "What makes you think I'm a Deviant?" Mine doesn't show. Hers doesn't either, assuming she has one.

"Why won't you tell me?" She pushes my shoulder, shoving me back. "Why should I trust you, if you don't trust me?"

Before I catch my balance, she shoves me again, then again.

"Stop it." I regain a strong stance.

"Come on," she taunts. "Show me what you can do."

"I hurt people, okay?" Understatement. I kill. Steam bursts from a machine behind us and I spin.

She snorts. "You don't look strong enough to hurt anything." She widens her stance. "Give it a go, then. Hurt me."

"I—my Deviance. It's not about strength."

"Show me."

I shake my head. "I'm not going to hurt you."

"Then we're done here." She steps back, starting to turn.

"No." I lunge toward her, grab her wrist, and she stares down at it until I let go. Maybe a demonstration won't be so bad—especially if I'm careful not to hurt her. Which means I have to trust my control. "Give me a minute."

She snorts with derision. Her skepticism and patronizing tone fuel my anger. Perfect. At least that will make my demonstration easier, my emotions easier to summon.

The telltale tingling builds behind my eyes. "Look at me."

She does, and I immediately latch on, feeling the pull that holds her to me, captured, helpless, but belligerent. She has no idea how easily I could kill her.

I choose her lungs, somewhere that she'll feel my power without my risking permanent damage—I hope. Squeezing, I use my mind to push all the air from her chest and I hold tightly so she can't draw more in. Panic rises in her eyes, her arms flap at her sides, and then one hand flies forward.

A fire starts in a pile of rags near my feet.

I break eye contact and jump back, then look around for something to smother the flames. Adele reaches into one of the laundry vats, pulls out a sack of wet fabric, and sloshes it onto the fire to douse it. Curses fly from her mouth faster and stronger than any of the off-policy language I've heard from Burn. The smell of singed fibers fills the air.

"I hope the detectors don't pick that up," she says once the fire's out and she waves the smoke to help it dissipate. "They're set low in here because of the steam." She examines the sack of what look like sheets that she used to put out the fire. It's marked with a tag showing an employee number. It must be someone in Management because everyone I know washes their own bedding. After satisfying herself that the fabric's not damaged, she tosses the sack back into the vat and then spins toward me, eyes narrowed. "How did you do that?"

I suck in a breath. "I didn't start the fire."

"I know *that*." She looks at me like I'm an idiot. "I started the fire. That's what I do."

"Of course. Yes."

"You didn't answer." She steps back from me, almost as if she's afraid.

I step forward. Her being afraid puts me at an advantage. "It comes from my eyes, and when it kicks in, I sense the insides of other people. I can grab hold and kill them."

Backing up, she stumbles away from me. "What are you? Some kind of monster?"

Her words are like a slap, but I raise my chin, bracing

for another. "If I'm a monster, so are you. I'm a Deviant." It's one of the first times I've said it aloud. "And I'm here to help you." Rescuing kids is much easier.

She swallows and runs her tongue over her teeth as if her mouth's gone dry. She puts her hands on her hips. "If you know people Outside, then prove it."

"I didn't say anything about Outside."

"But that's what you're talking about, right? Getting me Outside? Your people figured out how to live in the dust, right?"

I smile, neither confirming nor denying her assumption. "Night after next. Meet me in the alley behind this laundry, and I'll take you to meet my partner. He'll take it from there."

"I'm not meeting anyone or going anywhere until you tell me the details of your plan and where you're taking me." She leans toward me, waiting for my answer.

My body wants to climb out of my skin. I've always found a way to connect to the kids I've saved and gain their trust. But this woman is beyond stubborn. I can't mention Outside or the Settlement without violating every rule of my mission. Making a mistake like that wouldn't help me regain Rolph's trust.

When Burn saved Drake, he made contact with us directly, but now that I'm working on the inside we're supposed to have some separation to limit the FA's exposure in case one of our targets goes to the Comps. The less my targets know, the less they can reveal. If I'm the only one they know, I'm the only one at risk. Not the Extractor, not the Transport Team, not the Settlement, not the entire Freedom Army.

Adele's eyes open wide. "I just realized where I've seen you. You're that girl. The one who was kidnapped."

I freeze.

"Okay." She lifts her chin. "I'll meet your partner."

*Finally.* "Great. Meet me night after next at 0200 hours in the alley—"

"No." She shakes her head. "We'll meet tomorrow. Midnight. Here."

"That's not how it works. He sets the place. He knows where it will be safe for both of you. You can't arrange the meeting." And I can't guarantee I'll find Burn again before tomorrow at midnight.

"Well, then." Adele shrugs. "I guess there won't be a meeting."

On the way back to the barracks, I enter the room where I met Clay for my briefings, hoping Burn's there, determined to convince him to help me extract Adele and hoping he won't be such a jerk.

A shape moves in the corner. Whoever's in the room, they're too small to be Burn, and I brace for an attack. "Who's there?" I call into near darkness.

The shape steps into the light, and I realize what I saw was a trick of the dim light. Burn steps around the high stack of plastic containers, and his coat flares out above the tops of his heavy boots. "Came back for more, little girl?" His voice is cold and mocking.

I grit my teeth to absorb his dig and let it slide off me. "I spotted a new security camera in this alley. I'm not certain it works, but be careful on your way out."

"You think I'm afraid of a camera?"

"Burn"—I step forward—"you're wanted for kidnapping. They know what you look like." I don't mention the SIM avatar based on his likeness.

He rolls his eyes. "Let me worry about that. I certainly don't need your protection." His voice sounds the same, dark and thick, but he's changed so much in the months we've been apart. I refuse to tolerate his insulting behavior.

Whatever was between us is over. Clearly. My heart is cracked, maybe broken, but at least now I can stop thinking about him, which might eventually take one layer off my guilt for betraying Cal.

I will no longer make any concessions or allowances for Burn. He's had a tough life, but so have I, and I won't try to second-guess his behavior. He's not worth it. He's just an FA soldier I have to deal with to do my job.

I plant my feet solidly and straighten my back. "I found her."

"Who?"

"Adele Parry."

His shoulders twitch.

I try to restrain a smirk. "You didn't expect me to pull it off, did you?"

"Am I supposed to be impressed?" He glares and waits for what feels like a full minute. "So, where is she? I don't have all night."

"You think I do?" I stomp forward. "Do you have any idea how much I risk by meeting here? You're not the only one taking risks, you know." I hate that he's gotten the better of me. I've lost patience. I can't believe I ever cared for this guy.

He grunts. "Bring her here, then. Night after next. Two-thirty."

"Actually . . ." I try to figure out a good way to say this, but there isn't one. "She wants to meet in the laundry. Tomorrow. Midnight."

He shakes his head. "Who does she think she is, making conditions?"

"She's stubborn."

"And you're incompetent. Dangerous to others. Worse than your father."

My heart skips a beat. "My father?"

"You have no idea, do you?" Covering the space in two strides, Burn's in front of me, his face close to mine, and angry. "When your father was exed, people died. Good people."

I fight to stay calm. "You told me. That was the first time you changed into . . ." After turning into the monster he becomes, Burn killed a member of his own team, as well as the Shredders who were attacking my father.

Surprise flashes on his face. Did he forget he told me?

I lift my chin. "I'm going to meet Adele Parry in the laundry tomorrow. If you want to extract her, I suggest you come too."

He grunts and storms out, leaving me with no idea whether or not he plans to show up tomorrow night to meet Adele.

# CHAPTER SEVENTEEN

THE LAUNDRY IS QUIET. THE LAST SHIFT ENDED HOURS AGO and it's not as steamy as last night, but I hate this place.

I wanted to arrive early to check every space in here for danger, but Stacy took ages to fall asleep tonight and now I've only got five minutes until my scheduled meeting with Adele. With such a short time, it's impossible to walk the floor and check behind every vat.

Formulating a Plan B, I climb up a winding metal staircase at the side that leads to a catwalk.

The iron-barred door between the stairs and the catwalk is locked, but at least I've secured a better view and I don't see anyone on the floor below. It doesn't ease my fears. The laundry's full of shadows and large pieces of equipment, and there's no knowing what or who could be lurking. All I'm sure of is that I don't see Adele and I don't see Burn.

I hope he shows up.

"So, where is he?" Adele's voice echoes through the room, and I lean from the side of the stairs. She's standing in an open area in the middle of the room not visible from where I was standing.

I scramble down the stairs and out to meet her, deciding on the way that it's best to pretend that I've got a plan, that I've got everything under control. Even if Burn is gone from my life forever, I'll get word to Rolph somehow and he'll assign me a new Extractor. He has to.

"You'll meet my contact tomorrow night," I tell Adele. "At the originally scheduled time. If you want to live, you need to trust him."

"Trust him? I don't trust you." She pokes me in the chest, pushing me back a step.

I square my shoulders. "I guess you'd rather be discovered by the Comps and exed, then."

She grabs my arm.

My combat training kicks in. I twist and bend, taking advantage of her grip on me and pulling her forward. The much larger woman flips over me and lands on the cement floor with a thud. Cursing, she rolls over and slowly pulls herself up to her knees. "You little bitch."

"I want to help you."

"Oh, you're going to help me all right." She raises a hand and twists her wrist.

At least twenty other people step out from behind laundry vats and storage bins. I'm surrounded. Ambushed.

My heart rate triples in an instant—I was right to suspect

this location—but I fight to stay calm, to survey the situation and make a new plan. More than half of the people she summoned are teens, like me, but many are clearly older, and at least two are little kids. Keeping my head high, I plant my feet solidly, taking the stance learned in COT. "Who are these people?" I ask.

Adele steps toward me and tips her head to the side. Her neck cracks. "I'll ask the questions."

I cross my arms over my chest.

"Not so brave now you're outnumbered, are you?" She pushes me again, but I'm standing so strongly, I barely budge.

"Stop it, Adele." A boy steps from the ring of people surrounding me. "This isn't the way." He stands beside Adele and his light brown skin contrasts with her pallor. "This girl has information we need."

"Who are you?" I ask him. He's my age, maybe a year older, and so skinny he looks malnourished. But his expression seems kind. Compared to Adele, anyway.

He reaches his hand forward to shake mine. "Name's Joshua. Nice to meet you, Glory." I take his hand.

An electric shock zaps through me and I pull my tingling hand back. Everyone laughs and my cheeks burn.

"Sorry about that," he smiles and his brown eyes flash with what seems like friendly humor, not distrust. "I didn't hurt you, did I?"

I shake my head.

"Good. I was only letting you see what I am." He gestures around. "What we all are. This way our cards are on the table."

"You're all Deviants?"

"Wow, you're really smart," Adele says.

"And you're really sarcastic," I shoot back.

"Adele," Joshua says. "I'll take it from here."

She narrows her eyes. "I don't trust this girl. Not at all. Something's fishy. She's lying, and whatever you do, don't look into her eyes."

Joshua turns back to me and looks straight into my eyes. "You won't hurt me, will you?"

"Depends." I raise my chin.

He holds up his hands. "I think we all have the same interests here."

"Maybe." As apprehensive as I feel, this could be huge. I've found a few dozen Deviants who all need to be extracted from Haven to the Settlement. If she gathered these others together for me to help, maybe Adele trusts me more than I thought. With or without Burn's help, I need to find a way to get all of them out of Haven.

"Adele says you've been Outside," Joshua says.

I tighten my jaw. "I didn't say that." Although I suppose I implied it.

"But it's true."

I shift my stance, not answering.

Joshua steps toward me. "Can you put us in touch with your contacts Outside? The ones who want to overthrow Management?"

I fight to keep my expression neutral. This is treading onto very dangerous ground, and I'm not sure what I should tell this boy—a boy who I'm pretty sure could fatally electrocute me if he wanted. Plus, I never said anything to Adele about overturning Management. I keep my mouth shut.

"Why don't I go first?" He smiles.

I nod.

"We're rebels," he says. "We're working to overthrow Management. We have a plan to stop them from expunging Deviants and torturing us in that damned Hospital."

I lean forward. "How do you know what happens in the Hospital?"

A small boy steps forward. "I've been in the Hospital."

My eyes widen. If this boy's alive, then Mrs. Kalin wasn't lying. Some people do come out. "What happened to you in the Hospital?"

"I wasn't in for long," he answers. "But I heard the screams. It was awful." He's shaking.

"But you were released."

"Not exactly." He shakes his head. "The third day I was there, they marched eight of us through the halls—naked. A door opened and I escaped."

"Just like that?"

"Like this." The small boy fades from view, except for his clothes that remain suspended in mid air.

My breath catches. "You're invisible."

He reappears. "My Deviance got me in there. My Deviance saved me."

I turn back to Joshua. "You called your group rebels. What exactly do you want from me?"

"For a long time, we've suspected that there were others like us working Outside, but we've been unable to make contact, and some of us"—he shrugs—"let's just say that the idea of working with anyone who could survive in the dust isn't very palatable."

"So what are you doing to rebel?" I ask, and my skin crawls with the suspicion that this group could be connected to the terrorists. As much as I want to save every Deviant, and as much as I want to see Management's hold on Haven broken, what the terrorists do—setting bombs, killing innocent people—isn't the answer.

"We protect each other," Joshua says. "We hide the ones who need hiding." He gestures to the side, and a girl, whose skin is covered in fur, steps forward and nods.

"Is that all?"

Joshua's chin rises. "I've told you who we are. How about you tell me about your people. How do they survive Outside? How do they breathe in the dust? Where do they live?"

"I . . . I'm not authorized to say more." I draw my feet together and clamp my arms against the sides of my body in my best soldier stance. "I'll talk to my contacts and we'll get you all to safety. One by one. I promise."

"What good is your promise?" Adele steps forward. "I don't trust this girl. And after we bomb the Hub—"

"Quiet." Joshua cuts Adele off.

My chest freezes. "*You're* bombing the Hub?" I can't hide my shock, my revulsion. Adele just confirmed my worst fear; these people are the terrorists. Fury fires inside me. "No. Don't do it. That's not the way."

"Management must be stopped," Joshua says, and the group moves in more tightly around me. "Whose side are you on?"

"If you bomb the Hub"—pressure builds inside my head, my chest—"you'll be hurting more than just Management. Bombs, violence, hurting innocent people. That isn't the way. I can help you get Outside."

"All of us?" Adele says. "Every employee in Haven? You think Management's going to just sit back and let that happen?" Her forehead and nose wrinkle and she shakes her head. "I don't trust her." She beckons to the side and a large man advances.

Will I even make it out of here alive?

Searching for escape routes and assessing the situation, I glance back up to the catwalk.

I gasp. There's a Comp up there. I can't make out his face but the uniform's unmistakable. Trying not to react, I step up to Joshua and lean forward. "There's a Comp on the catwalk."

We look back, but the catwalk's empty.

"Check her." Adele grabs my wrist and the tall man she beckoned shines an ultraviolet light on my inner arm, revealing my COT mark.

"I knew it," Adele yells. "She's in COT. Probably one of those Jecs kids. This is a trap."

"No"—panic rises inside me—"I can explain." Do they think I brought the Comp?

The group scatters like rats—even Adele and Joshua—and I'm left standing alone. I need to think this through. I need to figure out a way to stop them from bombing the Hub.

A dark shadow moves on the catwalk. I spin and brace myself. How will I explain myself to a Comp? But the shadow vanishes. The Comp's gone.

# CHAPTER EIGHTEEN

KEEPING TO THE SHADOWS ON MY ROUTE HOME, I REPLAY the night's events. Joshua didn't seem shocked when I told him about the Comp. Is he working with them? If so, Belando was right. Not only are the so-called rebels planning to bomb the Hub; they've got a Comp on their side.

And I need a plan.

I could report them all to Mr. Belando, but some of those Deviants deserve to be saved—especially the kids—and how can I know which ones are guilty? Even the ones who are, if they're fighting for their freedom from Management— a group who wants to kill them—do the ends justify their means?

I'm one to talk, after the things I've done.

Mrs. Kalin might help me sort this out. Of anyone I've come across in Management, she seems the most open-minded, the most willing to see things from more than one side; but I'm still not convinced I can trust her. Not with these people's lives. And how could I explain to her what I was doing at the laundry? Or how I met Adele?

Talking to her isn't an option. Neither is going to Belando. Either choice would betray fellow Deviants. My loyalties have never felt so torn.

I wish I could discuss this with Cal. Always so calm and reasoned, he'd help me see what's right, but telling Cal any more than I already have will put him in danger.

What I need to do is meet with Joshua again. He seemed to be their leader, in spite of his youth. I'll convince him that they don't need to resort to terrorism. Once I connect Joshua with the FA, he'll follow Rolph's orders. Rolph didn't share details during the short time I was doing FA training, but I know the FA has a plan to overthrow Management.

I turn the corner and Burn's in my path.

Jumping back, I check the street for cameras, for Comps—for anyone. Burn's face is well known inside Haven and I don't understand how he's getting around undetected. "What are you doing out in the open?" I whisper. "You're being careless."

"*I'm* being careless? That's rich." He tips his head back and laughs. "I saw your little meeting."

"You were *there*?" My cheeks flare. "Why didn't you come out? You could have helped me convince them, and now I'm not even sure how to find them again." But I will. I found Adele and I can find Joshua. I don't need Burn's help.

Twenty feet behind Burn, two Comps step into the alley, and I pull him around the corner.

He pushes me away. "Keep your hands off me," he says. "I told you. I don't mess with little girls."

"You jerk." Anger rises hot and hard. "I hate you."

"Ha. That's not possible. You don't even know who I am." He grins, then his face, his body, his entire appearance starts to change.

I blink. Blink again. Then rub my eyes.

I've already seen Burn change into a much bigger, much scarier, out-of-control version of himself, but this is different. Instead of turning into that oversized, powerful monster, he's becoming shorter, slimmer, almost feminine. His clothes change too. This is some kind of illusion.

Closing my eyes I count to three. Something strange is happening with my vision. When I open my eyes, I skitter back on the pavement. "What?" I cry out. "How?"

Burn's no longer there. Instead, it's a woman, at least ten inches shorter than Burn, dressed in brown leather pants and a tight khaki t-shirt that's cut low over a well-endowed chest. Silver hair flairs out around her light brown complexion.

"Who are you?"

She sneers. "Get your ass off the ground."

I shake my head.

She leans against the wall.

Then she changes again—into my father.

My throat clamps shut. I know it's not him; it can't be. But it's like my dad's right there, just feet away from me, and

167

it's all I can do not to leap up and wrap my arms around this parental mirage.

But before I make a fool of myself, she—or he?—turns back into the leather-clad woman.

I stand and brush off my pants, and the woman stares at me from a face that's got sharp, fine features and distinctive eyes. They look purple against her caramel complexion.

"Who are you?" My voice shakes. I draw a deep breath. "Is this the real you?"

"The one and only." She shakes her head, and her silver hair sparkles under the moon light. "Name's Zina."

"Where's Burn?"

"How should I know?"

"It was you all along." My words come out on a weak breath.

"Of course." The smirk on her face is repugnant, and it's the same one I saw the other night on what I thought was Burn's face.

My mind cycles through my last two encounters with the person I thought was Burn. Burn is brooding, he's dark, he holds his emotions close to his chest, but he's not smug or taunting. He's not cruel. I hate that I was fooled, but I didn't know a Deviant could physically change so completely.

Still, I should have known something was up. Burn would never have treated me so badly.

"Has Burn even been inside Haven since I got back?"

"How the hell would I know?" Zina snaps. "I avoid that monster whenever possible."

I want to hit her for calling Burn a monster, but I keep my cool. "Why did you disguise yourself?"

"Why would I show my real face?"

"But why appear as Burn? Just to mess with me?"

Her laugh is deep and throaty. "*That* was a happy accident. I dress as that monster all the time."

"He is *not* a monster."

"He is not only a monster"—she steps close to me, glaring, clearly trying to intimidate me, and I hate that it's working—"he's a *homicidal* monster. I had no idea you and Burn even knew each other, never mind *knew* each other." Her nose wrinkles. "Talk about sick."

Her little girl taunts flash through my mind. "There's nothing sick about it. Burn and I are the same age." Close enough anyway. Burn doesn't know his exact birthday.

"I meant," she curls her lip, "that it's sick for *you* to be with *him*—a Shredder. He can't be trusted."

"Burn's not a Shredder. Burn hates Shredders. I've seen him kill them."

Grabbing fistfuls of my t-shirt, she yanks me toward her. "I know he's a killer. Believe me." She shoves me back. "But this isn't about him. It's about you."

"What about me?"

"I told you to stay away from Adele Parry."

I straighten my shoulders. If Zina's my contact with the Freedom Army now, I need to rise above her taunts. I focus on the dull brick wall behind her.

"Rolph wanted to find Adele and I found her. I found out other things too."

"Congratulations," she says flatly. "You're done now. Stay out of it."

"But you need to tell Rolph what they're planning. Once the rebels know that the FA has a plan they won't bomb the Hub."

One side of her mouth quirks up. "You don't know the first thing about what's going on."

"Then tell me."

She shakes her head slowly, milking the fact that she has knowledge I don't.

"Why do you hate me? What could I have possibly done to you?"

"You really have no idea, do you?" Her eyes narrow.

"Tell me."

"Your father and boyfriend teamed up to kill my brother."

"What? When?" My instinct is not to believe her, but I'm so confused I'm not sure what to believe anymore.

"The day your dear dad was exed," she says, "Burn put his fist through my brother's chest."

"Oh." The wind rushes out of me. Burn told me that he'd accidentally killed one of his team members the first time his Deviance kicked in. It must have been Zina's brother.

"Burn didn't do it on purpose," I tell her. "And he feels terrible about it." I pause, trying to catch my breath and gather my thoughts. "But why hold my father responsible—"

"Shut up." Zina slams me against the bricks and a sharp pain spreads across my ribs. "Your ass of a father can teleport. He could have saved himself. If he'd done that, my brother wouldn't have put himself in danger." She releases me and steps back. "And there are no excuses for your Shredder boy-friend. He feels bad? Well, boohoo. My brother's *dead.*"

I open my mouth to speak, but I'm no longer sure what to say. I understand why she blames Burn—to a point—but not my dad and not me. My dad didn't know he could teleport when he was exed. He didn't even know he was a Deviant. He was expunged because he confessed to killing my mother to protect me. But telling any of that to Zina seems pointless.

She steps way too close. "I'll never trust you. Never. And if you keep getting in my way . . ." She puts her finger to my temple. "Pow. You're dead."

Chills race over my skin. Her hatred for both Burn and me is palpable, and I want to see Burn so badly it aches. I know he's not a Shredder like Zina claims, but I want to know why she'd say that, and I want to make sure Burn knows he can't trust her. With any luck, Management will pick her up for kidnapping me, thinking she's him.

"Little girl, if I were you"—Zina runs for the end of the alley, leaps onto a ladder, and climbs—"I'd watch my back. You never know where I'll show up or as whom."

# CHAPTER NINETEEN

THE NEXT MORNING DURING CLASS, I CAN'T GET ZINA OUT OF my head. Now, not only do I really have no FA contact, I have an enemy, and everyone I encounter might be her in disguise.

As soon as I get time in the study room, I'll use Mr. Belando's passcode to find Joshua so I can try to convince him that bombing the Hub is the wrong tactic, not to mention just plain wrong.

"Glory!" Shaw's voice booms.

"Yes, sir?"

The class erupts in derisive laughter.

Shaw sighs. "List three reasons."

My cheeks heat. I have no idea what he's been droning on about, or what he wants reasons for. I'm not even positive what today's lecture topic is or what I was supposed to have studied last night. "I'm sorry. Three reasons for what, exactly?"

"Three reasons why you're a freak," Thor says, and Stacy laughs.

I turn toward her and when she catches my eye she stops laughing and turns to face the front of the room.

"Three reasons why Deviants are a danger to Haven," Shaw says, impatience coloring his voice.

It's an easy question. No wonder everyone's laughing. Every child in Haven learns this stuff before they start GT. "They hide among us. They're one step away from becoming Shredders. They won't rest until every Normal in Haven is dead."

The class laughs.

"Thank you for the pre-GT answer," Shaw says. "If you were four I'd congratulate you." He shakes his head. "Who can share a reason that's actually from the information you studied last night?"

Hands shoot up as my cheeks burn, and Shaw calls on Quentin.

"Deviants are different and different is dangerous. They have genetic anomalies that have eroded their humanity. They procreate more often than Normals and have litters, like animals from BTD called rabbits. If allowed to reproduce, Deviants would take over the population of Haven." He holds up a third finger. "Their blood and other bodily fluids are poison to Normals. They can kill Normals with a kiss. Was that three or four?"

"Four," Shaw replies. "Good work."

Anger rises inside and it's all I can do to keep my mouth shut. If Management spreads lies and no one disagrees, then how will anything ever change? But anyone who asks questions in Haven is immediately suspect.

The door to our classroom opens and Captain Larsson steps inside. I look down at my desk.

"Cal," Larsson calls out. "Step outside."

My insides flip, but Cal rises without question and follows Larsson into the hallway. Shaw resumes his lecture but I can't concentrate with my ears buzzing. Why would Larsson want Cal?

Shouts come from the hall and everything inside me clenches. The voice shouting loudest is Cal's. The wall of the classroom vibrates. Something or someone slammed into its other side.

Everyone gets up and rushes toward the door. I'm too small; my passage is blocked so I tug on shoulders, I push and yell. Finally, I drop and crawl under the final few sets of legs to get to the front of the pack now assembled in the hall.

Two Comps hold Cal as he struggles against them, and Larsson has his Shocker pointed directly at Cal's chest.

"No." I jump up from the floor. "Don't shoot him."

Larsson doesn't even turn.

"Let me go," Cal shouts. "I need to save him."

My body recoils at the tone of Cal's voice. I've never seen him this angry. I've never seen him out of control. I've never seen him defy authority.

"Cal, what's wrong?" I call out.

He turns at my voice, the Comps loosen their hold, and

he lunges forward, escaping their grip. Larsson fires his Shocker and its tag strikes Cal's chest.

The Comps grab him, and insulated from the charge by their thick gear, they hold Cal as his limbs shake and vibrate. His body twists—convulses—and his face distorts to a painful grimace, yet he doesn't fall.

Larsson increases the charge.

"Stop." I grab Larsson's arm to stop the torture. "Why are you doing this? What's wrong?"

Cal slumps to the ground and I run to his side. "What have you done?" I accuse everyone in the hall. "Someone. Tell me what's going on."

Larsson crouches beside me and puts a hand on my shoulder. I shrug it off.

"There's been an accident," he says quietly.

The Comps tug Cal up and I throw my arms around his torso, trying to push the Comps away. "Leave him. Can't you see he's unconscious?" I just want to hold him, to keep him from further pain.

"A set of scaffolding collapsed in the Hub today." Larsson's voice is even and calm. "A construction crew was on it, several stories up, preparing for the President's birthday."

"And?" My heart slams hard against my ribs. "So?" I can't make eye contact with anyone or someone will die.

"Three workers were killed," Larsson says. "Others were badly injured and are being admitted to the Hospital."

"Why is Cal so upset?" My voice shakes.

"One of the workers admitted to the Hospital was Cal's brother, Scout."

· · ·

The instant I'm allowed into the detention room, I rush to Cal's side, still shocked that Larsson granted me this visit. I sent a message to Mrs. Kalin, but I'm not sure when she'll get it or if she'll come. Cal's strapped down to the bed, metal shackles at his ankles and wrists and a thick strap of leather over his forehead to hold his head down.

I run my hand over his cheek. His skin's clammy. "Cal." I bend to get my lips close to his ear. "Can you hear me?"

His body jerks and his eyes snap open, full of terror. "Get me out of here. I need to keep Scout out of the Hospital."

"We'll figure out a way." But there is no way. Scout's already in there, but telling Cal while he's restrained seems pointless and cruel. He tugs against his bindings and blood trickles from his wrists onto the sheet.

I put my hand on his arm. "Stop struggling. You can't break those cuffs. You're hurting yourself."

He stops tugging.

"They won't remove those restraints until you calm down." I put my hand on his cheek and force myself to breathe slowly, doing my best to hide my own terror and grief.

My breath hitches. I wonder if Jayma knows yet. As Scout's dating partner, someone must have told her.

A tear slides down the side of Cal's face and I brush it off with my thumb.

"Get me out of here," he says hoarsely. "I need to save my brother before they kill him."

"Don't expect the worst," I say. "His injuries might not be that bad. Remember how Mrs. Kalin helped when you broke your nose? She'll help Scout too. I'll make sure of it. If she doesn't come, I'll go to her office and beg her."

"No." He bucks against the restraints again. "Her office is in the Hospital. Stay away from there. Get me out of these things. I'll break into the Hospital myself and get Scout."

I touch Cal's cheek and it's on fire, slick with sweat. I've never seen him like this. So angry, so out of control.

The door opens and I turn toward it. *Mrs. Kalin.* She came.

Her eyes are filled with concern. Warmth spreads through my chest and tension melts from my neck, my back, my shoulders.

She'll know what to do.

Cal fights against his restraints. "Don't kill my little brother. Please. Let him go. I'll take his place."

She walks to the side of the table and rests her hands lightly on Cal's arm. He turns his anger-distorted face toward her.

"Don't worry," she tells him. "I'll check in on your brother personally and make sure he's well taken care of. He'll be fine."

As Cal listens to Mrs. Kalin, an immediate change comes over his face; his entire body relaxes. "Really?"

"Of course. I care about every Haven employee, but a friend of Glory's?" She turns toward me and smiles. "I'll see that Scout gets special treatment."

"Thank you," Cal says. "Thank you."

The change in Cal is astounding, and I'm so grateful her presence calmed him. My whole life I believed that everyone in Management was unfeeling, that they considered us lower-level employees to be interchangeable, barely human, but Mrs. Kalin seems different. She cares.

As soon as I saw her, I felt better too, but my skepticism's returning. "Trust no one" has been my mantra since Drake and I were left without parents. Distrust is what helped me keep Drake hidden for three years, but I wish I could let it go—just a bit. I wish I could maintain the warm feeling I get when I look into Mrs. Kalin's kind eyes.

"Your brother's suffered several broken bones and a head injury," she tells Cal, "but the doctors are doing everything they can. The Hospital's the best place for him. He's in good hands."

"Did you hear that, Glory? Scout's in good hands." The relief in Cal's voice is incredible.

Too incredible? The hair at the back of my neck stands up. Did Mrs. Kalin do something to Cal when I wasn't looking? Did she slip him a drug? If a drug calmed him down, maybe that's fine. A big part of me wants to trust her completely, but I can't. The trust part of me is broken.

"You need to rest." Mrs. Kalin pats his hand. "I'll remove these restraints if you promise to get some sleep."

Cal nods as best he can with his head strapped to the table, and Mrs. Kalin reaches into the pocket of her white coat and brings out a syringe. If she didn't drug him before, she will now.

"I'm going to give you something to help," she says. "Is that okay?"

"Yes," he says. "Thank you."

She injects a clear liquid into Cal's arm. His eyes flutter shut. Then she turns to me. "How are you holding up?"

"Thank you for coming." My voice is shaking, so I draw a long breath. "Scout's not only Cal's brother, his dating partner is my best friend. I've known Scout since pre-GT. If there's anything you can do to help him get released, I won't ask for your help with anything ever again." My insides won't stop trembling.

"You can ask for my help whenever, however, and as often as you like." She rubs my upper arm. "You're like a daughter to me."

I nod my thanks, but keep my eyes on Cal who's breathing slowly now, clearly asleep. "The only thing I care about is getting Scout out of the Hospital."

"There's nothing to worry about." She tips my chin toward her with soft fingers and I look into her eyes. "Trust me," she says. "The Hospital is the best place for him."

I'm flooded by warmth that reminds me how it felt to be bathed in sunlight at dawn. Like anything's possible, like I'm safe, like everything is going to be okay. "When will Scout be released?"

"That's up to his doctors." Her light brown eyes flash kindness. "My team will do everything they can. Would you like to see him?"

"Yes, please." Excitement stirs inside me. What better

way to assure Cal and Jayma that Scout is fine? "When can we go?"

"How about now?"

"Great."

She turns and the relief I felt disappears, as if my trust was swept away with the swish of her white coat.

Nerves scramble inside me as I follow behind her. After all these years of fear, I'm going to enter the Hospital. The question is: will I come out?

# CHAPTER TWENTY

**M**RS. KALIN TYPES A PASSCODE ONTO THE SECURITY PAD by the Hospital's side door. 6-2-4-5-2-1. The numbers burn into my mind, and I'm shocked that she let me watch. Mrs. Kalin doesn't strike me as careless, so it's more likely the code gets changed every day, or there's a camera overhead to see who's at the door, or it's some kind of special keypad that only works for her. Entry can't possibly be granted with just a short passcode. And it's not possible she trusts me to see it. Is it?

"I like to sneak in the back door," she says. "That way I have a chance to get some work done, before my staff figures out I'm here and bombards me with questions and problems." She gestures for me to precede her through the door.

The heavy door clangs shut behind us, and my insides want to scramble out of my skin. I'm in the Hospital.

I blink against the bright lighting bouncing off shiny white walls and floors. I've never seen anything so bright, besides the real sun.

Mrs. Kalin strides down the hall, the heels of her shoes tapping a fast rhythm, and she's at a corner before I've even moved. She beckons to me from the corner, and I run past a series of closed doors to catch up. Trembling, I rally my courage. The only thing I was brought up to fear more than the Hospital was Outside, and that turned out safer than I expected—not all dust and Shredders.

Outside wasn't without peril, but it wasn't nearly as bad as I'd been led to believe. Perhaps the same will be true with the Hospital. Perhaps the rumor mill has exaggerated its terrors.

Mrs. Kalin stops at one of the doors. "Would you like to see one of our labs?"

"I want to see Scout."

"Don't worry. We'll see your friend, but let's make a quick stop for you to sign a confidentiality agreement. That way I can explain more of our research." She rolls her eyes. "Policy."

The room we enter is equally white and bright and filled with long tables covered by vials and burners and tubes. A vat, nearly twice my height and as big around, sits in one corner, and a man in a white coat stands on a catwalk above it, dipping a long stick.

"This is the water treatment lab." Mrs. Kalin gestures around the room. "We test filters here and continuously monitor the water pumped from the big lake for trace elements of dust."

"Have you figured out why the dust—kills people?" *Or turns Deviants into Shredders*, I think, but don't ask. I shouldn't let her know how much I know about dust.

She steps to the side of the room, types another code, and it brings up a display. I chide myself. Awed by my surroundings, I missed what she typed.

"Come here." She beckons.

"Read this"—she points to the screen—"and sign, if you agree." She hands me a stylo tethered to the desk. My nerves make it hard to concentrate, but I quickly realize that this is the confidentiality agreement she mentioned. Basically, if I divulge any information to anyone who doesn't have clearance, I'll be subject to an immediate transfer to the Detention Center without so much as an audit investigation. More likely, I'll be expunged.

But I sign. I want to learn everything I can in this place, and there's no chance I'm letting this confidentiality agreement get in the way.

"Good." Mrs. Kalin takes my stylo. "Now we can talk freely." She gestures to the equipment. "The filters safely remove all traces of dust from the water, as they have since the creation of Haven."

"That's reassuring." But she didn't answer my question.

"However, given the growing number of Deviants in the employee population," she continues, "we suspect that trace elements of the dust are penetrating the dome, so we keep tabs on the water and air vents to find the source."

Studying her expression and demeanor, I don't sense deception, so I nod. "What other kinds of research do you do here?"

She checks the dial on the side of a vat. "We have hundreds of ongoing experiments."

"Like what?" I try to keep distrust from creeping into my voice.

She steps toward me. "For example, we complete experiments on Normals to see the effect of adding small amounts of dust to their water and air."

"Without their consent?" I bite down on my tongue.

"Of course not." Her hand lands on my shoulder and gently squeezes. "Many Haven employees are willing to do their part for science, and we monitor our test subjects closely. No one's life is risked." There's no hint of deception in her eyes and I feel better.

"What have you discovered? Do any of them—change? I mean, does the dust hurt their lungs?"

"My, you are interested in science." She squeezes my shoulder again and smiles. "That makes me so proud."

I blush as she leans back against the table behind us. "We've discovered so many things," she says, "but our main aim remains to improve the quality of life and safety for *every* Haven employee."

She says "every" like she's telling me more, and I search her eyes for meaning. Could she mean Deviants too? I lean against the table opposite her. Mrs. Kalin has a knack for breaking through my trust barriers. It must be the sincerity in her eyes; and looking into them now, I believe that Mrs.

Kalin cares about me and wants to make a difference inside Haven. In fact, she might be the key to everything I want to accomplish.

A man in a white coat holds a clipboard toward us. Mrs. Kalin strides across the room and scans it.

I chew my bottom lip. If she's doing experiments with dust on people, then she must be figuring out some of the things that I already know—and perhaps things I don't. At a minimum, she must know that Deviants aren't really dangerous, just different.

It's no wonder she thinks Haven policies should change. Cautious hope rises in my chest.

She initials the clipboard and hands it back to the man. "Where was I?" She strides back to me.

"You were talking about how your experiments will help improve things in Haven."

"Yes." She nods. "Management has done its best, but with the growth in employee numbers, the increasing shortage of supplies, the continued barrage of Shredders, Haven can't go on like this forever.

"That's why my department is researching the effects of the dust on Normals. We must find a way to survive Outside, at least long enough for employees to search for the resources we need. And just imagine"—she pushes off her table—"just imagine if there are other survivors!"

I open my mouth to tell her that there *are* other survivors, that I've met them, that my father and brother live Outside, but a crash and a scream sound in the hall.

Pushing away from the table, I turn my head too

quickly. I fall to the side, then catch my balance. "What was that?"

"Probably a Shredder."

I tense. "There are Shredders in the Hospital?"

"Yes. We perform research on Shredders to discover how they can live on the dust." She smiles. "The creatures are well contained. Don't worry, you're safe."

Walking next to Mrs. Kalin along multiple corridors, I observe as much as I can. The Hospital isn't nearly as scary as I expected, but it's difficult to know what's going on behind the many closed doors.

Passing one with a small window, I crane my neck to peek inside. A man, his wrists tied to ropes stretched above him, is slumped, barely standing. Blood trails down his torso and face, staining the waistband of his pants. My hand flies to my mouth.

"Would you like to look inside?"

Turning sharply at the sound of Mrs. Kalin's voice, I nod.

"First"—Mrs. Kalin puts a hand on my shoulder and looks into my eyes—"let me prepare you for what you'll see."

"Okay."

"The man in this lab is a Comp who was badly injured Outside fighting Shredders." She shakes her head. "He sacrificed so much for our safety."

"What happened to him?"

"He was ambushed by a pack of Shredders. They tore off his mask and forced him to breathe dust." She shakes her head. "He went insane."

"Dust madness." My words come out on a shallow breath.

She cocks her head to the side. "Yes, that's a good name for what we've observed."

"Why is he bleeding?"

Her arm slides across my shoulders and she steers me toward the door. "The wounds you see are self inflicted. He's been restrained to prevent further self-harm. I've personally been testing our latest dust antidotes on him, but so far he hasn't shown much improvement." Her eyes become glassy.

"Dust antidotes?"

"To lessen what you called dust madness." She pats my shoulder. "Are you sure you want to go inside?"

I look through the window again. The man's tugging against his restraints and screaming. I shudder. She's right. I don't need to go inside. I've seen firsthand the effects of too much dust, and she's explained to me what happened to this poor man. "I hope you find an antidote that works."

"That's what this is all about." Mrs. Kalin smiles. "Making Haven safer for all. Shall we go see your friend?"

I nod, but as we proceed down the hall, my unease creeps back in with every step I take. My mind feels clouded and I feel like I can't trust my judgment. One minute everything here seems horrible, just like it was in my childhood nightmares, and the next Mrs. Kalin's reassurance washes the fear away.

A large double door opens as we pass, and I catch a glimpse inside. The room's lined with metal tables, a person strapped down to each one, and from my quick glimpse, a few are Deviants—several bleeding and writhing in pain.

I back up. "What's going on there?" I turn to face Mrs. Kalin. Even she can't make this seem humane.

"That's the rehabilitation room."

"Rehabilitation?"

She takes a deep breath and studies my eyes as if she's deciding whether or not to trust me. I fight to keep my Deviance under control so I won't hurt her.

"I signed the agreement."

"It's not that." She shakes her head. "You're too young to be exposed to this. I made a mistake in bringing you in here."

"No," I touch her arm. "I mean, I want to learn everything I can."

"You're such a brave young woman." Her smile touches my heart. "Your mother must have been so proud of you. I know I am."

My Deviance sparks behind my eyes, so I blink to clear the threat of tears and ban the emotions that would betray my secret if I let them take over.

She steps to the door, opens it, and guides me inside.

Now that we've entered, I'm positive some of these people are Deviants. The woman on the first table has what looks like a steel necklace that covers her entire throat and thick cuffs on each wrist. She's sleeping. "Is she—?"

"A Deviant, yes." Mrs. Kalin studies me as if looking for a reaction but I remain neutral.

"Why is she here?"

Mrs. Kalin checks the display on a machine at the head

of the woman's bed. "She's a volunteer."

"For what?"

"To help us figure out the link between Deviants and Shredders. The more we understand, the more we'll be able to figure out how to prevent the madness."

"And she volunteered."

"We give Deviants who haven't committed egregious policy violations this choice."

My stomach flips. "This or be expunged?"

She puts her hand on my back and I resist the urge to pull away. I turn and look into her eyes.

"Yes." She pauses for a moment. "Which would you choose?"

I look down to hide my fear. My stomach convulses, twisting in on itself. Does she know I'm a Deviant? I can barely breathe.

But when I look up, Mrs. Kalin's gaze remains calm and proud. "Speaking hypothetically, of course. If you were a Deviant, which would you choose?"

"I . . . I don't know."

"Do you really think you'd choose to be killed by Shredders over this?" She gestures toward the tables. "Our test subjects are well taken care of and grateful for the choice they made."

I look down the line of beds, eight on each side of the room, and everyone seems to be sleeping peacefully. No one's in pain. "I guess you're right. It is better than what the Shredders would do to them."

"It certainly is."

*But why don't all Deviants take this option?* I wonder. "Can I see Scout now?"

"Of course." We leave the room, and as we continue I keep my eyes forward. When she stops, she opens a door to a small room that's softly lit and quiet. I step in after her.

Scout lies on a bed. White sheets cover his body up to his neck, and his face is bruised and swollen. I rush to his side. "Scout. It's Glory. Are you okay?"

He doesn't open his eyes. I touch his forehead, one of the only places that's not bruised. He's warm and breathing. That's something.

"We're doing everything we can to help." Mrs. Kalin steps up beside me.

I lean into her, my body suddenly weak, and she wraps her arm around me. "Don't you worry. We will apprehend the terrorist who did this to your friend."

"Terrorist? I thought it was an accident."

Her expression hardens. "No, this was the work of a terrorist—a Deviant terrorist."

# CHaPTER TWEnTY-OnE

MRS. KALIN'S OFFICE IS THE OPPOSITE OF WHAT I EXPECT. Every other place in the Hospital is sterile and white and as brightly lit as the Hub, but her office is cozy and quiet and soft.

She guides me to a chair with an upholstered seat and wooden arms, and I sink into it gratefully. On the other side of a small desk, she sits in a high-backed chair and gestures for her System screen to wake. Then, twisting her hands, she adjusts the display so that it's visible to me, too, hovering above the edge of her desk.

She presses a few keys on her keyboard and a video starts. It's the Hub at night, based on the lighting and lack of pedestrians. The camera's focused on the lower levels of scaffolding, then it pans up to the top. Mrs. Kalin presses a key and the video fast forwards, the camera panning up and down, until there's a blur. She stops the video and backs up a few seconds.

A person dressed in black is standing at the base of the scaffolding holding a wrench.

I snap back in my chair. It looks like Burn, and I watch in utter horror as he loosens a bolt at the side of the scaffolding. He then loosens another and another. Burn rounds the far side of the scaffolding and loosens another bolt. The camera zooms in. Mrs. Kalin presses a key and the video pauses, focused on Burn's face. There's no doubt. It's him.

Blood rushes in my ears. I feel sick. Betrayed. Then my anger swiftly changes to hatred. My eyes tingle as my Deviance builds. The person on the screen can't really be Burn. It's Zina. But knowing that doesn't help. Someone I know did this on purpose. Someone I know killed innocent people and nearly killed Scout. Plus, because of Zina, the Comps will blame Burn.

"I realize this must be a shock." Mrs. Kalin leans over her desk toward me. "But I thought you should know that this heinous crime was committed by the same Deviant who kidnapped you."

I can't look at Mrs. Kalin. It's too dangerous. I can't even talk. I have no idea what to say. She has no idea how well I know Burn—the real Burn.

"I can see that you're scared," she says. "But don't worry. The Compliance Officers will find him. I'll keep you safe. There's no way this Deviant will escape detection again."

I hate to think that even someone as devious as Zina is

capable of this crime, and I wonder what Rolph will do when he finds out what she's done. She'll be kicked out of the FA, that's for sure, but with her as my only contact right now, how will I even get a message to Rolph to let him know of her crime?

I can't think about this right now—not around Mrs. Kalin—no matter how much I trust her, I can't trust her with this. It would be one thing to tell her my secrets, another to share those of others.

I flick my gaze up, and her eyes are filled with concern. I break eye contact as she reaches across the desk and takes my hand. "I'm so sorry that this happened to your friend and his co-workers. I promise you, this Deviant, and anyone he associates with, will be captured and killed."

Mrs. Kalin treats me to dinner in the VPs' dining room, but although the chicken meat is seasoned with something that makes my tongue tingle, and the carrots look as bright and sweet as the ones I ate Outside, the food tastes like dust. I can't swallow. Finally, Mrs. Kalin gives up on trying to get me to eat, and since it's past curfew, she has a Comp escort me back to the barracks.

I find Cal alone in the rec room with the lights off. The tape's off his nose but the bruising seems worse. I step tentatively toward him, unease chewing my insides. I have both good news and bad, and I'm not certain how he'll react to either.

The Cal I've known my whole life would be thrilled to know his brother's alive and recovering, but furious to learn that the scaffolding collapse was no accident. The Cal I've known my whole life would remain calm on hearing all this news. He'd think before acting.

Problem is, the boy I saw punching a hole in the wall, the boy I saw strapped down and bleeding as he fought his restraints, was not the Cal I've known my whole life. I think it's best if I keep the sabotage news a secret.

It won't help Cal to know any more about Scout's accident right now. It's a matter for the Comps to handle, and if Cal ever learns of my connection to Zina and the FA, he'll never forgive me—ever. The best thing I can do now is reassure him that Scout's in good hands.

Cal's head lifts. "Glory." He bounds out of the chair and runs across the room. Slamming into me, he lifts me in a tight embrace. "Where have you been?"

"I'm fine. Don't worry." I stroke his hair at the back of his neck and his body trembles as he holds mine hard against his. I keep my breaths slow and steady, hoping some calmness will soak into him by osmosis and replenish his normal personality. But who am I kidding? I'm far from calm. And the longer I'm away from Mrs. Kalin, the less I'm willing to trust her. At least she didn't keep me in the Hospital.

After what feels like ten minutes, he loosens his hold and backs up, pulling me with him to sit on a long metal bench against the wall.

"Are you okay?" I ask.

"Me?" He brushes hair back from my face. "When they released me, I couldn't find you. I was so worried."

"How are you?" I reach down to his wrists and find them bandaged.

"I'm okay."

I touch his cheek, and the reassuring prickle of stubble grounds me in reality and sends warm shivers up my arm to my chest. "I went to the Hospital."

Alarm shoots into Cal's eyes. "What? Really? Why?"

"I was with Mrs. Kalin."

He nods and his expression changes to one of visible relief. "How is Scout?"

"He was asleep." Or unconscious? "He's badly hurt, but alive, and Mrs. Kalin says he's got a chance at a full recovery."

Cal leans back against the wall. "Thank Haven. I started to think Mrs. Kalin's visit this afternoon was a dream."

"She was here." I study his expression. His calmness is eerie, especially compared to his reaction when he was pulled out of class this morning. "There are no guarantees, though," I add to make sure I haven't misled him. "He didn't look good."

Cal turns toward me and worry fills his eyes. "But Mrs. Kalin is helping him, right?"

I nod.

"Thank you."

"For what? I didn't do anything."

"Thank you for asking Mrs. Kalin to help." He takes my face in his hands and kisses me softly. "I'm so lucky to have you."

"It's me who's lucky to have you." I wrap my arms around his neck. Without Cal, I'm not sure how I'd cope.

His arms tighten around me, and I bury my face in his neck. He smells of soap and safety.

"What else did you see in the Hospital?" he asks. I'm snapped back to reality. How much should I tell him?

"It's not as bad as we imagined as kids." A vision of a Deviant man, spread-eagled and dripping with blood, zaps through my mind. I shake my head and the image vanishes.

"What's wrong?" he asks.

"I was thinking about the stories we used to tell each other about the Hospital."

"I always figured they couldn't be true." His voice is so calming it softens my skepticism and remaining doubts. "Back then, we thought Comps were all monsters too."

"Good point," I say. "Not everyone in Management is all bad, either." Management isn't setting off bombs or sabotaging scaffolding. And Management's hatred of Deviants is based on ignorance and fear more than cruelty. By backing the FA, did I choose the wrong side?

I shake that thought out of my mind and close my eyes. No. Everyone I've met in the FA—except Zina—is a good person who only wants to help others. I'll bet Mrs. Kalin will side with the FA once she knows about them. Images from the Hospital flash through my memory: Mrs. Kalin's reassuring smile, the clean sheets covering Scout, the soft warm lighting of her office.

A table of sharp instruments. Screams. Groans.

I tremble and snap my eyes open.

"Are you okay?" Cal asks.

"It's nothing." I give my head a sharp shake. "I'm just tired." And confused. And I need to visit Jayma tonight. She must be so worried about Scout.

I slide off Cal's lap and cross the room, stretching out the tight muscles in my back and trying to clear my foggy head of horrible images. I had so many nightmares about the Hospital as a child, and with all that happened today, with all the secrets and lies crowding my mind, I can't trust my own thoughts.

The room spins. I back up and drop onto a chair.

"What's wrong?" Cal dives down to one knee in front of me, his hands on my thighs. "You've gone white."

"I need sleep." My body feels strange. Like I'm floating. I should have forced myself to eat dinner. The past few days I've been so dizzy.

"Is Scout really okay?" Cal grips my arms. "Is there something you're not telling me?"

"He's okay. Really." An idea strikes. "You should see for yourself." Another trip to the Hospital—one when I'm better rested—will help me to clarify what I saw. Especially if Cal's along to compare notes with. "I'll ask Mrs. Kalin if you can visit Scout."

"You'd do that for me?"

"Of course."

He pulls me up and kisses me softly. My lightheadedness returns, but at least this time I understand its source.

I let myself nap for a few hours before sneaking out of the barracks and heading for the Pents. The narrow hall leading to Jayma's family's apartment is empty and quiet. Not surprising at this time of night when those workers who aren't on shift are asleep. I wind my lantern for more light, then duck under a piece of metal that holds the flimsy walls of the narrow corridor apart.

Pausing at the door, I can't hear any movement inside. I don't want to wake her whole family but I need to tell her that I've seen Scout, that he's alive.

I knock softly. No one answers. I knock again and it opens a crack.

"Who's there?" Jayma's father's voice drifts out in a deep whisper.

"It's Glory."

The door slides open and he grabs my arm, pulls me inside, and shuts the door quickly. I point my lantern toward the ground and it fades in the near darkness.

"Thank Haven it's you." He shakes his head. "I thought it might be someone from HR or the Comps."

"Why?"

He wipes sweat from his forehead. "Jayma's not doing very well."

I tense. "What? Tell me." My heart rate increasing, I look over to the thin screen that separates Jayma's bed from the rest of her family's home.

Her dad leans on the back of the door, looking so old and so tired. He's always been thin, but tonight his eye sockets are hollowed out with deep purple.

"She refused to stay at work after she heard the news." He tugs at the sleeve of his shirt. "She's torn up about Scout and says she's not going back to work." He slumps. "I can't lose her."

"I'll talk to her." I squeeze his thin upper arm. If Jayma misses work again tomorrow, she'll be flagged and in danger of being designated a Parasite and expunged. It might not happen right away given the backlog, but once she's flagged, her future in Haven will be bleak. She'll never get promoted and will more likely be demoted to sewage or another dangerous task.

Her dad slides down the door to land in a pile at its base, his head in his hands. Leaving him, I go behind the screen to discover Jayma's not asleep but sitting across her mattress, knees tucked into her chest and leaning against the wall.

"Hi." I kneel beside her.

She doesn't respond. Her eyes stare blankly ahead and I'm not convinced she's noticed my presence.

"I'm so sorry, Jayma. I can't imagine . . . But I've got great news." I get no reaction, and as I shift closer, I can feel the floor through Jayma's thin mattress. I've become so used to the luxury of my nearly two-inch mattress at the barracks. "I saw Scout."

Her head spins toward me, eyes wide. "His body? Have they taken him for composting yet?"

"No." I clutch her arm. She's cold. "He's alive. He broke several bones and hurt his head, but they're taking care of him, helping him mend."

She pulls away from me and her eyes narrow. "You're lying. You're one of them now."

I suck in a sharp breath. "No, I'm still me, Glory. Your

friend. Honest. The VP of H&S took me on a tour of the Hospital. She let me see Scout."

"Listen to yourself." Her voice is cold, so unlike Jayma. "You are part of Management now. How can you trust those people?"

"I saw Scout." My voice catches. "I touched his face. He's alive. They're helping him get better."

"Swear you're not lying." She clutches my forearm, her thin fingers digging into my flesh, awakening sore muscles and bruises from training. "Swear this isn't some kind of trick to get me to go to work."

"I swear, Jayma. I swear on my life."

Tears fill her eyes. Diving forward, she wraps her arms around me and sobs. Her tears wet my neck and I stroke her back, resisting the urge to cry too. Stress and fatigue have me on the edge of a cliff. If I give in to those feelings or take solace in tears, I'll plummet off the edge, and I'm not sure I'll be able to climb back up to accomplish everything left on my plate.

I still haven't found Gage's son. I still haven't identified the mole. And I still have no idea how to convince the rebels they shouldn't set bombs at the President's Birthday—only four days away.

When Jayma's breath returns, she takes one of my hands and grips it like she might never let go. "I feel like I'm living in a nightmare. Seeing things."

"I'm so sorry, Jayma. I wish I could have come sooner." I hug her again. "I know it's hard, but you've got to be brave. For Scout."

"You—you saw Scout? Really?"

"Yes. He's still alive and they think he's going to get better."

"I think I'm going insane from the grief." She draws a long, jagged breath. "I don't know what's wrong with me. I even thought I saw that Deviant—the one who kidnapped you."

I stiffen and push back to see into her eyes. "Where?" Did she really see Burn? Or was it Zina? Or could it be her imagination like she thinks?

"It was up on the roof." Her expression hardens. "He appeared out of nowhere and tried to talk to me, but I yelled, told him to go, and he disappeared." She shudders. "That's how I know it was my imagination. There's no way someone that big could move so quickly."

It sounds exactly like Burn. "Where did you see him? I need to know. What did he say?" It wasn't her imagination, but I can't be sure whether it was Burn or Zina.

Her forehead wrinkles. "He asked me to tell you to meet him."

"Where? When?" I'm not sure how I'll face Zina, knowing what she did to Scout. Still, if she's my only way to regain contact with the FA, so be it.

"He wants to meet you on the roof."

My chest tightens. "When?"

"Any night. He said he'd be watching, looking for you." She shivers. "So creepy."

"When was this?" My breaths quicken and my legs twitch, wanting to move. Wanting to run up to the roof this minute.

"Earlier tonight. Just after the moon light came on." She takes my hand and squeezes. "But don't worry. I was just upset about Scout—afraid for him—and it brought back memories of your kidnapping. I'm sure that's why I imagined that monster." Her eyes refill with tears and she slumps against the wall. "My dream was a bad omen. I'm going to lose you too."

"No." My hand shakes as I reach up to brush her hair back. The idea that Burn might actually be inside Haven both terrifies and thrills me, but it was more likely Zina. She approached Jayma to threaten me. To let me see how easily she can get to people I love. Nausea pushes up my throat.

What if Zina knew Scout was on that scaffolding work crew? What if she targeted Scout, knowing that hurting him would hurt me? Does she hate me, hate Burn, hate my father that much?

If Zina loosened those bolts to send me a message, then it's my fault that Scout fell and ended up in Hospital. My fault that his coworkers were killed.

Guilt swarms and rises inside me. What have I done? In my attempt to help others, I've endangered my friends. And since Zina can come and go from Haven, my brother and father might be in danger, too. I know she hates Dad.

"What's the matter?" Jayma asks through glassy eyes, and I shake my head.

"Promise me you'll go to work tomorrow?"

She nods but I'm not sure I believe her.

I kiss her forehead. "I need to go."

She grabs my shoulders. "Make me a promise too?"

"Anything."

"Promise me you'll never lie to me about Scout." She swallows hard. "Even if they kill him, you've got to tell me. Promise."

I hug her one last time. "I promise, Jayma. I won't lie to you and I won't let anyone hurt Scout."

# CHAPTER TWENTY-TWO

LANDING IN A CROUCH ON A ROOFTOP, I TURN BACK AND SEE nothing behind me. Still, I'm certain I'm being followed. I waited for an hour on the roof for Burn, but he didn't come. I can't wait any longer. And it's too late to go to Gage's wife's house tonight.

Talking to Jayma left me uneasy—paranoid—and I'm imagining Zina everywhere. She claims she can pose as anyone, any time, any place, and I'm chilled at the thought that she might be targeting my friends.

A shadow shifts on the other side of the roof.

I drop to the gravel and blink, staring at the spot against a low wall where I saw movement. Nothing's moving there now, so I creep across the roof and step onto the foot-wide bridge that joins this building to the next.

Underneath me, dozens of other makeshift bridges

crisscross, blocking my view of the ground over twenty stories below. This top bridge is narrow—two metal beams bound together—and it slopes down at an angle to the lower roof. I move quickly to maintain my balance and avoid plummeting to my death.

A bang startles me.

I waver to the side, catch my balance, and race across the final ten feet, jumping off the end to land in a crouch. The grimy flap of a rooftop dwelling opens and a man's face peeks out.

It's hours past curfew, but I stride toward him as if my being here is natural. He watches me through narrowed eyes, then his focus shifts to something behind me and alarm fills his eyes.

I spin but no one's there.

I take long breaths to slow my heart rate as I continue across the roof. When I reach the edge, I discover nothing more than a narrow metal ladder that leads up and across to a stone ledge around the next building. The rusty ladder's in bad shape and I scan it to gauge whether or not there are enough rungs to cross, or whether I'd be better off trying to jump the span.

I reject the latter idea. It's got to be twenty-one or twenty-two feet across, and the bridge below is lined with wrought iron spikes. Miss the jump and I'll be impaled.

I test my weight, the ladder bends alarmingly, and I almost decide to go back and find another route home; but I look over my shoulder and the man's still watching me suspiciously. I forge ahead.

Halfway across the ladder, a rung gives way under my foot, and I drop between the rails, grabbing one side.

Hanging by one hand I look down to the spikes below and wait for my heart to stop pounding so fast and so hard. It's only about twelve more feet to the ledge, but the ladder slopes up at a sharp angle and there are only three shaky-looking rungs between me and my destination.

Best to go hand over hand along the ladder's rails, rather than taking another chance on a rung.

From my position dangling under the ladder, getting onto the narrow ledge at the ladder's end will be a challenge, but it's either try or fall to my death. The ladder vibrates and bounces each time I move one of my hands, and I hope the hooks holding it to the concrete are secure.

A jagged metal shard digs into my palm, and pain shoots through my hand and up my arm to my neck. I can't let go. Five more feet and I'll be close enough to swing a leg up onto the ledge.

A dark shadow moves above me. Someone lands on the ledge.

"Give me your hand." The voice is deep and heavy. Burn.

I freeze. It could be Zina and she's more likely to kill me than help.

I twist to look back, but someone, probably the man I saw, has raised a panel that completely blocks my access back onto his roof. I suppose I should be grateful he didn't unhook the ladder to let it drop

"Stubborn as ever," Burn says.

I can't hold onto this ladder much longer, and there's

no way back. Ignoring my fear, I continue along the ladder's sides, blood dripping down my wrists and onto my forearms, my grip threatening to slip from the slick liquid.

"Let me help," Burn says.

"Is it really you?" Something in his voice makes me believe it really is him.

"Who else would it be?"

"Help me, then." I reach my hand up. Even if this is Zina, I don't have an option, so I choose to believe that it's Burn until I'm on the ledge.

Burn leans onto the ladder, grips my forearm, and pulls me until I'm leaning over the ladder's rails, a few feet from the ledge. The rungs creak under our combined weight, and he lets go and shifts his weight back onto the ledge.

"You can make it from there," he says as a statement, not a question. He sidesteps about ten feet along the ledge and ducks into an entrance to the building.

Panting, I pull myself up and onto the ledge and consider whether to follow him inside. I don't know of another route into this building, and every window I saw while hanging from the ladder was blocked.

Unsteady, I press my back into the wall and tip my head forward. The drop to the ground seems endless. I've traversed ledges like this more times than I can count and have never felt nervous of heights. Until now.

I cautiously sidestep, and when I reach the entrance— a hole bashed through the building's side to enlarge a former window—I grip a jagged stone, swing in, and then jump down the small distance to the floor.

Faint light glows from the end of the corridor and I squint to encourage my eyes to form shapes from the shadows.

Burn's large hand grabs my arm.

*Or is it Zina?* Revulsion grabs my guts and I pull back. "Murderer." The word bursts from deep in my gut. "My friend was on that scaffolding."

"What scaffolding?" Zina's impersonation of Burn's deep voice hums inside me and I resent how well she deceived me. She won't do it again. But something deep in my gut says this really is Burn. I wish I had some way to be sure.

"You need to put pressure on those cuts." Burn shifts and the dim light strikes his face, glancing off the hard lines of his cheekbones and glinting from his eyes—eyes that penetrate mine in a way that makes me feel like he can see inside me, see my heart beat, my lungs draw air, my mind form thoughts. *Is it Burn?*

Whoever it is in this very male body, he opens his long coat and pulls out a length of cloth. Not asking, he grabs my arm and binds my palm tightly. "Those cuts bled well, but rinse them when you get home."

I pull my hand away. "If you're going to kill me, get it over with. Don't go after my friends."

"Kill you?" He leans back. "Why would I kill you?"

"I know it's you, Zina."

"Zina?" He thumps a fist against the wall. "That bitch."

Suspicion fogs my mind and I back away. "How do I know you're not her?"

He lunges forward, putting one hand on either side of me against the wall to trap me. Typical Burn move, but I duck under one arm and run. Before I get far, he grabs me, holding me from behind.

"That bitch impersonated me?" His voice growls into my ear, and I try to slow my heart rate, my breathing.

His iron grip on me loosens and I shift my weight lower, hoping I can flip him over me and onto his back, but he's too big. I need another technique.

"Glory. Calm down. I can feel your heart racing. It's me." He holds me tightly. "What did Zina do? If she hurt you, I'll kill her."

"I still don't know you're not her."

He spins me to face him, but doesn't let go. His hands grip my shoulders. The tendons on his neck twitch and strain; his jaw hardens. If this is Burn, he might turn into his monster.

He releases me and backs off a few steps. "I can prove it's me." He digs under the neckline of his shirt and pulls out a string. "Look." Something glints as it hangs from the end.

My heart skips. My mother's ring. "Where? How?"

"I went back for it." He leans against the opposite wall.

I slide down to sit, energy drained by memories of the day I last saw that ring—not to mention the horrible truth of why I threw it away. I tossed it into the woods when I learned that I'd killed my mom.

For the three years that followed my horrible crime, I believed that my father, not me, was her killer. And my dad let me believe it. Let me hate him. Let himself be expunged to protect me. And all that time, I wore my mother's ring for comfort.

Burn pulls the string over his head and it ruffles his hair. "Here." He holds it out toward me.

My insides freeze. When Zina impersonated Burn she had him down, right to that signature coat—his appearance, his voice. Clearly she can use her Deviant ability to create a complete illusion and I have no idea how far that goes.

"Tell me about the ring." My voice shakes. "How did you get it?"

"I already told you."

"Not enough. I need details. Things only Burn and I know. Tell me everything that happened that day."

He slides down the wall to sit opposite me, and his long legs bend at the knee to fit in the small space, his boot an inch from my hip. "You tried to jump off a cliff," he says. "I stopped you. You were grieving, angry. You tossed the ring."

*No one else could know that.*

"I went back later to find the ring."

"Why?" My voice is small and breathy.

He rakes his hand through his thick hair. "I figured you might want it some day."

Emotions flood my mind, my chest, my eyes. I should close my eyes to guard against hurting him, but I can't take them off his face, his body, his eyes filled with heat and hunger. I can't believe I didn't see the truth sooner—both now and when it was Zina.

I can't believe I let her trick me. No matter how many months have passed, Burn would never have acted so cold. And as much as Zina got his appearance right, she didn't capture the utter power of his presence. She might have nailed his voice, but not the words he'd choose.

"It's really you." I drop a hand onto his boot beside me and swear I feel heat penetrating the worn leather.

"You couldn't tell?" His voice is quiet.

"I should have known. I'm sorry. The things Zina said . . ." I shift over to sit next to him, feeling lighter, freer. Now that I've found him, I've got an FA contact again.

Burn's quiet and I can hear him breathing beside me, feel his warmth. I want to tuck under his arm to feel safe, but who am I kidding? Nothing about Burn is safe.

"Have you seen Drake and my dad?"

He nods. "They send their—love." He has trouble getting the word out.

I lean forward. "How are they? What's going on?"

A door down the hall opens and a crack of light invades. Without a word, he takes my hand and pulls me up as he rises. We press back against the wall until the door closes, then move rapidly along the hall to a window and onto a rope that leads down. My cloth-wrapped hand slips but holds, and I let go after I hear him land on the street's surface. The drop is farther than I anticipate, but he catches me around the waist, easing my landing.

His hands stay around me longer than necessary, but when I look up into his eyes, he drops his arms down and dashes to the right, pulling me with him. A search-light trails down the lane ahead of us, and his grip on me tightens.

"Jump," he says an instant before he wraps an arm around me and he leaps. With the other arm, he grabs a railing, at least twenty feet off the ground.

"Pull your legs up," he whispers, and we both tuck just as the light passes under our feet.

Pressed against him, I feel his heartbeat drive into me as his scent brings back memories of pine trees, the hot sun, and passion.

"Ready?" he asks, and he lets go before I can answer. We drop back to the pavement and I follow as he runs through a maze of unfamiliar streets, some so narrow he has to turn sideways to fit his broad shoulders.

I'm used to running, but I'm sleep deprived and my lungs are on fire when he stops suddenly, checks around us, then opens a hatch at the bottom of a wall, pulling it up and into the street.

"Go through."

I drop and crawl through the entrance into the darkness, wondering how, or if, he'll follow. His hand hits my calf, then his body fills the entire hatch as he twists to squeeze his shoulders and chest through the space.

When he's in, he drops the hatch cover. "Your torch. Turn it on."

He just assumes I have one, and I grab and wind it. The faint light fills the small room full of piles of clothing that reach to the ceiling.

"What is this place?" I ask.

"Storage."

I don't ask more. The room's purpose isn't important. Not with everything else going on.

"You were going to tell me about Drake," I say.

He nods. "He's good. Shooting up like a weed, and strong. You'd never know he was ever paralyzed."

"Is he . . . is he happy?"

"How would I know?"

I look down.

He clears his throat. "He's fine. Tell me about Zina."

I look up. Burn's arms are crossed over his chest and he's scowling, looking even more intimidating than normal. "She pretended to be you. She said—" I stop myself from saying she'd claimed he had a new girlfriend. "She said you were a Shredder." The words burst out and I shake my head and laugh. I'd forgotten that ridiculous taunt until now. "She said a lot of crazy things."

His scowl darkens and fists form at his sides. "She and I don't exactly—get along."

"No kidding." I don't want to mention what she told me about Burn killing her brother. He probably already knows, and why bring up what I know is a painful memory? "She's a terrorist. You need to tell Rolph."

He looks up.

"Zina loosened bolts on some scaffolding in the Hub."

"Why are you so sure Zina did that?"

My heart sinks. "You mean it was you?"

His nostrils flare. "Me?"

"I saw the security camera footage. It looked like you."

He tips his head back. "Are you saying that the Comps think it was me?" His eyes narrow. "Great."

"Scout was on the scaffolding."

"Scout?"

"Cal's brother."

Burn's shoulders twitch at Cal's name and I swallow. "I think she did it to send me a message. To let me know she could hurt me."

He shifts. "Not everything is about you, Glory."

My cheeks burn. "It doesn't matter why she did it. You need to report her to Rolph." Once Burn tells Rolph, he'll punish Zina, take her off active duty at a minimum.

He leans forward. "What makes you think Rolph doesn't already know?"

"Rolph saw the security footage? You mean he already knows it was her and not you?" Smiling I shake my head. "I should have known Rolph would be on top of this. What's he going to do to her?"

Burn's chin rises slightly. "Why would he do anything? More likely Zina was acting under Rolph's orders."

# CHAPTER TWENTY-THREE

I STAGGER BACK AND SINK INTO ONE OF THE PILES OF CLOTHES and blankets. "That doesn't make any sense." My mind spins with fatigue and confusion.

Burn stays silent, watching me until I lose patience and push my way out of the soft stack and stride up to him. "Rolph would never have ordered Zina to sabotage the scaffolding. Not if he knew workers would be hurt. The FA would never do something like that. It was the terrorists."

"Potato, potahto."

"What does that mean?"

He shakes his head. "Just an old saying. Terrorists, freedom fighters, rebels, revolutionaries—it's a matter of perspective."

"Perspective? You're kidding, right? People died."

"It's war, Glory. The FA is fighting Management to free every Haven employee. Not just one or two."

"But sabotaging scaffolding, hurting innocent workers, makes the FA no better than the terrorists." I swallow a lump in my throat. "No. The FA would never stoop to their level." But I realize I barely know anything about the FA or their methods beyond doing extractions. I was recruited to help identify and save fellow Deviants, and Rolph refused to tell me about the big picture plans, in case I was caught. "The FA aren't terrorists."

Burn rakes his hair back. "Glory, Rolph sent me in here to make contact with the people you call terrorists so we can form an alliance. But the only name I have is Adele Parry, and I can't find her."

My breath catches. There's so much I could tell Burn, but not until I know where he stands.

"Those people set off bombs, Burn. They hurt people. It doesn't matter if we have the same goal. Their ends do not justify their means."

"Don't be naive."

"I am not naive. And I'm not a killer."

He raises his eyebrows.

I look away. We both know I'm a killer.

My mind reels with conflicting thoughts. How can I—someone who killed her own mother and took down at least three Shredders—be appalled by the terrorists' tactics? But I am. What I did to my mother was an accident—I don't even remember it happening—and when I killed the Shredders I was protecting people I love.

Plus, since meeting Mrs. Kalin, I've started to see

Management from another perspective. War isn't the answer. Killing people isn't the answer.

I straighten and clear my throat. "If that's the kind of tactic the FA uses, you're just as bad as Management."

"The FA's not like Management." He steps forward. "Not even close."

"Not everyone in Management is bad, you know. Not like you told me. Some of them see the problems in the current system and are trying to fix things—from the inside, without killing anyone."

He grunts. "Management kills all the time. They target the weak and the sick and anyone they see as a threat." He drops his head and his expression softens. "You know that."

"I don't know what to think anymore. But I do know that if Zina was acting under Rolph's orders, the FA nearly killed Scout, and Management saved his life."

Burn scoffs. "Saved his life?"

"In the Hospital."

Burn looks at me like I'm stupid, and I can't stand to look at him right now. I need to get away to think. I dive for the hatch but he grabs my legs and pulls me back. "You're not going anywhere until you calm down."

"Calm down?" I kick, connecting at least once. "Zina nearly killed my friend, Scout's in the Hospital fighting for his life, and you tell me you think Zina was justified in what she did? How can you tell me to calm down? I thought you hated Zina."

I struggle against his hold. My entire body's like a pressurized valve about to explode.

He flips me onto my back, pins me by the shoulders, and I buck to get him off. But he straddles me, sitting on my hips. I can't move. I'm better than this. He's big but I should be able to get free.

I stop struggling to make him think I've given up. The second the pressure eases from my shoulders, I sit—sharply—and slam my forehead into his nose.

He swears, lifting one hand to quell the blood flowing onto my chest.

I twist, trying to get away, but he pins me again and then makes his first major mistake. He looks into my eyes.

The emotional fuel I need is at the surface and I'm locked onto Burn in seconds. Without targeting anything specific, I twist and squeeze, and the shock in his eyes turns to pain. He rolls onto his back, pulling me onto his chest.

Unable to bear the pain in his eyes, I close mine.

He throws me, and I land against one of the soft piles of fabric. Panting, I to catch my breath. I'm full of shame for hurting him, but still angry.

Burn leaps to his feet. "Don't trust anyone in Management. They all lie."

"*You* lie. *Rolph* lies. When I agreed to work for the FA, no one told me I signed on to hurt innocent people. I won't be part of it."

"You didn't hurt anyone."

"The FA did, though."

He crouches in front of me and looks into my eyes—a

brave gesture, given what I've just done. "Think about the big picture. Think about the reality here and who you can trust. Management isn't taking care of your friend in that Hospital. Don't believe it for a second. He won't survive. Not in there. Not as you knew him."

I shake my head. "You're wrong. I've seen him with my own two eyes. I went to the Hospital."

Burn's head snaps back and he frowns. "I don't care what you think you saw in there. They controlled what you saw. Don't trust *anyone* in Management. And don't go into that Hospital again." He stands and offers me his hand. "As for your friend, Scout, I'm sorry. But he's as good as dead."

"He's not dead and I won't give up on him." And no matter what Burn says, tomorrow I'm going back to the Hospital—this time with Cal.

Burn helps me to my feet, then stays still, closer to me than he needs to. I can't back away without falling into the fabric pile. Less than a foot separates our bodies, and I'm aware of every inch, every molecule of air bridging the distance.

My anger dissolves. It's Zina I'm mad at—and maybe Rolph. I shouldn't take it out on Burn who's done so much for me and for Drake.

Burn, who went back for my mother's ring.

That thoughtful gesture reminds me how I felt when he first held me in his arms, when we first kissed, when he pressed his body against mine on that rock by the lake. Cheeks hot, I look up.

He's staring down at me, hunger in his eyes. "I'm sorry

about what happened. That day on the rock." His voice is soft and deep. "I never meant to hurt you. I'll never hurt you again."

My heart thumps so loudly I can barely hear.

He leans toward me and it's like time slows down. Instead of taking seconds, it takes minutes, hours, for him to close the space between us. The air grows thick. I can't breathe.

I step to the side. "I've got to go."

He averts his gaze. "Okay. I get it."

But I don't think he does. I don't think he understands why I can't stand so close to him, why I can't let him kiss me. It's not out of fear, not in the way he thinks.

I won't betray Cal again, and even if Cal weren't in the picture, I can't think about all of this right now—not with so much else at stake: while Scout's in the Hospital, and Jayma's depressed, and there's a mole inside COT, and terrorists are planning to bomb the Hub.

Nothing is easy anymore, nothing is black and white, and I feel as if my whole world has been yanked from beneath me, like I'm toppling end over end down a steep hill.

Burn's staring at the ground, hands jammed into his pockets, and I hate that I've hurt him. "It was so good to see you," I say, but my tone sounds phony and my heart thuds against my ribs. "I need to get back to the barracks before I'm caught."

His head snaps up and our eyes meet. "Come with me. I'll take you home—to the Settlement." His expression and words nearly knock me off my feet.

"I can't. I—not yet."

"I'll wait. I'll check back here for you—every night." His deep voice is barely audible. "Every night. I won't leave Haven without you."

# CHAPTER TWENTY-FOUR

THE NEXT DAY I'M STILL BUZZING FROM SEEING BURN, WHEN Mrs. Kalin takes Cal and me to the Hospital. Her eyes broadcast concern and she tucks my hair behind my ear as Cal reads the non-disclosure agreement. "You look tired," she says. "Are they working you too hard? Because I can speak to your instructors . . ."

"No." The warmth of her caring rushes over me. "Thanks, but I'm fine, really. Just stressed out about Scout." And a million other things I can't reveal. But just seeing her, just seeing how much she cares, sets me at ease.

And now there's pride mixed into her concerned expression. "Okay, I won't interfere," she says. "I guess it won't help your credibility if your mother asks your COT instructors to go easy on you."

My heart stutters. "My mother?"

She grins. "You know what I mean."

I nod and a smile spreads through my entire being.

"I know I could never replace your real mother," she says. "I can't just step in and fill her shoes, but I do care about you. To me, you are my daughter. You know that, right?"

I nod, feeling heat in my cheeks.

"What does this mean?" Cal points to a section of text on the screen.

He turns to face Mrs. Kalin as we walk over, and she says, "It's all standard. Nothing to be worried about."

Cal turns away from her and signs the agreement without reading the rest. A little strange for him to back down so quickly, but signing that agreement is the only way he's going to get access to his brother. I get that. I signed it too.

"Looks like we're all set then. Let's go see Scout." Mrs. Kalin's voice is cheery and bright and her light coat flares above her slacks as she walks. "I'm sure he'll be thrilled to have visitors."

Cal grins and holds the door open for Mrs. Kalin and me. I can't wait to see Scout again so I can report his progress to Jayma and snap her out of her funk.

Mrs. Kalin and Cal walk down the hall ahead of me and she tells him the basic information about the Hospital's research. It's what she described to me the first time I came here. The farther we walk, the more I remember my other reasons for wanting to come back here today. I want to be sure of what I saw. I want another witness so I can discuss the experiments and decide whether I'm right to trust Mrs. Kalin.

A shriek flies out from one of the rooms as we pass and I stop. "What's in here?"

"A research lab," Mrs. Kalin answers.

"Can we see?" I try the door and it's locked. The windows are blocked.

"Who screamed?" Cal asks.

She puts her hand on Cal's arm and he turns to face her. "Nothing to worry about. Some of the volunteers for our research have painful, pre-existing medical conditions before they're admitted. We do all we can to keep them comfortable." She turns to me, but full of nerves, I keep my gaze averted. "Nothing nefarious happens in the research labs. Just scientific experiments. Glory understands."

"Why don't you want us to see this room?" I ask.

"Why would you think that?" She smiles as she walks back toward me. "You can see inside every room in the Hospital. We have nothing to hide." She types a code into a pad and then pushes the door open.

I step in first and gasp.

Along one wall, six people are in shackles. Blood drips from their wounds into drains in the floor. Each, except the first who's a young man, is wearing a breathing apparatus that's connected to a vent that runs along the ceiling. A hospital worker, dressed in a loose blue jumpsuit, slides a sharp knife along the upper arm of the fourth subject who screams as blood runs from her wound.

I charge in. "What's going on? Why are you cutting this woman? What are they breathing?" The pipes that join the breathing apparatuses to the vent are labeled with numbers that range from 20 to 100 at intervals.

Behind me, Mrs. Kalin says something to Cal that I can't hear. I grab for the Hospital worker holding the knife, but Mrs. Kalin's hand lands on my forearm and I twist toward her.

"Calm down," she says, her voice stern. "Let me explain what you're seeing."

I shake my head, keeping my gaze focused on her forehead, trying to force down the anger and revulsion that's sparking my Deviance behind my eyes.

No one tells me the truth. No one. And if I look her in the eyes, I'll kill her.

I check on Cal who's studying a chart on the wall.

"These subjects are all volunteers." Mrs. Kalin shifts to force eye contact. "In this lab, we're studying the healing effects of the dust. Georgina here"—the woman in the jumpsuit nods—"is making careful and precise incisions on each of these patients as they receive varying doses of dust, so we can determine how much is required for healing."

I still feel uneasy, but what she's saying actually makes sense if I think about it. I look into her eyes and nod, pushing my questions away. She's right. How else could one properly learn how much dust it takes to heal without causing madness? I remember how terrified I was the first time I saw my father help Drake breathe in dust, and how crazy Gage seemed when he took in too much. It is important to learn how much is enough to heal without turning someone into a Shredder.

Cal steps over. "Are these all Deviants?" he asks. "We

learned in GT that Normals can't breathe any dust without choking."

She smiles. "That's what we used to believe, and I know they still teach it in GT, but through our research, we've discovered that most humans can tolerate small amounts of dust and still live. In fact, small amounts may be beneficial. This and other experiments are testing those limits."

Her eyes flash with sincerity, and guilt floods through me.

"I'm sorry for my outburst," I tell her, and she rubs my shoulder.

It's not as bad as I first thought. The subjects are secured to the wall for their own safety and they're not in any discomfort. Not really. No more than necessary. Everything seems so normal and civilized and supports what I learned and observed about the dust when I was Outside.

I can't figure out why I doubted Mrs. Kalin. Burn's warnings last night must have confused me and caused paranoia. I only saw this experiment in a bad light because that's what I was expecting to see.

I lose my balance, but Mrs. Kalin catches me before I fall.

Cal runs to my side. "Are you okay?"

"Glory's queasy at the sight of blood," Mrs. Kalin says. "No more incisions while we're in the room."

"Certainly," the Hospital worker says.

Cal rubs my back and I start to feel better. "I'm fine," I say. "Other than being embarrassed."

"No need to be embarrassed," Mrs. Kalin says.

At the doorway, I turn back, then blink.

Something's strange with my vision. It's as though a curtain keeps lifting and falling in front of my eyes. One minute everything looks normal and the next minute it's a horror show with people bleeding, writhing in horrible pain.

I turn back to Mrs. Kalin and my confusion fades. Everything here is just as she explained. I've been so warped by the Hospital horror stories that I heard as a child, and so confused by what Burn told me last night, that I can't see the truth when it's right in front of me.

Mrs. Kalin has been nothing but kind to me, and I was wrong not to trust her.

I turn away from her, and as I back out of the room, another thought slides into my consciousness. With these experiments going on, there must be a lot of dust floating around the Hospital. What if it's messing with my perception, and with Cal's? What if it's messing with Mrs. Kalin's, too?

Sitting on the barracks' roof next to Cal with what feels like our entire recruit class, I glance around to make sure none of the others are within earshot. I want to hear what Cal thought of the Hospital and it's our first moment alone. Our class had an oral exam at the end of the day, and we faced a panel of Comps and Instructors who threw numerous unpredictable situations at us, filled with conflicting information. In spite of the non-physical nature of the exam, everyone's tired and sprawled around the roof rather than in the rec room playing SIM games.

"Scout looked pretty good, don't you think?" Cal lies back on the roof, looking up at the twinkling stars. Clearly, the little LEDs get replaced in this section of the sky more often than the bits over where we grew up.

"Did Mrs. Kalin say when he'll be released?" I ask. Scout was only allowed one visitor at a time, so I waited in the hall when Cal went into Scout's room.

"Soon." Cal's forehead wrinkles.

"But when? Did she give you a date? Did she tell you any details about his recovery?"

Cal rises up onto his elbows. "Why are you being so negative? Mrs. Kalin said that everything was fine."

"Did you see anything that upset you at the Hospital?" I ask. "Anything that matched the stories we heard as kids?" I felt fine when we left the Hospital, but my suspicions won't quit.

"Did you see something upsetting?" he asks.

"I want to know your impressions."

He shakes his head. "It was like you told me it would be." He rolls onto his side and puts his hand on my waist. "I'm sorry for doubting you before."

"So, you didn't see or hear anything horrible at the Hospital?"

"Like what?"

"People being tortured, force-fed dust, sliced open, calling out for our help."

He balks. "No. Why? Did you see something when I was in with Scout?"

"No. I was right outside the room the whole time."

"Then why are you asking?" he says. "We saw the same things. People being treated for their ailments, comfortable in beds."

I draw a long breath and close my eyes for a moment. "I keep seeing strange flashes of things—horrible things."

He strokes my shoulder. "You need sleep. Sure, some of the patients we saw were in pain, but that's to be expected. They're sick and injured."

"But I wonder . . ." I nibble the inside of my lip. "It's almost like Mrs. Kalin's explanations for the experiments were too easy. Like she was reading off a script or something." If we were affected by dust in the Hospital, maybe Mrs. Kalin was too. Maybe everyone who works there has been touched by dust madness and it's affected their empathy, made them cruel like Shredders.

Cal's hand slides down my side. "You were right about Mrs. Kalin. She's someone in Management we can trust. Scout's in good hands."

I expel a long breath. Cal's opinion about Mrs. Kalin quashes my fears. Mrs. Kalin has done so much for me and she's been so open. Much better than the FA who failed to tell me their methods.

Cal slides over so our legs touch, and he leans over me. "You're worried about something. Talk to me."

"I thought that's what we were doing."

"You're like a little ball of stress." He tugs my arm. "What's going on?" He leans in close. "Are you still working for Mr. Belando?"

I nod. "Mr. Belando was right. I'm pretty sure there is a mole—a Comp."

His eyes widen. "Really? Who is it? How did you find him?"

"I'm not sure who it is yet. I just know there is one."

"Be careful." He kisses my forehead. "Promise me you won't do anything to put yourself in danger."

"Making out in public?" Stacy's voice comes from behind me. "I should report you."

Cal's hands fly from my body and I glare at my roommate. "Making out is a bit of an exaggeration, don't you think?"

Stacy, standing with one hand on her hip and chewing on a sliver of wood, doesn't answer.

"Cal," another recruit calls from across the roof. "Come over here."

He looks at me and I nod and smile. He leaps to his feet and strides over to join the other boys.

"He needs your permission to talk to other people?" Stacy shakes her head in apparent disdain.

I rise up to stand beside her. "He was being polite. Ever hear of the concept?"

She scoffs and I close my eyes for a moment to wash my anger away. I can't afford to waste energy on Stacy.

When I open my eyes, she's smirking. "Come with me." She gestures with her head. "We need to talk."

I shake my head. "We live in the same room. We can talk before lights out."

"We can't talk in your room." She leans in close and whispers. "Because Stacy's there."

I snap back. "Zina?"

Smirking at me over her shoulder, she strides toward the shadowed side of the roof. I choke back the urge to call out to the others, to tell everyone that this isn't Stacy, that it's the terrorist who caused the scaffold collapse—and goodness knows how many other deaths. But I have no proof. Unless I can get her and Stacy side by side, everyone will assume that I'm crazy.

Fear and anger plow through me, but I force myself to push it all down and follow, and as soon as we're out of the others' earshot I cross my arms over my chest. "My friend was on that scaffolding!"

"What scaffolding?" She grins, tipping her chin down and looking at me in a way that makes it clear she knows exactly what I'm talking about.

"How can you live with yourself? You're a murderer."

She shrugs, the sly grin not wavering.

My body shakes with anger, my insides twist with disgust, and I try to catch her gaze. Right now I could kill her, but I realize that makes me a hypocrite. Killing Zina might serve a greater good, but isn't that how she'd justify what she did? I won't stoop to her level.

She steps up so close I feel her breath on my face. Physically, she looks like Stacy, but while my roommate's a bully and unpleasant, the hate coming off Zina is palpable.

It's mutual. "You hurt innocent people—people the FA is supposed to be freeing. How can you justify that?"

"I don't know what you're talking about."

Fists form at my sides and it's all I can do not to use them. I want to confront her, to argue, but there's no point. She'll never admit what she did, and I can't prove it. "What do you want?"

"You've got a new mission."

"Fine. Give me their names and employee numbers." With all that's happened the past few days, I'll be happy to save a few Deviants. A new mission will be a welcome distraction, even if I have to trust Zina to get the kids to safety.

"It's not an extraction," she says. "This mission's more important."

I step back. "I'm not doing *anything* under your orders. You aren't my FA contact anymore—if you ever were." Zina is a liar. And even if she has a legitimate mission for me, now that I know more about the FA's tactics, I'm no longer certain I want to be involved.

"Believe me, I'm not coming to you by choice." Zina makes a face as if she's eaten bad meat.

"Fine, get someone else."

"Rolph needs your special talent."

I frown.

"He wants to send a message to Management, to hit them where it hurts." She crosses her arms over her chest. "You've got access to Senior Management. Next time you get close to the VPs, kill one."

I shake my head. "No way. I'm not killing for Rolph. Not for anyone."

She rolls her eyes. "I told Rolph you weren't strong enough, that you couldn't do it."

"I *could* do it." My stomach tightens. "I *won't.*"

"Don't be scared," she says. "Assuming you can do what Rolph says, the VP's death will look like natural causes."

"I'm not committing a murder. And this doesn't even

make sense. If it looks like natural causes, how would it send a message?" Zina's setting me up.

"You let Rolph worry about that part."

"I won't do it." I lift my chin. "Unless the FA has another extraction for me, I'm done. Finished with the FA." Killing is wrong, no matter what justification.

She widens her stance. "This isn't a request, Soldier. It's an order."

"And if I refuse?"

She smirks. "Then, little girl, you are done. If you refuse to follow orders, we can't trust you and"—her eyes narrow—"you know way too much about us to live."

Back in the barracks, I jump up onto my bunk and close my eyes. I can't stop shaking. Zina was clear: do what the FA asks or I'm dead.

Her power to transform herself is terrifying. It's so much more than I ever thought a Deviant could do. I curl on my side and tuck my hands under my pillow.

Nothing makes sense. I thought my life was complicated when I was sneaking out of the COT barracks nightly to save Deviants, but now that duplicitous life seems simple and easy. It might have been dangerous, but at least I had a clear purpose. At least I knew I was doing some good. At least I knew whom to trust.

Now everything's turned upside down. Someone in Management has become the closest thing I have to a mother, the Hospital is saving Scout and making it safe to live Outside, and the FA asked me to kill.

I need to talk this through with someone, but whom? I'm completely cut off from Dad and Drake, and I can't talk to Cal without betraying the FA, putting him in more danger.

And I can't talk to Burn. I no longer understand him. I know he feels terrible when he kills—I've witnessed it, talked to him about it—so how can he reconcile what the FA and terrorists are doing?

His mere reappearance has turned me inside out, flipped me end on end, spun me so fast I feel dizzy, unable to see my path clearly. If I could roll back time, my life might regain an ounce of its normalcy, a pinch of its purpose.

I need to do an extraction. If I find someone, Burn will get them out.

My eyes snap open. *Gage's family.* I found them in the System days ago, and based on what I read, his son Tobin's in danger. As an added bonus, extracting Tobin will get Burn out of Haven and away from the rebels. I still don't know how I'm going to stop them from bombing the Hub, but I can make sure Burn doesn't take part.

I slide my hand under my pillow and my fingers strike something—a slip of paper.

Shaking, I read the word Laundry, along with tomorrow's date and the time of 2300 hours. Given the location, it seems safe to assume that this is a time and place for a rebel meeting, but who left this note here?

My chest freezes. *The mole.* Whoever the mole is, he's on to me. He knows I met with the rebels, and he has access to my room.

# CHAPTER TWENTY-FIVE

I SHAKE THE FABRIC FLAP THAT FORMS THE DOOR TO GAGE'S family's apartment, and a woman lifts the door, holding a knife.

Graying hair frizzes up around her face as she stares at me with fierce eyes. "Get away. Leave us alone." Her voice is scratchy.

"Wait." Risking my fingers, I grab the edge of the fabric as it drops. "Theresa, I knew your husband. I want to meet you and your kids."

I poke my fingers through a gap between the fabric door and its metal frame, risking an attack from that knife. The raspy breathing tells me she's still close by on the other side, probably hoping I'll give up and leave, but I hold my ground.

Finally, the fabric lifts to form a long triangular opening.

"Hurry," she says.

I slip inside and she cranks a small lantern. A frail-looking girl, who seems younger than fourteen, clings to her side.

"You must be Kara." I smile. "I'm Glory." I want to tell them that Gage survived his expunging, but I can't. It's against FA protocol to mention anyone Outside, and besides, until I'm certain I can help reunite their family, mentioning him seems unfair. "I knew your Dad."

Theresa grabs a fistful of my t-shirt and pulls me forward. "Don't you talk about that man to my daughter. He was a Deviant. He was expunged. We're trying to forget we ever knew him."

"Sorry." I lift my hands in surrender. "But Gage was kind to me. When I heard what happened, I wanted to meet his family. I'm sorry it took me three months to come by." She drops my shirt and I look around the small space.

"Where's Tobin?" I ask.

Kara lets go of her mom and backs up a few steps. Fear invades Theresa's angry eyes. "Who?" Her voice shakes.

"Your son."

"I don't have a son." Theresa's voice is clipped and her hand trembles as she raises it to push stray hairs behind her ear. "Where did you get the idea I had a son?"

"Theresa." I take a tiny step forward. "It's okay. I would never ever turn him in. No matter what."

She flinches. "Can't turn in someone who doesn't exist."

"Okay." My gut twists. Theresa's unpleasant, but I get her denial. She doesn't trust me and wants to protect him.

"I must have misunderstood when Gage said he had two kids."

Her head jerks to the side. "That man was a liar. Typical Deviant." She spits the second word out like poison.

I look down. "I guess I didn't know him as well as I thought."

Her eyes narrow. "How *did* you meet him?"

I smile. "In the Hub, in line for the ration store." Anticipating this question, I came prepared.

Theresa squeezes her arms tight to her sides. "He never went to the ration store. I did."

"Every time?" I tip my head, keeping my cool. Then I smile and nod, like I'm remembering. "That must be why he asked my advice about which line had the freshest vitamin powder. I'd forgotten." I shake my head. "Mostly, I remember all the nice things he said to me about you and your kids."

Her shoulders jerk. "Kid. Singular. I have one child. A daughter."

My heart rate goes up. The more she denies Tobin's existence, the more I want to save him. Assuming I'm not too late. A chill races through me. Gage told me that someone close to him betrayed him to the Comps. I'm starting to wonder if it could have been his wife. If that's true, how terrible. I feel sick. What if she did the same thing to Tobin? Could she turn in her own son?

"I'm going to boil some water," Kara says from the far side of the small room. "Would you like a drink?"

Theresa spins toward her daughter, then back to me. "Yes. Sit." She gestures to a spot on the floor. "Where are my manners?" Her voice is flat. "Have a drink before you go."

I lower myself to the floor as Kara takes a small pot filled with water out of the room, presumably to use whatever stove they have access to up in this Pent. The actual room's a different shape but about the same overall size as the one I grew up in. I'd guess about sixty square feet. But at least our apartment had a door and solid walls on all sides, reportedly because it had been used for clothes storage BTD. This apartment was clearly partitioned off from a much larger space.

"Kara is even prettier than Gage described," I tell Theresa after her daughter's out of the room. "He talked about you all with such warmth and love."

Theresa's cheek twitches. "Can't trust anything a Deviant says. They're out to destroy Haven."

Staying cool, I don't answer. I'm treading on dangerous territory. I scan the room, looking for possible hiding places.

"My home not good enough for you?" Theresa says. "You look well fed. Your folks in Management?"

"No." I shake my head. "I was just thinking how homey this is. It's so much like the Pent I grew up in." And there's no way Tobin's in here. The only furniture is a single mattress rolled up against the wall and a small metal box. There's nowhere to hide.

"You really from the Pents?"

I nod.

She bends forward and puts her head in her hands. "It's so hard. We had enough trouble feeding the kids with two of us, but now with me alone . . ." Her voice trails off and she looks up and away from me, eyes glassy in the fading light.

"Kids?" I say.

She shakes her head. "Kara. One kid."

"You can trust me," I tell her.

She leans back. "With what?"

"With anything you want to tell me." I reach forward to the lantern and turn the crank; she doesn't object.

"Have you known any Deviants?" she asks. "I mean, besides my late husband?"

I nod, hoping this is my opening and she'll admit Tobin exists and tell me where to find him. "My father was expunged over three years ago."

She shakes her head. "You know how it is for my Kara, then. How horrible it was to learn of her father's betrayal and be left with only one parent."

"My mother died—before my father was exed."

"Oh." She leans toward me, and her expression softens. "So it's just you? All alone? You poor thing."

I don't respond, not wanting to lie again but not wanting to mention Drake, or that my father survived his expunging, although I'm not sure how much more risk it would create at this point. I'm exposed. If this woman did turn Gage and her son in to the Comps, I could be next.

"Ah." She takes my wrist and taps on my bracelet. "I see you're not alone." One side of her mouth crooks up and her eyes turn wistful. "A young man." Her fingers slide over my dating license. "What's his name?"

"Cal."

"And does he have a good work placement? Is he happy?"

My stomach clenches. "He's in Construction and Maintenance." It's not a complete lie. He was assigned to C&M for over two years before starting COT.

Kara returns, dips a tin mug into the steaming water, and passes it to me. "Sorry. We're out of flavor powder until ration day."

"This is wonderful." I take the mug of plain water and let the steam fill my nose. "Yum."

She serves her mother, then herself, and sits down cross-legged beside me.

"Are you enjoying GT?" I ask Kara. "What's your favorite subject?"

She shrugs and I remember how annoyed I used to get when adults would ask me about GT and my classes, as if it were the only possible topic to bring up with a kid. But with the denial of Tobin's existence like a shield between us, I can't think of anything else to discuss. I need to make them comfortable so they'll trust me.

Kara's hand bumps into my leg. At first I ignore it, thinking I'll embarrass her if I draw attention, then she does it again. I slide my right hand down my leg to the floor near her hand and she passes me what feels like a slip of paper. Where would Kara get the rations to buy paper?

Without looking toward her, I slide the paper up my leg. Pretending I'm scratching an itch, I tuck it into the waistband of my slacks.

"Have you graduated GT?" Kara asks, her cheeks pinking.

"Yes, last quarter."

"Where did you get placed?" Theresa asks, and I sip my water, trying to decide how to answer. I've run out of lies and the energy to create more.

"I'd better get going." I hand the mug to Kara and stand. "I just remembered how early I have to get up tomorrow. It's past curfew so I'll have to be extra careful getting home."

"Where do you live?" Kara asks.

"In the Pents over in the far eastern sector." At least that's where I used to live.

"You've got a distance to go then." Theresa starts to stand and I offer her a hand, surprised when she takes it and lets me help her. Her palm is rough and cold.

"Thank you so much for the hot drink," I say. "It was so nice to meet you both. I'm so sorry about, about . . . Gage." There's no delicate way to discuss an expunging.

Theresa unclips the hooks locking the fabric door, "Come by again."

"Thank you," I say, but I can tell by her tone that she doesn't mean it. Still, I'll be back. I need her to trust me if I'm going to help Tobin. Next time I'll convince her I can keep him safe.

Walking down the hall, the folded paper from Kara digs into my skin and I stop under a faint light in the hall to unfold it.

It's an address and the word: roof.

Tobin. Have I found him? Even if Theresa wants to deny she has a son, Kara hasn't forgotten her little brother.

Thinking of Drake pricks the backs of my eyes and

makes me want to find Tobin right now. But I should talk to Burn first to set the extraction plans. If Tobin's hidden on the roof, his sister must be bringing him food. He can sit tight one more night.

# CHAPTER TWENTY-SIX

"WHY IS THERE A WALL OUTSIDE HAVEN?" ANSEL ASKS AS we all study the map that our instructor, Mr. Mendell, projected onto the wall at the front of our classroom. The map shows not only the footprint of the dome, but also the big lake to our south and the wall that surrounds Haven about a mile out.

I'm trying to pay attention. I'm genuinely curious to know how Mendell will explain the wall that's kept secret from most residents, but I'm distracted, anxious for the end of the day.

After I talk to Burn and rescue Tobin, I need to attend the rebel meeting and talk them out of bombing the Hub. The President's Birthday is the day after tomorrow. Complicating matters, Zina's still out there and might be trying to kill me. With all that going on, how can I be expected to pay attention in class?

"Does anyone have any ideas?" Mr. Mendell asks.

His communicator beeps and he puts his hand to his ear. "Glory Solis."

"Yes, sir?"

"You have a visitor," he says. "Main desk."

I rub my palms on my legs as I head toward the classroom's door. Everyone stares. The last one called out of class was Cal. Being called out of class usually means bad news, but as I close the door, I realize my visitor must be Mrs. Kalin. Maybe she has news about Scout.

I rush down to the front desk, and my feet skid on the floor when I see who's there: Jayma's dad.

He steps toward me, the color drained from his face. "Glory, I need your help."

"Anything." My heart thuds.

He glances around. "Where can we talk?" The purple circles under his eyes are darker.

I step farther from the desk and into the corner of the room that's hidden from the one working surveillance camera in the room. "We're fine here," I say. "But keep your voice down."

"Jayma's worse." He shakes his head. "She was better after you visited and even went to work yesterday, but she lost concentration, forgot to lock her sorting bin, and caused an accident."

I grab his arm. "Is she okay?"

"One of her co-workers pushed her out of the way of the falling scrap metal, but she's had a negative review posted to her HR file. Audit is investigating and says she's never going back to work again."

"I'll come by tonight and visit. But it'll be late." I'll visit her after my other tasks. So much for sleep.

"It's beyond that." He looks around. "Given all the terrorist activity lately, they're investigating her for sabotage. They made her audit a priority."

My veins turn to ice. "Jayma? That's crazy."

Worry furrows his brow. "Even if the auditors conclude it was an accident, she'll have a black mark against her in her file that will affect her for life." He slumps against the wall. "And that's not the worst. The Comps can't see her like this. They'll put her in the Hospital." He closes his eyes. "I can't lose another child like that."

My guts constrict. "Where is she?"

"Hiding in the north factory district in an alley near the building where I work. She's behind some chemical waste storage bins in NS27—assuming they haven't found her already." His hand shakes as he reaches forward to grab my arm. "Help her. Please."

"Don't worry." I hug Jayma's dad, trying not to show my fear. "I'll do everything I can."

After eating a few bites of food and tucking the rest into a scrap of cloth, I sneak out of the barracks to find Jayma while the sun light is still on. The COT group is spread between the study room and the rec room, and I'm hoping no one misses me other than Cal. I told him I was meeting with Mr. Belando—lies piled upon lies upon lies, but if I'd told Cal the truth he'd have insisted on coming.

At least Jayma is easy to find. I discover her huddled right where her father hid her, and she comes with me without question. But as we travel, her pace consistently slows. If she doesn't pick it up, we'll be caught.

At the end of a rope bridge slung between two buildings, I turn back to face her. "You need to move faster."

She looks up through streaming tears. "Leave me. I just want to die."

My stomach tightens. "You don't mean that."

"I do." She grasps the rope strung along the bridge's edge and looks down. The bridge sways.

I dash back and grab her arm. Fighting the urge to wipe her wet cheeks and hug her, I force a stern look on my face. "You're putting both of us in danger. Is that what you want? For both of us to fall off this bridge or be arrested and exed?"

She shakes her head.

"Then wipe your face." I hide my fear and keep my voice stern. "You can't see through those tears. You'll trip or cause another accident."

She winces.

I pull her in tight. "I'm sorry." Mentioning the accident she caused was mean. "But we need to move quickly and find you a place to hide."

We're near the Exec Building and only a few blocks from the Comp barracks. The sun light is dimming, and if I don't get back soon, I'll be missed. I'm not sure what I was thinking in leading her this way except that, with everything I've got to do tonight, I want her close by. Plus, I know that there are no functioning cameras on the Exec Building's roof, and I might be able to find a way into that big metal container.

As soon as I get her hidden, I'll head to that fabric storage room where I last saw Burn. He said he'd check back for me and I hope he meant it, but I won't take Jayma there until I'm certain it's safe. Besides, she'll panic when she sees him. I'm not ready to face that.

"Jump on my back." I turn away from her. "I'll carry you."

"No." Her voice hitches. "I'm sorry. I'll move faster. I don't care what happens to me, but I won't let you get in trouble."

I simultaneously want to hug her for cooperating and shake her for saying she doesn't care about herself, but at least she's agreed to get moving. I take advantage and race across the remainder of the bridge, grateful when she matches my pace.

At the end of the bridge, I climb up a ladder and roll over the building's lip onto the roof. Jayma follows and I reach back to help her stand.

"Halt," a loud male voice reverberates off the sky above us, and I spin, ready to fight.

It's a Comp in full-armored uniform, his Shocker at the ready. A physical battle is futile. So is running.

I raise my hands to show I'm no threat.

"This is a restricted area," he says from behind his mask. "What are you doing up here?"

I step forward slowly. "I'm in the Comp training program.

Are you sure this roof is restricted? I thought it was cleared for our exercise." I shake my head as if frustrated. "I knew I took a wrong turn a couple of buildings back." I pull up my sleeve, so that if he shines his ultraviolet light he'll be able to see my mark that brands me as part of COT.

But he doesn't pull out his light, and when I get within four feet of him I plead, "I'm on a training exercise. I was supposed to get this Civie volunteer across the city and to the barracks without getting spotted. I'm so close. I need to get back before dinner or I fail. Can you give me a break?"

"You're too small to be in COT."

He lifts his visor. Lines furrow his forehead. "My sister wanted to be a Comp. They wouldn't even let her into the Entrance Trials. Said she was too small. She's bigger than you."

"I'm super lucky because Mr. Belando, the SVP of Compliance?"—I continue after he nods—"He took a special interest in me. He really wants me to graduate to prove his decision wasn't a mistake, and if I fail this exercise . . ."

The Comp's Shocker lowers slightly.

I take another step forward and whisper, "Between you and me? The last time a recruit beat me in a combat bout, Mr. Belando kicked him out of the program for cheating." I lower my voice further. "The kid didn't cheat."

The Comp shifts his head back, as if physically absorbing the information. "You mean Belando will blame *me* if I turn you in? Write a bad evaluation for my HR file?"

I shrug as if I'm wishing he wouldn't, but it's out of my hands.

Worry builds in the Comp's eyes, and he lowers his gun and cocks his head to the side. "Go then. Quickly. There's a ladder on the other side of this roof. It leads to a bridge that ends up near the back door of the barracks. No one's supposed to know about it"—he narrows his eyes—"so don't tell your friends. When I was in training, some of the boys used it to sneak out that way to see their dating partners at night."

I know exactly which bridge he means and I'm sure half our class knows about it. "Thanks. I won't tell anyone. I promise." I reach back for Jayma but she's crumpled down into a ball on the roof. I roll my eyes toward the Comp and mutter, "Civies." Then I pull her up by her shoulders and whisper, "Come on. Let's go."

She slumps along behind me, trying to run, but it's like her legs are weighted down with heavy chains. When we get to the ladder, I look back and the Comp waves.

We get onto the narrow bridge that leads to the fourth floor of the Comp barracks, and halfway across I stop to let Jayma catch up. I point to a landing jutting out from the adjacent building, about fifteen feet below us and at least ten feet to the right. It's a risk to jump to, but I can't take her into the Comp barracks. "See that landing?"

"Uh huh." Her voice is thin and pale.

"Can you make it?" I know normal-Jayma could, but I'm less sure about depressed-and-possibly-suicidal Jayma. She likely hasn't eaten since Scout's accident.

She nods, but there's fear in her eyes. I decide that's a good sign. If she's scared, then maybe she's not planning to jump to her death.

"I'll go first." I stare down at the platform. I've gone this route before without trouble. The platform is five feet long and about four feet deep. It's metal, but not too slippery, and while there are spots of rust, it easily held me the last time I jumped. Its lack of a railing makes aiming easier, but staying on harder. Nothing's perfect.

I flex my legs on the bridge and then power out, stretching my body, using every muscle to propel myself forward. The wall behind the platform rushes toward me and I realize mid-air that I over-shot the jump.

My hands slam into the concrete wall, arms absorbing the force, and I drop down the last five or so feet to the platform. My palms sting and a pounding pain radiates from my wrists, but I've made it. And Jayma will see that my jump was overkill. Hopefully, that'll give her confidence.

Standing across from and above me, she spins to the side as if she heard something and then flings herself off the bridge and down toward me. I slide into the far side to give her more room, and she lands on the lip of the platform. Unable to catch her balance, she sways back. I dive down, my knees land on the platform, and I grab her legs.

But I'm too late. Gravity pulls her back, and my hold low on her legs doesn't help—she's tipping back—so I let one leg go and she lets it fly back as counterbalance. Bending at the waist, she reaches for me.

Terror flies from her eyes. She's doubled over, one foot

still on the platform, the other dangling back. On my knees, I clutch her arm with one hand and the calf of her leg with my other. My knees slide forward across the metal platform.

We're going to slide off.

I stretch a leg back and fumble with the toe of my boot, searching for one of the rusty holes near the wall. My toe catches and I pull Jayma forward. Her elbows land on the platform, but both legs drop off. I grab under her arms and pull while she shifts and twists her body to help.

I feel the shift of her weight coming onto the platform. We've beat gravity, but I refuse to let go. I wrap my arms around her thin torso and pull her fully onto the platform, falling down beside her. Panting, we cling to each other. I want to look into her eyes, to reassure her, or maybe myself, but the backs of my eyes sting, and it nearly kills me that I can't risk looking into my best friend's eyes when I'm so full of emotions.

"Thank you," she whispers and we lie there, regaining our breath and composure.

"Guess you didn't want to die after all." I pull myself up to sit.

She rolls onto her back and bends her knees. "Guess not."

I stand and offer my hand. "Come on. There's a rope around the corner. It's not easy to get to, but from there we can climb to the top of this building." If that metal box isn't empty, I'll hide her in the shadows behind it for now.

She lets me pull her up. "What building are we climbing onto?"

"The Exec Building."

She steps back. "It's too dangerous."

"It'll be fine. Trust me." She might be right, but I won't admit it.

Jayma nods and follows me as I carefully move from one window ledge to the next until we're around the corner and within reach of the rope.

# CHAPTER TWENTY-SEVEN

AFTER LEAVING JAYMA, I CHECK THE FABRIC STORAGE ROOM for Burn, but he's not there, so I decide to go after Tobin. Cal must be wondering where I am, and if I don't get back before lights out, everyone will know I'm missing. But if Tobin's hiding place is sound, maybe I can hide Jayma there too.

Reaching the top of a rope, I peek over the edge of the building that Kara named in her note. This can't be right. The sky's so close to the roof that I can't press up with my arms to get onto its surface without smashing my head. Instead, I swing one foot up, hook it over, and roll onto the roof.

Grime instantly coats my hands and clothes, and I'm not sure how I'll explain the dirt. Right now that's the least of my worries. The air chokes me and I pull the neck of my t-shirt up and over my mouth as a makeshift filter. But I can't hold it in place as I crawl over the roof on my hands and knees, and even down so low my back strikes a low hanging beam in the dark. Giving up on crawling, I press my belly down and slither.

Shining my torch around, I'm glad that I cranked it to its maximum charge before getting off that rope. Without the light, I'm not certain I'd see anything in the disorienting blackness.

The light beam strikes an old ventilation unit in the sky above, but the blades of its fan are so thickly covered with oily grime that it's hard to imagine the last time it spun. No wonder the air's so bad up here. The vents are broken. I'd guess it's been decades since any fresh air has moved across this space, and the worst of the industrial smoke that escapes from leaks around factory stacks has gathered here, building up thick, black residue caked with ash, like a lake of oily sludge.

"Hello," I call out. "Is anyone up here? Tobin? I know your dad. Kara told me where to find you. It's safe. Don't worry." My gut says that Kara wouldn't have sent me up here as some kind of cruel prank, but even if Tobin was once here, there's no guarantee he is now.

I creep forward, stop to shine the light around, and pull my t-shirt back over my mouth to draw a less-choking breath.

Something rustles off to my right. I shine the beam and catch movement. "Tobin?"

No answer. It might be a rat, but seriously, no rat would live up here. It's horrible. Plus, above a factory there's nothing for rats to eat. I crawl toward the movement and a cool rush of air hits my face. Rush is an exaggeration, but compared to the still, dank air, a mere puff feels like a breeze on the top of a hill Outside.

I redirect the light toward the spot where I saw movement, but the torch has faded so much it's next to useless. Pressing onto my belly, I free both hands and crank the lantern until it glows brightly again. Ahead of me there's a low wall that blocks my view of the roof's far edge.

My combat and patrol training click in, urging caution. It's dumb to be crawling blindly toward something or someone I can't see, but this isn't combat. It's a rescue. I hope.

I crawl forward, the torch illuminating sprays of black dust each time I set my hands down. Soon I'm near the wall. About three feet beyond it, the roof's edge abuts the sky—or seems to—but I realize whispers of fresh air are flowing up from the side of the building and escaping through the small gap between the roof and sky.

"Tobin," I say softly. "If you're here, I'm a friend. I'm here to help you. Kara sent me."

There's no response so I continue forward until I can peer behind the wall. Nothing.

My light fades again, and I flatten to free my hands to work the crank. Ahead, in the darkness, the shadow of a head appears, then disappears against the sky as if someone poked up over the side of the building. Surely he's not hanging off the building's edge waiting for me to leave? That thought almost makes me go, but I've come this far. If it is Tobin, I can't leave him behind. I must find a way to make him trust me.

Leaving the torch uncharged, I creep forward, slowly,

willing my eyes to adjust to the near darkness. The edge of the roof looks smooth, no hint of fingers holding on and I hope that doesn't mean he's fallen.

"Tobin, please," I say. "Come up. It's safe, I promise."

His head slowly reappears in silhouette, then his shoulders. I'm not sure what he's standing on, but he's not holding onto the edge of the building.

"Hi." I reach out one hand. "My name's Glory. Are you okay?"

He moves quickly. Light glints off something and I realize he's got a sharp piece of metal in his hand.

"Stay away or I'll slit your throat." His voice breaks with early adolescence and fear.

"I'm not here to hurt you."

He lunges forward, knife first, and I grab his forearm.

"Let me go." His voice shakes and the back of his t-shirt bulges like he's storing the rest of his belongings over his shoulders.

"Drop the knife and I'll let go."

"Not a chance. You'll stab me."

I drop my lantern and press down on his knife hand with my other elbow. His fingers unfurl from the pain. I grab the knife and throw it as far as I can to the side.

"There," I say. "Neither of us has a knife now."

The back of his t-shirt's almost throbbing, as if whatever's under it is alive, and I hope I'm not up against two people here.

"Tobin—"

"How do you know my name?"

"I know your dad."

"My dad's dead."

"And I talked to your sister." I decide it's best not to mention his mother. If she rejected him like I suspect, bringing her into this might backfire. "Kara told me where to find you. I can help."

"Help?" His voice quivers. "How can you help?"

I pull forward and see that his legs are hanging over the side of the roof. There's only a small gap between his body and the sky, but below that there's a platform, and the air is definitely better here.

"How did you find this place?" I ask, and he doesn't answer so I pose another question, keeping my voice light, unthreatening. "Is that a platform? That's a pretty cool hiding place."

I shift forward again and loosen my grip on his forearm. Our heads are only a foot apart now and I pull forward again. He lurches and his backside bangs the sky.

"Careful." Our faces are close now, and I smile and let his arm go.

"I can take care of myself." He pulls away and pushes back to slip through the gap and out of sight.

I quickly pull forward and peer over the side. He's cowering on a platform that's about five feet long and three feet wide and wedged between the building and a beam of the sharply curved sky. The two ends of the platform are open. If he fell there'd be nothing to stop his descent for at least fifteen stories. Still, I'm glad he's not living on the grimy roof.

"How long have you been here?" I ask.

He shifts and rubs his back as if it's itching.

"When's the last time you ate?"

He shrugs.

"Here." I hand him some food I have tucked in my pocket. He grabs a chunk of meat and gobbles it eagerly.

I survey his space again. It's isolated but the access is terrible. Tobin and Jayma wouldn't be spotted here, but this far west side of Haven is too far from the barracks. I'll have problems delivering food and water if they have to wait a few days for Burn to plan an escape route. Plus, I'm not sure Jayma will be up for crawling over this grimy roof.

"Is there another way onto your platform?" I ask. Still eating, he shakes his head. "Listen," I say. "I really can help you. I have a friend and he knows your dad too. He can get you somewhere safe, somewhere that they don't care that you're a Deviant."

He almost loses his balance on the edge of his platform.

I reach down. "It's okay. I'm a Deviant too. Let me help you. It's what I do."

"What do you do?"

"I help Deviants get to a place where the Comps won't bother them."

He licks his fingers and I cringe at the amount of grime that was on them when he took the meat. "No. What do you do?"

For an instant, I worry that he's asking about my work placement, but then I realize he wants to know the same thing Adele did. He wants to know my Deviance.

"When I get super scared, or angry, when I feel emotions really strongly, I can hurt people, using my eyes."

He leans forward. "Show me."

I shake my head. "It's too dangerous."

"You're lying. You're not a Deviant."

"I can't just turn it on at will." I have, but I can't risk hurting him.

"Liar."

"Tobin, it's late. I have another friend who's hiding too. I want you both safe, but I don't have all day." I realize my tone sounds impatient. I am impatient. I want to return to the barracks before lights out so I'm not missed, then sneak out again for the rebel meeting once Stacy's asleep.

"I'm not going anywhere with you," he says, "until you prove you're telling the truth."

Frustration bubbles up inside me, threatening to turn into anger. "Fine." I focus on his eyes as my ability leaps to life and sparks behind my eyes. I think of his lungs and squeeze.

Alarm builds in his eyes. Fear.

I snap my head back and close my eyes.

"What did you do to me?" Tobin's eyes are still wide when I reopen mine. He's shaking.

I reach for his arm. "Are you okay? I told you my Deviance was dangerous."

"I'm okay." He pulls onto the roof. "Where are we going?"

"Do you trust me?"

He nods.

"Then let's go."

. . .

"This is the Exec Building." Tobin backs away from me, looking like he might make a run for it.

"You promised to trust me, remember? You'll be safe here." I'm actually not sure he'll be safe, but I've yet to come up with a better plan.

I guide Tobin across the roof to the big metal box where I left Jayma, and we slip through the bent panel that's doubling as a door. I'm pretty sure this metal box used to house some kind of heating or cooling system for the building from BTD, but all the machinery and parts have long ago been repurposed. It's surprising the shell still exists. No chance would all this metal still be around or uninhabited if it was on the roof of any other building.

Jayma's sitting in the corner, staring ahead, and doesn't seem to notice we came in. Not a good sign.

"Jayma, this is Tobin." I crouch and wave my hand in front of her eyes. Finally, she shifts them to look at me.

"Tobin could use some company," I tell her. "Can you hang out with him until I can get you both somewhere safe? I really need your help."

At the word "help" she shrugs, but the gesture's so slight I'm not positive her shoulders moved.

Tobin stretches his arms forward, accentuating the lumps on his back. I'm still so curious about his Deviance but don't want to ask questions that might spook him now that I have him somewhere temporarily safe.

"Jayma." It looks like she hasn't moved since I was here

hours earlier. "Come outside with me for a minute so we can talk."

She doesn't move, so I reach down, grab her hand, and tug. "Come on," I bend over and whisper. "You need to help me. I can't take care of this kid without you."

She lets me drag her up, swaying slightly, confirming my suspicion she's been sitting in one position for a long time. We squeeze out past the bent panel, and after a few steps across the roof, she doesn't need my help to walk anymore. She scans, searching for danger, and I take this as a good sign.

"How are you doing?" I ask.

"Who is the kid?" she counters. "What's going on, Glory? Why are you so dirty?"

"Tobin needs help. As soon as I can, I'll get you both somewhere safe."

"Like the roof of the Exec Building?" Her voice is cold and full of sarcasm.

I reach for her. "No. Someplace where there are no Comps, no Management, no Shredders. Someplace really safe."

She crosses her thin arms over her chest. "No such place exists."

"Yes it does. I've been there, and you're going to love it."

"If it's so great, why aren't you there?" Her skepticism is better than ambivalence.

"I was there, but I came back to Haven to help others get to safety."

Her eyes get wider and she backs up a step. "Are you taking us to the place where your kidnapper held you?"

My stomach churns. I close the gap between us and take

her hands. "Jayma, I need to tell you something and you need to promise you'll never tell anyone—ever."

She nods.

"And promise me you'll listen and keep an open mind, no matter what?"

She shrugs.

My heart is racing and I draw a long breath. "That guy, his name is Burn and he took me and Drake Outside, to this beautiful and safe place." Her brow furrows but I continue. "I was never kidnapped. I went willingly. Burn didn't kidnap me. He was saving Drake."

"Drake is alive?" A smile bursts onto her face, then vanishes, and she pulls her hands away. "No he's not. You're lying. Why would you say that? How is it even possible? No one can live Outside."

"It's true. And Burn will take you too. He can save you."

"Save me? Why do I need saving?" Her voice trails off as if she realized the answer while asking.

"You're suspected of sabotage." I grab her hand. "If they don't ex you, they'll put you in the Hospital for your depression."

She steps back. "I thought you said the Hospital was safe?"

"Yes, well . . ." She's got me there, and explaining my divided opinions about Mrs. Kalin would make things too complicated right now. I don't have time.

"Scout's dead, isn't he?" She shakes her hand free and drops down, wrapping herself into a tight ball. "You lied."

"No." I crouch and rub her back. "I saw Scout the day

before yesterday. So did Cal. Scout was fine then. He was still unconscious, but he was alive, and they're helping him get better." I'm no longer certain, but Jayma doesn't need to know that. Not now. "Burn will help get Scout out of Haven too. You can be together."

She lifts her head. "Really?"

I pull her up. "Really. You'll be so happy Outside. Believe me."

She shakes her head and backs away from me, shaking.

Putting my hands on her shoulders and concentrating to control my emotions, I look into her eyes. "You have to believe me. It's possible to survive Outside, even for Normals. I've been to a place where there's fresh air and light from the real sun and a whole lake full of water. More water than you could ever imagine. There's fresh food too—everything tastes amazing—and people are happy. That's where Drake is and—" I stop before mentioning my father. I'm already asking her to absorb too much at once.

"How do they breathe Outside without drowning on dust?" Wonder creeps into the skepticism in her voice.

"There's barely any dust where they are, and if a storm blows some in, they wear masks." As all this information tumbles out of me, I feel lighter, easier—almost giddy. I want to tell Jayma everything about me, every secret I'm keeping.

"What about Shredders?" she asks.

"There aren't many around there, because of the lack of dust. But guards keep watch, just in case."

"And Deviants? No Deviants are allowed there, right?"

My lungs squeeze, my giddiness crushed. "Everyone

lives happily together." She can decide what that means. I've already told her more than I should. I can't tell her I'm a Deviant—not yet. "We should get back to Tobin. He really needs your help. He's alone and he's scared."

She nods. "Okay. I'll help with the kid."

I pull her into a hug. "I knew I could count on you."

We head toward the makeshift shelter. An alarm rings.

Jayma jumps and I pull her into a shadow. My heart racing, I keep us hidden, but soon realize the alarm's not about us. If we'd triggered it, Comps would be swarming over the rooftop by now.

"Come on." I pull her out of the shadows and help her climb into the box ahead of me.

Jayma screams.

# CHAPTER TWENTY-EIGHT

I FOLLOW QUICKLY AND ASSUME AN ATTACK POSITION, READY for whatever is threatening Jayma and Tobin.

She's pointing across the shelter, her mouth still open, but her scream has gone silent. Her face is so pale in the torchlight that her freckles look like black spots. I don't think I've ever seen her so frightened. Tobin has backed into the far wall, tucked into a shadow.

"What is it?" I keep my fists up, my legs flexed, ready to fight.

"Deviant," Jayma says, her voice high and tight. "T-Tobin. Not a Normal."

"Oh." I step toward her, my body relaxing. "Don't worry. He's harmless." I turn toward Tobin and beckon him to come out from the shadows. "You are harmless, right?" I hoped that Tobin's Deviance could remain a secret, but clearly that's no longer an option.

Tobin takes a shaky step forward. His face hits the light first, then his bare chest. Nothing unusual. Then he takes another step and I gasp. Wings. Silver wings spread behind Tobin from high on his back. When I step forward, his wings flap, creating a current inside the small space.

I can barely breathe. "Do they work?"

"Do they work?" Jayma steps up beside me. "*That's* your question? This kid is a Deviant who somehow tricked you into helping him, and that's all you ask?"

Tobin reaches for his t-shirt.

"Leave it off, if you're more comfortable," I tell him. "I bet that t-shirt binds your wings when they come out. Did the alarm startle you?"

He nods and grabs the shirt, holding it to his chest.

Jayma clutches my arm, her fingers digging into my flesh. "He's a Deviant," she whispers hard into my ear, as if I'm not fully comprehending the situation.

I turn to her, take her shoulders, and draw a deep breath to calm my emotions before I look into her eyes. This is it. The moment of truth. The moment I've both yearned for and dreaded. But if I don't tell her now, she won't believe anything else. She won't trust me. She won't let Burn save her.

"Jayma, I already knew that Tobin's a Deviant." I swallow.

"And you brought him here? Why didn't you turn him in? What's going on?" Her voice is shaky, her eyes full of confusion.

"Jayma, we're friends, right?'

"Forever." Her brow wrinkles.

"Friends forever, whatever?" My insides shake, but she nods.

"Tobin's a Deviant"—I draw a long breath—"and so am I."

She backs away from me. "You are not." She reaches for me as if pleading, but when I reach toward her, she tucks her hands behind her back.

My throat nearly closes. "I am. So is Drake. That's why I had to hide him. That's why I had to get Drake out of Haven." The words come out quickly, as if they're trying to keep pace with my racing heart.

"No." Her head shakes vigorously. "No. The Comps came for Drake because he was a Parasite."

"That too. But Jayma, Drake can walk now. Once he got Outside, his legs got better."

"How? That's not possible." Jayma backs up and slams into the wall. The vibrations from the impact are dulled by the alarm that's still ringing.

"Jayma," I step closer and smile. "I don't completely understand how it happened. I just know what I saw. Drake can walk." Telling her what little I know about the dust's healing but addictive qualities would only confuse her. I'll save that for later.

"Why did you say you're a Deviant?" Red spots flare

on her cheeks. "To make him feel better?" She gestures toward Tobin, whose wings are now folded back in. He's sitting on the floor, head down.

"I *am* a Deviant, Jayma." My voice cracks and I try to wet my mouth. "I'm so sorry that I didn't tell you, that I couldn't tell you."

"When did you find out?" Her nose twitches as her shocked expression shows hints of disgust. "What's *wrong* with you?"

Her question is like a slap, but instead of letting it knock me down, I absorb it and take a deep breath. At least Jayma's got her spark back.

"I realized I was a Deviant about nine weeks after my fourteenth birthday." That was the first time I killed a rat with my eyes. No sense mentioning that my Deviance first kicked in at thirteen without my knowing or remembering. If I mention that, I have to explain what I did to my mother. That confession can wait until everyone's safe.

"And Jayma," I say, "there's nothing *wrong* with me." How do I explain this? It goes against everything she's been brought up to believe. "You know how good I am at killing rats?'

She nods.

"That's what I do."

"Your Deviance kills rats? How?"

"I'm not sure. I look into their eyes and—"

Her eyes open wide. "That's why you hate making eye contact. You kill people too." Her voice quavers.

I try to make eye contact but she won't let me. I ache inside. "I would never—ever—hurt you, Jayma. Never. I don't use my Deviance anymore. Not even on rats. I'm learning to control it."

"Deviants won't rest until they control Haven . . ." Her voice trails off and I can see her thinking—see the wheels spinning and jamming and reversing inside her mind.

Not literally—I'm not using my Deviance—but I can see it all the same. When you know someone as long as I've known Jayma, when you've shared your secrets, your hopes and fears, you can tell what they're thinking without special powers.

"I know what we were taught." I keep my voice even. "We were taught that Deviants are dangerous, that they're monsters. Evil." I shake my head. "It's not true. I'm not evil. My brother's not evil. Does Tobin seem evil?" I pause. "I'm still the same person you've known your whole life."

She finally looks at me. "You never told me." Her voice is shaky. "Why?"

My ears clog. "I'm sorry, but I couldn't be sure you'd understand. I couldn't put Drake at even more risk than he already faced, I . . ."

"I understand." Her lips twitch. "I'm hurt, but I understand." She looks straight at me, eyes wide. "Does Cal know?"

Guilt lands on my chest and I shake my head. "I want to tell him, but I can't. I'm so afraid. He doesn't even know I've been Outside."

"Oh, Glory." She steps up and squeezes my upper arms. I pull her into a tight hug, so glad my friend doesn't hate me.

"Wait," Tobin says from a few feet away. "Is that where your friend is planning to take me?" His voice is shaky, full of fear. "Outside? Where I'll die or turn into a Shredder?"

Jayma rushes over to him and takes Tobin's hand. "Don't worry. You'll be safe. There's fresh air and a lake and . . ." She struggles to remember the things I've told her.

The alarm stops and I peek out. "I need to go. Will you two—"

"We'll be just fine," Jayma says. "Don't you worry about us."

Grateful, I slip out and slump back against the metal.

Jayma knows I'm a Deviant. The relief's overwhelming and I feel almost boneless.

I've been so afraid for so long, but maybe I should have admitted the truth long ago. She's my best friend; I should have trusted her to understand and accept me for my differences.

It's time to tell Cal.

Thinking of this, anxiety creeps back in. Just because Jayma's accepted the truth—for now—doesn't mean Cal will. He's so devoted to the rules. But Burn was right. I have to learn to trust. I have to use my judgment to decide whom to trust.

Jayma and Tobin are trusting me.

A sinking feeling further fuels my unease. What if I've made promises I can't keep? What if Burn can't or won't save them? What if I never see him again?

I consider heading out to look for Burn again now, but the moon light just turned on and I should go back for bed check. If my absence hasn't already been noticed, it will be. Besides, I need more time to decide whether or not to tell Burn about the rebels' meeting.

His mission is to find them, but I'm not sure I want him to.

I have until Stacy's asleep to decide.

# CHAPTER TWENTY-NINE

MY CONFIDENCE RETURNS WHEN I SUCCESSFULLY SNEAK back into the barracks without notice. Finding Tobin and telling Jayma I'm a Deviant have made me believe I can do the impossible, that I can save them, that I can stop the rebels from bombing the Hub, that I can save everyone.

If I'd told Jayma I was a Deviant years ago, I'd have had someone to talk to besides my little brother. I feel lighter than I have in a week, stronger than I have since I learned that Clay and Arabella were killed.

After my shower, I briefly consider getting a few hours of sleep, but if I fall asleep I might never wake, and I can't miss the rebels' meeting.

Instead, I slip into the rec room and Cal comes over to sit next to me. He takes my hand, kisses my cheek, and doesn't question where I've been. Other than him, no one takes notice. I was made for spy work.

Soon, the lights blink and, with a groan, my classmates set down their games and file out of the room. I get up to follow, but Cal pulls me back into the darkened and empty rec room.

"We should get to our rooms before lights out." I squeeze his upper arm. "We don't want to get caught." The sooner I get to bed, the sooner Stacy will fall asleep and the sooner I can sneak out. I want to tell Cal the truth but there's no time. Not now.

Cal bends his head close to mine and wakes delicious feelings that further pump my confidence and clarify my thoughts.

I know who I am, I know what I am, and I know what's right. Cal needs to know the truth. But not tonight.

"Stay with me a few minutes," he says, his voice low and deep. "I've barely seen you all day."

I nod, and he kisses me in a way that makes me feel stronger, ready to take on the world. When our lips part, I reach for his neck to pull him back down. I need more strength to face this night.

But he resists. "We need to talk."

"Now?" I stroke his neck. "For months you wanted me to kiss you, and now you want to talk?"

He moves his lips close to my ear. "What's your plan?"

Everything tenses as I try to remember what I've told Cal and what I haven't. "My plan?"

"Is Mr. Belando helping?"

"Mr. Belando?" My mouth goes dry.

"You disappeared earlier. I know you were on an undercover assignment. Have you found the mole? Have the Comps stopped the terrorist threat?"

"I—I can't talk about it."

Cal's eyes are filled with worry, but also trust. The worry's well founded but the trust almost kills me. It's time. I need to tell him everything. I've treated Cal badly on so many levels, and it's time to make it right no matter what it costs. Besides, if I'm going to rescue Scout from the Hospital, I need to tell Cal. I need to give him the choice to leave Haven with his brother. I'd never forgive anyone who took Drake away without telling me.

Jayma accepted the truth. Cal will too.

"Okay." My heart thumps. "I'll tell you what's going on."

He cups my cheek and kisses my forehead. "Let's sit." He starts back toward the chairs.

"Cal." My mouth's so dry it won't open. I suck on my cheeks.

He turns back and I glance up at his trusting face, trying to keep mine neutral and knowing I'm failing.

"You can tell me anything," he says. "You can trust me. I'd never betray you."

"I'm a Deviant." My voice comes out in a croak and my heart races, banging in a sharp, hard staccato.

Cal doesn't speak for what feels like an hour, and I watch him, his profile lit by the soft light from the hallway. His expression runs from shock to amused to angry, and finally he speaks. "That isn't funny."

"No, it's not." I draw a long breath. "But it's true. I'm a Deviant."

"You're not. I know you're not." He grabs my hand. "Why are you saying that? If you were a Deviant, I'd know."

I thread my fingers through his and hold tight. "I've known since I was fourteen. My brother's one, too, but his Deviance is harder to conceal because the skin on his torso and arms turns hard like armor when he's scared. That's why I had to keep him hidden."

"You kept Drake hidden because he was injured." Cal's voice is cold. His jaw hardens. "Your brother's dead. Why are you talking about him like he's not?"

My stomach twists. "Drake's *not* dead. He's alive."

Cal wrenches his fingers from mine and strides across the room. His hands grip his hair and pull. His shoulders rise and fall as he stands near the door, and for an instant, I'm scared that he might call out to report me. But this is Cal. He's thinking. He's torn. I've just ripped his sense of loyalty to shreds.

As I wait for his reaction, my muscles cramp and twitch. I want to run to him, to explain, to wrap my arms around him to make him understand, but I know this boy. He needs time to absorb what I've said.

He turns abruptly and stomps toward me.

I gasp. He's so angry. So hurt.

"What's *wrong* with you?" he asks.

I reach toward him, afraid to make contact. "I should have told you sooner. I should have trusted you. I'm sorry. I shouldn't have lied. "

His brow furrows. His eyes narrow. "You're a liar, yes, but that's not what I meant. What's *wrong* with you."

My head snaps back. "There's nothing wrong with me."

"But you said—"

"I can hurt people," I blurt, knowing full well what he meant.

"I got that." His voice is cold. "You're a Deviant."

I reach for him but he pulls back.

"Not all Deviants hurt people, Cal. In fact, most don't. We aren't evil like Management tells everyone. I promise."

His jaw twitches. "But you—" He shakes his head. "You admit that you hurt people."

"Yes."

"How?"

"With my eyes." I look down. "I don't understand how it works, but when I get angry or really afraid—when I feel negative emotions strongly—something behind my eyes changes, and if I look into someone else's eyes, it's like I can feel the person's insides. I feel their blood flowing. I can sense their internal organs and understand how they work. Then once I do, I can grab on and . . ." All this barely makes sense to me. How can it make sense to Cal?

"That's why you won't look at me."

I snap my gaze up and nod.

"Who have you hurt?" His voice is low but still hard.

"Rats," I answer. "Up on the roof of our Pent. That's how I caught so many."

His face lights up with realization. "I always knew you didn't use a net. No one's that quick. Not even you." Admiration washes onto his face and I step toward him.

Just like Jayma, he gets it. I should have put more trust in my friends, especially in the boy that I've always loved. I've wasted so much energy hiding secrets, and it's such a relief that he and Jayma, my closest friends, the people who love me, accept me for who I am.

"I'm so glad you understand." I smile. "Listen. I'm hiding Jayma. She's in trouble. Do you want to come with me to see her? She's on the roof of the Exec Building. It's easy to sneak over. I go up the air vent from our hall to the roof and then—"

He frowns and backs away.

It feels like a punch. A lump forms in my throat.

"Why did that Deviant terrorist kidnap you?" he asks, his voice cold. "Are the terrorists converting all the Deviants to their cause?" He shakes his head. "None of this makes sense."

I swallow so hard it hurts. "I was never kidnapped. The boy who they think kidnapped me—his name is Burn. He saved Drake. Burn had to get him out of Haven before Drake was exed or put into the Hospital."

"You went with that monster on purpose?" The shock and pain in Cal's voice is clear. He backs away and crosses his arms over his chest. "You know his name?"

"He's not a monster." My cheeks heat. "He's a boy my age, and he's brave and strong, and he saved me and Drake. He's been through more than either of us could ever imagine. Don't call him a monster."

Cal's arms drop to his sides as if he's suddenly lost muscular control. "He's the reason you've been so distant since you got back." He shakes his head. "I thought you

were traumatized, but that wasn't it, was it? The distance
. . . you not letting me touch you . . . it was all about him."

My mouth drops open. My tone and my words revealed
more than I meant them to. And Cal's figured out things I
wasn't even sure of myself until now. I can't speak. I don't
know what to say.

"What happened while you were gone?" Cal's chin rises.
"Do you love him?"

I jump forward and put my hand on Cal's arm, but he
pulls away.

"Cal, when I met Burn, I thought you'd betrayed me.
You'd just joined the Jecs. I thought you'd turned Drake in to
the Comps. I thought you were the reason the Comps came
that night. I was confused."

Hurt floods his expression, but then he closes his eyes.
All I can hear is my heart beating as I wait for him to say
something, do something. It feels like hours pass.

His eyes reopen and his expression is eerily blank. "It's
him you want." He twists the dating license on his wrist as
if it hurts. "I can tell by the way you talk about him. I should
have known. You barely let me touch you when you came
back. You could have just said."

"No." I reach forward but drop my hand before it makes
contact. "I'm sorry. I was confused—maybe I still am—but
Cal, I don't know what I'd do without you." My heart rises in
my throat. "You have to believe me. I didn't mean to hurt you.
I don't want to now."

"But you're *confused*." His voice is cold.

"Cal, I feel like you're part of me. I wouldn't know how to

breathe or to walk or to talk if you weren't part of my life. I thought you'd betrayed Drake. I thought you'd betrayed *me*, and it felt like I'd died. And since I got back, having to keep all these secrets made me feel divided, like I'd been cut up into little pieces. I didn't even recognize parts of myself anymore. That's why I was distant."

"But you've always kept secrets." His voice is clipped. "You're a master liar. You play a different part for everyone you know." He glares down at me. "How do I know you're not playing me right now?"

My chest is imploding, my whole world collapsing. "I'm not. Please, Cal. Everything I've said tonight is the truth, and everything that's happened between us since I've been back has been real. The truth. What I feel for you is real." As I say it, I believe it.

"And what about him?" He drops my hand. "The Deviant? What do you call what you feel for him? Is that real too?"

"I—" I promised myself I'd be honest with Cal from now on, and I'm too tired to do anything else. "It would be easy to tell you that I feel nothing for Burn, but it's not true. He understands me in ways you can't."

Cal winces.

I feel sick. "You have to understand, Cal. Burn saved my life. He saved Drake's life. He brought us to our dad."

"Your dad?" Cal staggers back. He tucks down with his hands on his head, then springs back up. "Your father is dead. He was exed over three years ago. I saw it." He rubs his hand over his hair. "Has this all been lies?"

My heart crashes against my ribs. "No. Not tonight. Everything I've told you is true." I back toward the couch. "Please. Sit down. Let me explain." I sit, and he steps closer but stands above me, looking down.

"My dad's alive," I tell him. "He and Drake live Outside."

"Impossible." Cal's voice is curt.

"No, it's true. Management lies about what it's like Outside. I know. I've been there. There's more dust around Haven than other places. Management does it on purpose."

He shakes his head, his expression hard. I'm losing him.

"Based on what you saw at the Hospital, even based on what we've learned in our COT classes, you must realize not everything we were taught in GT, and what they share with lower level employees, is true." I can't catch my breath.

"So you're telling me your dad is a Shredder now?" Cal's voice is laced with disgust.

"No." I bite my lip. Why won't he understand? "When Dad was exed, Burn—and some other people he works with—saved my dad from the Shredders."

"Burn again." Cal's nostrils flare and his eyes narrow. "Even if that's true, your father killed your mother. He should have paid for that."

I press my hand against my forehead, and cowardice chokes my ultimate confession, the one thing I'm still holding back. Cal's right. My mother's killer should be brought to justice, but I am that killer—me—and even though I started this conversation wanting to tell him everything, I can't. Not now. Not that. If I tell him, he'll never speak to me again.

Cal can't turn me in. The stakes are too high. I need his

silence, if only until I save Jayma and Tobin. And I need to get Scout out of the Hospital. And I need to make sure the rebels don't bomb the Hub. The confidence I felt an hour ago has vanished. "Are you going to turn me in?" My voice comes out in a whisper.

Cal widens his legs and glares. "Are you a terrorist? Because if you had any part in that scaffolding collapse"— he bends down toward me—"I won't bother to turn you in. I'll kill you."

The fierceness in his eyes punches into me, and I have to turn away before I answer. "I had nothing to do with that. I'm trying to *stop* the terrorists." And I thank Haven that no one showed Cal the footage of Zina and Burn loosening the bolts.

Cal puts the heels of his hands on his temples, clearly having trouble absorbing all I've told him. "And Mr. Belando? Were you lying about all that too?" His eyes fill with horror and hate. "Are *you* the mole?"

"Of course not."

"Thank Haven for that." His tone's sincere, not sarcastic. He paces across the room and back a few times, and I press my hand to my chest to keep my heart inside.

He drops down on the couch beside me, a few feet away, but it's progress. He just needs to think through all I've told him.

I'm in so deep, pulled in so many directions, that it's hard to know who or what poses the greatest danger right now. But I feel sure it's not Cal. I should have told him the truth sooner. Calm, cool Cal, loyal to a fault. He'd never turn against me, even if he can't accept me as a Deviant. He didn't turn against me when he found out I was hiding Drake, even though he was a Jecs.

I place my hand softly on his shoulder. "What are you thinking? Do you have any questions? I'll tell you whatever you want to know."

He sits back and turns toward me. "What am I supposed to think? I thought I loved you, and you've just told me that you're something I've been taught all my life to despise, to fear. Not only that, it's obvious that you know something about the people who hurt my brother. Information you're holding back from the Comps." His head bangs against the concrete wall behind us.

"Careful."

Not responding, he sits there, staring forward in silence. Anxiety swirls through me, eating away at my composure. He needs more time to think, to process all I've told him, but I can't afford to wait. If I don't leave right now, I won't have time to look for Burn before the rebels' meeting.

I grab his arm. "You'll keep quiet, right? You won't tell anyone about me? About Jayma? I need time to get her to safety."

"Safety?" He shakes his head. "You're hiding her on the roof of the Exec Building. How can that possibly be safe?"

I look at him with a million questions in my eyes. Pleading.

He jumps to his feet.

"Cal." I chase after him. "Don't do anything before talking to me. Please. Promise."

He spins back. "You've got a lot of nerve to ask me to promise anything."

# CHAPTER THIRTY

ANXIETY KEEPS ME AWAKE UNTIL STACY'S ASLEEP. AS SOON as I hear her snoring, I start to get off the bed, but discover another slip of paper. Panicked, I risk cranking my lantern and I hide the light under my blanket to read.

The note says, "Laundry compromised." Then it lists another address.

My stomach tightens. It's not like I had any doubts that the mole had found me, but now I feel as if I'm being watched by a thousand eyes, as if I've been fooling myself into thinking I can do anything in secret.

Does the mole know about Jayma and Tobin? I need to make sure they're safe, even if it means I don't have time to find Burn before the meeting.

My feet hit the floor at the side of the bunks and my legs scream in pain. Stacy snorts in her sleep and turns over, but doesn't wake. I sneak out of the room, then through the grate in our hall, and up the ventilation tubes that lead to the roof.

Slipping onto the roof, I hear a clang down lower in the vent and thinking I'm caught, I freeze for a moment, but no other sound follows. Keeping low, I race across the roof and race to the Exec Building.

When I slip past the bent panel, Tobin's sitting on the floor, his wings spread, and Jayma's behind him, running her hands over his feather-like fronds. Somehow she got him cleaned, and his skin tone's naturally darker than I thought, almost olive. He takes after Gage more than Theresa.

Jayma turns toward me and smiles. "Hi."

I sit down next to them. "Looks like you're feeling better."

She tips up one shoulder in a half-shrug. "Tobin's wings get stiff when he's cooped up."

Tobin turns and his wings drop down behind his back. I want to know if they retract entirely but it seems rude to check. Of all the Deviances I've seen, his is one of the coolest, and I wonder if he can actually fly like the bird I saw above the lake near the Settlement. It might not have occurred to him to try. He's never seen a bird.

"When is your friend getting us out of here?" Tobin asks, his face painted with eagerness.

"Be patient." Jayma touches his arm and I smile inwardly, glad she has a project, someone to take care of. Now I need to live up to my end.

"Soon," I say. "I'm going to meet with him right now. I'll tell you the plan tomorrow."

"What's it like Outside?" Tobin asks. "Will I really be able to let my wings show?"

"Yup. Once you get to the Settlement, anyway." I realize there's no harm in my using that word. It's not as if it's a map to lead the Comps there, if the unthinkable happens.

"Have you got everything you need?" I ask Jayma.

She nods. "The maintenance workers' water up here isn't locked. We got Tobin cleaned up."

"Thank you so much." My heart swells with love for my friend.

"I'm the one who should thank you," she says.

I want to argue, but there's no time. "I need to go, but I'll get back here as soon as I can."

After leaving Jayma and Tobin, I slip through the hatch into the storeroom, hoping to find Burn but terrified he won't be there. Tobin and Jayma need him. I need him.

He said he'd wait for me, that he wouldn't leave Haven without me, but maybe he's had second thoughts. There's no movement in the darkness, no sound, and I wait motionless for my eyes to adjust.

Burn draws out of the shadows. "I knew you'd come back."

"Show me the ring."

"It's me."

"I need to be sure."

Swallowing the distance between us, he draws me in and bends close to my ear. "I don't think I should need a ring to convince you." His deep voice vibrates through me, and his breath heats my neck.

My legs go weak as his lips hover over my throat, my cheek, my hair, never touching but scorchingly close. Engulfed in his arms, I want to ignore reality. But I can't. I push back.

"Show me the ring."

Cupping my head in his hands, he bends and captures my lips in a kiss. My hands fly to his chest, but they refuse to push. I'm not sure I want them to. My resolve weakens along with my common sense. My fingers glide over his chest absorbing his heartbeat and heat.

I break the kiss. "No."

He releases me and I stagger back.

Air rushes from his chest. "I thought you'd know it was me."

I have no doubt. It's Burn. "Show me the ring."

Hurt flashes on his face.

I look down. I don't want to wound him, but I'm with Cal—assuming he ever speaks to me again.

If Burn believes I don't have feelings for him anymore, it will be easier for him to accept that I'm with Cal.

Although, if I'm honest, I realize I want it that way because it'll be easier on me.

"Zina came to see me again," I tell him, to change the subject.

He digs out the ring and holds it forward. "Did she hurt you?" He reaches for me, but I step back and his hand slices through the charged space between us.

"She gave me a mission and claimed that it came directly from Rolph."

"What mission?"

"She wants me to kill a VP." I look down, then straighten to defy my fear. "She claims if I don't do it, she'll kill me. But frankly, her death threats are getting old."

He takes my shoulders in his huge hands. "I won't let her hurt you."

"I can take care of myself. If she threatens me again, I'll grab her by her cold heart and squeeze. Assuming she's got one." I grin, hoping to lighten the mood.

Burn's dark gaze is so strong, so intense, that I can't control my emotions. I shift my focus from his eyes to his mouth, but his lips remind me of the kiss.

Warmth spreads inside me, and his hands, still on my shoulders, create a strong sense of comfort and security. But I'm not positive that even Burn could protect me from Zina. She can appear anytime as anyone. How would anyone protect against that?

"Do you think the mission really came from Rolph?" I ask.

He drops his hands and rakes his hair back. "Could have. Things are moving quickly."

"What's going on?"

"Lots."

"Good or bad?"

"Some of it good, some of it—" He stops short. "We've

made contact with other groups of survivors Outside." He frowns. "Rolph's made some questionable allegiances, but the FA's numbers and capabilities are growing."

There's more, I can tell. Something he's not telling me. "What?" I ask. "Is it my family?"

"They're fine. I'm not telling you more because it's too dangerous for you to have details while you're inside."

"You don't trust me." I cross my arms over my chest.

"I trust you." He steps closer and the heat from his body penetrates mine. "I don't believe what Zina said."

My shoulders fly back. "What did she say?"

"Zina told Rolph you're feeding the Comps information about the FA. She thinks you tipped them off and got Clay killed."

I feel like I've been punched. "I'd never. No."

He shakes his head. "I believe you."

"Why would she say that? Why does she hate me? She barely knows me."

"It's not about you. It's about me and your dad and her brother. Plus, you should have told someone as soon as you were put into Comp training. Finding out didn't help build trust with Rolph."

Guilt pushes inside me. I begged Clay not to tell Rolph when he first found out. I've held so much back from so many people, and after my conversation with Cal, I feel like the most untrustworthy person on the planet. "Do you still trust me?"

His hands grasp my arms and draw me forward. "How can you even ask that?"

Avoiding his eyes, mine land on his chest, and the sight of his body, its breadth and strength, muddles my thoughts. I close my eyes and try to ignore the heat from his fingers as it radiates through me, urging me to slide forward and into his embrace. But I can't do that. I'm with Cal, and Burn's too dangerous.

Burn seems to have forgotten that his Deviance means we can never be together. On the other hand, he kissed me and didn't change. Is it possible that he's gained more control over his Deviance?

"Look at me." He crooks a finger under my chin and urges it up. "I trust you because I know you. I know who you really are."

"Who am I?" My voice comes out weak. I thought I knew just hours ago, but I don't know—not anymore.

"You're Glory," he says. "You're strong. You're good. You're loyal."

I lurch back, breaking the physical bond between us. *Strong?* Maybe. *Good?* I'm less sure. *And loyal?* To whom? My loyalties have never felt more divided.

Burn's eyes narrow at my silence, so I lift my face toward his again. "You're right. I am loyal to my friends, to my family. But there is something I haven't told you. Something I didn't tell Clay."

He nods, encouraging me to continue.

"Mr. Belando thinks I'm going to spy for him. He's ordered me to find you again, to infiltrate the FA, and to feed information back to him." I look into his eyes and shake my head. "I would never, ever, betray you or the FA."

"I know." His arms lift a few inches, like he's going to touch me.

It's too much. This time I'll cave, so I increase the distance between us.

My back hits the door. "As for me being good, I'm confused. I'm not sure I know what that word means anymore, especially after you told me that Rolph sanctioned the scaffolding collapse."

He shakes his head. "Sometimes bad things have to happen to bring about good."

"That's no excuse. Scout is still in the Hospital."

His eyes emote sympathy, but he doesn't respond.

"The FA put Scout in the Hospital. That makes us responsible. You need to help me get him out."

"Not possible."

"I've got the access code for the back door."

Burn doesn't respond so I continue. "I found Tobin, Gage's son. He is a Deviant and you need to get him out, too."

"I don't *need* to do anything."

"Yes you do." I step forward. "And Jayma. You need to get her out."

"What? Why? She's not a Deviant." His eyebrows rise. "Is she?"

I shake my head. "She got depressed after Scout went into the Hospital. She caused an accident at work. If you don't get her out of Haven, they'll ex her."

Burn doesn't argue, which I take as tacit agreement. "When should I bring them here?" I ask.

"Where are they now?"

"Hidden. In a metal box on the roof of the Executive Building."

He charges forward. "Why there?"

I put a hand up between us. "It's the only place I could think of. Mr. Belando disabled the cameras up there so I could get to and from our meetings. It's the best I could do."

His fingers form fists, then unfurl. "No. That's good. That works. Leave them there for now and I'll let you know when to move them. Right now I've got other priorities. I need to complete my mission."

"The rebels." My stomach roils. I can't hold back the information I have. Not when he's helping my friends. "The rebels are planning an attack on the Hub on the President's Birthday."

"Rebels?" He steps forward. "An attack on the Hub? What do you know? How did you find them?"

My stomach tightens. "I found Adele Parry and she led me to them."

"Why didn't you tell me?" His brow furrows. "If they're planning an attack I need to tell Rolph. You need to take me to them."

"I don't *need* to do anything." I throw his words back at him.

He crosses his arms over his chest and raises an eyebrow.

"Don't worry," I tell him. "I'll take you to meet them." I can only imagine the rebels' motives for bombing the Hub, but maybe Burn can convince them not to. At a minimum, I hope they'll postpone their plans until they can discuss them with Rolph and the rest of the FA.

# CHAPTER THIRTY-ONE

THE HEAT FROM RAGING FIRES ASSAULTS ME AS I LEAD BURN into the building that was on my note.

"What is this place?" he asks.

"Metal recycling, I think." Piles of metal scraps lie all over the concrete floor, sorted by type, and at the far end of the long room, workers are pouring liquid fire from a vat into molds.

Adele steps out from a shadow. "You were supposed to come alone."

"You wanted contact with people Outside." I nod toward Burn.

"Your kidnapper." She shakes her head in what looks like disbelief. "I recognize him."

"I wasn't kidnapped," I tell her.

"The plot thickens." She crosses her arms over her chest.

"I'm here representing the Freedom Army," Burn tells her. "My mission is to make contact with your group so we can coordinate our efforts against Management."

She raises her eyebrows and nods. "Then you'd better meet Sahid." She gestures for us to follow.

We walk past raging fires, which wash the space in yellow light, to the far corner and then through a door to a room that's lined with piles of unsorted metal, some of which must have come from Outside, based on the rust. Burn tugs out a long piece with a sharp edge. "This would make a great knife."

"Leave it," a voice says, and we turn to see a man with brown skin, about my dad's age, his dark hair sparked in places with silver.

Burn drops the metal and straightens. My nerves vibrate along with the sound. This room is cooler without the fires, and the light is harsh.

"Are you Sahid?" Burn asks. "I'm here representing the Commander of the Freedom Army."

The man nods. "Are you really from the Outside? The girl claimed to have contacts, but some of us don't trust her." He looks at Adele.

"Clearly Adele was wrong," I say. "And now that you've made contact with the FA, there's no need to set bombs inside Haven. No need to hurt more innocent employees. Setting bombs is not the answer. There are other ways to change things. If we coordinate—"

Adele grabs my arm. "You don't tell us what to do."

Burn glares at Adele and she drops my arm.

"We don't take orders from either of you," she says, although it's clear she's intimidated by Burn.

Sahid raises his hand and Adele backs off. "There's much to discuss and no time to waste."

"I agree," Burn says. "Let's talk."

Sahid narrows his eyes and his jaw twitches. A long elegant finger taps on his opposite arm. "We've got a mission in less than forty-eight hours. How can your people help?"

"Bombing the Hub?" I push forward.

Sahid turns toward me. "Who told you that?" He turns to glare at Adele.

"Is it true? You can't do it. You'll hurt so many innocent people."

"Nothing's been decided." He gestures for Burn to follow him. More people come out from the edges of the room until we're surrounded. Sahid and Burn talk in hushed tones just out of my earshot, and I want to listen but tension builds inside me. I want to scream at these people. I want to accuse them of being monsters, but looking around, it's clear they're not monsters.

They're just like me. Many of them were here the night I met with Adele. I spot Joshua. He nods and I instantly recognize the resemblance between him and Sahid—their brown skin and long noses. I'll bet Sahid is his father.

Just observing these people, knowing their faces, their approximate ages, some of their first names, I have more than enough information to feed Mr. Belando.

But I don't want to turn fellow Deviants in. If I turn them in, these rebels will be exed, but if I don't, they'll bomb the Hub.

I step closer to Burn and Sahid.

"How are you keeping ahead of the Comps?" Burn asks.

Sahid gestures for someone to join him, and a muscular male body steps out of the shadows.

I freeze. My throat closes and every muscle inside me tenses.

It's Captain Larsson.

I back up into the crowd but Larsson turns and stares straight at me; he doesn't look shocked.

Is it Larsson, or Zina? I wish I had some way to be sure.

Is Larsson the mole?

I spin, scanning the crowd, checking my exits, and I spot Zina at the edge of the crowd, her arms crossed over her chest.

Larsson grabs my arm. I try to pull away, but he's too strong.

"Are you the mole?" I ask in a hushed voice.

"Mole?" he asks. "What are you talking about?" His eyes narrow. "Whose side are *you* on?"

"Whose side are you on?" My heart is racing so fast I think my chest might explode.

As he looks at me, I can tell he's got as many questions about me as I've got about him. Every scenario I consider that explains his presence turns out badly for me.

If he's here on Comp business he'll assume I'm a terrorist. If I claim I'm here spying for Mr. Belando, no one will trust me. If Larsson's a terrorist, he's against me in other ways.

Confusion clouds my mind. I can't safely ask or answer any questions. All I can think of are the ways his being here makes my situation worse.

I wrench away, but he grabs me again. Before I can react, Burn grabs Larsson, pulls him off his feet, and throws him. One of the piles of metal rains down on top of the captain.

I run.

Burn's at my side. "Who is that?" he asks as we're crossing the other room.

"He's a Comp. The Captain of COT."

Burn pushes the door to the building open, and we race down the narrow alley between this factory and the next. The moon light is barely reaching between the walls of brick and stone and concrete that press in on both sides. After the bright factory, it's hard to see.

"Get on." Burn reaches for me and I climb onto his back, piggyback style. He leaps and grabs onto the bottom of a ladder. After climbing the ladder, he pushes off and grabs the bottom of a small balcony that sticks out from the next building.

We're hanging and I'm about to reach out and grab a slat to relieve some of the weight, but he pushes down with his arms—doing an exaggerated version of a chin up—propelling us up in one forceful motion. His feet land on the platform with a clang.

I've seen Burn's strength before, but nothing like this. He's become stronger, even in his unchanged form, and it thrills me as much as it scares me.

He leaps off the platform to a rope that's hanging down from the roof and pulls us quickly, hand over hand, until we're at its top. Without stopping to wait, he runs across that roof and leaps to the next, then the next, until we're at least twenty blocks from the metal factory. He stops and twists his body as a signal that I should jump down.

I survey our surroundings. We're near the edge of the north quadrant and the sky is only about six or seven feet above, sloping sharply, and almost devoid of blue paint. Burn's chest heaves as he takes long breaths of the hot air, and droplets of sweat spray back as he pushes his hair off his face.

"Did you see Zina?" I ask.

"Yeah."

"Did you know she'd found the rebels too?"

"We don't exactly swap plans."

"And the Comp, do you think he's part of the rebel group? Or do you think he was there as a spy?" I know these are questions Burn can't possibly answer and I'm expecting a gruff response, but instead he slowly shakes his head and looks down at me with questions in his eyes.

I turn and pace a few feet. "I panicked. I shouldn't have run. I'm sorry." I turn back to Burn. "I got thrown when I saw Larsson. He hates me."

Now that I'm calmer, I realize it's probable that Larsson is the mole. He could easily have planted the notes I've found. But I can't be certain. Nor can I be certain of his motives. He could be on either side.

"Don't worry." Burn rests his hand on my shoulder. "Something didn't feel right in there." He looks up to the sky and pushes his hair back again. "At least I know how to reach Sahid now. Once I get him in touch with Rolph, my mission's complete."

I close my eyes for a moment, my mind finally clearing. "What do I say to Larsson in class tomorrow?"

Burn shakes his head. "Your cover's blown. You can't go back to the barracks."

My stomach spins and twists. "But I need to go back. I'll be fine."

I'm not sure how, but I need to convince Burn. I won't accept that my role inside Haven is over. There are so many more Deviants to rescue and the bombing to stop. I can salvage my cover.

"No." He takes my shoulders in his hands. "It's too dangerous. I'll get you out of Haven as soon as I clear a route. Meet me tomorrow night. "

I back out of his grip, wondering if he's right. If my cover is blown I'm no good to anyone. I might be arrested. "You need to save Tobin and Jayma."

He curses. "I'll come back for them once you're safe."

I back away. "No. Not a chance. I'm not leaving Haven without them and I'm not leaving without Scout—or Cal." I add that last name without thinking. Although he's not in any specific danger, the idea of leaving Haven without Cal is unthinkable.

"Cal?" Burn says his name like it's dirt.

My heart races. "He's my dating partner. If I disappear,

they'll suspect him. I can't leave him." I hold up my dating bracelet and Burn lurches back as if I punched him in the face.

"I thought you were just pretending to be with Cal." The veins on his temples pulse. "I thought he was part of your cover. You said you two were done."

"I—" My face heats and I straighten my shoulders. "You were the one who said you were done with me. And Zina said some really horrible things when I thought it was you."

"I didn't. She did."

"I know it wasn't you, now, but I didn't know at the time, and . . . Cal's been supportive and understanding. He's been my only real friend since I've been back." My stomach flips and churns. My cheeks are on fire. In spite of how I left things with Burn, in spite of his insisting we could never be together, if Zina hadn't said those horrible things, I might not be recommitted to Cal. But I am. Assuming he'll still have me.

"You were gone." My mouth's dry. "You'd told me we could never be together. What did you expect?"

Fists form at his sides. "I was wrong. You're not loyal."

"You want to talk about loyalty?" Anger builds inside my chest. "You claim your control has improved. Well, how do you know that, unless you've been practicing with other girls?" Even if Zina was lying when she claimed Burn had a girlfriend, her idea must have come from somewhere. Where there's smoke there's fire. "Has your new girlfriend been introduced to your monster?"

At the word monster, his head snaps back. It's a word I

swore I'd never use again with him, and I want to shovel it back. It's too late.

He lowers his head. "Do you love Cal?" His voice is a low growl.

"I—" I don't know how to answer. My head's swimming in a sea of confusion. "I'm not leaving Haven without him."

Burn stares at the rooftop. I'm focused on his fists. They're growing. His whole body's growing.

Clearly he hasn't got his Deviance under control. I should run—he might kill me—but I can't leave him like this. And what if he goes after Cal?

"Burn, I'm sorry." I cautiously step forward. "Calm down. I didn't mean to hurt you—and it's certainly not Cal's fault. Don't be mad at him because of me."

His head raises and his eyes turn red. His normally huge coat pushes out to its seams and tears along the right shoulder. Impossibly huge muscles press on the fabric and the hem rises from the tops of his boots to over his knees as his thighs surge and shape into hard mounds. If I can't calm him down, he'll kill someone— maybe me.

Shaking his head, he stomps around the roof, vibrating it under my feet, and he repeatedly punches his fist into his palm so hard the sound hammers my eardrums. He's going to break his hand.

"Burn, I'm sorry. Calm down. Don't be jealous of Cal."

At Cal's name, Burn races toward me.

I duck, but before reaching me, he leaps and his fists slam into the sky fifteen feet above us.

The metal screeches as he breaks through. The sky's panels bend and tear into jagged edges. Insulation showers down, blowing down on me as air from Outside invades.

Burn disappears, and booms from his footsteps vibrate the sky as he runs across the outside of the dome. They fade quickly and vanish. I hope that he got away without being shot by a Comp on patrol. I didn't hear a gunshot, but I can't be sure.

From this angle I can see only the merest hint of the inky night sky, and it makes me want to follow through the hole. But I can't stand here staring and yearning. I won't be alone here for long and I can't explain what happened. I'm not even supposed to be out of the barracks, never mind on a rooftop standing below a gaping hole.

Movement startles me and I spin.

Larsson strides across the rooftop, and I race for the other side, planning to jump, hoping there's another roof below to catch me.

"Stop," he yells. "There's nowhere to jump to from there. You'll be killed."

I don't trust him, but I don't want to die, so I skid to a stop, then windmill my arms to catch my balance on the roof's edge. He wasn't lying. Below me, a pile of metal scraps juts up, waiting to spear me.

Larsson grabs me around the waist and pulls me back from the edge.

I struggle to get free.

"Get out of here," he says, his voice hard in my ear. "The Comps are coming." His eyes and voice seem sincere.

"But the hole in the sky. What? How?" I can't form complete thoughts.

Loosening his grip, he looks up through the hole and wipes insulation and dust from the sleeves of his shirt. "It's happened before."

"What?"

"Shredders have breached the dome before, not to mention the wall around Haven."

"The wall?" I don't want Larsson to know I've seen the wall, but I can't imagine anything, even a tank, going through that huge, thick barrier, never mind Shredders.

"An explosion took down part of the wall the day your class viewed the expunging. It's still not repaired."

I gasp. The loud boom. The blowing dust. The squads of armed Comps marching in the distance. I take a step back. Does Larsson really think that a Shredder made this hole in the sky?

Or does he think Burn is a Shredder? Zina's accusation nags at the back of my mind.

Larsson's takes my shoulders and turns me. "Run. Now. Go back to the barracks. I'll take care of this mess."

I nod, not understanding what's going on, but grateful. I need to remember what's important right now. Even if my time rescuing Deviants is over, I need to save my friends. And now I need to do it without Burn.

# CHAPTER THIRTY-TWO

CAL AVOIDS ME THE NEXT DAY. HE WON'T EVEN MAKE EYE contact, and I've never felt so alone. By the end of classes, it's been more than sixteen hours since Burn burst through the sky, and I haven't heard a word about it. No alarms, no rumors, no special bulletins. It's as if it didn't happen.

At least Larsson was absent from training today and I didn't need to face him. I lean against the wall in the rec room. The President's Birthday is tomorrow and I have no idea whether or not the rebels still plan to set bombs.

Watching Cal and the others play games, I press my hands into my knees to try to keep my body from shaking. I've run out of options, and I'm considering going to Mr. Belando to give up Sahid. At least that way the bombing will be prevented. Then I just need a way to get Tobin, Jayma, and Scout out of Haven.

There must be an entrance to a tunnel somewhere in that fabric storage room Burn took me to. If I can find a route that leads us past the wall, I feel sure I can find the way to the Settlement. As long as we don't run into Shredders.

If Scout is still unconscious, I'm not sure how I'll transport him. I bite my lip. Cal needs to come.

I leap up and pull Cal away from his game. "We need to talk."

He pulls his arm out of my hands, but nods.

"Give it up," Stacy says. "He's done with you."

I ignore her and lead Cal down the hall until we're out of hearing range. He stands with his feet shoulder-width apart and stares above my head, which hurts more than I can bear. It's not clear whether it's because he hates me, or whether he's afraid to look me in the eyes now that he knows the truth.

"Where were you last night?" he asks. "Stacy says you were gone most of the night."

I cringe at the mention of her name. "I needed to get food to Jayma."

"That took all night?" His voice drips with suspicion.

"Did you report me?" I ask in a low voice.

His gaze snaps down to meet mine. He shakes his head slowly.

"Did you tell anyone?"

He leans against the wall and rubs his face in his hands before answering, "I haven't done anything."

Relief washes through me. "Thank you."

"I didn't say I wasn't going to. I just said I hadn't."

I look up at him, searching his blue eyes for a hint of compassion or affection, a tease of what I normally see when he looks at me, but there's nothing but disappointment. Down the hall, a light flickers.

"Is that it?" he asks. "Because if we're done, I was in the middle of something."

"Sorry to interrupt your *game*." My tone is harsher than I intend. "It's only my life at stake. No big deal."

His eyes fill with fire. "I don't know what you expect from me, Glory. You drop a hundred huge bombs and then expect me to carry on as if nothing happened."

"I'm still the same person." I grab his wrist. "Please, tell me what I can say, what I can do, to make you understand."

He's silent and his jaw shifts as he looks at me with hurt in his eyes. Hurt is better than hate. Hurt gives me hope.

"I need your help. Jayma needs your help. So does Scout."

His head snaps back at his brother's name. "What's wrong with Scout?"

I lean in close, relieved when he doesn't pull back. "I'm going to break him out of the Hospital."

"Why?"

I move my hand near his but don't touch him. "I don't think he's safe there."

"Leave him alone." He pulls back. "What's going on with you? You're the one who told me to trust Mrs. Kalin."

"Cal," Stacy calls from the rec room entrance. "Are you coming back? You promised to show me how to jump higher with the SIM controller."

I reach for Cal, but he's already backing away from me, questions and doubt in his eyes.

I'm well and truly on my own.

My legs aren't fully under my control as I pace in the halls, trying to calm my nerves, to think. Everything's muddled, but one thing is clear: I need to get Tobin and Jayma off that roof and to the fabric storage room—tonight. Cal knows about my hiding place on the roof and I'm no longer sure I can trust him. Plus, I have no idea where Larsson's gone and what else he might know.

Stacy's bunk is empty when I enter our room, and the glue holding me together melts. I drop down to the ground in a heap.

"What's wrong with you?" Stacy says, and I spin to see her standing next to the door.

"Nothing." I turn on the floor and lean against the edge of her bunk. "I'm just tired."

"Don't try to fool me." A knowing smile pollutes her face. "I know."

Alarm courses through me. "Know what?"

She crouches down and puts a hand on my shoulder. "About Cal. That he dumped you."

I suck in a breath, and her lips twitch in delighted response. She pulls her hand away. She's bluffing. Cal didn't dump me. Not exactly. Not officially. Not yet.

"I don't know where you're getting your gossip from, Stacy, but I suggest you check your sources." I stand and pull up onto the top bunk.

She looks up at me, gloating. "Oh, my source is pretty reliable."

"Didn't your mother teach you it was rude to eavesdrop?"

"I didn't eavesdrop." A grin spreads on her face.

I toe off one shoe, then the other, keeping silent and hiding my emotions. I need her to go to sleep so I can leave, although I'm not sure why I'm bothering to maintain the ruse that she doesn't know I sneak out.

"I heard the news straight from Cal," she says.

My head snaps up, and her smug look makes me want to kick the expression off her face. But instead, I lie back on my bed and stretch out as if I'm ready to fall asleep. Maybe she'll take the hint and sleep too.

Stacy leans on my bunk, her hands on the coarse, gray sheet and her face close to my shoulder. "Cal pretended to be sad, but I could tell he's relieved. And he made it clear he dumped you to be with me."

"Liar." I sit quickly and my head slams into the ceiling.

"Careful," she says. "Losing a dating partner isn't any reason to hurt yourself. You'll get over it."

My head throbs. "Stacy." I lie back down. "I need to sleep. Just shut up and leave me alone."

She's quiet for a few merciful seconds but I can hear her breathing next to my bunk. "Suit yourself, but don't wallow. Cal and I will do our best not to flaunt our relationship in front of you—not that you offered me the same courtesy. Just know that as soon as he gets your license hacked off his wrist, we're going to head to HR to apply for ours. Hope that's okay. Not that I need your blessing, but I know sometimes

HR interviews former dating partners before approving a new relationship to make sure there was no sexual harassment. I hope you won't lie to interfere with our happiness."

I don't answer. Finally I hear the creak of her landing on her bunk below me.

Jealousy stings the million tiny wounds I'm already feeling. The thought of Cal confiding in Stacy rakes my pain, and when I close my eyes I imagine him laughing with the other recruits, telling everyone how he dumped me. Tears build behind my eyelids but I fight against them.

No matter how angry Cal is, he wouldn't do that. He'd never mock me. He'd never mock anyone, and I don't even believe he told Stacy what she claims.

I won't allow myself to believe her. I've got enough on my mind. I pull long, slow breaths through my nose, pushing them out through my lips.

*Relax. Ignore Stacy. Ignore the pain. Relax.*

I need to focus on one thing at a time, and the highest priority right now is getting Tobin and Jayma out of Haven and getting Scout of the Hospital . . .

I wake with a start. It's dark. I fell asleep and have no idea how late it is. Stacy's snoring so I grab the bundle of food I snuck at dinner and slide off the bunk, dropping silently to the floor. Fumbling in the dark, I discover my shoes haphazardly at the side of the room. Stacy must have kicked them over there.

Glancing at a clock, I wince. It's hours later than I planned. I was hoping to search the storage room for a tunnel entrance before bringing Jayma and Tobin there. A small part of me hopes I'll find Burn, but after last night, I know I can't count on him. I can't be sure he's alive.

I sneak out, and after I pull onto the Exec Building's roof, I keep low and run across to the metal box.

I open the slat and slide through the gap. Jayma and Tobin don't have a light on, so I wind up my torch, keeping it pointed down so the sudden brightness won't hurt their eyes.

Once the beam's working I lift my arm slowly. Strange. I expected to see Jayma sleeping against the wall opposite the entrance. I pan to the other side, and my heart races out of control.

I step into the center of the box and spin, dragging the light around me, striking all four walls, every corner of the space. But no amount of light will change the truth.

They're gone.

I climb into my bunk less than an hour before the morning bell is due to ring. It's not as if sleep would be possible, even if I had hours. My mind darts a million places, testing alternate plans and scenarios, and my body's ready to spring, to run, to fight. I spent the entire night searching for Burn, for Tobin, for Jayma. I cannot, I *will not* give up until my friends are safe.

The storeroom where I meet with Burn was empty, as was the place where I used to meet Clay, and the tiny platform where Tobin was living before I found him. I checked the roof of our old building in the Pents too. They're gone.

Vanished. I'm consumed with panic that they've been reported. I failed them. They'll be expunged.

I have no idea who could be responsible for reporting them. I thought I heard someone behind me in the vent the other night. It could be Mr. Belando or Cal or Zina or Larsson—it could even be Stacy. But at this moment, who might have turned in Jayma and Tobin is moot. If the Comps have them, knowing the culprit won't bring them back.

Unable to sleep, I get down off my bunk to pace the halls and think. On my third lap, Cal steps into the hall.

I stop, holding my breath. He looks down and backs into his room like he's pretending he didn't see me.

"Nice," I say. "Run. Don't even talk to me. You're such a coward."

He steps back into the hall and strides toward me. "I'm not a coward. I just don't want to see you."

My heart seizes. "Ready or not, we need to talk." I stride toward the rec room and I'm relieved when he follows.

After we enter, he glares at me in the near-darkness, jaw twitching. "What do you want now? Do you have more secrets to spill?"

"I think Jayma was caught last night. If I find out you had anything to do with it—"

"I didn't turn her in." Genuine distress flashes in his eyes, then he looks away and his voice lowers. "But I'm not surprised they found her."

My chest caves. "How can you be so cold? So cruel?"

"Do you think any of this is easy for me?" he asks. "With everything you told me—" He closes his eyes. "You hid her on the Exec Building. No wonder she got caught." He shakes his head. "Maybe it's for the best."

"How can you say that? We're talking about Jayma. Someone you've known your whole life, my best friend, the girl your brother loves." I gasp for air. "She'll be exed."

The color drains from his face, but he frowns. "More likely they've taken her to the Hospital to treat her depression. Maybe she'll even be able to spend some time with Scout."

My mouth gapes open; then I snap it shut. Cal still firmly believes his brother's safe.

The morning bell rings and I jump.

Nothing's resolved but we've run out of time, and although I haven't asked Cal the questions I want to, our short discussion has clarified his position. He hasn't forgiven me.

With everything else going on, I'm ashamed at how much that hurts, at how painful it is to see the change in the way he looks at me. Not only do I no longer have a dating partner, I no longer have a friend. No allies in my corner.

The door into the rec room swings open to reveal Stacy. Seeing me with Cal, her eyes narrow, then her self-satisfied smirk appears, and she turns back into the hall. "I found her. She's here."

Thumping comes down the hall—the unmistakable sound of Comp boots in formation. Stacy steps out of the way and holds the door open as the first men plow through, their Shocker guns raised and pointed directly at me.

My lungs collapse.

Larsson comes into the rec room behind the Comps.

"What's going on here? Why are you arresting one of my recruits?"

One of the Comps turns toward him and lifts his visor. "She's a terrorist."

"You have evidence to support this?" Larsson asks. "You're not taking one of my recruits until I see evidence." He crosses his arms over his chest and stands firm.

As much as I've despised Larsson, I could hug him right now. Not that his support will do me much good if the Comps have evidence of my hiding Jayma and Tobin.

The door swings open and Mr. Shaw steps in, bright red spots on his cheeks. "The charge is now murder."

"What?" I can't draw breaths. They can't possibly know about my mother. My knees want to crumple. I don't let them. "Please . . . Explain what's—"

"Silence," one of the Comps yells.

"Who was murdered?" Larsson asks. "Someone tell me what's going on."

"Last night, this recruit tampered with the food in the Exec Dining Room," Shaw says. "Seven members of Senior Management were poisoned this morning and it was just confirmed. Mr. Belando is dead."

A collective gasp sucks the air from the room, and my terror turns to a sharp pain. Mr. Belando's dead? I never liked him, never trusted him, but the thought that he was poisoned is horrible. And they think I did it.

I look up. Larsson is staring at me, eyes wide and questioning as if he thinks I'm guilty. My stomach turns somersaults. "It wasn't me. I didn't do it. I swear."

"Shut up." The big Comp slams the butt of his stun gun down on my shoulder and forces me back into a chair. Searing pain races down my arm and up my neck.

"Hey," Cal says, but another Comp grabs him.

"Why would you think it was my recruit?" Larsson asks. "Recruits aren't allowed out of the barracks at night."

Larsson's defending me even though he knows full well I've been out of the barracks at night. Maybe there is one person left I can trust, assuming it's not too late to matter.

"We have proof." The head Comp turns on the display screen in the rec room, and after going through a short series of menus and passcodes, a grainy image of a kitchen appears on the screen. The date and time are displayed in the bottom corner, the seconds and minutes clicking away at about 0230 this morning.

A small person, about my size and shape, steps up to a pot of porridge and empties the contents of a small bottle into it. She turns her head and I gasp. The image is grainy, it's hard to be sure, but it does look like me.

*Zina. It has to be Zina.* I didn't kill a VP like she ordered, so she took matters into her own hands.

Terror clamps my throat, my heart, my belly. She's found a way not only to carry out the assignment I refused, but also to carry through on her threat to kill me. She might not be driving in the knife herself, but I'm as good as dead.

"That image." Cal steps forward and points to the screen. "It can't be Glory. It looks a bit like her, but it's not. It can't be."

"How do you know?" Larsson asks.

"I know because she was with me last night. We were together the entire night. In the gymnasium."

"Do you swear that she was with you?" Larsson asks. "Because if you're lying, you'll be arrested too." The warning in his tone is clear. He's telling Cal to stay out of it.

"Glory was with me the entire night," Cal says, his voice strong. "That video image is grainy. It could be anyone. But it can't be Glory. She was with me."

"No." Stacy bursts in. "You weren't together last night. You two broke up."

Cal steps to my side, crouches down, and takes my hand in his. "Last night, I begged Glory to take me back. I love her. We were together last night. All night."

I risk a quick look toward Stacy but she's backed into the corner and I can't see her face.

A Comp grabs me by the arm and pulls me out of my chair. "We'll check out your alibi, but right now, I have orders to take you into custody."

# CHAPTER THIRTY-THREE

"YOU'RE GOING TO WEAR A PATH INTO THE FLOOR."

I spin back to see Larsson at the small, wire-covered window in the door to my four-by-four cell. It's small, but not that much smaller than the apartment I shared with my brother for three years after our parents were gone.

The lock clicks, the door swings open, and Larsson steps inside. "We only have a few minutes before they realize I disabled the camera and sound surveillance for your cell."

"Do you know what happened to my friends?" I ask. If he doesn't already know about them, I have no choice but to tell him.

"What friends?" He leans against the rough concrete wall.

"Did someone from the rebel group find them? Are they safe? Has anyone been exed?"

"No one's been exed, but I honestly don't know what you're talking about."

"I was hiding a Deviant boy and a friend who was falsely accused of sabotage."

He shakes his head. "They're probably still wherever you hid them."

They're not where I hid them, but I don't think Larsson's lying, and I've got so many other questions, so many other problems to solve. Today is the President's Birthday. I need to get out of here. I need to do something to stop the bombing.

"Why did you poison Belando?" he asks. "The guy was a jerk, but why target him?"

"That wasn't me." My knees tremble so I start pacing again as I ask, "What happened to the hole in the sky? Why did you help me? Why were you at that rebel meeting? Who are you, really?" A million other questions run through my mind, but those seem okay for starters.

He grabs my arm. "Calm down."

I pull away. "Calm down? You've got to be kidding."

"Being frantic won't help anything. Calm down and talk to me and I'll answer your questions."

I back up, then slide down the wall to sit.

Larsson's knees crack as he sits down beside me. "Hang in there."

"You said you'd answer my questions."

"I reported the dome breach. It got repaired quickly and quietly using a special crew of workers that Management trusts." He cracks his knuckles. "Now it's my turn for a question. How did that Shredder smash the sky? Did you see it? Why were you at that meeting? Are you a Deviant?"

I raise my eyebrows. "That's a lot of questions."

"Answer one."

"Which?" My heart is thumping hard. Larsson seems sincere—so different from how he was during training—but I don't trust him.

"I know your father was a Deviant," he says. "Are you?"

"Do you think I am?"

He shakes his head. "No. If you were a Deviant, I'd have noticed it during training. We put you under plenty of stress. I assume you support Deviant rights because of your dad?"

I nod, but my neck feels stiff.

"Were you really kidnapped?"

I snap my gaze toward him and slowly shake my head. "No. Burn helped me rescue my brother from the Comps. My turn." But what to ask first? "Why did you pick on me during training?" I can't figure him out. Perhaps this will help.

He frowns. "You're too small to be a Comp."

"So you said. A million times."

He bends one leg and rests his elbow. "I didn't want you to get killed. You'd never have lasted your first rotation Outside. I figured if I made you quit, I'd save your life."

"And Cal?"

"I put pressure on him to up the pressure on you."

I nod. His answer seems honest, and what I suspected.

"My turn," he says. "Why were you at that rebel meeting? Are you working for that Freedom Army? How did you meet them?"

"That's more than one question."

He raises an eyebrow.

"I met the FA when everyone thought I was kidnapped. I went to the rebel meeting to try to stop them from bombing the Hub." I twist away from the wall and sit cross-legged facing him. "Did you have anything to do with that last bombing in the Factory district?"

He shakes his head and relief floods me. "Why?" he asks.

"Mr. Belando said they found a training tag from a Shocker in the place where the rebels built the bomb."

"Ah." He nods and blows air through his lips. "I was there. I tried to talk them out of planting that bomb." He shakes his head. "I can't believe I dropped a tag."

"Why are the rebels setting bombs? Why are they hurting innocent people?"

Larsson shakes his head. "Adele's driving it. She believes the only way to weaken Management is to undermine their authority and prove the Haven Equals Safety slogan wrong. She thinks they can get people on their side that way." His brow furrows. "What's your relationship to Mr. Belando? Why did he push you into the COT program?"

I study his face for a moment and decide to tell him the truth. "Mr. Belando recruited me after my kidnapping. He figured that either I wasn't telling him everything or that I'd forgotten details and would eventually remember more about where I was held. He wanted me to work undercover for him and betray Deviants. He figured that I could reconnect with Burn, convince him I'd become a sympathizer, and betray him. But I would never—" I stop myself, still unsure of how far I can trust the COT Captain.

"I support Deviant rights too." He leans forward onto his knees. "My younger brother—he was a great kid, wouldn't hurt a fly—but the second his Deviance emerged, the bastards exed him. I was a rookie Comp at the time. To test my loyalty, they made me watch as those monsters tore my little brother apart." His voice shakes. He slams a fist on the floor. "That day, I swore I'd do whatever it took to keep others from being killed just because they're different."

"But you're still a Comp."

"Sometimes it's easier to change things from the inside."

I nod. That's what Mrs. Kalin claims to be doing too. If I believe her.

"Some days," Larsson continues, "I do feel like a hypocrite as a Comp, but at least in COT I'm not the one doing the killing. Plus, when I get wind that the Comps are going after a Deviant, I let Sahid know and he tries to get to them first and hide them."

"So you are a rebel."

"I guess so. Kind of."

"Can you stop them from bombing the Hub today?"

He shakes his head.

I leap to my feet. "But you need to do something. I can't stop it from in here, and I won't be able to do anything once they ex me." My voice shakes and sadness slams into me.

I turn away from Larsson so he can't see my despair.

He touches my shoulder. "You won't be exed. I'm not sure

how you've done it, but you've got friends in high places."

"What do you mean?"

"The President himself is pushing to have you transferred from here to the Hospital." He tips his head. "How do you know the President?"

"I don't." My moment of relief is replaced by dread. Why in the world would the President be intervening? "Why the Hospital?" Am I going to be a subject for one of Mrs. Kalin's experiments? My insides twist, but I fight to stay strong.

Larsson looks over at the door. "The President's in the Detention Manager's office right now, expediting your transfer. Compliance is in a bit of a shambles with Belando's death coming so soon after Mr. Singh's."

"I still can't believe someone killed him."

Larsson spins toward me. "It really wasn't you?" His eyes narrow.

"It wasn't me."

"You don't need to lie. Not to me." Skepticism paints his face. "I saw the tape, and Zina told the rebels about your mission. Apparently your orders came straight from your army commander."

I fight to control my breathing, my heart rate. I can't stand being accused of a murder I didn't commit. "Do you know what Zina can do?" I ask. "Do you know how her Deviance works?"

He shakes his head.

"That was *her* on the tape. Not me. She can impersonate people. She alters her appearance. She pretended to be me when she poisoned the food. She sabotaged that scaffolding too."

He leans back and his brow furrows. "Why would she frame you?"

"It's not about me. It's about my dad and Burn. I don't believe the orders she gave me came from the FA."

Larsson's quiet for a few minutes. He rubs his chin and says, "Too bad Cal got caught up in all this."

"Cal?"

"They've arrested him."

Panic grabs at my chest. "Why?"

"The alibi he gave you was blown. Stacy claims she talked to him in the rec room last night at the same time he claimed to be with you."

My heart rises in my throat and fists form at my sides. "I could kill her."

"Watch what you say." He looks up at the camera.

I grab his arm. "Did you lie? Is the camera on?" Has this whole conversation been a trick to get me to confess?

He shakes his head. "Sorry. Just habit."

I lean in closer. "Stacy hates me. She came forward to hurt me, but she might recant her story if she thinks it will help Cal. Talk to her. Please?"

A guard knocks on the door.

"I'll see what I can do." Larsson shoots me a grim smile before leaving my cell. "Good luck."

As soon as he leaves, the lights in my cell go out.

. . .

A light shines in my eyes. I wake with a start and scramble to my feet, backing into the corner of the cell.

"Calm down," a male voice says. "If you cooperate, I won't hurt you."

"Who are you?" I ask. "What are you doing?" His light's directly in my eyes so I can't use my Deviance, but as soon as this man lays a hand on me, I'll use my combat skills to take him down. Then I'll escape.

"Grab her," another voice says, and the light drops from my eyes. I lunge at the legs of the man holding the torch and knock him off balance.

We land on the floor, but before I can leap up, a boot lands square on my back, pushing the air from my lungs. Another set of hands restrain my legs, and prone, I struggle to grab onto something, anything. A boot lands on my out-stretched arm. The other's squished under me.

A sharp pain pinches my neck. "Done," one of the men says. "She won't give you any more trouble."

The pressure of their bodies lifts and I try to fight back, but my muscles won't move. No matter how hard I try, nothing happens. The room fades to black.

# CHAPTER THIRTY-FOUR

I WAKE UP IN DARKNESS AND TRY TO SIT, BUT SOMETHING'S holding my limbs, and there's pressure on my forehead. I'm strapped down.

"Where am I?" I shout, but my voice comes out hoarse and echoes in the space. "Help," I shout again, and lights snap on, blinding me. I hear a door, then heels clicking over a hard surface.

"You're awake," a voice says.

"Mrs. Kalin?" My mind is fogged. The light's bright, and my eyes sting behind closed eyelids.

A warm hand lands on my arm. I can't open my eyes, but I know it's her. A motor starts and my body tilts until I'm raised to a forty-five degree angle. My eyes open a slit, I blink, and Mrs. Kalin comes into focus, wearing a white coat over her usual gray slacks and sweater.

"Where am I?" I ask, even though I'm fairly certain I'm somewhere in the Hospital. My mouth feels as if I've swallowed a bucketful of dust.

"You're safe." She looks at me with kindness in her eyes and I feel better.

"Why am I here?" I ask. "Why am I strapped down?"

"I brought you here so we could talk." Her eyes flash kindness and I can't believe I stopped trusting her. She cares about me.

"Why did you poison that food?" She rests her hand on the strap on my forehead. "What was your strategy in going after Belando?"

I don't answer. I have no idea what she wants to hear, and I want to please her. My head's still spinning, likely from the aftereffects of the drug.

"Don't worry," she says. "I'm not angry with you, sweetie. I'm just not certain of your motives. Belando was easily controlled."

My stomach tightens. What does she mean? What answer will please her?

I look directly into her eyes. If I really can listen in on people's thoughts, maybe I can figure out what she wants. Gathering my Deviance, I lock onto her mind, but it doesn't feel safe, it doesn't feel controlled. I might hurt her.

*This girl is stronger than I thought*, I hear in her mind. But I also feel my ability squeezing, tightening like a belt around her brain.

Mrs. Kalin's hands fly to her temples and I break eye

contact, releasing my hold. "Are you okay?" My chest tightens.

"Just a headache." She blinks a few times, then narrows her eyes, looking at me askance. "Nothing to worry about."

I shift on the tilted table. "Can you take these off? The straps are digging into my wrists."

"Certainly." She smiles and steps behind the table. "As long as you tell me why you poisoned that food. What was Mr. Belando up to?"

My trust wavers. "Are you gathering evidence for the Comps?"

From behind me, she rests her hand on my shoulder. "I swear I will not repeat a word of what you tell me—to anyone."

I glance around the sterile white and stainless-steel room—the parts I can see from the table.

"There are no cameras in here," she says.

I can't move my head. She rounds the table and looks directly at me. I lock on again, focusing on her mind.

Synapses snap—hers and mine. Something is wrong. Something's strange.

*You trust me*, she thinks. *You love me. You'll do anything I ask.*

My entire body tenses, every nerve fires at once, and I struggle not to show my emotions. I struggle not to hurt her as I realize why I've found it so easy to trust Mrs. Kalin, why I only trust her when I look into her eyes.

Mrs. Kalin is a Deviant.

And like me, she activates her Deviance with her eyes.

But she doesn't hear thoughts—at least, I hope she doesn't. No. Mrs. Kalin's Deviance is more chilling. Mrs. Kalin plants thoughts.

No wonder Cal was so easily placated after Scout's accident. No wonder she convinced us that the experiments in the Hospital are humane. No wonder she got me to trust her.

I draw long breaths to calm myself, to focus, to keep control. I sense her in my mind, and her influence casts a strange veil that doesn't replace reality, just alters it. I fight to hold on to that awareness and how it feels when she's there.

As long as I'm conscious of what she's doing, I should be able to isolate my real thoughts. But still foggy from the drug, I'm not sure I can.

My body tenses. "I trust you." I repeat the thoughts she's planting. "You love me and want nothing but the best for me."

"That's right." She undoes the strap on one of my wrists.

"Mr. Belando was a threat," I say. As long as I can mislead her, I know I'm still in control. "Mr. Belando wasn't like you. He didn't understand that changes need to be made inside Haven. He refused to understand."

A smile spreads on Mrs. Kalin's lips like she just ate the most delicious dish in the world. She releases my other wrist, then bends down to kiss my forehead lightly. "I knew I was right to make you my protégé."

"Protégé?" Our eye connection is broken. I want to listen to her thoughts again, but increasing our connection is a two-way street. I have to limit eye contact or she might gain the upper hand.

She bends to release my ankles and then the straps across my chest and hips. I step off the table and rub my legs.

"Glory," she says, "it's time for me to be completely honest with you, and for you to be completely honest with me." She takes my hand. "I know what you are. You're Chosen, like me."

"Chosen?" Her use of the word that the settlers use for Deviants fills me with hope. If she's like me, a fellow Deviant, should I trust her? Does she know there's a better life Outside? Does she know about the Settlement, the FA?

"Yes. Chosen," she says. "You and I, our minds have evolved, adapted. That makes us better than most people, capable of doing things Normals can't."

"Deviants."

"No." She wrinkles her nose in disgust. "Not like Deviants. Deviants' bodies have changed in crude ways. With them, the transformation is physical, not intellectual. Deviants are aberrations of nature and humanity—mistakes of nature." She squeezes my arm. "But they aren't without their use. In fact, Deviants are playing an important role in helping me discover the key to harnessing the power of the dust." She looks directly into my eyes. "Remember, because this is important. Deviants are not like us. They're inferior."

"Deviants are inferior." The words come out of my mouth without my thinking, and I blink, suddenly dizzy, sick to my stomach. I've let her into my mind. But as long as I can recognize when she's planting thoughts, I might be able to fight her. "Chosen people use their minds, not their bodies."

"Exactly." Her grin reappears. "And with you by my side, we can save humanity. We can find a way to live Outside in the dust."

I make eye contact again but she turns away, and I suspect she knows she can't influence my thoughts quite as easily as she can other people's. I must keep straight which thoughts are mine and which are hers.

"If you're going to be my protégé, my daughter,"—she tucks my hair behind my ear—"I need to be sure I can trust you."

"You can." I focus on her eyebrows, conflicted between wanting to use my Deviance to hear her thoughts and risking her influencing mine.

She shakes her head, cocking up one side of her mouth. "I know my abilities don't work well on you."

My breath catches, but I try to cover. "What do you mean?"

"Glory," she shakes her head. "You are a very talented girl, but I need to be certain you're on my side. I need to be sure you won't betray me. To that end, I need to see a first-hand demonstration of what you can do."

"What I can do?" I still haven't admitted to my Deviance. I need to tread carefully.

She tips her head to the side. "I saw Mr. Belando's surveillance footage of you killing rats with your eyes."

My body tenses.

"You don't think it was a coincidence you were placed in Comp training, do you?"

Panic rises like bubbles in my chest. "No, but . . ." Mr. Belando's explanation never completely made sense to me.

"I told Mr. Belando to keep an eye out for people like you." She rolls her eyes. "Belando was an easily manipulated asset. He forwarded directly to me all observations of employees who might be using their minds in extraordinary ways, and he cancelled all Compliance audits of employees showing signs of being Chosen." She puts her hand on my shoulder. "The other candidates he found proved disappointing, but I've had my eyes on you for some time."

"Why not just approach me? Why the ruse? Why COT training?" I'm asking too many questions. Her lips have pursed.

"It was a test of loyalty, of your abilities, your control." Her voice is clipped and she looks directly into my eyes. "I do what's best for you, whether or not you fully understand."

I try to smile but it wavers, my cheeks vibrating from the effort. I feel her inside my mind, trying to make me trust her; and in spite of my efforts to hold her out, I do trust her. At least, I believe what she's telling me right now. I believe that she thinks she knows what's best for me. She has been looking out for me. The three years Drake and I lived without being discovered make so much more sense to me now.

"I want to trust you, Glory," she says, "but first you need to do something for me."

"What?"

"Just a simple demonstration of your Chosen abilities."

I nod. "Do you have a rat?"

"Sweetie." She shakes her head. "Killing a rat will not

be sufficient proof. To earn my trust, and for me to be sure you're the right one to serve at my side, I must see your talents work on more than rats. I need to see you kill a human."

My stomach twists. "I—a living person?"

"Yes, and I have the perfect test subject in mind."

"Who?" I try to keep the quaver out of my voice.

"Your friend Scout."

My head snaps back. "No." I back away. "How could you possibly ask me to do that? I've known Scout my whole life. He's my best friend's dating partner. Cal's brother. I can't. I won't." But I've given her more information than I wanted to. Ammunition to hurt me.

I look down. It was ammunition she already had.

She snaps her fingers to draw my attention. "Look at me," she says. "It's for the best. The life of one boy is trivial. Besides, he's barely alive and a worthy sacrifice in the fight for humanity. You'll be ending his pain."

Once again, I feel my mind shifting, my focus waning. If Scout is suffering, perhaps he will be glad to die. Mrs. Kalin is searching for ways to help Normals live in the dust. Every death in the Hospital is for the greater good.

No. Those are her thoughts.

Dizziness threatens, but I hold on. I cannot let her plant thoughts in my mind, but neither can I let her be certain that she can't. If I refuse to make eye contact, she'll know I'm on to her. I need her to believe that I'm under her control. Problem is, I'm no longer sure that I'm not.

I nod. "I understand. I'll do it. Where is he?"

# CHAPTER THIRTY-FIVE

MRS. KALIN LEADS ME DOWN A SERIES OF EMPTY CORRIDORS, and I scramble to come up with a plan—a way to save Scout and escape with our lives—but the aftereffects of the drug, and my fight to keep Mrs. Kalin's influence out of my mind, have left me foggy.

I can't remember the last time I ate, what time of day it is, or how long I was unconscious. "Did we miss the President's Birthday?"

She rubs my arm. "No, sweetie. It's tonight. And don't you worry. Impress me now and I'll take you to the executives' private reception."

At least I know what day it is now, but I don't know whether or not the rebels still plan their attack. Maybe Larsson got to them in time, or maybe Burn had Rolph intervene. Either way, there's nothing I can do about it from here.

Right now I need to save Scout—or at least avoid killing him myself.

Mrs. Kalin stops in front of a door, turns, and looks me directly in the eyes. "You are about to see some very important, top secret experiments essential to our cause. We cannot save humanity without sacrifices."

"No gain without sacrifice," I say, then swallow hard and blink. I didn't mean to say that, but at least I realized it afterward.

She pauses and tips her head to the side, studying me. My heart thunders in my chest, but I keep my expression neutral and keep my focus just below her eyes.

Apparently satisfied, she turns, types a code into the keypad, and the door swings open. I chide myself for not watching and memorizing her access code. I need to keep alert, on my toes. But it's so hard right now. Denying her complete control of my mind is taking so much concentration.

I choke back a gasp.

The room is lined with tall metal cages barely wide enough for people to sit. As we enter, the cages rattle, screams ring out, and the stench of blood and human waste is unbearable.

Some of the cage inhabitants are loose; others have their limbs restrained, tied to the bars with heavy metal chains and shackles. Some of the captives seem more Shredder than human.

My desperation rises as I search each cage to find Scout, hoping that he's not in this horrible room. I hope my *agreeing* to kill Scout was enough and Mrs. Kalin no longer expects me to do it. Maybe she's showing me this room for another reason.

The Shredder in the cage next to us chews on his cage, and the heavy wires are doing more damage to his mouth than he's doing to them.

Gagging, I look away.

"When did you last clean this room?" Mrs. Kalin says, and I turn to see that we aren't alone. There's a man, also in a white coat, except his is splattered with blood.

"Right away." The man races to pick up a hose. He pulls a lever and a strong stream of water flies out of the hose, slamming into a man and tossing him back against the bars of his cage. Filthy water runs into a trough along the back wall and into a drain.

Mrs. Kalin pulls my face around with her hand and looks me directly in the eyes. "We are not barbarians. We make our volunteer test subjects as comfortable as possible. See? They even get baths."

"You're very kind." I fight a shudder and try to sound sincere. Then I scan the cages again. *Please don't let Scout be in this room.*

One of the cages holds a scrawny man with wispy, gray hair. Dirty, bloodstained clothes hang from his skeletal frame, and jagged scars and fresh wounds mar his thin, papery skin. Clearly lacking the strength to stand, he is being held upright against the back of his cage by a rope strung under his arms. His head is slumped forward.

"Is he alive?"

"I'm not certain." Mrs. Kalin answers, and I realize I spoke my thought aloud. She gestures for the man with the hose to come over, and he directs the punishing spray at the old man's body.

His face rises in pain and shock, and our eyes meet.

His anguish rips into me and I look down, unable to maintain eye contact, ashamed that I'm not doing anything to stop this.

"Oh, this is most unfortunate," Mrs. Kalin says, and I see that she's walked to the other side of the room to the front of a cage containing a body that's crumpled on the ground—a body that didn't move when sprayed with the hose.

She beckons, and fighting nausea, I cross the room to join her. My legs shake with each step.

She unlatches the cage and the body falls out, landing on its back, face up.

Bile rises in my throat, then tears, then anger. It's Scout.

I dive down and gather his body into my arms, but he's cold and stiff, his body covered in bruises and cuts and burns. "No," I shout. "No. This is wrong. So wrong. No experiment is worth this. You're torturing people, killing them."

Anger racing through me, I look up to Mrs. Kalin. "You're a monster."

She looks into my eyes. "Of course I'm not. You know better," she says. "I'm the closest thing you have to a mother. I love you. I care about you. I understand you. I'm all you have."

She's right. I love her.

I break eye contact and bend over, panting, trying to regain my own thoughts.

I need to fight back. I need to resist the comfort she offers, my instinct to please her, my desire to be loved. She is *not* all I have, but I have to give her credit for evoking my mother. It nearly worked. She's been playing me since we first met.

She rubs my back and I rise, letting her pull me into her comforting arms, but I will not cave. I need to repress my grief over Scout. I can't afford to feel such strong emotions right now. I need to maintain my control.

"I know you'll miss your friend," she says. "But look at the bright side. Now you don't have to kill him."

I hold onto her tightly. I can't let her see into my eyes or she'll know the truth. She'll know how much I hate her.

"Leave us," she says to the man. He turns off his punishing hose and exits.

Emotions cloaked, I release Mrs. Kalin and back away, keeping my gaze from hers.

"It's for the best," I say. "Scout gave his life for science. It's a noble death. For the greater good of all Haven."

"That's right." Mrs. Kalin beams. "I knew I was right about you."

"What else can you show me?" I ask her. "I want to learn everything."

"Not so fast." She wags a finger. "You still need to complete your test."

I back up a few steps and look around the room to cover my reaction. After all that—after finding Scout dead—she still expects me to kill someone?

336

Her eyes narrow. "I thought you understood what's at stake." She walks around me in a slow circle. "But if you'd rather I hand you back to the Comps to be expunged . . ."

My chest constricts. I can't justify killing an innocent person, even if it's to save my own life. But I don't want to die.

"I'm not heartless," Mrs. Kalin says. "I'll make it easy for you. You may choose anyone you want for your demonstration. Look around"—she spins, hands out toward the cages—"pick anyone. Let me see what you can do."

The old man groans. I turn toward him. He looks at me, his eyes pleading, and it's easy to imagine that he's asking me to kill him, giving me permission, but I have to be sure. If I can hear thoughts, I can find out what he wants.

I step closer to his cage and notice there's blood seeping through his t-shirt from what must be a huge wound in his abdomen. His eyes are glassy, and while I'm no expert, he seems close to death.

"Show me. Come on." Mrs. Kalin steps up beside me and I can feel the eagerness wafting off her. "Prove that you're Chosen and I'll keep you at my side. I'll protect you, treat you like my daughter."

At the word "daughter," my anger and my determination to live spark to life. I already am someone's daughter. Even if they are a long way away, my father and brother are waiting for me on the Outside. I can't give up hope of seeing them again.

Given Mrs. Kalin's capabilities, few people will ever be able to challenge her. She can talk anyone into trusting her, following her. Glory was also convinced that Scout was safe in the Hospital for awhile. I can't let her control every mind in Haven. If I'm dead, she wins.

I need to make her believe that I'm with her—until I find a way to stop her.

If she wants to see the full extent of my talent, I'll show her, even if it goes against my vow not to use my Deviance to kill. There's no other choice.

I look into the man's eyes and lock on in an instant.

*Let me die*, he thinks. *Please. Now. I can't stand the pain.*

I latch onto his heart and feel its weak beat accelerate as I grab hold. I feel his blood flowing. One tight squeeze and he'll be dead.

I turn away. I can't do it. I can't take another life. Especially not someone so helpless. I want to help this man, to ease his pain, but this isn't the way. The only life I'll save by taking his is my own. It's not a justifiable reason to kill. No. If I'm going to do something so horrible, I need to kill Mrs. Kalin.

A crash distracts me. I turn.

A Shredder has broken out of his cage and is charging toward us. Mrs. Kalin lunges for a red button on the wall, but the Shredder grabs her and digs its teeth into her shoulder.

"Hey," I yell. The Shredder looks up. Blood drips from its teeth.

Mrs. Kalin looks into my eyes. "Help me."

The pain in her eyes, her pleading, tightens my chest. I can't let the Shredder hurt her.

I shift my eye contact to the Shredder's and grab hold.

Focusing on its brain, I hold tight and twist. The Shredder screams and the sound is horrible, like metal on metal, but it releases Mrs. Kalin and she drops to the floor.

Holding the connection, I transfer my concentration to the Shredder's heart and sense the thickened blood flowing, the slow beat of its heart. If Mrs. Kalin wants a demonstration, I'll give her one. This monster hurt Mrs. Kalin. Hurt my new mother. I aim for the vessels leading in and out of its heart and drive blood in, while squeezing off the exits. Pinching hard, I force more blood toward its heart and the Shredder's eyes bulge. I can sense its heart expanding, filling with the thick sludge Shredders have for blood.

It screams again, clutches its chest, and tears at its flesh, baring ribs. I squeeze—hard.

The Shredder's heart explodes.

Blood dark as tar bursts from its chest. The Shredder crashes to the floor, and Mrs. Kalin screams as the body lands across her.

I push the dead monster away from her. Mrs. Kalin's covered in Shredder blood, her face filled with terror. From her knees, she reaches up and pulls me into a tight embrace. "You saved my life."

Workers rush in. Noise bombards my ears. Someone pulls Mrs. Kalin off me and hands her a mask she places over her face. It's dust, I realize. She's breathing dust to heal her shoulder wound. Thank goodness she'll be okay.

A man in a white coat pulls me up. His lips move. I hear sound, but no words. All I can hear is blood rushing in my ears. I'm dizzy, but I can't pass out. I won't let it happen. I drop to sit on the floor and fight to comprehend what just happened—what I've done. I've killed a Shredder to save Mrs. Kalin.

A moment ago I wanted to kill her, and yet all I can do is wonder whether or not I've passed her test.

# CHAPTER THIRTY-SIX

Mrs. Kalin nods with approval as I step into the main room of her apartment, bathed and wearing the dress she bought me last week. At the time, I thought she was just being kind, but now I suspect she was planning for today.

She's wearing a shiny gray dress and is cleaned up too, which can only mean that her apartment has more than one room with cleaning facilities. In the Pents, rooms with running water are shared by hundreds of tenants, and Mrs. Kalin appears to live alone with her marriage partner in his huge, multi-room apartment.

"Where is Mr. Kalin," I ask.

"There is no Mr. Kalin." She adjusts a tall pointed glass object that's sitting on a wooden table. Is it just for decoration?

"But I thought that the title Mrs. was reserved for women in marriage contracts," I say.

"The title Mrs. commands more authority, so I choose to use it." She gestures toward a sofa. Rich, deep orange fabric covers plush cushions that are as thick as a metal girder. The comparison to a girder ends there. I sit and sink into the softness, the cushions absorbing me, enveloping, caressing, and soothing every ache.

But I can't afford to relax.

Mrs. Kalin has barely let me out of her sight since we left the Hospital, but neither has she made eye contact. I almost want to grin at the turmoil this must cause for her as she weighs further attempts to influence my thoughts against the possibility I might explode her heart like I did the Shredder's.

I should do it. If there was ever a case for the ends justifying the means this is it. Mrs. Kalin is dangerous.

All I need is the right place and time. If I do it here, the Comp guard outside will know I killed her. More importantly, before I kill Mrs. Kalin, I need her to do something for me. Scout might be dead, but I need to do everything I can to ensure my other friends are safe—if they're still alive.

"Tonight," she says, "after the President's Birthday, you will move into my spare bedroom. Would you like a drink of lemonade?"

"Move in?" *She has a spare bedroom?*

"Of course." She opens a shiny box and pours a pale translucent liquid into two matching glasses. "You aren't an orphan anymore. I've already filed the HR paperwork for your adoption. I'm your mother now." She smiles, making eye contact. "As your parent and mentor, I'll make sure you live up to your full potential, and I won't ever let anyone hurt you, ever again."

My mind buzzes and I can't find words to reply. In fact, the thought of having a mother again warms me. How could I have thought she was dangerous? I blink. Remembering. She's not my mother. Those weren't my thoughts. "I—I need your help."

"With what, sweetie?" She closes the shiny box.

"With Cal. He was arrested. And two of my friends are missing. I need to know that they're safe."

She hands me one of the glasses and sits down on a chair near the sofa that doesn't look nearly as comfortable as the seat I'm in, yet more luxurious than any chair I've seen before today. Even its arms are covered in fabric.

Holding her glass in both hands, she leans forward and rests her elbows on her tightly-drawn-together knees. Her dress shines like metal. "You saved my life, Glory. I'll help in any way that I can. What makes you think your friends aren't safe?"

My mouth goes dry. I take a sip of the liquid and my eyes open wide. "What is this?"

"Your first lemonade." She winks. "It's just a lemon squeezed into water with some sugar."

I've heard of lemon, but never tasted one. "What's sugar?"

She tsks and leans back in her chair. "I can't wait to introduce you to some of the rarer things Haven has to offer."

The lemonade is tart and sweet at the same time and I take another sip, marveling at how something can both shock and refresh. It's delicious. I smile at her, then look down. I need to be more careful. I still feel a semblance of myself, even though I'm not positive which thoughts are my own. I need to keep my priorities straight.

"Tell me what's wrong." Her voice is comforting, and if she can help, I don't care if she's influencing me.

"One of my friends—her name's Jayma—she's suspected of sabotage. She's innocent. The other is a Deviant boy I . . . I stumbled upon. I was hiding them, hoping I could help them. They disappeared."

"I had no idea those children were your friends." Her hand traces over the arm of her chair. Then she looks up into my eyes. "I'm sorry. It's too late. They're gone."

"Gone?" My throat tightens. I try to latch on to her gaze to see if I can focus on her thoughts, but she turns away.

"Gone where?" I ask. "Please. I need to help them. If you can do anything, Mrs. Kalin—"

"Call me Mother." She looks into my eyes again. "I wish I could help but it's too late."

"Too late." My heart squeezes and tears fill my eyes. She walks over, sets my lemonade on a table, and draws me into her arms. Once in her embrace, I want to let everything go, to take the comfort she offers.

Dizzy, I blink a few times to force back the tears and regain my focus. I can't let her take over my head. "And Cal? When can I see Cal?"

She holds me by the shoulders and looks into my eyes.

"No need to see him again. We'll find you a more suitable mate."

"But—"

She holds up her slim-fingered hand. "Even if you think you love him, you're young. It's not real. You'll get over it. Besides, love isn't what matters in a good match. What matters is combining your DNA with another's to create children, future employees for Haven. And someone who's Chosen cannot be wasted on such an ordinary mate."

Her words are comforting. My shoulders relax and my breathing slows. "Yes, I'll find another mate. One more suitable," I say. I'm still myself enough to know she's not right, though.

"Good." She returns to her seat and takes a long sip of her lemonade.

Head swimming, I take another sip of mine. I'm walking a thin line. I need to let her look into my eyes often enough and long enough that she'll think she's influencing my thoughts, but not long enough to actually let her, or to chance that it will last.

I'm not sure whether I'm winning the battle. I'm weak. I'm sad. I'm defeated. And I'm ashamed at how much better it feels to let myself accept Mrs. Kalin's comforting influence. My own thoughts right now are too horrible to bear.

I look into her eyes and keep my voice steady. "Even if Cal won't be my mate, I'd like to see him. I'd like to say good-bye."

She shakes her head. "I'm sorry, that's not possible. There's no time. We need to leave soon or we'll be late for the birthday celebrations. It's important you attend today's ceremony."

Remembering the possible terrorist attack, I shiver. "Why?"

"Because you deserve something special, of course. You deserve to have some fun." She smiles, but I look away, avoiding her eyes.

I've failed Tobin and Jayma. I've failed Scout. I need to focus on saving Cal. "I know you think I'm special and all that—"

"Chosen. You were Chosen."

"Does that mean I can't even talk to people who aren't Chosen?"

Her fingers drum on her glass and a cloud of impatience crosses her face. She makes eye contact, then looks away, clearly apprehensive. "Of course you may talk to people who aren't Chosen—you and I are quite rare—but you can't talk to Cal. It's simply not possible."

"Why not?"

She leans back in her chair and drapes one arm over its back. "Because tonight, during the celebrations, he'll be expunged."

I leap out of the sofa down onto my knees in front of her. "No, please. You need to stop it."

She runs her hand over my hair. "I'd help, sweetie, but it's not up to me. He was found guilty of fraud during a Compliance investigation. My hands are tied."

"But you got me released."

"That's different. You're Chosen. You're my daughter."

"But if you convinced the President that I wasn't guilty, how can Cal be guilty of trying to get me cleared of a crime that I didn't even commit?"

She shakes her head. "It's not that simple."

I grab her hands. "I saved your life. Can't you do this one thing for me?"

She looks me in the eye. Her expression's cold. "I saved your life too," she snaps. "If not for me, you'd be heading for an expunging yourself—and don't you forget it."

# CHAPTER THIRTY-SEVEN

My knees shake as I step into the viewing gallery high above the Hub and directly opposite the largest viewing screens, which look five times larger from here. The room is painted a deep red and the furnishings gleam in chrome and polished black leather. My gaze dances over more beautiful objects and opulence than I ever imagined existed—never mind all in one place. But I can't be distracted.

The room opens up onto the Presidential Balcony, jutting out over the Hub's edge.

I wonder if Mrs. Kalin wanting me here is another cruel test. I almost hope that it is. Perhaps if I stay calm and do as she asks, she'll change her mind and pardon Cal. I must keep my wits about me, my thoughts my own, but my defenses are wearing down. I'm so tired and my head aches from the effort of barring her from my mind.

"Glory," Mrs. Kalin looks me directly in the eyes. "You should be honored to be here. I know that today was difficult—you faced some bad news—but I'm proud of how you've handled it all."

"Thank you."

"How is your shoulder?" I ask her.

"Much better, dear. Thank you for asking." She leans in close. "The dust helped. It's nearly healed."

I nod, dismayed that I'm happy she's feeling better, proud that she trusts me enough to share this classified information.

The room is filling with every member of Senior Management, and with Mrs. Kalin's hand on my back, my last defenses collapse and I give in, feeling like the luckiest, most important girl in Haven. Comps in full uniform are stationed in each corner of the room, with two more on the balcony, Shockers at the ready.

I'm special. I'm safe. I'm Chosen.

"I'm proud of you," she says, her kind eyes flashing, "and I need you tonight. Tonight and every day going forward."

"You need me." Every fiber inside me yearns for her approval. I can't wait to hear her tell me she's proud again. I'll do anything to earn it.

"You displayed great skill and bravery today," she says, "I know it was difficult."

"Very difficult."

"But we must act now. For the good of all the people in Haven."

"What do you need me to do?"

Mrs. Kalin pulls me to the side of the balcony where we can't be overheard. Lights flash on the screens all around the Hub, not helping my focus.

"In a moment," she says, "the President will go to the microphone to make his Birthday salutation."

I nod. "Tell me what you need."

A soft smile spreads on her face and warms me inside. "I need you to give him a gift."

"A gift? I didn't bring a gift." Panic grabs me. I'll disappoint her.

She cups my cheek. "Don't worry, sweetie. You'll be presenting a gift on behalf of all the Employees of Haven."

"Such an honor." Music swells and I turn my head to find its source, but she draws my attention back with soft fingers on my chin.

"It is even more of an honor than you realize, because you'll deliver something else along with the gift."

Excitement builds inside me; it's all I can do not to bounce.

"Seeing your power in the Hospital today, I know that it's finally time. With you at my side, I'm ready. It's time for the President to go."

"Go?"

"Yes. It's time for me to take charge." She leans closer. "Tonight, I'll be promoted to President."

"Really?" I grab her hands. I feel like the flashing lights and grand music are for our personal celebration.

"Yes. Haven will be so much safer under my direction, even if a small percentage of the population resists."

"Resists." The word clicks something inside me and I remember what she can do, that she can affect minds. I feel numb. I turn and see an image of Cal on the screen across the Hub. He's being held by Comps at what I recognize as the exit they use for expungings.

I blink. No matter what Mrs. Kalin's doing to me right now, even if she's in my mind, I need to please her to save Cal.

Mrs. Kalin turns my face back to hers. I want to please her; she's my mother now. It isn't just her influence affecting my decision. Or is it? I'm confused.

"If you do this for me, I'll save your Cal."

Air and hope fill my lungs. "I'll do anything."

She puts her hands on my shoulders and stares directly into my eyes. "The future of Haven is in our hands. Yours and mine. Some lesser-minded individuals will resist—it's inevitable—but we'll eliminate the most simple-minded, like the former VP of Compliance."

"Mr. Belando."

"No." She purses her lips. "I saw no signs of resistance in Belando. I'm referring to his predecessor, Mr. Singh."

My mind buzzes. I once wondered if Mr. Belando had killed his former boss, but it was Mrs. Kalin. She's so powerful, so strong. And she's my new mother. I'm so lucky.

"He had to go," she says.

"He had to go," I repeat. "For the greater good."

A huge smile spreads on her face. "Yes. I knew you'd understand. And while I convinced the President to release you from prison, he's showing signs of resistant thinking. I can't let him hurt us, hurt you, hurt the future of Haven."

"You'll keep me safe. You'll keep us all safe."

"Always." She smiles and squeezes my shoulders. "Once the President is terminated, you and I will reform Haven together. Once I have access to all the Communication Department's screens and control over the System, I'll explain our way of thinking to every Haven employee. Those who resist . . ." She leans in. "You will eliminate those threats."

"Eliminate the threats." My mind slides in and out of her control. It sounds so reasonable as she says it. Why wouldn't I eliminate threats? But then I blink a few times, and what she's saying sinks in. She wants me to kill everyone whose mind she can't control. She wants me to use my Deviance to kill, starting with the President. Tonight.

"It's time for us to rule Haven," she says. "Together we can raise the standard of living. We can make Haven the wonderful place we know it can be—a place where employees are rewarded for their talents, where promotions aren't based on connections or your parents' job placements."

That does sound better than the status quo. She listened to my ideas. "Tell me how I can help." I blink and a mist passes through my mind, clouding my thoughts.

Mrs. Kalin is my mother now. She's the smartest, most wonderful person I've ever met. "Tell me." I lean forward. "Please tell me how I can help."

She cups my cheek. "When you hand the President your gift, you will demonstrate your unique talent. You'll show me you're truly Chosen. You'll make his death look like natural causes—a heart attack. No one can suspect my hand or yours in his death."

"No one will suspect."

"You understand what I need you to do, Glory?"

"I do." If she's asking me to do it, it can't be wrong, and I want more than anything to please her. I was motherless for three years. I won't disappoint my new one.

She leans her lips close to my ear. "Glory, it's time to live up to your name. It's time to make a glorious act. It's time to terminate the President."

Guiding me, Mrs. Kalin steps up to one of the other men in the room. A boy of about ten stands at his side, holding a small box. "Mr. Alast," Mrs. Kalin says. "This is my daughter, Glory. Glory, this is the Senior VP of Human Resources."

The man extends a hand and I shake it. "Very nice to meet you, sir."

"Mr. Alast," Mrs. Kalin grabs his attention. "Glory is going to present the President with the gift on behalf of the employees of Haven."

The boy turns to Mr. Alast. "But I was picked."

Mrs. Kalin leans down in front of the boy and puts a finger under his chin to guide his gaze up to hers. A pinch of jealousy grabs me.

"You'll get a chance another year," she tells him. "This is the girl with the honor today."

The boy smiles. "Yes, this is the girl who will have the honor." He hands me the box. My jealousy fades. I've never felt so happy or special, so loved and appreciated, not even when I was little. My original mother's face flashes through my memory.

Something inside my mind snaps and shifts, and I stagger back, losing my balance.

"Are you okay?" Mrs. Kalin asks.

"Yes, I'm fine." I struggle to sort my thoughts. I just agreed to kill the President.

I'm losing my mind. Listening to Mrs. Kalin makes me feel so secure, so happy, so strong, so safe, but she is *not* my mother. My mother is dead. Dead because of my inability to control my Deviance. And now Mrs. Kalin wants me to use it to kill.

If my mother had survived my attack, she would have forgiven me more easily than I've been able to forgive myself. My mother loved me—unconditionally—even when I was acting like a brat. Plus, I have a father who loves me in spite of what I did.

I cannot allow Mrs. Kalin inside my head again. I cannot allow her anywhere near the most precious places in my mind, the ones containing the emotions reserved for my family.

Mrs. Kalin is *not* my family and she's using my most cherished memories, my most sacred emotions, against me. I hate her.

A cheer rises up from the Hub below us and I look over to see that the President has stepped to the edge of the Balcony.

"It's time," Mrs. Kalin says and gently pushes on my back.

"It's time," I repeat. She must believe I'm still under her control.

"You know what you need to do," she says.

"I know what I need to do."

"Good girl." Mrs. Kalin squeezes my waist as we walk. "I'm so proud of you."

I keep my eyes forward as I step next to the President at the edge of the balcony. The crowd cheers again. My image, many times larger than I really am, is projected onto every screen around the Hub.

"And offering the President a gift, on behalf of his loyal employees, is Jonathan—" the announcer's voice breaks off. "There must have been a last minute change, but I'm sure whoever this young woman is, she is thrilled to be representing her fellow employees."

The crowd cheers again and I can almost feel the sound as it rises to fill the air above the Hub and onto the balcony.

Mrs. Kalin steps up to the announcer's microphone and, given the President's expression, I assume her speaking wasn't part of the program.

"Fellow employees," Mrs. Kalin says, and the camera pans to her face. Everyone in the Hub is looking into Mrs. Kalin's eyes on one of the screens. "This is a special day and I've chosen a very special girl to represent all of us: my daughter, Glory." She gestures for me to step to her side, and when I do, the crowd roars again.

Basking in the adoration and excitement, I glance at an image of Mrs. Kalin on one of the screens. She beams at me with pride and love in her eyes and my mind almost shifts, but I keep hold of myself. I will not let this feeling, no matter how marvelous, take over.

The people at the Settlement use the word Chosen to mean Deviant, but it takes on such a different meaning the way she uses it. She thinks she's better than everyone else and wants to rule Haven—completely—using mind control. From what I've seen, she'll be able to do it, especially if she has me kill anyone who resists. Every time I look into her eyes, I find it harder to resist.

If she succeeds, no one in Haven will be safe. Or will we all be safer? I can't decide. But even if she can make us all safer, at what cost? Is safety worth losing our ability to think for ourselves? Our free will?

"It's time," she whispers, and I turn toward the President.

Looking at him, memories of how he gloated onscreen the day my father was exed flash into my mind, and they draw emotions to the surface that are powerful enough to kill. But as despicable as he is, killing the President won't solve my problems—or Haven's. It will only create more.

The President is the lesser of two evils.

I turn to the microphone and rise up on my toes. "On behalf of the employees of Haven, please accept this gift." I hold the box toward him and he smiles as our eyes meet. My Deviance sparks, but I keep my gaze focused on his far-too-smooth-for-his-age forehead.

"Thank you, young lady." The President takes the box and the crowd bursts into song, wishing him a happy birthday.

A loud bang draws my attention—an explosion at the

edge of the Hub. Smoke billows from three different roads leading in.

Crowds emerge from each of the smoke clouds, and from their dress and their weapons it appears that at least some have come from Outside. I spot what looks like the FA insignia on a flag.

Mrs. Kalin takes my arm. "Now. Kill him. While everyone is distracted."

The President is speaking into the microphone, trying to calm the crowd, but it's hard to hear him over the shouts below. Someone in the crowd has a megaphone and is calling for everyone to rise up, telling them that they don't need to live under Management's oppression anymore.

"Join us!" the man says. "Rise up!" He's too far away for me to recognize him. "Haven does not equal safety. Not with Management in control."

The man with the megaphone is shot by a Comp's Shocker and falls to the ground in convulsions. Someone picks up his megaphone and continues the messages. That man is shot too. The Comps converge on the newcomers.

The camera focuses on our balcony, displayed on all the Hub screens, and zooms back to show the building below.

I gasp. Burn is climbing up the scaffolding beneath us, toward the Presidential balcony. He'll never make it. He's going to be shot. If he hasn't been spotted already, he will be soon.

Mrs. Kalin's beside me, watching the mélée. Her hand lands on my shoulder and squeezes, fingers digging in.

"Now," she says, through gritted teeth. "Now! I need to get this crowd under control. See how ineffective the President is? If we don't act quickly, we'll lose Haven to the Shredders."

I turn toward her, not even trying to hide my fear, my doubt.

"You can do this," she says, her eyes connecting with mine. "Don't be afraid. I believe in you. I am so proud."

Calmness floods through me, then determination. She's right. The President has lost the employees' confidence. He's not fit to lead. He's got to go. Only Mrs. Kalin, my new mother, will be able to restore safety to Haven.

"I'm proud too," I tell her. "Proud that I was Chosen. Proud that you're my mother." I hug her and then head for the President.

Burn appears at the railing at the far side of the balcony. Given all the confusion, no one but me seems to have noticed him, and the moment I see his face, my thoughts clarify.

I remember who I am, which thoughts are my own.

When I came back to Haven I vowed not to use my Deviance to kill. I vowed to stop using my powers because of what I did to my mother, but Burn was right. Sometimes the ends do justify the means. Denying what I can do is the same thing as denying who I am. I'm Glory. My emotions can kill.

And this is my chance. I need to kill one last time. I need to kill Mrs. Kalin.

I turn toward her and, with my Deviance sparking, I look into her eyes.

"The President," she says, her voice low and hard. "Kill him. It's the best thing for us and the best thing for Haven."

"The best thing for Haven," I repeat back, hoping she'll be tricked into thinking her mind control's working, but I maintain my concentration, my focus, and I latch onto her eyes. My entire body shakes from the effort of maintaining control. I need to hold on. Her heart's racing and I hear and feel the rush of her blood as the organ pumps. I sense her heart as if it's my own. Then I squeeze.

Her expression shifts. She knows what I'm doing. She knows that her mind control's no longer working on me. She knows that I'm winning.

*You don't want to kill me*, her thoughts invade mine. *You love me. You don't want to kill your own mother. Not again.*

Not again. Those words are like a stab to my guts. My thoughts flip back and forth, flashing like a strobe. I can't kill my mother a second time. I don't want to kill Mrs. Kalin. I love her.

No. She's invading my thoughts. I hate her. She's dangerous.

Pressure builds inside my head and I raise my hands to quell the searing pain. I have to hold on. I can't let her win. She's too strong.

I break eye contact; I'm panting; my head's screaming with pain.

"Guards," Mrs. Kalin yells. "I've been betrayed. This girl isn't my daughter. She's an impostor. A Deviant terrorist here to assassinate the President."

The Comps on the balcony turn toward me, Shocker guns pointing. If I'm hit with multiple tags at once on full power I'll die.

Mrs. Kalin grabs the microphone, looks directly into the camera, and says, "This girl is dangerous. We can't wait for an expunging. We must terminate her now or she'll kill us all." She turns toward the President. "Immediately."

"Kill her. Kill her," the crowd shouts from below. The President frowns.

Burn pulls over the side of the balcony. I shake my head at him, trying to get him to go away. There's no need for him to get caught up in this mess.

I turn to the screens where my image is projected. There's a huge red dot on my head where the laser sights from at least six Comp guns are merged into one. This is it. I'm going to die. I might be able to disable one of the Comps using my Gift, but that would leave five. Even if the President doesn't order my immediate execution, Mrs. Kalin can easily use her power to get one of the Comps to act under her orders.

"Mr. President," Mrs. Kalin captures his attention and, from the look on his face, his mind too. "This Deviant must die," she says. "Now."

The President grabs my arm. "I'll kill her myself." He pulls me toward the edge of the balcony.

"No." Burn charges forward, rage on his face. Almost instantly, he transforms, growing to more than seven feet tall, his muscles nearly bursting his coat's seams.

The President releases me and drops down in a crouch, covering his head.

The closest Comp points his Shocker at Burn but before he can fire, Burn picks up the Comp and tosses him over the balcony. Stunned, I watch as the man falls to his death.

Another Comp shoots his Shocker and the tag strikes Burn's arm. Electricity courses through him and Burn roars, growing even angrier. He pulls the tag off his coat, tearing a hole.

In a full rage, Burn is enormous, ghastly, out of control. Like this, he is like a Shredder—not so much in appearance as in his drive to kill.

He swings his arms, knocking people down like they're flies. The Comps back away and the VPs run off the balcony into the building. Only two Comps remain.

The President's still crouched in a ball near the railing. Burn lunges for him and lifts his body, as easily as a child lifting a ball.

"No," I yell as Burn tosses the President over the balcony's side.

Below, a roar rises from the crowd and it's not clear whether they're happy or horrified. Probably both, and I realize Mrs. Kalin got what she wanted. The President's dead. Where is she?

Burn roars at the few remaining people, who are hiding behind the Birthday decorations, and I spot Mrs. Kalin. She's pressed against the wall, waiting, watching. Burn heads toward the remaining people. If I don't stop him, he'll kill everyone.

"Burn, stop." I grab his arm, and he turns and looks into my eyes.

"Please," I shout. "This isn't you."

His chest rises and falls. His eyes are red, full of rage. Terror builds inside me. He's hurt me before. I have no idea how much control he has over his actions when he's transformed. Does he even recognize me? Will I be the next one thrown over the balcony? Or crushed beneath his fists?

I do know that once this is over, he won't even remember what he's done, but I need to try to get him to listen to me now. I need to stop him from killing anyone else.

"This isn't the way," I say while holding onto his huge arm. "It's not you. You don't want to kill."

Something in his eyes shifts and understanding builds inside them. I hope.

An explosion bursts down below and I turn. People are racing out of the Hub, pushing and shoving, climbing over those who've fallen. It's out of control.

Burn grabs me around the waist and leaps.

From below on the balcony, Mrs. Kalin stares up, her mouth hanging open, shock on her face.

I'm happy that I've stopped Burn from more needless killing, but I missed my chance to kill Mrs. Kalin.

# CHAPTER THIRTY-EIGHT

BURN SLINGS ME ONTO HIS BACK AND CLIMBS, SWINGING UP from one window ledge to the next. With him transformed into his larger self, I can barely reach my arms around this neck and his power pulses under my fingers.

Clinging, I turn and look down. Forty stories below us, the Hub's in chaos.

He reaches the top of the building and pulls us onto the roof. I drop off his back onto its surface.

Two Comps race toward us, Shockers pointed. Burn pushes me behind him and charges. One of the Comps shoots and misses. Burn swats the gun out of his hands and then throws the uniformed man across the roof as if he weighs nothing.

"Look out," I yell, but I'm too late. The second Comp shoots, and his aim's better. The electrically charged tag strikes Burn's bare neck and sticks. He convulses and drops to his knees.

The Comp moves toward Burn, turning up the charge on the tag. I race forward and grab the Comp from behind, trapping his arms. He's too big and easily breaks my hold. Anticipating this, I drop off him and land in a strong stance.

He turns. I tuck, reach for one of his arms, and flip him over me onto his back. He lands with a thud, and I straddle his chest, pinning his arms, then flip up his visor to expose his eyes.

It's Williams, a Comp who often helped Larsson during our combat training.

I latch onto him with my Deviance, fighting to remember how I put that rat to sleep. Can I do it again? Can I disable this man without killing him? I focus on his brain, concentrate on making him sleep. His body goes slack. I've done it—I hope—and I dig my fingers under the side of his helmet to feel for a pulse. He's still alive.

Burn, about fifteen feet across the roof from me, has changed back into his normal self but he's still convulsing from the Shocker tag. Angry with myself for not helping him sooner, I lunge for Williams' weapon and turn it off. I race to Burn and pull the tag off his neck. It leaves an angry red ring.

"Glory." His voice is weak. He brings his hands to his head. "What happened?"

"You've got to get up," I tell him. "More Comps will be here any moment."

He stands, but it's clear that he's weakened. I'm not used to seeing Burn this way, and I drape his arm over my shoulders and walk, his body heavy above mine. We reach the edge of the roof. The next building's close, its roof no more than ten feet across and twenty feet down.

"Can you make it?"

He nods, and I jump first, rolling after I land. He follows, but when he gets up, he's sluggish, limping. We need to find somewhere to hide.

"Over here," a voice calls out and a man's head pokes out of a hatch on the other side of the roof. "Hide here."

Hearing a sound behind me, I turn, seeking the source but not seeing one. If the Comps don't know where we are already, they'll find us—soon. Burn needs time to recover, but what if the man in the hatch is leading us into a trap? Burn staggers, nearly losing his balance. We don't have a choice.

"Come on," I tell Burn and we run for the hatch. A few feet away, I recognize Larsson.

Burn and I follow him under the hatch.

The space is small. The three of us barely fit. Larsson has a small lantern and cranks its handle once the hatch is sealed.

He raises a finger to his lips.

The thump of Comp boots penetrates the space, vibrating through the walls around us. I wonder whether this small space leads somewhere else, whether we should move, but Larsson remains still. Burn sits with his head in his hands and we wait. Any moment the hatch might lift and we'll be exposed. The lantern fades away to darkness.

What feels like twenty minutes later, Larsson cranks his lantern and light fills the space. "I think they've moved on. I'll check."

"Thank you," I say.

"We need to get to the west quad," Burn says. "Do you know the best route?"

Larsson nods. "I'll take you there."

"Why the west quad?" I ask.

"Best route out," Burn says. "There are Comps all around the North side of the dome because of the invasion and the expunging."

I panic at the word expunging. Is Cal already outside the dome being torn apart by Shredders?

Larsson opens the hatch a few inches and looks out. "Stay down. I'll be back as soon as I make sure the coast is clear." He climbs out and closes the hatch above us.

"I need to get Cal." I watch Burn carefully. Mentioning Cal might be a huge mistake—what if he changes again?—but I mean what I say. There is no way I'll leave Haven without Cal, not if there's a chance he's still alive.

"You're too late," Burn says. "He was exed."

"You don't know that. We never saw the door open, and I won't let another one of my friends die."

"Another?" Burn asks.

I nod, my eyes prickling with tears. "Scout's dead. They killed him in the Hospital. Plus, Tobin and Jayma were expunged."

"Who told you that?" he asks.

"Mrs. Kalin."

He shakes his head. "She was lying. Jayma and the kid are in the storage room where you and I met."

"No, I checked. They aren't there."

"They're in a tunnel waiting for me to get you."

Happiness pushes through my fear and anxiety. "I looked for a tunnel entrance in that room. I couldn't find it."

"Good," Burn says. "It's well hidden."

The hatch opens.

"Now," Larsson says. "Quickly, while the Comps are all focused on the riots in the Hub. We've got a chance to escape, but it's got to be now."

We climb out and Burn and Larsson start across the roof heading west. I don't move.

Burn notices and turns back. "Now, Glory."

I shake my head. "I have to get Cal."

"It's too late." He widens his stance.

Larsson's mouth twists. He knows something.

"Is it too late?" I grab Larsson's arm. "Have they exed Cal already?"

Larsson lifts a hand to his ear and adjusts his communicator. "Cal's still inside the dome. The Comps holding him by the door are waiting for new orders. With the chaos, they don't know what to do."

I straighten my shoulders. "Then we need to get him."

"No." Burn shakes his head. "It's the opposite direction. It's him or those kids."

I back away. "I can't leave Cal. I won't. Promise me you'll get Tobin and Jayma to safety."

Without waiting for him to reply, I run north and jump off the edge of the roof.

# CHAPTER THIRTY-NINE

I RACE ACROSS ROOFTOPS TOWARD THE NORTH EDGE OF Haven. If I can get into the tunnel where our class watched the expunging, I can find the door out of the dome. I'm certain.

Spotlights bounce off the sky and the air's filled with sirens and smoke. Every route I try is blocked, but I can't stop to figure out what's happening or who's winning the battle. There's no time to be careful.

I leap to lower and lower buildings, and the sky comes closer above me on each one as the dome slopes toward the edge. Finally I spot it: the building that leads to the tunnel.

Finding a rope, I climb down four stories to the street surface. I run nine or ten blocks, my lungs burning and a copper tang in my mouth.

The door's marked, "Danger. No Entrance." Hanging at the back of the group that day, I didn't see the door before it opened but I'm sure it's the one Larsson led us through. At least it's my best guess.

I open it and enter a dark hallway. About five feet along, lights snap on, and as I race forward, more lights follow as if they're chasing me down the hall.

The corridor ends at a door, and when I open it I'm certain I've found the right place. This is definitely the hall we traveled down to view the expunging. Passing the door to the viewing room where our class watched, I hear voices around the next corner—the corner that should be near the door leading Outside. I stop and then move forward with more caution.

"How do you know it wouldn't be better?" a male voice asks.

"Haven equals safety," replies another. "Without Management, without the P&P, Haven will devolve into chaos, Shredders will break in, holes will open in the dome, and we'll all drown in dust."

"Maybe we'd just get better food," the other man says. "Maybe what we've got would be divided up more fairly. You heard what that guy with the megaphone said."

I peek around the corner. Cal is sitting against the wall, his hands and feet tied, a gag in his mouth. Two Comps in full gear are leaning against either side of the corridor, their visors raised.

The larger of the two turns. He sees me.

"What are you doing here?" He points his gun—an Aut with bullets. From his voice, I know he's the one who wondered about the better food. The smaller one quoted Haven rhetoric. Perhaps I can divide and conquer.

I raise my hands in surrender. "I'm one of the COT recruits. Captain Larsson sent me here to observe the expunging."

Cal opens his eyes wide and struggles, but he's bound too tightly.

"We weren't briefed," the big one says. "We didn't get any notice we'd be assigned a recruit today."

"You're not even in uniform." The smaller one frowns. "Unless torn red dresses are the new issue at COT." He laughs.

"It's her." The big one charges toward me. "You're the girl who tried to kill the President. We saw it on screen." He points to a TV high on the wall. "You're Mrs. Kalin's daughter. She's got everyone looking for you."

"She also calmed that Shredder who killed the President," the smaller one says. "She saved people's lives. That thing would have killed everyone." He turns to me. "How did you do that?"

He thinks Burn's a Shredder. I don't correct him.

The smaller Comp reaches for his gun. Cal swings his bound legs and knocks him off his feet. The larger Comp turns on his communicator. "Assistance required. Code Red. Location NQ15."

The Comp whom Cal knocked down isn't moving and blood drips down his forehead from under his helmet. I need to act. Even with all the chaos, a Code Red will bring more Comps. Too many.

"Hey." I draw the other one's attention and instantly lock onto his deep green eyes. I summon my Deviance without even pausing to build my emotions.

It's not necessary. Using my Deviance is becoming too easy.

But even if that makes me a monster, I can't afford to think about the consequences now. If I need to kill these Comps to save Cal, so be it. I should have killed Mrs. Kalin when I had the chance. I won't hesitate again.

Fixed on the Comp's gaze, I concentrate on slowing his heart rate, slowing his brain waves, and making him sleep. He staggers back into the wall. "What . . ."

He drops to the floor.

"What the hell did you do to my partner? What *are* you?" The other Comp has regained consciousness. "You didn't even touch him."

I spin toward the Comp whom Cal knocked down, and he raises his hands in surrender. He's removed his helmet and is rubbing his bleeding head. "Don't hurt me." He puts his Aut down.

I pick up his gun and tuck it into the back of the belt on my dress. "Give me your knife."

He pulls the blade from its leg sheath and slides it across the floor. Grabbing it, I slice through the ropes binding Cal's hands and he removes his gag as I cut the rope around his ankles.

The bigger Comp crawls across the hall to his partner and checks for a pulse. "He's still alive."

"He'll be fine," I say, although I'm not certain. "Is that the way out?" I point to a door with a bright red light above it.

"No," the Comp says. "That leads Outside."

"Perfect." I reach for the handle.

Cal puts his hand over mine. "Are you crazy? What are you doing?"

"We need to go out. We've got no other choice. Trust me." We're too late to go back and join Burn in the tunnels. I have no idea how Cal and I will survive our self-inflicted expunging, but we've got to try. It's not safe inside Haven.

"You'll die out there without masks," the Comp says.

I pull out the Aut and point it at him. "Give him your mask," I tell the Comp. I know I can breathe in some dust without choking or going mad. Cal might die.

"Leave if you want," the Comp says. "I'm not going to stop you."

I don't lower the gun. "Your mask."

"There are spares. Over there." He points down the hall.

"Get two," I tell Cal, then turn back to the Comp.

"Why are you letting us go?" I ask as Cal's getting the masks.

"I saw what you did on the balcony."

"So you're afraid of me?"

"I don't know." He wipes blood from his forehead. "Everything's messed up. I heard what those people said who burst into the Hub about Management controlling our lives. All I could think was maybe they're right. Maybe we *should* question Management. Maybe things *do* need to change." He shrugs. "If you're with those people, I'm not sure I want to stop you."

Cal returns with two masks. "Are you sure about this?"

I nod. "Put it on."

The Comp I knocked out stirs.

The one helping us grabs his partner's Aut and hands it to Cal. "Good luck."

I sling my mask on and open the door.

The light is blinding. I take Cal's hand and walk forward, shielding my eyes with my other hand. The wind's blowing and dust strikes my cheeks like tiny needles. I'm grateful we picked up the masks.

"The light is so bright," Cal says. "The air's so hot."

"It's the sun." I wish I had time to explain it, or let him see the miracle of the world for himself, but the dust is thick here and I have no idea what we're facing. Since an expunging was planned, I feel certain that Shredders must be nearby and waiting. The Comps usually tip them off to make sure that the victims are attacked soon after they get out the door. This guarantees a good show for those watching in the Hub.

My eyes slowly adjust, and as we trudge forward, the air starts to clear. A loud rumbling comes from far off to the right and I turn to see what it is, but Cal tugs on my arm. "Glory." His voice is low and filled with tension.

Forty feet to our left is a pack of Shredders—at least ten. They spot us and shout.

"Run!" Still holding Cal's hand, I race diagonally to the right. We need to get away from the dome and away from those Shredders. In the distance, ruins, sections of old buildings from BTD, jut up from the dust. We might find somewhere to hide if we can outrun the Shredders.

Something whooshes past my ear and a long metal shard lands in the dust. A foot to the left and it would have been in my back—or my head.

The rumbling noise increases. The ground trembles.

"What's happening?" Cal shouts.

I shake my head, then turn.

The tank. At least it looks like the tank that took Burn and me to Fort Huron, but it can't be the same one. Burn made it explode. I stop. Which is worse, the Shredders or those cannibals at Fort Huron? I shift direction. What will we do now? Shredders on one side and those military people on the other.

Cal stops and my hand slips from his. "Wait," he yells. "There's someone waving at us from that huge metal thing. They're trying to get our attention."

I stop and turn. Glancing over my shoulder, I see the Shredders have abandoned their chase, likely scared off by the tank. Then I see the FA insignia on the side of the tank. Do I dare hope?

The tank stops and a large body climbs out of the hatch. It's Burn. I race forward.

"Get in here," he yells. "We don't have much time."

I make Cal climb up the tank first; then I follow. Burn offers his hand. He yanks me up and my body slams against his. He wraps his arms around me. "You made it."

"Jayma and Tobin?"

He nods. "They're inside."

I wrap my arms around his neck. "Thank you."

In his arms, I feel safe. I don't want to let go.

"Get down," he says. "Comps."

A loud bang comes from the direction of Haven and there's an explosion about ten feet to the left of the tank.

I shoot down the ladder. Burn follows, and the tank starts moving even before he's fully closed the hatch.

I land on the floor of the tank and am thrown back. Cal jumps up to cushion my fall and then draws me into his lap.

"You came back for me," Cal says. "You saved me." He pulls me into a kiss.

Adrenaline, anxiety and stress pour out of me, and it feels as if Cal's extracting my pain with his kiss, soothing every fear and ache with his caress. The world and my troubles wash away, and it's just me and Cal. He knows what I am and still loves me. We've escaped Haven. I don't think I've ever been happier.

The tank goes over a bump and we break apart.

Reality floods back. We aren't alone.

My cheeks, my entire body, are on fire. I shift off of Cal's lap to sit next to him on the bench. I glance at the others. Jayma's grinning across from me, next to Tobin who's struggling to keep his wings contained. I turn toward Burn.

He's staring at the floor, hands clenched into fists on his knees.

What have I done? If his full Deviance kicks in while we're in this tank, none of us will come out alive.

"Burn?" My voice is drowned out by the sound of the tank.

I cross the small space and sit down next to him, putting a hand softly on one of his fists. He raises his head to look at me. His jaw's tight, teeth clenched, and his eyes are dark and sad.

"I'm sorry." My words are inadequate.

He shakes his head.

"I—we got caught up in the situation. I—"

He shakes his head again. "Nothing to explain. You're with Cal. I get it. I've accepted it." He looks down. "It's not like we can ever—you know." He pulls his hand out from under mine and turns away.

My heart sinks. I never meant to hurt Burn and I certainly don't want to hurt Cal. I'm not even sure, given a choice, which one I want to be with, and I can't begin to sort out my feelings right now.

We go over another bump and Jayma squeals. Tobin's wings sprout again and she helps him contain them. Cal watches them in awe. I turn to Burn beside me, but he quickly looks away. My heart sinks, but I can't fix this now.

The ride is rough as we cross the dangerous hot zone that surrounds Haven, and I can't help but think how the bumps symbolize my life. I may have escaped Haven alive, but so much is unfinished, so many obstacles lie ahead.

The FA and the rebels are battling the Comps inside the dome, but Mrs. Kalin is still alive. If she takes the Presidency and makes daily broadcasts to the employees, how long will it take before everyone inside Haven is under her control—including the FA soldiers and rebels?

She told me that some people are resistant to her power—I know I am—but even I found myself falling under her spell.

I need to warn the others. I need to go back. I need to stop Mrs. Kalin.

"Brace yourselves," the driver shouts from the front. "We're going through the wall."

I grab one of the handles above my head, bracing for whatever comes.

# ACKNOWLEDGMENTS

The second book in a series is a challenge: meeting the expectations of fans of the first novel, while simultaneously entertaining readers new to the world, and I'm deeply indebted to everyone who helped me bring *Compliance* to the page.

First I'd like to thank the readers who loved *Deviants* and were kind enough to let me know. You make everything worthwhile.

As always, I am forever grateful to my critique partners Molly O'Keefe and Ripley Vaughn, without whom my books might not get written. Or at least not as well. Thank you for not letting me get away with anything, and for making the process a lot more interesting and fun. Thanks also to Stephanie Doyle who read a draft of the manuscript before reading *Deviants*, and to Mary Sullivan and Michele Young.

I must also thank the vast and varied writers' community I'm proud to be part of, including members of RWA, SCBWI, CANSCAIP, Backspace, #torkidlit, and Monthtowrite. Particular shout-outs to Danielle Younge-Ullman, Bev Katz Rosenbaum, Claudia Osmond, Debbie Ridpath Ohi, Nelsa Roberto, Megan Crewe, Chevy Stevens, Diana Peterfreund, Eileen Cook, Eileen Rendahl, Barrie Summy, Kwana Jackson, Misty Simon, Alli Sinclair, Danita Cahill, and Marilyn

Brant, and dozens of others. I'm going to kick myself for not listing. TRW peeps; you know who you are.

A shout-out to everyone at "the office" aka F'Coffee, and at Broadview Espresso. Thanks for putting up with the strange woman with the pink hair huddled over her laptop for hours on end, hogging the plug.

Thank you forever to my enthusiastic agent Charlie Olsen. Your continued belief in me means the world. And thank you to everyone else at InkWell Management, especially Alexis Hurley for her efforts to have this series translated into other languages. And a special thank you to eighth grader Kirsten Traudt, who read and wrote a helpful and insightful report on *Compliance*, while doing an internship at InkWell.

Finally, but by no means least, thanks are due to Lindsay Guzzardo who helped me unwind and reweave the multiple plot lines in this story. And thank you to everyone at Amazon Children's Publishing, including Margery Cuyler, Deborah Bass, Amy Hosford, Jenny Parnow, Erick Pullen, Timoney Korbar and Katrina Damkoehler. Go team!